SILVER HIGHWAYS

KATE LANCE

SEA
BOOKS
PRESS
seabooks.net

Print ISBN: 9780987211361
Ebook ISBN: 9780987211385

Published by Seabooks Press
seabooks.net

BY THE SAME AUTHOR

Fiction
Embers at Midnight
Testing the Limits
Silver Highways
Atomic Sea (As CM Lance)
The Turning Tide (As CM Lance)

Non-Fiction
Alan Villiers: Voyager of the Winds
Redbill: From Pearls to Peace

Dedication

To Tony Larard (1939-2016)
farmer, pearler, skipper
and rebuilder of the luggers
E.W.S., *Intombi* and *Ida Lloyd*

CONTENTS

I. RUNNING BEFORE THE WIND

I was so young then—only fifteen when first I met gentle Sam Lee, cynical Danny Whalen and beautiful Gideon Meade. They were the mates on a barque captained by my father; his final command before retiring to Melbourne with Mama, my sister Rosa and me.

We were out from England on my first deepwater passage and I was dizzy with fascination at shipboard life. Danny Whalen kept saying he was driven to distraction by all my questions and climbing and curiosity but, oh, I just wanted to *see*.

I wanted to understand everything I possibly could, yet there was so much no one would tell me.

It was 1906 and every certainty I had was about to be overthrown.

'So it goes over and under, through the loop, around and out this side?'

'No, that side,' says Mr Meade, beside me on the bench.

I push the tail of twine through the loop and pull it tight. 'There!'

'By Jove, Miss Lucy, that knot could moor the mighty *Preussen*,' says Mr Meade, his blue eyes kind. He gazes at Rosa, seated in a deckchair beside us. 'Miss Fox, do let me show you—'

'I would not care to be shown, Mr Meade,' says Rosa. 'I do not intend to moor anything, ever at all.' The flick of her fan stirs a red-gold ringlet against her throat.

My sister is wearing her second-best white muslin and looks cool and fresh. I wish I did. My dark blue dress, despite its stylish sailor's collar, only soaks up the heat—and even in the shade of the awning how hot it is! I can smell melted pitch in the seams of the deck and something far worse in the stagnant water lapping around *Willowmere*'s hull.

It often puzzles me why Rosa is so unfriendly to Mr Meade. With his golden hair and merry smile I think he's terribly handsome, although sometimes his voice is a little loud. But I suppose it has to be. A first mate does a lot of roaring at the crew, especially when they're a long way up in the rigging.

A trickle of moisture tickles the back of my neck and I wipe it away, still surprised at the feel of my short hair. Not long before we sailed I suffered a fever and my head was shaved to cool me down. It's a common enough remedy and no one has remarked upon it, but for the first time I feel a little abashed.

'The scarlet fever was most unpleasant, you know,' I say. 'I felt hotter than even today and Mama was forced to cut off all my hair.'

'Indeed?' says Gideon Meade, as Rosa sips her tea and gazes without interest at the horizon.

'Mama said it might grow back wavy.' It's hard to tell with only an inch of mouse-brown pelt.

Third mate Danny Whalen looks up from a battered copy of *Reed's Seamanship* and scratches his russet curls. 'You know, trousers on and up the rigging we'd think you're one of the deck boys.'

'Up the rigging? Oh, please *may* I, Mr Whalen!' Every day I watch the sailors with envy as they climb from this hot deck to the cool wide sky, and long to join them and see the clouds and our tumbled wake and the far horizon.

Gold sparkles from Danny Whalen's earring as he laughs. 'I didn't mean it like that, child. Of course you can't go aloft.'

Of *course* a girl can't climb the rigging: how foolish of me to even imagine it. Rosa looks gratified and I feel cross at the unfairness of life.

Sam Lee, the second mate, joins us. He lifts his faded cap, brushes his straight black hair off his forehead and squats lightly beside Danny, his white shirt open at the neck. Sam Lee is quiet and kind, and doesn't roar nearly as much as Mr Meade, although the men still do what he says. Yesterday I decided he was also terribly handsome, but suddenly I dislike everyone.

'And why is *your* hair all cut off, Mr Lee?' I say. 'You did not suffer the scarlet fever. Must not every Chinese wear the pigtail?'

He gazes at me patiently. 'I am a free man, Miss Lucy, I am not ruled by the Emperor.'

'Indeed you are not, Mr Lee!' says Gideon Meade. 'Why, Sam is only half a Chinee, his father's an English lord and he may do as he pleases. When we were at school—'

'Miss Fox, Miss Lucy, I believe your mother wishes to speak to you,' says Mr Lee. 'Danny, a squall is coming in from the east. Would you mind keeping an eye on the apprentices?'

Danny Whalen shuts his book with a snap and hurries away with Sam Lee, and I hear the familiar thump of feet on the deck as the men go to their duty. I gaze at the book and sigh. What *interesting* lives sailors lead.

Rosa is already at the stairs to the saloon before Mr Meade is even on his feet, his eyes still warm at the memories of his school days. Yes, I think, Gideon Meade is much handsomer than Sam Lee: and he's certainly a finer man than that Danny Whalen, who might have a gold earring but is only third mate after all.

Our pretty barque *Willowmere* is sailing from England with a cargo of iron spars and timber for the building of busy young Melbourne, but sadly our small world has come to a halt just a few weeks out on a four-month passage. We're completely becalmed in the middle of the Atlantic and I *do* wish we'd get moving.

Papa's younger brother Edward is already established in Melbourne and we're going to live in a new house at the seaport,

Williamstown. Mama has been busy for weeks choosing suitable papers and fabrics and, as I follow Rosa down into the saloon, she looks up smiling. Rosa pulls out a red velvet chair and sits, smoothing her skirt. I lean on Mama's shoulder and gaze at the samples spread out on the table.

'My dears,' she says, 'I believe I've found just the wallpapers for your rooms. Rosa, what do you think of this one? A little old-fashioned but the pink and pale green would suit you so well.'

Rosa remains silent.

Mama turns to me. 'Little Lou, what about something modern for you—coral and blue and olive all twisting so, isn't that pretty?'

'Oh, *yes*. Look Rosa, it's like my silk shawl—'

Rosa still says nothing. She's sulked all the way down the Thames, through the Atlantic and into the Doldrums, and she certainly isn't going to stop now. It's probably something to do with that Lieutenant in his red coat who waved her goodbye at the dock.

'Are you uncomfortable, darling?' Mama says. 'Perhaps you would breathe more easily without your corsets. I'm certain there cannot be the slightest objection in this weather.'

'I would *never* go without my corsets, Mama,' says Rosa. 'It would not be seemly.'

'Always be open-minded, my dear. After all, the human body is a work of art.'

Rosa's pretty lips tighten and she looks away. Mama often takes us to galleries and tells us about the paintings, even the ones of people without any clothes on, until Rosa goes pink with fury. Mama adores the modern styles, like Japonisme and Arts and Crafts, and tells us thrilling stories of her days among the avant-garde as an artists' model.

Her name then was Annabel Joyce, and her dramatic profile and waist-length auburn locks made her a favourite. In the famous canvas *Ophelia Drifting*, her eyes amused, her body barely concealed by flowers, she caused a small scandal at the Academy.

One night at a soiree she happened to meet Papa; quiet, hawk-nosed Nicholas Fox, fiercely proud of his first mate's ticket. Some months later she accepted his hesitant offer of marriage and, she says, she has never regretted it. I love to think with a shiver how my own being so depended upon that chance meeting.

That evening after dinner I climb the companionway stairs to the deck. The air is still and the stars in this new equatorial sky barely twinkle. I notice a figure near the charthouse looking up with a spyglass.

'What can you see?' I ask.

Sam Lee replies, 'Jupiter, Miss Lucy, and its moons.'

I feel shy. 'I cannot see them.'

'Here, use the glass. It has four moons and you may sometimes discern one or two off to the side of their parent.'

The brilliant light wavers as if we're under the sea. 'Yes, there is one to the left and another, almost joined to the star! Are they truly *moons*?'

'Indeed, Miss Lucy, but their parent is a planet not a star. It wanders, so it is not as useful to mariners as the fixed bodies.'

After a silence I say, 'Today, Mr Lee—I am so sorry. I was unhappy and my words were not kind.'

'Please, it is of no account. I've known far worse. Mr Meade may recall our schooldays with pleasure but I do not.'

I cannot imagine any man as fine as Sam Lee at a disadvantage, but suddenly think of a small child, black-eyed and solemn, thrown into a world of large golden lads.

'Was Mr Meade a good friend to you at school?'

'Unlike the other boys we both dreamt of the sea, and in the end we became stout companions,' says Mr Lee. 'His parents were not pleased, but when we apprenticed together and they saw our crude shipmates they decided they liked me a little better.'

I think he might be smiling.

'And if your father is an English lord, why is your name Lee?' I say.

There's a brief silence. 'My mother was not married to my father,

Miss Lucy, so I carry her name.'

I know for some reason this is a terrible thing. The other girls whisper about it, but I don't know why.

'Did your father look after you?'

'He provided for my education. However, he is no lord, merely a second son. He was sent out to Hong Kong to make his fortune, and did so managing my mother's company.'

I think I must have misheard. 'Your *mother's* ...?'

There's no mistaking the amusement in his voice now. 'Company. Yes, my mother is a prosperous merchant trader.'

The mysteries of babies are as nothing to this!

'But how can that possibly be, Mr Lee? I've never heard of a woman merchant trader.'

'She is clever, she works hard, she wishes to prosper. It is not impossible.'

'Papa always says the finest occupation for a woman is to run her husband's household and bear his sons.'

'Indeed—' I wonder why he hesitates. 'But my mother Min-lu is someone rather like you, Miss Lucy, always finding the world of endless interest. She lives in Melbourne so perhaps one day you may meet. Please excuse me now.'

Mr Lee takes out his timepiece and checks it in the light of the compass binnacle, and calls out the order for eight bells. The watch changes over and I go below to the quiet saloon.

At one end of the table my mother is brushing Rosa's long hair, while at the other end my father rustles through papers irritably as he deals with the never-ending demands of ship management.

I enter the small washroom off the master's cabin (wonderfully modern with its bath and water-closet), and prepare for bed. I say good-night to my family and climb up to my bunk in the small cabin I share with Rosa, and lie quietly, my thoughts racing.

Meet! Meet a Chinese woman, a *merchant* woman? What if she has tiny feet all bound up and long sharp fingernails and red lips and an opium pipe? I'm not at all certain I'd like to meet someone like that.

Then again, I think, turning over with a sigh, I probably wouldn't be allowed to anyway.

The ship barely moves next day, then at last a few clouds appear and the air ruffles across the water and flutters and fills the limp canvas. Waves begin to gurgle and slap against the hull and *Willowmere* begins to make her stately progress towards the Equator.

Day after beautiful day follows. The sailors hang a plank below the bow so the bosun can repaint the ship's figurehead, a gentle-faced redhead in green with a sheaf of willow fronds. I think she has a look of Mama, but of course she isn't nearly as pretty.

One evening I stand at the stern in the soft breeze. All my life I've listened enthralled to Papa's sea stories, but this is my first true ocean passage. Mr Meade loves to tease me with tales of terrible storms and waves that tower like cathedrals, but on a night like this it's difficult to believe.

Behind me I hear Danny Whalen say to the pimpled apprentice at the wheel, 'Christ, Brownley, that wake's as crooked as a snake. Watch the compass, not the women, you poxy lubber.'
I know there are harsher things he could have said. The sailors curse all the time, and some words must be worse than others because they often look worried if they notice me nearby.

I watch the ship's wake. It's hardly as crooked as a snake but does show a pretty wriggle along its shimmering path.

'Mr Whalen,' I say. 'Our wake looks like a silvery path taking us across the world, a highway on the sea. Is that why the moorings outside the ports are called the roads?'

'Good God, you've a strange way of thinking, child. I haven't the slightest notion of highways or roads, silver or not. Brownley you fool, stop snickering and steer straight.'

I sigh. I join my parents and find them chatting to Mr Meade, although Rosa is silent and unsmiling, her arms crossed, her hair pale in the moonlight. She is being unfriendly once more to handsome Gideon Meade, when just this afternoon I'd seen her returning his pleasantries, turned away from quiet Sam Lee beside her.

My sister must have a strange way of thinking too. But then, nobody ever calls her a child. She's eighteen and will soon find a husband. I'm not a child, I think wistfully, although surely my sister had not been quite so—flat—in front at fifteen.

Next evening Danny Whalen's voice calls from high in the mizzen mast, 'Captain Bowline, ahoy! Have ye any lubbers aboard?'

Papa plays his part well. 'Who are you, stranger, aboard my ship, and what brings you here?'

The voice roars, 'I am Neptune, King of the Seas, and no lubber may pass where I hold Court. I shall board tomorrow at five bells in the forenoon watch as you cross to my southern realms!'

I laugh with delight. At last I'll get to see the famous ceremony of Crossing the Line. I hear some of the men reminiscing cheerfully about the tortures they've seen inflicted upon first-voyagers and the apprentices become pale and quiet.

Next morning a canvas bath is filled with water, then Neptune and his court clamber over the bow. Danny Whalen, with a trident, wobbly crown and yarn beard, grins and swaggers along the deck to his makeshift throne with his queen Amphitrite on his arm, a red-cheeked Swedish seaman with rope ringlets and two cooking bowls tied to his chest.

The apprentices are forced to eat some concoction, thrown into the bath and held under for a worryingly long time. Dripping and retching, they accept their parchments of welcome to King Neptune's domain. There's also a parchment for Rosa, who takes hers with a cool smile, and another for me (although in this weather I think I'd have preferred the dunking).

Later there's music. Danny Whalen has his jaunty fiddle, three sailors tootle along on penny whistles and the bosun squeezes a concertina, and they play jigs and shanties and melancholy airs until late into the night.

I sit quietly in a corner under Mr Meade's supervision, although I hardly need his protection: the crewmen are good-natured and well-behaved. As on most deepwater ships they're drawn from a mix of nations, and include the shy blond Swedish lad who played Amphitrite, a Yankee from a whaling ship, a scowling dark Finn, a large Pacific Islander named Thomas, a small Malay with a curved knife, a Dutch cook called Piet, and a couple of unfriendly apprentices from London.

In these glorious days of running before the wind, the sails are full on the swaying masts, the rigging creaks and the water rushes and rustles along the hull. Our wake curves away to the blue horizon behind us and the horizon itself stretches further than I ever thought possible.

At midday as usual I join Mr Meade to take the noon readings. He taught me how to use the sextant to locate our position on the ocean, and now I shoot the sun with him and the apprentices. Of course Mr Meade's reading is the official one, but I'm pleased to notice mine is almost as accurate as his, and it's certainly better than that of the scornful apprentices.

Papa approaches us, his hands clasped behind his back, and Mr Meade says, 'Sir, Miss Lucy would have us but a quarter of a mile from our noon reckoning—she has the mark of a fine navigator. A credit to her upbringing of course,' he adds quickly as Papa frowns.

'I'm far from certain she will have call for such accomplishments in her life, Mr Meade.'

'But Papa, if I marry a captain we'll be able to talk together of his daily tribulations.' I say.

He has grown stern and tired these last few months and his hair and moustache have turned grey. 'A *captain*, young miss!' he growls. 'You'll do better than that, I hope. All that worry and separation. No indeed, a nice young bank clerk would suit you admirably.' He walks away.

'Perhaps, Miss Lucy—your mother wishes to see you?' says Gideon Meade uncertainly.

The pimply apprentice Brownley nudges the mean-looking smaller boy (I think of him as Ratface). 'Maybe ye'd better go do some *sewing*, missy, instead of playing at sailor.'

'Get below, you young ...' Mr Meade cannot think of anything both satisfying and proper as the boys run giggling down to the mid-deck and disappear.

'It's all right. I don't mind, really.' I sigh and gaze at the blue sky filled with tumbling white clouds, and walk over to the companionway and down the stairs.

As I enter the saloon I hear my mother say with surprising sharpness, 'I will not put up with this tedious behaviour any longer, Rosa. We must behave with politeness to all the officers.'

Rosa, flushed, stands at the end of the table. 'I do not have to be amiable to *everyone*, Mama. I do not like him, that's all. He looks at me as if he sees my soul. He has no right!'

'Mr Meade?' I ask. Rosa groans in fury, and in a flurry of white muslin dashes into the tiny cabin we share and slams the door.

'Mr Lee?' I try again, but my mother tuts with exasperation. Danny Whalen, then. He has a bold eye, my mother says, although I'm not sure how that lets him see Rosa's soul.

I sit down at the table and open my sewing box, and decide to complete one side of my petticoat hem with a new stitch the sailmaker showed me. In green, for starboard.

There are two watches, port and starboard. Each takes a turn on deck for four hours then goes below to sleep, so at any time half of the men are awake and alert. In the evenings they relax, and music often echoes from the foc's'le—penny whistles and Danny Whalen's fiddle and the bosun's concertina. I listen from beside the charthouse, humming and tapping my toe. Rosa says I'm mad.

The off-duty officers usually join us for dinner every evening. Mr Meade and Danny Whalen take charge of the port watch, and meals with them are a cheerful affair. Sam Lee leads the starboard watch, and meals with him are quieter, although he gets on well with Mama because both have an interest in modern novels.

Weeks have elapsed since we were becalmed, and this evening the talk is of today's great change in course. *Willowmere* has been turned away from the steamy coast of Brazil and is now sailing south-east towards the winds of the Roaring Forties.

'Mr Meade showed me the mighty Amazon on the chart today,' I say. 'He said there are blue butterflies and green sloths in South America. Can this possibly be true?'

Sam Lee smiles. 'For once, Miss Lucy, he is not joking. There are indeed such oddities.'

'Have you ever seen the famous Pampero, Mr Lee? I read about it in the *Illustrated London News*. They say it comes off the pampas plains in a great storm, fierce and freezingly cold.'

'I have, but it was only a squall. We were fortunate, as I believe it can be ferocious.'

'I shall retire now,' says Rosa. 'I have the headache.'

I leave my parents and Sam Lee sitting over coffee and climb the stairs into a world of cloying heat. The day has been hazy, the clouds suffocating and low. Lightning is flickering around the horizon and thunder rumbles in the distance.

The lightning shows the large form of Gideon Meade with the helmsman, and the lookout at the bow, the small Malay with the curved knife. But he's not a dog of a Malay, he explained politely to me today when showing me a clever knot. He's from Koepang in Timor and his name is Borue.

I look over the side of the ship, and gasp. Instead of black water there is astonishing brilliance, diamond-like flashes that seem to echo the lightning, while behind us *Willowmere*'s silvery wake has become a miracle of tumbling light. This must be the famous phosphorescence I've read about, but never quite believed could be real.

Large creatures—sharks, dolphins?—flash in sudden green-blue fire towards the ship then swerve away, while shoals of little fish turn and twist in glittering clouds between the eerie forms of jellyfish. I had never *imagined* so much life was darting and flickering beneath us.

I watch entranced for ten minutes or so, then hear a whispering that, strangely, seems to come from the ship's sparkling wake itself. The noise grows louder, hissing, growling, and I lift my head and say, 'Mr Meade, what can that be?'

He turns and listens, then frowns and roars, 'All hands on deck— *lower away topsails*!'

A wall of wind and rain slams into us.

Willowmere judders and groans and heels steeply, and I'm flung against the rail. Men sleeping below leap awake and run to join the turmoil on deck, climbing the rigging to take in the sails. Forks of lightning are striking the sea around us and the thunder is almost continuous.

Soaked through in moments, I can only cling to the rail and watch the men aloft in astonishment. Lit up by brilliant flashes, they struggle with writhing balloons of canvas high on the yards and yell through the tumult of chains clanging, cables shrieking and decks drumming in the pelting rain. As the sails are reduced the ship gradually rights herself, but now she rushes through the foam, two helmsmen desperately trying to hold her on course.

An hour passes before all the canvas is secured. One sail blows out with an explosion, the gloomy Finn has his head cut open by a swinging block, and apprentice Brownley slips and is just saved from plunging to the deck by the massive fist of Thomas the Islander.

When everything is quiet again, it is Gideon Meade who discovers me sitting near the stern, ecstatic, cold, forgotten in the dark.

'Was that a *real* Pampero, Mr Meade?' I can barely get the words out for shivering.

'Good Lord, Miss Lucy! You must go below—your mother thinks you're in bed!'

I try to stand but I'm too stiff, so he helps me across the deck and down the stairs to my horrified mother. She sits me by the fire in the saloon, wraps me in a blanket and rubs my short hair with a towel, scolding me all the while.

But nothing can diminish my contentment. I have seen the Pampero.

2. THE SKIPPER'S DAUGHTERS

Rosa is of the opinion I should suffer for my foolishness, but I do not get even a cold.

'You would have done it too, once upon a time,' I say, tired of everyone's reprimands. 'You used to like adventures, Rosa. Why have you become so ... *sensible*?'

It feels like an insult but she says demurely, 'I must be a lady now, Lucy. One day you must too.'

I remember her telling me wonderful stories as children, her brown eyes dreamy as if gazing into another world. We would play at being animal-flowers from the garden: Rosa was a golden tiger-lily and I was a little mauve snapdragon. (When Rosa decided the snapdragon was to be cut for a vase of flowers, I sobbed for hours.)

Her curls hide a faint childhood scar on her eyebrow from when she'd jumped off a roof with an umbrella despite Mama's desperate pleas, fiercely convinced she could fly. Now I stare in bewilderment at my sister. What could have happened to change her so?

As *Willowmere* sails south the days begin to stretch out. It's no longer dark after dinner but pink with sunset, the air gusty and cool. One evening Sam Lee is leading the watch on deck, staring at the fat curves of the sails against the sky, and I look up too.

Mr Lee calls for the watch to take in the upper topgallants and men take hold of the lines and jerk the ropes to a rhythm chanted by the bosun. Others run aloft and lean over the yard-arms, balancing on the footrope as they fasten the canvas. *Willowmere*'s rolling eases. The men climb down and gather beside the cookhouse to wait until the ship needs them again.

I gaze at Sam Lee, his dark eyes still intent upon the curves of the sails. I consider his golden cheekbones and the clean line of his jaw against his black hair.

'Do you like being Chinese, Mr Lee?' I ask.

'Great *God*, Miss Lucy!'

'I'm sorry. Was that rude of me?' I understand some of my questions are permissible and others are not, but as yet I'm not sure which are which.

Sam looks at me in silence then takes a breath and says, 'Not rude but ... unexpected. In truth, I forget what I am at sea. Not white, not yellow, not the butt of jokes, not threat to English womanhood. As it happens, Miss Lucy, I do not like being anything but a sailor.'

I feel my eyes sting but do not understand why. 'I believe you're a very fine sailor, Mr Lee, and you must certainly become a captain soon.'

His face eases. 'I've taken my master's ticket, Miss Lucy, but it might be quite some time before I'm a captain. Indeed, I may not remain in square-riggers at all.'

'Oh. What would you do instead?'

'My mother's business exports pearlshell, so I wish to travel to Broome in north-west Australia. That is where the divers in their great copper helmets harvest the shell from the bottom of the sea.'

'My goodness! You would become a *diver*?'

He laughs. 'I think not. However, those divers work from wooden ketches, and a man might make his fortune with a few of those well-found vessels.'

'But are there not terrible cyclones? And enormous *clams* that snap shut upon divers' legs?'

'Indeed there are cyclones, although I am less certain about the giant clams.' He gazes at me. 'In Broome, men from Asia comprise much of the industry. Some, like myself, are half-castes—boat-owners, pearl-buyers, merchants of the town. Perhaps in such a place my race may be of lesser importance than my skills.'

'How wonderful, Mr Lee! And there might at very least be giant octopuses,' I say hopefully.

The corners of Sam Lee's mouth curve. 'Broome is a fine port, with its rust-red rocks and jade-green waters, but regretfully I've heard nothing at all of octopuses.'

The gusty wind increases and spray dampens my face. Mr Lee calls out for a reef in the lower topgallants, then goes to the wheel to instruct the helmsman. In the fading light I see the waves are higher than before and patchy with foam.

I shiver and go below to my sewing. I'd argued, persuasively I thought, to finish the other half of my petticoat hem in red (for port, to complement starboard), but with a sad lack of imagination Mama has insisted I unpick it all.

Willowmere is just a small three-masted barque, with an iron hull, timber decks and steel masts, a mere six hundred and fifty tons register. She's certainly not one of the great square-riggers of three thousand tons or more that spread, so they say, a whole acre of sail.

She looked substantial enough when we boarded, but as we were sailing down the Channel a handsome four-master came from behind and slipped past us. *Willowmere* was like a child's toy beside her and I stared in awe until the gigantic ship was gone.

Willowmere may not be large, but as the winds push her further south she shows herself to be sound and seakindly. The men have been busy lately replacing her old canvas with her strongest sails to prepare her for the great storms we'll soon meet. Above and below, the moveable gear has been fastened, and lifelines strung along each side of the open deck. The hatches, well-sealed in London with tarpaulins, are now secured further with planks.

Wrapped in coats and scarves, Rosa and I watch as the last of the hatches is battened down. Out on the rising sea the high green swells are curling over and foaming into pale, lacy spindrift.

Passing by with a coil of rope, Danny Whalen says, 'Do you know, when the waves look like that they're called the skipper's daughters? You should be honoured.'

I clap my hands in pleasure. 'Is that true, Mr Whalen? They're called the skipper's *daughters*?'

'Indeed, child,' he says with a grin. 'They say when a man sees the skipper's daughters he should head for safe harbour as fast as he can.'

Rosa rolls her eyes in disdain.

Later that day the wind strengthens and *Willowmere* begins racing through the sea. As the rigging shrieks, water pours over the sides and swirls along the deck and out through the clanging washports, while men grab the lifelines to stay on their feet. I gaze, thrilled, at the wild seas: we have reached the Roaring Forties and now we're sailing our Easting down.

Rosa, less thrilled, is seasick below in the cabin. To her disgust I'm never seasick. Mama also enjoys the exhilarating air, walking arm in arm with Papa. Sometimes he murmurs to Gideon Meade or Sam Lee, who relay his commands to the watch. A sail is adjusted, the rolling eases, and Papa regards the taut billows above him with satisfaction.

There are two helmsmen on the wheel all the time now, fighting to keep the barque balanced between storm and sea. *Willowmere* rolls down the steep grey waves, slicing so deeply the wind almost fades away, then she lifts herself up to the next summit, hesitates for a breath, and begins her slow fall once more. The waves may not be quite as high as cathedrals but they're certainly as awesome.

The great terror—men only whisper it—is of *broaching to*: losing our rushing way from a broken rudder or carelessness at the helm, and turning, slipping side-on, lying helpless beneath one of those collapsing dark mountains. Ships can be lost in moments if broached, and many are.

The sailors let their beards grow in the freezing weather. They sleep for four hours below in sodden clothes and damp blankets, then labour without a break on watch. Illness is rare, the hard work a challenge the men meet with their own strength. Our food is good (unusual on a British vessel, says Papa) and Piet the Dutch cook is friendly, even tolerating Mama in his tiny galley when she bakes for special occasions.

Despite the danger and grinding effort, *Willowmere* is a happy ship.

Piet brews coffee for the officers and men at the helm, and sometimes I help take the steaming mugs from the galley to the stern. One gloomy evening, apprentice Brownley and I carry the drinks along the rolling deck, stopping now and then to brace ourselves against the stays, spray pattering on our oilskins.

At the steps to the deck I let Brownley go ahead (when I went first one night he tried to make me slip). He takes mugs to the helmsmen while I carry one to the charthouse, off the stairs that lead down to the saloon.

I open the companionway door, turn and close it against the spray, then open the inner charthouse door and hand the mug to Danny Whalen, who looks up from a large blueback chart on the table.

'Such an effort to get around in this weather!' I say. 'Do you think it will improve soon?'

'Thank you, child.' He takes the mug in both hands, shivering. 'The barometer's rising, so there's a chance tomorrow will be finer. Lord, that's good.'

I brace myself against the wall as the ship rolls. A pencil slides across the chart and lodges at a curled edge. The lamp hisses from the corner and I peer at the lines Danny has just marked.

'How far did we come today?'

'A good two hundred miles. Look there, we're well into the South Atlantic now.'

I read aloud a warning printed on the chart. '*South of this curved line, Ice-bergs are more or less numerous throughout the year.* Did you ever meet icebergs when sailing around Cape Horn, Mr Whalen?'

'Lord, yes. You can almost smell them, the air's so suddenly ice-cold. They glimmer at night too and make your hair stand on end. But I've only been round the Horn twice, child, and the first time was no worse than the Irish Sea.'

He puts down his coffee and moves the weights off the edges of the chart. It rolls itself up into a blue canvas cylinder and he places it back in its pigeon-hole. I remember something that's been puzzling me.

'Why don't you ever call me Miss Lucy, as everyone else does?'

His green eyes crinkle. 'Ah, when you're a fine young lady in your silks and laces I'll call you Miss, but till then you're just a strange little mite, with all your questions and climbing and curiosity.'

'But that's not fair. I always have to be polite and call you Mr Whalen.'

He thinks for a moment. 'You know, you're quite right, it's not fair. Why don't you just call me Danny like everyone else? Truth is, I'm always looking round for my father when anyone says Mr Whalen.'

'Is he a sailor too?'

'No. A schoolmaster in Dublin,' says Danny. He picks up his coffee again and swallows. 'Taught me to play the fiddle. He's dead now, consumption.'

'Your mother must have been very sad when you went to sea.'

'I've a brother and two big sisters, she's in good hands. She always knew I'd go away.' He finishes his coffee and hands me the mug. 'There, child. Give my thanks to Piet.'

'I shall. Good night, Danny.'

The harsh weather eases a little, although we're still rushing through broken seas. Mist streams past the mast-tips and spray freezes in icicles along the rigging.

Rosa starts coming to dinner again, pale and slim, delicately beautiful. She's pleasant enough to attentive Gideon Meade and even chats to quiet Sam Lee. Yet she ignores Danny Whalen who, rather than trying to look deep into my sister's soul, seems almost amused. Later, I lean on the rail beside him, watching choppy grey swells criss-cross their way to the horizon.

'Is it hard to play the fiddle like you do, Danny?' I ask. 'I used to take violin lessons, till the teacher got cross when I didn't do my scales. But I'd like to learn some of the songs you play. They make my toes tap.'

'Well, that's a good start. Fiddle music's for dancing after all—you just play over and over with rhythm and a soft hand, and feel the lilting inside and hear how the notes slide together. When your feet start moving you're doing it right. I suppose I can show you one or two tunes.'

'Thank you, I'd like that. I'll get my violin out of the luggage tomorrow.' After a companionable silence I ask, 'Danny, why does Rosa always make you look as if you're trying not to smile?'

He chuckles, his curls shaking. 'Well, I'm sitting there thinking—beneath all that peaches and cream she's as tough as the bosun and crazy as the Finn. God help anyone getting in the way of whatever Rosa wants.'

'But Rosa's just wilful. Mama says she's truly kind and loving at heart, but sometimes she feels things so terribly deeply.'

He gazes at me for a moment. 'Then take care, child. Often people who feel so terribly deeply don't bother themselves overmuch with how anyone else feels.'

Papa becomes unwell, a cough that turns bronchial and feverish. Mama attends to him with patent medicines and herbal teas and he recovers, but is too sick to leave his bed for a few days.

We've been at sea for seven weeks, and suddenly Christmas is upon us. Mama packed a few old decorations which we hang on the aspidistra, I make paper chains to dangle from the skylights and Piet the cook produces plum pudding, but because of Papa's illness it is a quiet time.

Mr Meade and Danny sit down to Christmas lunch with Rosa and Mama and me. I've just finished another fiddle lesson with Danny and I'm ecstatic.

'Mama, I already know *Over The Ocean* and *The Old Grey Goose* and I'm learning *Aggie Whyte's* now. It's such fun!'

'*Aggie Whyte's* what?' asks Rosa.

'Just *Aggie Whyte's*,' says Danny mildly. 'It's a reel.'

Gideon Meade says, 'Now Miss Lucy, that kind of thing isn't suitable for young people. What about Mr Brahms' waltzes instead? *That's* what I call good music.'

'I could hardly agree more,' says Rosa. 'And what's worse, she insists on practising over and over in our cabin. It's simply dreadful.'

Danny's eyebrows move slightly and he has that look on his face again.

In the evening Sam Lee joins us for Christmas dinner. He and Mama discuss a recent novel about an arranged marriage and scandalous divorce and I'm enthralled. As the pudding is served, Papa called out to Mama and she leaves to attend to him.

There is silence. Coals in the small cast-iron fireplace crackle and the saloon rolls slowly side to side in a rhythm we barely notice now.

Rosa pushes the last piece of pudding idly around in her plate. 'And are you also destined for an arranged marriage, Mr Lee?'

'I believe you may have confused Chinese customs with those of India,' he says. 'No, Miss Fox, I am free to marry anyone I please.'

'Will she have tiny feet, all bound up,' I ask, 'and wear embroidered silken kimonos?'

He laughs. 'Miss Lucy, kimonos are the dress of Japan, not China. And my mother is from the Hakka people. They never adopted that cruel practice and she certainly would not permit me to marry a woman with bound feet.'

He watches Rosa's bowed red-gold head and I see he's no longer smiling.

She looks up. 'Then I wish you joy in your search for a bride amongst the Hakka. I believe I will take some fresh air before retiring. Good night.'

Sam Lee stands as Rosa leaves the saloon, then sits again slowly.

'Goodness,' I say. 'She doesn't usually like fresh air, especially not at these latitudes. But Mr Lee, why don't you marry a white woman then, since you're just as much English as Chinese?'

I notice his expression. 'Oh. Is that another unexpected question?'

Sam rubs his face with his strong brown hands. 'A difficult one indeed, Miss Lucy. There are many who find the idea of an Asian man with a white woman unthinkable.'

He gazes at the fire. 'In the recent depression some women chose to marry hard-working Chinese men, market-gardeners, carpenters, shopkeepers, and found good lives with them. But their contentment is not something much dwelt upon by the newspapers, which never cease to spout venom upon the topic.'

'I've seen the cartoons they print, and they draw the coloured people so they look ugly and frightening, not at all like you or Borue or Thomas the Islander. That's so unkind.'

'But those unkind people are powerful, Miss Lucy, and a woman would have to be very brave to marry a half-caste man—she and her family might never again be received in society. So you see I cannot take a white wife, it would bring her too much suffering.'

'That is unfortunate, Mr Lee. I believe you would make a very good husband.'

He smiles. 'Thank you, Miss Lucy, but I suspect the world does not see anything—anything much at all!—in quite the same light as you.'

I laugh, then say shyly, 'I do not mind if you simply call me Lucy, you know. Danny and I have already agreed such formality is not warranted in our present circumstances.'

'Of course. Perhaps a touch of distance is appropriate when your father is present, but otherwise, should you also feel moved to address me as Sam, I would be honoured.'

Papa seems better and takes dinner with us again. He's in a good mood and, perhaps inspired by the eerie icicles all over the ship, the conversation turns to ghostly sea stories.

'And the barque had been lost in that *very* position—but it was fully one hundred years before!' finishes Gideon Meade, who looks rather pleased at the gasps of surprise and laughter.

'I'm certain Mr Whalen also has a thrilling tale for us all,' says Mama as she serves the coffee.

Danny rubs the russet curls on his chin and says, 'Ah no, Mrs Fox, I've no tales at all.'

'That's not true,' I say, 'you have lots!'

He glances at me in exasperation, takes a sip of his coffee and says, 'I have one, but I fear you may not sleep well in these waters again.'

Rosa says, 'I imagine that's highly unlikely.'

'We shall see. Well. This happened not far from here to a shipmate of mine, a good man. It was a moonless night, freezing cold, the barque running along at four bells in the churchyard watch—'

'Two o'clock in the morning,' I whisper helpfully to Rosa.

'—and suddenly they heard an uncanny howling out of the darkness. A frightful wailing cry, he told me, like voices in agony. The men stood still on deck, hair lifting on their necks staring out into the darkness, listening in horror.'

'Good heavens,' says Mama faintly.

'The screams rang out again and even the men asleep below came running, terrified, up to the deck. They were six hundred miles from the nearest land—what could it possibly be? Then the ghastly

noise came a third time. It rose to a peak of unbearable torture—
and then what was worse, he said—what was worse, it died away in
the most terrible, terrible, *whimpering.*'

Rosa is still, her eyes fixed upon him. I'm biting my lip.

'They all stood stock-still, even the captain, silent, the ship
ghosting along. They waited, peering out, then slowly began to
breathe again, began to move, to murmur, to ask what in God's
name it could have been. None of them, not even the oldest hands,
had ever known such a thing. Whales, perhaps, they whispered, or
the screams of sea-lions, seals groaning on an iceberg, a sea-serpent
arisen from the deep, or...'

He stops for a moment, staring at the cast-iron fireplace. An
ember crackles and flares.

'Or perhaps it was simply some boatload of poor, shipwrecked
desperates, watching the lights of their only salvation passing
beyond and away from them forever.'

There is silence.

'And what was it?' asks Mama.

Danny looks up and shrugs. 'I don't know. They never knew.
They moved on, the ship must always move on, we all understand
that. It cannot retrace its passage, not in these waters, not in the
dark, not for anyone.'

There's more silence.

Papa harumphs, 'Indeed.'

Mama rises and begins to gather the cups, her eyes anxious, and
Gideon Meade says quickly, 'Sea-lions, I'm certain of it, they make
an extraordinary racket.'

'A most unsatisfactory tale,' says Rosa. 'I shall retire now and I'm
sure I'll sleep very well.'

As good-nights are exchanged, I take my coat and slip up to a
corner of the deck. I stare into the freezing night—the light winds,
the ship ghosting along, just as in Danny's story. I hold my shaking
hand to my mouth and try not to make any noise.

He comes up behind me. 'Jesus, child, it was just a tale.'

I wipe my cheeks. 'It wasn't just a tale, Danny. You said your shipmate was a good man.'

I see a glint from his earring as he looks out to the dark. 'He was, Lucy, and I trusted his words. He's been gone three years now, poor sod, lost on *Loch Long*.'

'It's so terrible. The sea is so cruel.'

'And don't you forget that, child, when you're playing at your knots and navigation and admiring the billowing sails—never, *never*, forget that. Go to your mother now and don't cry. We're all safe tonight.'

The wind dies down and for a day or two there's pale sunshine. The crew spread torn sails out along the deck and sit side by side, patching and mending. I can see Danny next to Thomas the Islander, grinning and telling him a joke.

I've discovered Thomas comes from Torres Strait, where he was once a diver for pearlshell and can swim down an amazing fifty feet with only goggles to protect him. I wonder if Sam knows that? Perhaps Thomas can go with him to Broome.

Beside me Gideon Meade is looking up at the rigging, light glancing off his golden beard.

'Why do we have a third mate at all, Mr Meade?' I ask. 'I thought a barque of this size would have only first and second.'

'Ah. As it happens, this was to have been my first command, but your father's seniority saw him kept him on as master for this leg of the voyage. So Danny is acting third mate although he's rated second, and Sam Lee is acting second, although he should be first. However, once *Willowmere* reaches Melbourne we shall all take up our correct stations.'

'Were you sad not to be master this time?'

He smiles wryly. 'In truth, Miss Lucy, it was something of a blow, but our job is always to pull together for the ship. Rank does not account for much in a Pampero, after all. I will have my chance soon enough.'

'When we get to port we must celebrate your command. You will be Captain Meade then!'

He cannot hide the pleasure in his blue eyes. 'Indeed, I cannot pretend I am not anticipating our arrival. And with my improved prospects perhaps I may hope for even greater joy in my life.' He glances at Rosa, arm in arm with Mama as they stroll the small deck.

'I am not entirely certain my sister is fond enough of the sea to become a captain's wife,' I say, 'but I do wish you the best of fortune.'

'Thank you, Miss Lucy.'

'And after Melbourne where will you take *Willowmere*?'

'To Newcastle, New South Wales, for coal. Then the West Coast, Chile, for nitrates, and home by Cape Horn. It will be a harder voyage than this one but we must lift whatever cargo we can. Steamships get all the best trade nowadays.'

'Would you ever go into steam, Mr Meade?'

He strokes his moustache. 'There is nothing on this earth quite so fine as life on a wind ship, but yes, in a few years I believe I will go into steam. It is the way of the future.'

'And the other mates?'

'I believe Sam Lee has plans for his own small fleet, the shell-fishing ketches—and may he remember us all when he makes his fortune with a great pearl! Danny Whalen? No, he will never leave sail, he would sooner die.'

I gaze at the life of the ship around me. The moody Finn is at the bow on lookout, the Swedish lad at the wheel, his eyes alert on the compass. Two men are working aloft and someone off duty is playing a melody on a penny whistle.

I can hear the gruff voice of the sailmaker instructing an apprentice, and the murmur of quiet words as the sailors stitch a canvas that, dry, weighs half a ton. No one knows what it weighs when it's wet, but the crewmen know how to rig it and set it and handle it to steer the barque anywhere they wish to go on the seven seas.

What kind of world would have no use for these clever men and their great vessels crafted out of centuries of experience? I laugh to myself at the very notion.

The fair weather becomes just a memory. The seas are again massive, the waves vicious and irregular, pale foam flying from gunmetal peaks. Clouds roil and race across the black sky and the rigging shrieks. *Willowmere* is now running under lower topsails and staysails alone.

Squalls of rain drive in and away, sometimes hail, sometimes sleet, always freezing. The men tie soul-and-body lashings around their waists, wrists and necks to try to hold a little precious warmth inside their oilskins, but they're wet through all the time.

Red-eyed and grey-faced, they stumble below to eat and fall asleep, then turn out again just a few hours later to deal with the incredible storms. Water swirls even on the floor of the saloon.

'It's only a few inches, Rosa,' says Mama irritably, soaking it up with a towel. 'When your father and I were off the Canaries in 'eighty-six there was a foot of water in the cabins.'

Scowling, Rosa climbs into her berth. 'I'm not coming out and what's more, if Lucy touches that fiddle again today I'll throw it overboard.'

I beg to be allowed to go up on deck in my oilskins for a few moments but my tired mother refuses to consider it. In the grey afternoon she goes to lie down in the cabin beside Papa, whose chest has again taken a turn for the worse.

Rosa is reading, flipping the pages of a novel in the lower berth, then she puts the book down and begins to doze. Sitting in the top berth with my arms wrapped around my knees, I realise no one is awake to tell me what to do.

I quietly get down, slip on my seaboots and oilskins and climb the companionway. I can hardly push open the door for the wind, but finally squeeze through before it slams shut again.

Mr Meade is clinging to the rail forward, roaring something to the crew. The helmsmen notice me with surprise, then must cope with the kick of the wheel as a sea strikes. It is said they're forbidden to look behind, in case they go mad from terror at seeing what is approaching.

I stumble down the sloping deck to catch hold of the port rail. Waves tower above the barque as she rolls and pounds through the broken foam, down the side of one mountain, up the side of another. The noise is beyond anything I've ever known.

Mr Meade turns and sees me and begins yelling and waving his arms but I can't hear him. He stares beyond me, horror on his face. I glance back and see a black peak, rearing, breaking, descending like an avalanche.

I'm caught up in freezing noise and darkness, and tumble against the deckhouse. Gideon Meade reaches me as the wave ebbs and I fall to the deck in great pain. He throws me across his shoulder, yanks open the companionway door and runs down the steps, roaring, 'Mrs Fox, *Mrs Fox!*'

He lowers me onto the dining table and from the corner of my eye I can see blood pooling from my head. Mama starts to remove my coat and I lose consciousness from the pain. I remain mercifully unaware as Mr Meade moves my arm, broken above the elbow, back into alignment and binds it.

Mama sends for Mr McPhee the sailmaker to attend to my head wound, a task he performs often enough for the crew. He trims the hair around the cut and closes it with dainty, perfect stitches. They put me in the lower berth of our cabin, then Mama takes turns with Rosa to stay with me.

3. IN THE RIGGING

I remain unconscious for a day then open my eyes, confused, and Mama gives me water. Half a day later I wake again, my words a little slurred, but I begin to understand I've been in an accident. I cannot focus and sometimes I cry from exhaustion.

'Don't fret, darling Lou,' my mother says, stroking my cheek. 'Your body has had a terrible shock and will take time to recover. You'll feel better bye and bye.'

'I'm so sorry, Mama, so sorry to be such a bother. I just wanted to *see ...*' And I weep.

'Aye, you just wanted to see,' says Danny when he comes to visit. 'I told you it's no game, child. Ah well. I believe you cannot read at the moment. Would you be wanting to hear some of the more cheerful works of Mr Dickens?'

Gideon Meade says solemnly, 'Miss Lucy, I would be no friend if I did not say you put the vessel herself into danger, causing me to leave the deck at that time. Your punishment therefore is to study this copy of the classic tome, *The Black Book of the Admiralty.*'

'How can that be a punishment, Mr Meade?'

'Well, those rapscallion apprentices would certainly think it so!' And to my great pleasure he helps me through a few pages of sailing lore every day.

Sam brings me gifts from the men—a small perfect model of *Willowmere* from the starboard watch and a beautiful ropework mat from the port watch, woven with the message 'Get Well Shipmate.' I weep again.

I just manage to hold back the tears the day the sailmaker removes his tiny stitches. Mama says the scar is faint, but the hair around it is again trimmed to the scalp, just as it was promising to grow out in pretty waves.

'No need to mourn for your hair, girl,' says Danny. 'No one'll notice it anyway once they're seeing those bruises. Myself, I can't believe the colours.'

The officers sometimes sit with me during their precious off-duty hours. Mama is grateful; Papa is improving but still demands her attention. Interspersed with Mr Dickens, I hear all about a small typhoon Danny ran into near Siam, and an elephant he rode once in Calcutta, and a pet monkey he got from the bosun of a tea clipper.

Sam tells me about his two little half-sisters, Filipa and Izabel, born from his mother's marriage to a man from Macao named Leo Peres. Mr Peres died from a fever and Min-lu and her daughters now live in a fine house at Williamstown. It's apparently not far from our new home, so perhaps I will get to meet a merchant woman after all.

Mr Meade reminisces about his idyllic childhood in Oxfordshire, his happy days at school, his mother's garden parties and the wise sayings of his father, the Bishop. If Rosa is nearby he tries to draw her into conversation too, with occasional success.

Gideon Meade's broad shoulders and golden good cheer are sometimes a little overwhelming in the tiny cabin, but Sam's presence is always a comfort: his quiet voice and thoughtful dark eyes leave me with a sense of peace. As usual, Danny sparkles with mischief, but I notice the tales he tells me are light-hearted ones and I'm grateful he avoids the harsher side of sea life.

The officers sit on a chest at the foot of my bunk in their heavy coats and seaboots, their bearded faces tired and fiercely alert at the same time. My concentration wavers and sometimes I see them as if meeting them for the first time.

They're all tall yet so different: Gideon muscular, Danny rangy,

Sam elegant. But their hands are oddly alike—the size of soup-plates—probably from years of hauling on ropes. My broken arm hurts a great deal and the prospect of hauling on anything again seems sadly remote.

Indeed, I'm suddenly more aware of bodies than ever before. One morning I call for Mama, afraid I've suffered an internal injury in the accident. She explains I'm now a woman, and I notice I'm not as flat under my chemise as I used to be. But I certainly don't feel like a woman. I wonder if these odd changes are what turned Rosa into such a bore.

Mama also gives me some extraordinary information about husbands and wives, and I begin to realise the complicated forms of males in classical art are not merely decorative, as I'd always assumed, but also functional. I've visited farms so am not entirely ignorant, but it never occurred to me that humans could behave so oddly too.

I puzzle about this strange new world, about clothes and positions and surely, the terrible embarrassment of it all. Do people set up appointments to make babies with each other? Do they talk? Does it hurt?

Now I feel waves of shyness with the officers and wonder if they notice the changes in my body. Everything is suddenly different and I hate the feeling of constraint that's come over me.

By the time I'm allowed out of my bunk, *Willowmere* has passed the Cape of Good Hope and is half-way across the Indian Ocean. Even with Mama's help it takes time to get up the stairs, my hip and knee are so painful. Next morning I climb again, then sit on the deck watching the waves and sunlight and sails. After a few days I begin to feel better, but my arm still hurts and has nothing like its former strength.

Papa has recovered from his fever but his temper is worse than ever. We have two compasses on board, one near the wheel and the other, the master's own standard instrument, at the fore of the poop deck. Gideon Meade mentions he's noticed a discrepancy between the two, but Papa just harumphs.

On deck a few days later Mr Meade says, 'Sir, I am still concerned about the accuracy of the standard compass. The discrepancy seems larger now.'

Papa explodes. 'It's been with me for twenty years, mister, and it's never been wrong. Are you sure it wasn't you who got the deck compass wrong when the ship was swung? You're not master of this vessel just yet, you know!'

He strides forward and roars at the men near the deckhouse to brace a sail. I see a quick look pass between Mr Meade and Danny, who turns away and busies himself with tidying a line that's already perfectly coiled.

Later, I ask him what's going on. Danny says, 'Ah, the captain is always right, you know that, it's how it has to be. You can't be having a pretty conversation in the middle of a hurricane.'

'But what if Papa is wrong?'

He hesitates. 'He's a good master, your father. Many things can happen on a voyage, girl, and most of them are out of anyone's hands. We just have to be doing our best.'

Danny has started calling me *girl* lately, instead of *child*. Is it apparent, after all, I am growing up? It's only later I realise he didn't answer my question.

One night at dinner Sam politely asks how my arm is mending.

'Not very well. It's weak and I fear it will never be flexible again.'

'You must move it more, Miss Lucy,' says Sam, 'put weight upon it, strengthen it. I had a shipmate once with a broken arm. He was almost crippled, but the mate made him climb the rigging no matter how he complained, and soon it was as good as new.'

'Climb the rigging, Mr Lee? Oh, I would so much like to do that.'

'Climb the *rigging*!' says Papa. 'A girl—in skirts! On my ship?

Impossible.'

Mama looks thoughtful. 'But Nicholas, I have my cycling bloomers in the trunk. They're perfectly modest and we're all aware that exercise is essential for growing young women.'

Rosa rolls her eyes.

'Papa, if my arm is useless no one will ever want to marry me.'

He frowns. 'Well. Certainly a point of consideration. Annabel, are you quite certain such a thing would be seemly?'

'Of course, darling. Lucy's health must come first. She'd be safe and supervised, with the assistance of the officers, naturally.'

'Indeed.' He gazes at his plate for a while.

I wait, hands clasped beneath the edge of the table.

'Very well. But only on the lower rigging and by *God*, Mr Lee, the men had better behave themselves.'

'I shall make certain of it, sir.'

Sam and I glance across the table at each other and hide our smiles.

'Now you understand you must always climb on the windward side of the rigging so you're pressed towards the shrouds, not away?'

'Yes, Mr Lee.'

'And always grasp the shrouds, never the ratlines—they're sometimes rotten. Now, up and around, have you got hold? You be ready here, Thomas, to catch Miss Lucy if she falls. Up a step— there, how does that feel?'

It feels terrible. I ease my aching left arm and use the right for balance, and take another step and another. But I must place weight on my sore arm, that's why I'm here. Another step. I lean my head on a ratline. Another. I stop.

'Come down now, Miss Lucy. Just do a little this first day.'

Thomas the Islander helps me down and onto the deck.

'Thank you Thomas, Mr Lee.' My voice is unsteady. 'I'll try again tomorrow.'

I lean on the rail beside Mama, catching my breath. 'I do enjoy wearing your blouse and cycling bloomers, Mama. I feel as if I can do almost anything in them.'

She ruffles my hair. 'Good. My brave Lou.'

It's Sunday so the men are free of routine work, and I gaze ahead to the foc's'le deck. Men are washing their clothes in buckets, others are shaving off their cold-weather beards or getting a haircut from Sig the Bosun, an acknowledged master of the tidy trim.

Danny sits playing a quiet tune to himself on his fiddle, and some of the men lie in hammocks enjoying the sunlight. It won't be long now before we reach Melbourne and I must strengthen my arm before then.

The next day I climb the same few steps up the rigging and the pain is still sharp. Yet every day I go a little further and the aching is less. Finally I can reach the masthead, and few days later I can climb up and down again twice before I'm forced to rest.

'Surely that's enough exercise for now, Lucy,' demands my father at dinner.

'Oh no, Papa, my arm's still so sore and stiff, I must keep working it.'

'You'll get muscles like a deckhand! Annabel, I do not see anything at all amusing in that.'

'My dear, just look at Lucy's arms—so thin, nothing at all like a deckhand's,' says my mother. 'I believe she should continue, her efforts are doing her good. See how excellent her colouring has become?'

'She's still got hardly any hair on one side,' says Rosa unkindly. I'm surprised—at dinner she's usually demure—but then, the officers aren't with us tonight because the mainsail blew out earlier and they're helping bend another. I wonder if she's harbouring a secret passion for Mr Meade or Sam Lee (not Danny, it's obvious she can't stand him).

Today she was chatting to the officers but the conversation was ordinary until Gideon Meade said perhaps we could meet for a picnic after we reach Melbourne, and Sam said he would bring his little sisters too. Rosa replied she did not believe she would be free for picnics because Mama would need her assistance with the new house. But if she harboured a secret passion for Sam or Mr Meade wouldn't she want to go on an outing with them?

Later I say to Sam, 'I'd love us to have a picnic. I cannot fathom why Rosa is being so contrary.'

He gazes at the waves. 'I think perhaps she is not used to the fact of circumstances even she cannot alter. Rosa does not wish to be constrained by anything.' He smiles. 'In some ways you're rather alike.'

Oh dear. I do hope I'll never become as complicated as my sister.

The Southern Ocean is notorious for its storms, but instead we have days of glorious weather. It's February 1907, and summer-time in the Colonies. The men wear open-necked shirts while Mama and Rosa and I are in light cotton dresses. The ship sparkles as every surface is chipped or cleaned, polished or varnished, ready for the day we sail—*smart as new paint*, says Sig the Bosun—into Melbourne's Port Phillip.

Sig gives me a nice new haircut too, leaving it light and wispy around my face, hiding my scar. Danny says I look just like his pet monkey from the tea clipper, only taller.

It's taken time to be able to hold the fiddle properly again, but now I've learnt nine tunes and practise them with Danny whenever I can.

One day he says, 'Like a goose's neck, girl. Lighten the grip on your bow.'

'But my teacher in London said to hold it very firmly.'

'Aye, that's the problem. It's not so much your left hand, it's your right that needs to forget what it's doing and just—flow.'

'Oh, I *see*. The way a goose waves its neck!'

We play the reel again and I can feel how much the rhythm is improved. I'm often surprised at how seriously Danny takes his music: there are few jokes and his concentration is intense. Even within my small experience I can tell he's a good musician.

I still exercise my arms on the rigging. By now no one pays attention, although Thomas the Islander usually hovers protectively nearby. I love the strength that's bloomed in my body, and the only discomfort I feel now is from well-worked muscles, not damaged bones.

For variety I climb the rigging on a different mast each day, and today it's the foremast. As I reach the foretop platform I hook an arm through the rigging and gaze around. At first the deck seemed a frightful distance below, but now I'm used to it. I love the sight of the swooping lines of canvas and cables and blocks: the sinews and joints of this great spiderweb construction.

I yearn to go higher, but at this point the men have to swing themselves out and up to reach the platform above. My arms are not strong enough for that, but there's an opening against the mast called the lubber's hole, small enough for me to get through.

I quickly check—no one is watching—and I wriggle through and up onto the platform. Nobody yells at me to get down, and before I can lose my nerve I step onto the next line of rigging and keep climbing till I reach the cross-trees. I hold on tightly as I gaze around in triumph.

The mast swings in a slow wide arc, side to side against an immense blue sky. The deck below is very small indeed. It curves sweetly into the bowsprit, slowly rising and falling. Twin white bow-waves surge out and mingle with the long wake ruffled behind us as far as I can see.

'Oh my,' I whisper in awe. 'Oh my.'

I hear a shout on deck and look down guiltily, but it's only an order to the crew. Five men move to the fore rigging and start to climb—I can feel the vibration. Perhaps they're just going to the foresail, I think hopefully. But they swing up onto the topmast rigging and continue towards me.

The Swedish lad is the first to see me, saying in surprise, 'De *flicka* is dere!' He goes red as he swings onto a footrope six feet below me and moves out along the yard. Ratface the apprentice mutters, 'Girls!' as he clambers towards the other end. 'You should not be here, Missy!' says a horrified Thomas the Islander. The Finn just stares at me suspiciously from under his black eyebrows.

Borue the Koepanger laughs. 'You get to royal top soon I think, but now please hold tight!'

He step onto the footrope and leans over the yard with the others as they begin to unbend the sail. Another canvas below on deck is ready to replace it. I watch the men as they release blocks and lines and the upper edge of the sail. They work quickly and efficiently, swaying and balancing, occasionally muttering or cursing.

I gaze at the Swede's fair hair and supple brown arms and capable hands, and for the first time I wonder if being married might not be quite so bad after all, despite the embarrassing things people have to do.

The men lower the old sail to the deck and the new one is hoisted and fastened into place. Then, as they swing themselves sweating back onto the rigging, Borue says, eyes mischievous, 'You wait one minute then come down, maybe your daddy not see you after all.'

When everything is quiet I climb down to the deck.

Danny is standing there, arms crossed. 'If you're wanting to join the port watch so badly I've got a great patch of rust needs chipping in the forward hold.'

I hesitate, considering the prospect.

'*Jesus*, girl, I'm hardly serious! So what chance d'you think I'd have of getting my ticket if the skipper's daughter goes head-first into the deck on my watch?'

'Danny, I'm so sorry! I never thought of that. Did my father see?'

He blows out his breath in exasperation. There's silence.

'No, thank Christ, but you took a year off everyone's life. Don't do it again.'

The sky grows hazy and for several days we cannot take sextant readings, so our position on the chart is calculated by dead reckoning from the ship's speed and direction. It's less accurate, naturally, says Mr Meade, but it's clear we're on course as expected.

'Rather a relief,' he says. 'We must make our way between King Island and Cape Otway. Fifty miles apart so you might think it easy, but the waters off Victoria can be cruel. There were many wrecks here in Bass Strait before the lighthouses were built.'

'And were there none afterwards?' I ask.

'Some. But we shall be safe, do not fear.'

'Are the compasses in agreement now?'

'A minor discrepancy still exists.' The wind ruffles his golden hair. 'However, the standard compass is a fine instrument, so we work to that. We are well prepared for the difficulties, and soon we shall sail into the vast haven of Port Phillip. And then, Melbourne...'

'You are dreaming of your promotion now, Mr Meade,' I say teasingly.

'I cannot deny it, Miss Lucy.' He smiles. 'How very much I look forward to landfall.'

That evening the beam of the Cape Otway lighthouse appears in the distance and everyone cheers.

Mama holds a small party in the saloon to celebrate our journey's end. The fire is lit and the reflections of candles flicker on the polished panelling. There isn't much room to spare once the officers, bosun and sailmaker join us in the small room, but it doesn't matter.

It's the first time I've seen Sam and Danny in their brass-buttoned coats and stiff collars. They're freshly-shaven, their hair trimmed, and they seem both familiar and rather magnificent at the same time.

Mama hands around drinks and small savouries, and the chatter and laughter increases. As it's a special occasion I'm permitted to have a tiny glass of sherry.

Danny leans over and growls to me, 'Ah, me hearty, ye'll be wantin' your tot of rum soon, then?'

'Indeed I will sir, once I'm done chippin' that rust you've got for me in the forward hold.'

'Never you bother yourself with Danny's scurvy crew, Miss Lucy,' says Sam. 'I need a good upper yardman for the starboard watch.'

Papa looks puzzled at the idea of anyone thinking I'd make a good upper yardman, but Mama distracts him with a savoury and everyone starts talking about what they'll do when they reach Melbourne.

Gideon Meade is on watch but comes below for ten minutes to sit, blue eyes content, beside Rosa. I overhear 'picnic' and am pleased to see Rosa smiling at him at last.

When the evening is quiet again and I'm preparing for bed, I hear the familiar voice of Mr Meade reporting to Papa, as the deck officer must do every night. The fog is coming up, he says, but he's put an extra lookout on the foremast and they're casting the lead every ten minutes.

I lie in my berth and distantly hear the watches change over at midnight. Water gurgles along the hull, rolling with the rhythm that's now woven into my sense of balance. Such a comfort to know my family, and the friends who've become like family, are safe together in this tiny perfect world.

As I drift into warm sleep, I think, you did it *Willowmere*—so far, so strong, so brave, so beautiful.

And I wake to cold grey light from the porthole, and urgent steps and raised voices on the deck above.

4. THE FIGUREHEAD

I stumble on deck to see grey-yellow cliffs—*cliffs*?—just half a mile ahead of us. After that I only remember moments as if lit up by lightning flashes, like the night of the Pampero. Mama, hair flying around her face, catching my arm. Get warm clothes, get Rosa! No corsets, no petticoats, just *hurry*! Running below, yanking a dress over my nightgown, buttoning my boots, hands shaking.

On deck again, men hauling, yelling, the helm hard over. The ship turning little by little away to starboard. Papa, grey-stubbled cheeks, hands clenched on the rail, staring. Sam, Thomas and Sig the Bosun on one side of the foredeck. Danny, Borue and the Finn on the other. Gideon Meade concentrating on the helm, the sails, roaring orders to the whole ship.

Willowmere turning, turning away from the cliffs and the little white beach, almost away, almost away ... and then a shock of abrupt stillness. Silence, then a groaning quivering judder, the screeching of tearing steel, the fore-topmast exploding, collapsing, sparks like fireworks.

Rigging all over the foredeck, men chopping with axes, men crawling free—men groaning, crying. Trying to tie my lifebelt, Mama helping, her own not yet done up—be brave, my darlings. Rosa's shocked eyes reflecting flashes of blue distress rockets. The bosun calling out to Papa, *twelve feet in the bilges sir, and rising*.

Hands helping me over the side into the lifeboat, huddling close to Rosa, Sam in charge, Thomas at the tiller, men at the oars, men working the blocks. Dropping into the sea, my stomach turning over, pulling away, then waiting, watching, blood pounding in my ears.

The second boat, Gideon in charge, Mama sitting down, apprentice Brownley, the Swedish boy at the tiller: the boat lowering, slowing, tilting, tipping, something *wrong*, people like dolls flying into the sea. *Mama*!

Our boat moving, slowly, agonisingly, towards the figures in the water—Gideon holding up the Swede (blood in his fair hair) pushing him into the boat, swimming away. Rosa crying out, there, there she is! Sam standing, white shirt, diving in. My mother's red hair floating out around her like *Ophelia Drifting*, then she's sinking, sinking. I can hear myself shrieking, high, like a gull.

Gone. *Gone*?

Sam looking back at us in despair for an instant, then turning, diving under choppy waves, up for a breath, down again—a long, long emptiness—then up, oh God, in his arms, he has her! Pushing, pulling her over the side, Mama coughing, shaking, clinging to me and Rosa, sobbing.

The third boat away now, Papa there, Danny there. Men still hauling people from the water, some moving; some not. Two boats alongside in the grey dawn, words shouted between Danny and Sam, then turning, rowing towards the land, the pale beach, the breakers. A wave lifting us, flying forward, the keel scraping and grinding on the sand. Safe, all safe.

Landfall.

I remember Gideon Meade's confident words. 'How very much I look forward to landfall.'

Surf rushing, wind crying, someone whimpering. Carefully getting out of the boat, people helping, lifting, carrying. Clinging, supporting Mama, stumbling. Not daring to look back at our great broken vessel grinding in anguish on the reef.

Gathered on a stretch of dry sand near rocks beneath cliffs. The Finn with a broken ankle, several others with bleeding cuts, the sailmaker ripping up shirts to bind what he can. The Swedish boy, blood seeping through a rough bandage, unconscious but breathing. Two figures lying still, not breathing.

I stare around, confused. Where's Borue? The apprentices? Piet the cook? Sig the Bosun? Oh—Borue, there—his arm around the shoulders of sobbing Ratface. Inside a great silence I walk to the still figures, one a deckhand I don't know very well and the other Brownley, the unkind apprentice. I cannot move or think. Danny takes my arm and leads me back to the others.

'I don't like him, Danny, but he mustn't be dead. He shouldn't be like that.'

'No, no, girl, that he should not. Come sit by your mother.'

A long whistle, a call from high on the cliff, a figure among the scrub. Someone climbing across rocks of the cliff-face, down a rough track.

'Ahoy!' yells Gideon.

A man with a white beard slithers down the last few yards of cliff and falls on the sand, and Gideon helps him to his feet. The man says, catching his breath, 'Saw your rockets—out mustering sheep —the boy's riding to the homestead—not far—'

He sits down, puffed. 'Ewan Campbell, farmer. By God, what a sight, the ship—you poor, poor people. Matches, I've got matches here, make a fire, for the Lord's sake.'

The men gather driftwood and branches, and soon a small fire flickers in the morning chill. Rosa and I huddle close to Mama, trying to keep her warm. Papa is coughing occasionally, holding the ship's logbook and sitting beside the navigational instruments, thrown in the lifeboat at the last moment.

I see Gideon speaking to Sam, ticking off his fingers. Together they look around, count again, then Gideon rubs his face with his hands and Sam stares out to sea.

A long time passes. Danny goes to Gideon and says something quietly. Gideon nods. Danny speaks to large Thomas and they lift one of the bandaged men—the Yankee, who hardly seemed hurt at all!—and carry him over to the other group: now there are three bodies, unmoving.

I cling close to Mama, who hasn't said anything for a long time. I hope she's resting. Her clothes are dry on the outside now but she's still shivering. I gaze around at every face and realise the cook, friendly Dutch Piet, never even made it off the ship, and I stare at the flames of the small fire, my eyes stinging. People murmur every now and then, but whenever they stop it's horribly quiet.

After hours and hours there's a shout from the top of the cliff and a group of loud men start down the rough track, carrying narrow stretchers. They help Mama and the Swedish boy and the Finn onto the stretchers, and lift them slowly up the cliff, cursing and calling out to each other.

Rosa and I go with Mama and Sam stays close by, taking our hands over the roughest parts. Danny helps carry the instruments from the ship with Papa, who cannot seem to stop coughing.

The wounded men limp, supported by the healthy men. I look down at one point where the scrub opens up and can see the three dark figures still lying on the beach.

'Sam, we can't leave them behind in the cold—'

'We'll bring them up later, Lucy, don't worry. Later.'

At the top of the cliff the wind is strong, the grey clouds low. Someone wraps a blanket around me and gives me water from a canteen. There are two bullock carts waiting, but I can't get to them as everyone else is moving around and talking loudly.

Mama and the Swede are beneath blankets in one cart, Sam and Rosa beside them, bracing them. Rosa's red-gold hair has fallen out of its usual knot and her dress is muddy. In the other cart, the Finn is lying down and Papa, white-faced, is sitting beside three bandaged crewmen. Gideon speaks to him and Papa nods wearily, then they shake hands. Suddenly the carts move away.

They've forgotten about me. I stand staring after them, tears coming to my eyes, but Danny murmurs, 'Let them go now, girl, they've got to be getting to the doctors quickly. There'll be another cart for us soon, then we'll follow.'

Someone builds a small fire on a rocky patch near some bushes. Our rescuers and the rest of the men gather there, murmuring, waiting for a can of water to boil.

Bizarrely, the ground seems to sway beneath my feet as if I were still on board. I hear a faint groan of steel over the rush of wind and water, and for the first time since we reached shore I look back to the ocean, to *Willowmere* impaled upon the reef. I walk carefully to a flat boulder near the edge of the cliff and sit, and a few minutes later Danny joins me.

'Well, that was a bastard of a day,' he says thoughtfully.

In silence we watch the ship, sails still set as if she would be proudly on her way at any moment. A fallen mast is broken at a horrible angle, its threads of cables flying loose, looped and tangled over the deck, almost covered by water. The hull seems to quiver under the impact of the waves.

Gideon brings us two mugs of black tea and says to Danny, 'I'm taking a party down to the beach to bring the others up.' His face is grim.

'I'm so terribly sorry, Mr Meade, such—' I cannot finish.

Gideon puts his large arm around my shoulders and hugs me for a moment.

'There, there, Miss Lucy. We've been very lucky, all told. Indeed we have.'

I sip the tea, huddled in my blanket, watching *Willowmere* in silence beside Danny. After a long time a rhythmic metallic groaning grows suddenly sharp, then the mainmast sails shake, and slowly the main-topmast leans over and flutters and gracefully collapses.

'I can't bear it,' I whisper. 'She was so beautiful and strong and now she's dying.'

'She's not dying. She's only a bloody ship, just iron and steel and timber and endless work, nothing special.' After a moment Danny sighs and rubs his face. 'Ah, I'm a fool, of course she's special. But ships'll always let you down in the end, Lucy, no matter what you do ...'

He takes a ragged breath, and I see his eyelashes are damp.

'You called me Lucy then. And you did on the night we told ghost stories, too.'

He smiles fleetingly. 'Well, that's what happens, girl, whenever you're driving me to distraction with your questions—'

'And climbing—'

'And curiosity, aye.'

'Don't be sad, Danny. Everything will be better soon.'

It's late in the day when they bury the men under three clumsy crosses made from branches. The clouds have moved away and the air is still. Gideon leads us in the words of a prayer, one side of his tired face outlined by the sunset.

Most of our rescuers ride away then, to get back to their small settlements before it's dark. We sit around the fire, huddled in blankets, the moon rising almost full. Farmer Campbell killed a sheep earlier—thankfully well away from me—and now it's cooking over the embers. Occasionally quiet voices rise above the swish of the dark sea. *Willowmere*'s metallic groans are growing fainter.

I ask Mr Campbell how long it will take the carts to get to the nearest big town, where the doctors are.

'Colac is fifty miles inland from here, lassie, so twenty hours or so if they don't rest the bullocks.'

'Twenty hours?'

'Aye, but another cart will be here in the morning, so you'll all be there by tomorrow night, God willing.'

Oh, Mama. I feel so alone and shy at being the only female here. I finally whisper to Danny, my face hot, 'I need to go into the bushes but I'm afraid of wild creatures.'

He shows me to a small clearing away from the camp and

tramples around it for a few moments.

'No wild creatures here now, you'll be fine. But just shout ahoy if an elephant turns up and I'll come back and take it for a ride.'

That makes me smile so I don't worry about the little noises in the scrub around me. Later, after some damper bread and hot meat and more black tea, I wrap myself in my blanket and fall into a deep sleep.

At dawn the bullock cart arrives. I take one last look at *Willowmere*, now broken in half, her stern beneath the water. I sigh and clamber into the cart. Only six of us remain from the ship now —me, Gideon, Danny, Mr McPhee, Borue, Thomas and Ratface. Farmer Campbell and the last few rescuers now mount up, and after our heartfelt thanks they ride away.

The cart sets off along dusty tracks between scrubby bushes which turn into tall stands of olive-coloured trees. The bullocks trudge up and down hills, with scattered farm holdings appearing every now and then. The tall trees are called eucalyptuses, Gideon says. Across a field—they call them paddocks here, he says—I see two kangaroos nibbling grass and for a moment I'm so charmed I almost forget what has happened.

Gideon holds the ship's logbook and Mr McPhee cradles the valuable navigation instruments. I notice Danny has somehow managed to save his fiddle too, tucked beside him in its battered case. We stop for a lunch of more tea and damper and mutton, then late that night we arrive at the town of Colac.

The last five miles I lie asleep, cradled by large Thomas the Islander, then wake with a start to lanterns and voices. Gideon speaks to a group of people then turns around to say the men will go to the Shire Hall to sleep and I shall go to Widow Burton's house.

'But Mama—Papa—Rosa, where are they?'

Gideon says, 'I'm sorry, Miss Lucy, you may have to wait a little longer to see them. They've all gone on the noon train to Melbourne. Your mother and the Swedish lad Nilsen need to be treated at the hospital. We shall travel to Melbourne tomorrow too.'

I almost weep with disappointment. 'Courage, Missy,' whispers Borue and pats my arm.

Widow Burton is kind and efficient and has already organised some underclothing and a grey silk dress for me. She raises her eyebrows a little at my short hair. It was the scarlet fever, I murmur, and the Widow nods sympathetically.

When I'm getting ready for bed I realise I'm still wearing my nightgown under my dress, the nightgown I put on after our celebration, our premature celebration. Was that really just two evenings ago?

Next morning I'm surprised to see in the mirror how much I've grown since leaving England, and surprised too at my new waist in the grey dress. At the station the men wear a collection of donated clothes and hold parcels of food from the townspeople. Danny has his fiddle case in a sack.

'Was it damaged yesterday?' I ask him.

'A bit of salt, probably good for the tone. I couldn't leave it. My father's.'

A small deputation from the town, a reporter and a cluster of curious onlookers are there to farewell us, then finally we settle into our seats as the train puffs away. I sit beside Gideon Meade and watch the passing bushland.

After a time I say, 'What will happen to Papa, Mr Meade?'

'There will be a Court of Marine Inquiry, Miss Lucy. It shall not affect his career, he's on the point of retirement, but nonetheless it will be painful for him.'

'And your career?'

He pauses. 'I do not know. I shall have to face the Inquiry too, and afterwards? There are few enough vacancies for Masters in Sail at the best of times, and even fewer for those who have lost a ship. I may have to consider moving into steam sooner than I had expected.'

'But it wasn't your fault—'

'We do not know where the fault lies, Miss Lucy. I rack my brains wondering what might have gone wrong—the compass, the fog, currents, a lee shore? Thank God we have the logbook. Still, I simply do not know how it happened.'

He looks so grim I can say nothing more.

Outside the window the bush gives way to fewer trees and more paddocks. We stop at Geelong, then more paddocks, market gardens, then Werribee, with cottages and hotels. The trip seems endless, then suddenly there are houses in narrow streets and glimpses of wider streets with trams, and the engine is huffing clouds of black soot. We arrive at Melbourne.

As we step down from the carriage Sam comes towards us. He's dressed formally in a brass-buttoned coat and high collar, his black hair brushed back. He has never looked so handsome, nor so sad.

Sam briefly greets Gideon and Danny then turns to me and takes my hand. 'Lucy, your father asks that I bring you to the hospital as soon as possible. Your mother is still unwell.'

To Gideon he says, 'The company has not been forthcoming with assistance, so I've arranged for us all to stay at my mother's house in Williamstown.'

'Surely there won't be room—' says Gideon.

'It is perhaps more accurate to call it a mansion.'

'Mansion, you say?' asks Danny.

Sam smiles. 'I think you'll find it extremely comfortable.'

He gives directions to Gideon, then we climb into a taxi-cab. As the horse clip-clops along I say, 'Please tell me, Sam. I thought Mama was not hurt, why is she still in hospital?'

'She took water into her lungs, Lucy, and now she finds breathing difficult.'

'But she will recover, will she not?'

'The doctor has every hope for her recovery, do not fear.'

'Then why do you look so unhappy, Sam?'

'I did not realise—' he pauses. 'No, perhaps it's because I'm unsettled by—the difficult things that have occurred, not your poor Mama. The doctors had to operate on the Swedish boy Nilsen and he's still unconscious. Your father's bronchitis is of concern, but he stayed with his brother's family last night while Rosa and I sat with your mother. Rosa has been magnificent.'

I feel a touch of comfort, recalling that Papa's younger brother Edward is established here in Melbourne and will be able to help us. Soon we arrive at the hospital and so much has changed. Papa is grey-faced with a tremor in his hands, and Rosa is different too. No longer irritable, somehow both gentle and strong, her face glows when she sees us arrive.

Mama is in a single room propped up on pillows, her auburn hair plaited into loose braids. She weeps a little when she hugs me. 'You look so grown-up, darling,' she whispers.

'A kind woman in Colac gave me the dress, Mama. Are you feeling better? Can we go home?'

'Not yet I'm afraid. I'm sorry to be such a bother.'

'Oh, Mama, that's just what I said to you when I was hurt. Of course you're not a bother—it's my turn to help now. I'll sit with you while everyone else has a rest at Uncle Edward's.'

Rosa hugs me and Papa says, 'My dear, that would be a great help, we're exhausted. Edward has had the telephone installed and the Sister will show you how to call us if necessary. We'll go shortly but will return first thing in the morning.'

Later, Mama is able to sip a cup of tea. She doesn't want her roast beef dinner but she swallows a little mashed potato, and I eat the rest. Then she sleeps, but cries out softly several times.

I curl up in an armchair near her bed, feeling that strange slow swaying as if I were still standing on *Willowmere*. I think of the gentle-faced figurehead—the one that looks like Mama—gathering silt and seaweed on the hidden reef. I wonder what's happened to my violin, and the never-to-be-completed petticoat, and the woven mat that says 'Get Well Shipmate.' My familiar things becoming unfamiliar deep beneath the ocean.

I fall asleep, but wake just before dawn when Mama sits up, gasping for breath as if she's dreaming too what it's like under the water. I lie beside her and hold her until she relaxes again into a doze. I notice how hot she is, how laboured her breathing.

I find the nurse and she comes to Mama's bedside, and takes her temperature and times her pulse with a watch. She goes to call a doctor, then shows me how to telephone my uncle.

'But they won't be awake yet and they're coming here in a few hours—'

'Ring them now, Miss. They must get here sooner than that.'

I don't understand. They said Mama would recover, why the haste? Then I see the doctor's face after he examines her. He takes me aside and says, 'How old are you, my dear?'

'Fifteen ... almost sixteen.'

'Your mother has developed a dangerous inflammation of the lungs. You must be brave.'

I am brave sometimes, but I don't know if I can possibly be brave enough for this. I sit beside the bed holding Mama's hot hand. She opens her eyes and smiles and whispers, 'There, there, my darling Lou.'

She smiles again when Papa and Rosa and Sam hurry into the room, but after that she is silent, her eyes closed. Hours pass and her agonised breathing becomes lighter and fainter until I do not recognise the moment it ceases.

Afterwards, strangely, I remember no sound, just the sight of my father pressing a handkerchief to his eyes, Sam's face harsh with sorrow, Rosa clutching his hand and sobbing. A carriage, the masts of ships at the ends of passing streets, an ornate door, Uncle Edward there, with a look of Papa—and plump Aunt Bertha, without the slightest look of Mama.

A parlour, a cup of tea, but no Mama beside us to drink it. What shall we do, what shall we do?

5. THE HOUSE ON THE STRAND

'Don't be sad, Danny,' I'd said when we sat gazing at shipwrecked *Willowmere*. 'Everything will be better soon.' How instead could we have come to this moment, this inconceivable moment?

Uncle Edward, Aunt Bertha and Elspeth stand to one side of the grave. Rosa leans on Papa, Gideon on her other arm. Danny and the crew are beside me, with Sam and two Chinese people. There is no one else. All Mama's friends are in far-away England.

The minister finishes; the gravediggers throw earth upon the coffin. Rosa groans and collapses and Gideon supports her while Aunt Bertha offers smelling salts.

Danny takes my arm for a moment and murmurs. 'Hold on, girl.'

We walk away along an avenue of rose bushes, scented and pretty in the warmth: Mama would have loved them so (I wince at the thought). Sam introduces his companions—his mother, Lee Min-lu, a small woman in fashionable black silk, and his uncle, Lee Bao-lim, a mature man in a long dark robe.

Min-lu expresses her condolences in perfect English, and I'm touched at the kindness in her brown eyes. No opium-pipe after all, I think, and almost laugh at my own foolishness. How Mama would have enjoyed the joke.

Funeral meats await us at Uncle Edward's house. The food is probably excellent but it tastes like blotting paper, and all I want to do is hide away and sleep. Papa stands beside the mantelpiece, holding a plate, nodding his thanks stiffly to sympathisers.

I hear Rosa saying, 'We certainly shall, Aunt Bertha, it's what

Mama would have wanted.'

Aunt Bertha's face is worried. 'But you're welcome *here*, my dear, we have enough room and every comfort—and Williamstown is so far away—'

'The house will be perfectly comfortable once we've completed it to Mama's design, and the seaport is just twenty minutes from the city by train.'

'*Train?*' says Aunt Bertha, appalled. 'Good heavens, only tars and Chinks take the train!'

There's a hush as she realises, too late, what she's said. Gideon smoothly restarts the conversation with a comment on flourishing Williamstown. He's staying at Sam's mother's house with the crewmen: a mansion, Sam said. His uncle Bao-lim has a grey moustache and a long dark plait—a queue—down his back. He's speaking to Danny and nodding thoughtfully.

Rosa's voice is unsteady. 'We shall be grateful, Aunt Bertha, for your kind hospitality until everything is ready, but then we will set up our own household, as Mama would have wished.'

There is no more argument and I'm glad. I want our own place too. Papa says the furniture and house are already paid for, so we lost only clothes and mementos with *Willowmere*. And the heart of our family.

Papa is still troubled by his cough and finds it hard to sleep. He doesn't say much, but sits in the morning room pretending to read a book. I notice it's always open at the same page.

It seems as if the painting and papering of our new house takes place with agonising slowness: after the past few months of freedom my life at Aunt Bertha's seems to ache with tedium. There are so many little rules too, very few of which are ever explained to me until I've broken them.

Our cousin Elspeth is not very happy to have us there, either— her young man, Ronald, is rather too taken with Rosa. Elspeth and

Ronald 'have an understanding,' Aunt Bertha mouths to me one night, but she still frowns at the sight of Ronald anywhere near Rosa.

It reassures her whenever Gideon comes to take tea. 'Such a handsome man, our Mr Meade,' she says afterwards, adjusting her combs, 'and what a marvellous prospect for any woman.'

Papa is still so dazed it falls to Rosa to organise our finances, aided by Sam and an impressive silver-haired lawyer who works for his mother. Rosa always seems to be able to get away from here whenever she wants, I grumble to myself, helping Aunt Bertha rearrange her linen press for the third time this week. *She* doesn't have to bother about lavender sachets.

I realise it's now the middle of March. My sixteenth birthday has come and gone, and no one even remembered it. Oh, Mama. You would have.

Life becomes a little more interesting when I start going out with Rosa to buy rugs and curtains and linens for the new house, but the day we look at wallpapers is painful. We come upon the patterns Mama chose for us—old-fashioned pink and pale green for Rosa, coral and blue and olive for me—and we weep together afterwards in the carriage.

Our new house is ready on a fine morning in April, a topsy-turvy autumn April, here on the other side of the world. Rosa unlocks the front door with a large key, and sunlight shines through coloured glass around the door onto the long polished hallway. I run up the staircase to the balcony and gaze over the masts of Hobsons Bay to the distant steeples of Melbourne.

Horse-drawn carts deliver our new furniture and *Willowmere's* crew and officers help us move it inside. The men are still in Melbourne as they're not permitted to leave until the Court of Marine Inquiry is over. Mr McPhee the sailmaker proves himself handy once again when it comes to hanging the curtains—a stitch here and a fold there and he has them draping as beautifully as silken staysails.

At last all is ready for us to move in. The house, situated on the fashionable Strand waterfront at Williamstown, is a handsome two-storied bluestone building with wrought-iron balconies. At the rear it has a kitchen garden, a greenhouse and a small orchard of young fruit trees.

We take a carriage from Aunt Bertha's place. She seems sorry to see us go, although Elspeth looks relieved. Papa sits silently beside Gideon, who directs the driver and sees to everyone's comfort.

As we arrive I take a deep shaky breath. The air is scented with woodsmoke, the trees are olive and russet, the still waters of the bay are a mirrored blue. A new house, a new life.

I catch Rosa's eye and am comforted—we've become closer over these long painful weeks. Her childhood recklessness seems nearer the surface now, but it alternates with a sweet absent-mindedness that's unusual for her. We are all changed so very much.

The staff stand at the door to welcome us: Mrs O'Brien, the housekeeper, with arms like a wrestler, Alice, the shy maid in her neat white cap and long apron, and gruff Harry, the gardener and stable-hand. *Willowmere*'s crew also line up on the veranda to greet us too. I see the Swedish boy, Nilsen, is out of the hospital at last.

We're shown the sailors' latest handiwork in the large kitchen—shelves, pantry doors and a meat safe—then we take tea in the drawing room. With everyone packed in it's a tight fit and Alice the maid, flustered by Danny's grin, nearly drops the tray.

The men sit gingerly on the new furniture. Thomas the Islander is twice as wide as his flimsy morning chair, Borue seems to disappear into the depths of a couch, the Finn scowls and rests his broken ankle on an ottoman, and Mr McPhee occasionally glances at his curtains with an air of satisfaction.

When on duty the crewmen must be silent unless addressed by an officer, so the conversation is stilted (although Mrs O'Brien's magnificent fruit cake may also be a factor). I notice Ratface the apprentice keeps his head bent over his plate, although he looks up once and his eyes are red. I realise how oddly subdued he has been of late.

The next few weeks bring much noise and activity as people come and go—there's still much to be done. Windows and French doors light up the elegant furniture in the Japanese style Mama loved so much, and the house exhibits every modern convenience: handsome tiled fireplaces, bright gas lights, bathrooms upstairs and down—even the telephone is installed.

I'm pleased to notice Rosa's new mourning clothes are in our mother's style too: soft blouses and draped skirts, with no more stiff corsets. She still shows that odd air of absence which has begun to puzzle me, but then there's no time to think about it: the Court of Marine Inquiry is upon us.

'By the readings and dead reckoning we were at least ten miles from the coast, as the logbook makes perfectly clear,' says Papa.

'Yet the weather was cloudy, Captain Fox,' says stern-faced Judge Stevenson, flanked by his two expert Assessors. 'How could you believe your course to be accurate?'

'There was certainly a possibility of error, but not large, at any rate.'

'I have been informed there was some difference of opinion regarding the accuracy of the two compasses aboard.'

'Yes, there was. However, the standard compass was of the highest quality. I took it that the binnacle compass was in error—perhaps not adjusted correctly—so I trusted to the standard instrument.'

'Your cargo comprised iron girders, Captain Fox. Surely that is a well-known threat to the accuracy of magnetic devices?'

'I can only repeat, sir, we adjusted the compasses accurately, taking into account the effects of the quantity and position of the cargo.'

'And if the cargo had shifted during the voyage?'

Papa hesitates. 'We were aware of the possibility during a storm in the South Atlantic, but the watch reported no shift. Certainly there was no change at all to the trim of the vessel.'

I notice Sam look across at the nearby sailors with a thoughtful air.

'Despite what you say, Captain Fox, a compass error is not out of the question. Yet even so, how could the vessel have sailed so close to the coast? You had two men on lookout, did you not?'

'Naturally. The night was foggy but we took soundings every ten minutes; we should have seen the danger in enough time to escape. Even with our proximity to the coast we might have gotten away but for the reef in our path.'

'The Inquiry would like to hear now the exact circumstances of the incident, so I call upon the first mate, Mr Gideon Meade.'

Papa moves stiffly to sit beside Sam and Gideon comes forward.

'Mr Meade, your watch was on duty at the time, was it not?'

'Yes, sir. We had the morning watch, starting at four o'clock. We realised the ship was in danger at about ten minutes past two bells —just after five o'clock. Dawn was breaking and the fog had lifted, and the forward lookout suddenly reported land five hundred yards ahead, half a point on the port bow—'

'Where were you, Mr Meade, and the third mate, Mr Whalen?'

'I was in the chartroom writing an entry in the log and Mr Whalen was checking on a problem with a pump. I immediately ordered the helmsman to take her hard a'port—'

'Why did the lookout aloft not see the land sooner?'

'I do not know, sir, I cannot fathom it. We roused all hands to wear ship, we began to turn away safely, we should have been in no danger of the shore, but then the hidden reef ripped her apart—'

He stops for a moment and takes a breath.

'The bilges filled within ten minutes and we launched the lifeboats. The second lifeboat jammed at the davit, throwing people into the water, but we managed to rescue most. In all, two men drowned, one was crushed on the ship, and another died of injuries after we reached shore.'

'Thank you, Mr Meade, please step down. We shall adjourn for luncheon.'

We walk to a nearby hotel where Papa has booked a private room for our meal. Rosa and Gideon stroll ahead with Papa.

'Sam,' I say, 'when the iron girders were mentioned what were you thinking?'

'Ah, you noticed. I suddenly remembered sending Rawson and the Yankee down to check if the cargo had shifted in the storm. They reported no change, but now I wonder, were they careless? Any shift could have affected the compass ...'

Danny is listening. 'That may be reason enough to have taken us off course, but how could the lookout not have seen the bloody shore? There was light enough, the fog was gone—a man on the mast can see for miles.'

'Asleep?' suggests Sam.

'I'd hailed him just minutes before and he'd replied all clear.'

'Who was the lookout?' I ask.

'Brownley, poor lad,' says Danny.

'Ratface—Rawson—was his best friend,' I say. 'He's been very strange since the wreck. I wonder if he knows something he's not saying.'

Back at the court Danny and Sam take Rawson into a corner. After ten minutes Sam comes to Papa and murmurs something while Danny stays with Rawson, who's now sniffling into a handkerchief. Papa hurries off to see the Judge.

When the court reconvenes Rawson is called forward, still clutching his handkerchief.

'Wilfred Rawson,' says Judge Stevenson sternly, 'I believe you have some knowledge of the events that may have led to these unfortunate circumstances.'

Rawson moans. Why, he's as young as me, I realise in surprise.

'You were on the middle watch at midnight, were you not?' prompts Assessor Captain Watson.

'Yes, sir,' Rawson whispers.

'And what did the apprentice Albert Brownley say to you as you came on duty?'

'To ... to watch Piet the cook, sir. He saw him with half a bottle of sherry, cleaning up after the party. He said to nick the sherry and hide it near the fore-shrouds, so he could have it later.'

'And what did you do?'

Rawson sighs in despair. 'I watched him—Piet. He put the bottle in the galley cupboard, then went below. I took it, like Albert said.'

'And then what happened?'

'I winked to Albert when the watch changed over. I saw him put the bottle in his coat, then go aloft. I went to my bunk and the next thing I know is all hands on deck. We was on the halliards together just before she struck, and he kept saying I didn't *see*, Wilf, I just didn't *see*! And then he drowned ...' Rawson sobs.

'Step down, Wilfred Rawson,' says Judge Stevenson. He whispers to the Assessors, then says, 'We may have established reasons for the barque *Willowmere* to have been off course and for the lookout's dereliction in his duty. We shall reconvene tomorrow to establish further facts of the vessel's wreck and abandonment, and after consideration shall then deliver our finding.'

Rawson has another painful day in court describing how he and the Yankee went only part-way into the hold to check the state of the cargo: the girders seemed to have moved a little but the men were exhausted, it was the end of the watch, they did not want to have to restow them. They reported no shift at all. Papa puts his hands over his face.

The Court presents its findings. Papa is reprimanded for not investigating the discrepancy between the compasses, although compared to the lookout's drunkenness it is agreed that navigational errors were but a secondary cause of *Willowmere*'s loss.

Gideon is commended for his efforts to save the ship and fined ten pounds for allowing a member of his watch to be drunk on duty. Sam is fined five pounds for Rawson's misdeeds and commended for rescuing people in the water. Rawson is sentenced to gaol for six months.

'But that's not fair!' I say to Danny outside the courtroom. 'Gideon didn't know the lookout was drunk, and Sam didn't know Rawson stole the sherry.'

'They were leading the watches, girl, they were responsible. That's how it is at sea.'

'But Rawson's so young, he shouldn't go to gaol.'

'It won't be easy for him, but he signed on, he had an adult's responsibilities. It's no game, remember? We lost everything—the ship, your mother ... oh Christ, I'm sorry, don't cry.'

'It's just too much, Danny, it's all been so hard. And Papa—it's as if he's barely there—and Rosa too, she hardly speaks, she just drifts around as if in a dream.'

'Aye.' Danny doesn't say anything more and we rejoin the others at the courtroom. I don't remember until later the set of his face at the mention of Rosa.

The following week Papa and the officers must also attend the Coroner's Court. I'm not allowed to go as Papa says such places are not suitable for a girl. The Court returns a verdict of misadventure in the three deaths. The culprits, Brownley and the Yankee, are dead and beyond any punishment.

Gideon is often at our new house, taking tea with Rosa and Papa and keeping an eye on the sailors (to whom Alice the maid now appears to be rather partial). The men help out with cabinetwork and moving furniture between the rooms: they're finding it hard to get new berths because shipping is quiet at this time of year. Mr McPhee and Sig the Bosun open a sailmaking loft above a Williamstown warehouse.

Danny starts studying for his ticket, Master in Sail. Gideon teases him, saying he should have learnt his lesson by now and be going into steam, but Danny just smiles and says nothing. He doesn't offer to go on teaching me the fiddle, and in any case I don't feel like looking to replace the instrument lost with poor *Willowmere*.

The gloomy Finn signs on to a four-masted barque heading for Seattle for timber. He comes limping to see me before he leaves, scowling from under his black eyebrows as usual. To my surprise he hands me a small dancing reindeer made of bone.

'From antler, I carve it. I am sorry for your *aiti*—your mamma. She make us very happy on ship.'

It's the most the Finn has ever said, and I dash up to Papa's room and find a good woolly scarf, and present it to him, shaking his hand. I think his expression lightens for a moment.

'Well you'd better not give away all your father's woolly scarves, or he'll go mighty cold this winter,' says Danny. 'But maybe Bao-lim'd run you up a bulk order. I'm thinking, myself, of asking him for some silk sheets for when I go back to sea.'

Sam throws a small parcel at him, which Danny catches, grinning, and replaces on the shelf. 'The beds at my mother's house don't really have silk sheets,' Sam says confidingly to me, 'but Danny is sadly unfamiliar with any level of civilisation beyond a wet hammock.'

Today we're visiting the Lee Trading Company. We've already greeted Min-lu and Bao-lim in their offices at the front of the building, and now Sam has taken us through to the rear to see the warehouses.

I gaze around at the sacks of rice marked with vivid slashes of red, and the shelves of neatly-tied packages—tea, noodles, spices and dried mushrooms, Sam tells us—and the bottles with bright labels with sauces and vinegar and wine. The air itself smells edible.

The next shed has glass skylights and is vivid with colour. Light shimmers from bolts of silks and satins, and glows from layers of velvets and wools piled on shelves around the shed. I want to stroke everything I can see, and I gather up a handful of weightless gold silk with a scent of cut hay and have to restrain myself from burying my face in it.

I reluctantly follow Sam and Danny as they head towards the third warehouse. But this one doesn't seem very interesting to me —just rows and rows of wooden crates—then Sam says, 'Look more closely, Lucy,' and lifts the lid of a crate. 'Here you are, here's our pearlshell.'

I gasp at the shimmering iridescence. Sam hands me one of the plate-sized shells and I run my fingers over its silvery smoothness.

'Oh, Sam, that's just *beautiful*! Now I understand why you want to go to Broome.'

'Ah, Broome, indeed. When I can.'

'Aye, I'm thinking you'd better get there pretty damned soon,' says Danny dryly. 'You never know, they might run out of shell otherwise.'

I don't quite understand his tone, but there's no time to think about it. When I arrive home I find the Swedish boy Nilsen waiting for me. They call him a boy for his shyness, but he's closer to Rosa's age. He's signed on as deck-hand on a steamship to Britain, and has come to say farewell.

I ask Mrs O'Brien to make up a package of fruitcake and biscuits for his voyage: I know how scanty the food can be on some ships. We take afternoon tea and Papa joins us, but he wanders out at one point with an absent air and does not return. We speak about the voyage on *Willowmere*, awkwardly at first and then with ease.

His name is Mattias Nilsen, he tells me. He shows me the terrible scar on his head from the shipwreck, and I part my brown hair, three inches long now, to show him Mr McPhee's fine handiwork. We both agree his scar would have been much neater had the hospital the foresight to employ a sailmaker for surgery.

Later, as we shake hands at the door, he leans over and kisses me, first on the cheek, then gently on the lips. I breath the warm scent of his skin and feel the softness of his moustache.

'*Hej då*, Lucy. Maybe we meet again, bye and bye.'

'*Hej då*, Mattias. I hope we do, bye and bye.'

Not so shy after all, I think later, and touch my lips in delight.

6. A NEW FAMILY

I cannot sleep that night for remembering Mattias Nilsen's kiss, so different from anything I've ever felt before. I'm hungry too. I'd been distracted at supper and hadn't eat any of Mrs O'Brien's apricot pie, still sitting almost untouched in the pantry.

My bedroom is upstairs so I can see the ships on the bay, and Papa's is beside mine. Rosa sleeps downstairs in a pretty room that opens onto the side veranda.

We're alone in the house: it turns out that Harry the gardener is Mr O'Brien (or close enough, Danny says), so Mrs O'Brien shares his rooms above the stable, while Alice lives nearby with her widowed mother.

I put on my dressing-gown and slippers and tip-toe downstairs to the kitchen at the rear of the house. As I pass Rosa's room I hear her rustling and murmuring in her sleep.

In the spice-scented pantry I cut myself a slice of apricot pie and take a bite, tangy and sweet, then go to the back door. Outside, the air off the sea is so fresh I close my eyes and pretend I'm on *Willowmere*'s deck.

I open my eyes and take another bite of pie. The moonlight gleams on the narrow paths of the kitchen garden as I stroll, gazing up at the night sky. Then I hear a faint noise and turn.

The door of Rosa's room opens and my heart thumps as I see two shadows emerge. They become one for a long moment, then slowly separate. The Rosa-shadow moves inside and the door closes. The other, the set of the shoulders utterly familiar, walks away along the veranda.

At breakfast next morning Rosa comes late to the dining room. Papa looks over his newspaper, harumphs, and goes to his study. Rosa nibbles at a piece of toast and gazes out of the window. I realise she's not in her best looks. Her eyes are a little puffy, her jawline softer than usual.

'Don't examine me like that, Lucy,' says Rosa. 'I've been sick, as on the ship.'

'But we're not on a ship now.'

Rosa tuts with exasperation, then takes a breath. 'I'm going to have a baby.'

'A *baby*! Rosa, how?' I feel myself flush. 'Oh, Lord, how stupid of me. But ... oh, *Rosa*.'

'The father—'

'I know. I saw you last night, both of you, by accident.'

We gaze at each other in silence then I say, 'How, when?'

Rosa stares out the window. 'It was so strange. On the ship, whenever I was near him I disliked him. I couldn't bear how I felt! But after he saved Mama from drowning he looked into my eyes. Then I knew.' She runs her fingers through her curls. 'He was so good to me when she was ill. And I wanted him, Lucy: you cannot imagine how terrible—how wonderful—it is to love such a man.'

'But what about Gideon?'

'It would have been convenient to return his affection, but it's Sam I love.'

'Oh, Rosa—what on earth will you do?'

'We're going away to get married. Tonight. That's why I'm telling you: I need your help. You must take Papa out somewhere, I don't want anyone here.'

'But Sam told me he should never marry a white woman, it would bring her too much suffering.'

'I do not care, not in the slightest. He is *mine*.'

'Rosa, I love you both but this may be the wrong thing to do. Papa will be so hurt and Sam's mother too—it will touch us all!'

'What do you suggest I do, then, Lucy? Give birth to a bastard child?'

We look at each other in despair.

'Of course I'll help, whatever you need. But how can I get Papa out of the house?'

'The newspaper, here, the advertisements,' says Rosa. 'Perhaps there's a public notice, a presentation, something you might want to attend.'

'Let me see. There's a carnival in Newport—but at night there would be too much drunkenness for Papa to take me to that.'

'A talk at the Mechanics' Institute—*Getting the Most From Your Kale*? No, it's next week and dear God, even you couldn't pretend to find that interesting.'

'Here's something,' I say. '*The public are cordially invited to attend the launch of a fine schooner from the slip at C. Blunt Boatbuilder, Friday the 17th of May.* That's tonight!'

'Can you persuade Papa?'

'I'll try. And when we get back I'll say you're asleep and he'll suspect nothing until morning.'

'I shall leave him a letter,' says Rosa, faltering a little. 'Oh Lucy, this is so frightening.'

'Where will you go, Rosa?'

'To Ballarat—it's only a day or so away. So many Chinese from the goldfields already live there, no one will take the slightest notice of our marriage. Sam has already organised the banns.'

I take my sister's hand. 'Mama would have helped you, I'm sure she would have! And I will too.'

It's not hard to persuade Papa to take me to the schooner launch. He's been watching progress on the vessel with interest as he takes his constitutional every day. Just before we're leaving Rosa complains of feeling unwell and says she wants to stay behind. She hugs us both at the door.

As we walk down the street Papa says, 'I do hope Rosa's not sickening for anything, she's not normally so affectionate. Perhaps we should return—'

'Oh no, Papa, I'm sure she's well, I believe it's simply a feminine frailty ...'

Of course he can say nothing more to that. We arrive as the sun is setting and I pull my coat around me in the autumn chill, still hardly able to believe such news—Rosa and Sam, *lovers*!

The boatyard is brilliant with gaslight and flags, and the schooner so handsome that after a time I feel comforted. I'd have wanted to attend this launch no matter what, so it's not really a deception, I tell myself.

Gideon and Danny are there too. Gideon is disappointed Rosa has not come but I hint again her indisposition is of a feminine nature, which rules out any chance he might drop by to enquire about her health. Papa asks after Sam, and Gideon says he's visiting a friend at Geelong. Everything seems to be working to plan.

After speeches the Lady Mayoress breaks champagne on the bow. The winch squeaks and the cradle moves down the rails, and the schooner slides into the water with a small splash and a cheer from the crowd.

It isn't as enjoyable as I'd expected, but at least—perhaps—everything will be fine: if only Danny would stop looking at me like that. He drops behind and catches my arm as we're walking back along the main street.

'Apart from seasickness I doubt Rosa's ever been indisposed in her life,' he mutters. 'To say nothing of that friend at Geelong Sam's never even mentioned before. What's going on, girl?'

'I don't know, Danny.'

'Yes you do. Oh sweet Jesus, don't tell me—they're not eloping tonight?'

I hesitate.

'Yes, of course they are, the bloody *fools*. I can't believe it. It'll destroy both your families, and Gideon too! And *you*, haven't you got an ounce of self-preservation?'

I've never seen him so angry, not even when I climbed the foremast.

'I didn't find out until last night myself, Danny—and she needs my help, there's a baby ...'

He stops and closes his eyes for a moment.

'Oh good God. Of course, a baby. Well, nothing more to be said. Let's just sit back and enjoy the spectacle, eh?' He takes a breath. 'I'm sorry, girl, this is going to be hard on you.'

I do not understand what he means.

I still do not understand next morning when I give Papa the letter left behind a porcelain shepherdess on Rosa's dressing table. He goes pale and the note drops from his hand.

'Samuel Lee? My second mate?' Papa has forgotten he no longer has mates or a ship to command.

I read the note. In Rosa's confident loops it says, *Dearest Papa, soon I shall be a married woman, wed to Samuel Lee, the finest man I've ever known. We wish to spare our families the trials of marriage preparations at this difficult time. We shall return in two weeks after our honeymoon in the countryside, and pray you will then forgive your impetuous and loving daughter, Rosa.*

She was always his favourite, the one to whom he could refuse nothing. He stands and goes to the window. 'But he is not white,' he says in wonder. 'Does she not *realise* what that will mean?'

'Sam is a good man, I'm sure they'll be happy,' I say, my heart aching for him.

'And so soon, so soon. Barely three months since ...'

I see Papa grow still, staring at nothing, and know he has realised Rosa is with child. He sits down again and puts his head into his hands.

'Please ask Alice to bring me tea, Lucy, then tell her I am not to be disturbed.' He looks up, his face exhausted. 'I do not wish to know what hand you had in this—debacle—but perhaps you would be so good as to take the note to the family of Mr Lee and see for yourself the outcome of this extraordinary act of selfishness.'

I remember Danny speaking of Rosa, warning me: *Often people who feel so terribly deeply don't bother themselves over-much with how anyone else feels.*

I tie the ribbons of my bonnet under my chin, hands shaking and eyes large in the mirror. I put the note in my reticule and walk down the street in the cool morning air. I greet Mr McPhee and Sig the Bosun, smoking their pipes on the footpath near their sailmaking loft, and am surprised at how normal I sound.

I stop outside the gates of the great house. I haven't been there before but I know there are two wings. Bao-lim lives in one and Min-lu and her daughters in the other, with reception rooms in the middle.

The Chinese man who answers my timid knock at the large carved doors sends a servant to call Bao-lim, and leads me into a drawing room decorated with giant ceramic vases and intricate silk paintings and carved wooden screens.

Bao-lim enters and bows and asks me to sit down. He's wearing a dark blue silk robe and a round black cap with a gemstone on the crown. I hand him the note, unable to say anything. While he's reading it a servant brings a tray and offers me a small steaming cup. It's tea, he says, but there's no milk and it has jasmine flower petals floating in it.

I sip, and sip again. 'Oh, how *nice*.'

Bao-lim folds the note and hands it back to me. 'Thank you. We had such a letter from Sam too and my sister is distraught. You understand what this will mean to us?'

I shake my head.

'This is a very strange country,' he says, stroking his beard. 'Its people wear Chinese fabrics stitched by Chinese tailors, use furniture built by Chinese artisans, eat food from Chinese market gardens. Yet still we are barely tolerated. We suffer assaults and hear endless demands for our expulsion—and we are told we bring this upon ourselves because we work too hard.'

'But what is that to do with Sam and Rosa?'

'What incites the fury of these barbarians to the extreme is the prospect of a white woman in marriage to a Chinese man. I fear my family will be bearing the brunt of my nephew's foolish actions for some time to come.'

'But if Sam and Rosa show the world they love each other and their marriage is good?'

He's puzzled. 'Most white people—and most Chinese—would see that as the worst possible consequence. The races should always remain pure.'

Min-lu appears at the door. Her dress is olive green silk and I saw the style in the latest Paris journal. Her glossy black hair is swept neatly around her head and anchored with golden combs. She nods to Bao-lim, who leaves the room, then she sits beside me. I think she's been crying.

'You're shocked too, Lucy, I see. My brother knows how difficult it is for Chinese people here, always afraid of what new attacks will descend upon us—but perhaps even he does not understand how hard this will be on those of us who love Sam and Rosa.'

I put my little teacup down on the tray.

'Please believe me, I didn't know! At least, not until it was too late—and Rosa, I can never stop her doing *anything*! And I do want Sam to be happy, except now Papa's so worried—but Mama would have helped them, I'm sure—oh, dear ...'

A tear runs down my face and Min-lu gives me a handkerchief. She says carefully, 'I wonder if there is a baby? Sam would not usually be so hasty—'

'He'd still have wanted to marry her anyway!'

'Ah,' says Min-lu, suspicion confirmed. 'Yes, I believe you are correct. Well, we must make the best of it. Lucy, they will have to go away until after the baby's born, do you understand?'

'But where?'

She thinks for a moment. 'Of course ... they must go to Broome. Everyone knows Sam has plans to go there to work a pearling fleet. I have a house in the town and know a good woman who will help Rosa with the birth.'

'But Broome is so far away—'

'That is what will protect them.' She smiles. 'And I have another idea. Before they go we'll hold a grand reception to celebrate their marriage. People may whisper all they like but we'll make it such an enviable, glorious occasion there will be no room for petty scandal.'

I gaze in awe at the small clever woman beside me. What a relief to be able to share the weight of responsibility with someone else.

'Oh, thank you *so* much, Mrs Lee ... Mrs Peres ... I'm sorry, I don't know what to call you—'

'Min-lu will do, Lucy. It may have happened rather unexpectedly,' she says, her brown eyes amused, 'but it seems we have now become family.'

Heavens, *family*—with people who drink perfumed tea and trade silks and spices and luminous shells. How interesting life has suddenly become.

At home, Papa is still locked in his study but I begin to feel a little more hopeful. I curl up in an armchair in the sitting room, hoping soon things will return to normal. Then the doorbell rings insistently and Alice answers.

She barely has time to walk back down the hall when Gideon pushes past her and my heart sinks. I'd almost forgotten him.

He cannot speak at first. He stands at the window, takes off his hat and runs his fingers through his fair hair. Then he turns, looming over me.

'Is it *true*? My God—I see it is. And did you know?'

'Not until the last moment, Mr Meade—Gideon—I'm so sorry.'

'She deceived me, she deceived us all. And Sam—my friend, my trusted friend! I cannot conceive of such a betrayal.'

'It was not intended, I'm sure of it! How could they tell us? We were in mourning, we had the Court of Inquiry to deal with—'

'Still they let us go on believing, let me go on believing there was a chance ...' He puts his hand to his eyes.

I feel such pity. 'I'm certain they have only the highest regard for you, Gideon, and would never have wanted to hurt you.'

There's a silence. Gideon lifts his head and looks at me.

'You stupid little girl.'

It's as if he's punched me in the belly. Yet some small part of me is unsurprised, and I know suddenly I've always been a little wary of that great golden joviality.

'I've lost everything,' he says. 'Your father stole my first command and sank my ship. My crewmen shamed me in open court and I may never again have a chance to be master. My closest friend has lied to me and the woman I planned to marry has publicly mocked me. And you say they did not want to hurt me?'

'It's not like that, Gideon, surely you cannot believe—'

'And you. With your prattling and disrespect—your disgraceful lack of femininity—yes, and your lies to facilitate that hussy's elopement: you too.'

He smiles and that's worse than his anger.

'You don't understand yet, do you? What your whore of a sister and that chow have done to you?'

I gasp.

'Your reputation is lost forever,' he says, as if discussing the weather. 'Every man will believe you a slut and treat you accordingly. You will never marry and you will have no children, unless they're bastards like Sam Lee. You—'

'Stop it! For heaven's sake, *stop*. How can you say—'

'You will end your days as an opium addict, a harlot too raddled for even the nightsoil carters to bear to touch—'

The door opens. Mrs O'Brien stands there, almost as tall as Gideon himself, and crosses her beefy arms. 'Pardon me, Miss, but I believe I urgently require your presence in the kitchen. This *gentleman* was just leaving, I take it.'

Breathing deeply, Gideon stops and stares, expressionless, for a long moment at Mrs O'Brien. Then he places his hat on his head and says, 'Farewell then, little Miss Lucy. And may you one day suffer as I do now.'

He pushes past Mrs O'Brien and we hear the front door slam.

'The gall! Are you all right, Miss?'

'I—yes, I think. Please, may I have a cup of tea, Mrs O'Brien? And thank you.'

'Certainly, Miss. But no gentleman at all, that one. I can't believe anyone could say such things.'

But at last I understand what Danny had meant.

I sit late into the evening, thinking. Mrs O'Brien brings me food on a tray but I can't eat much. At about seven o'clock the doorbell rings again and I flinch. Alice shows Danny into the room.

I look up, expecting another scolding, but he just sits down across from me and says, 'I reckon you're thinking—well, that was a bastard of a day.'

'Oh, Danny, yes. As bad as losing *Willowmere* all over again. I didn't understand Gideon would be so outraged.'

'I suppose if you've always had everything—beloved son of the British Empire and all that—it comes as quite a surprise when you don't get your own way.'

'He called Sam and Rosa and me terrible names and said my reputation is lost and I would end my days—oh, I cannot even say it.'

'Let me guess. Was it something about about raddled harlots and nightsoil carters?'

'Well ... yes.'

'He always says that when he's cross. He's English, don't forget, not too creative with the old invective.'

'But he said I would never marry.'

'Indeed? Tell that to the Swedish lad. I've never seen anyone so intent on getting back to Melbourne one day.'

I smile a little despite myself. 'How did you ...?'

Danny grins. 'I don't miss much.'

After a few moments he says, 'This—Gideon—is pretty ugly, but he's right. People are going to treat you badly once your family's become involved with the Chinese.'

'But Danny, you've got to know them, Min-lu and Bao-lim, they're so clever and kind and interesting.'

'They certainly are, and I'd die for Sam Lee and probably he for me. But Chinese have no rights here, they're treated worse than dogs, and anyone linked to them gets treated the same. Still, I expect you'll survive, and your Papa'll be fine. And Rosa, by God she'll just flourish in the fuss.'

'And Sam?'

'Sometimes Sam's too ... trusting. I don't know. But I do know if you're not going to eat Mrs O'Brien's excellent pudding you can hand it over here and I'll take some sustenance, thank you very much. Once again you've driven me to distraction with your questions and curiosity–'

'But no climbing this time!'

'Aye, there's an improvement.'

Next day Uncle Edward and Aunt Bertha drive up in their carriage. Elspeth is not with them, presumably to avoid contamination. They go with Papa into his study and shut the door. Later, Aunt Bertha emerges and takes tea with me.

'Oh my, you're so pale, Lucy. What a difficult time. Has there been—any word?'

'No, but we expect they'll be back soon.'

'Your father said Mr Lee's family are planning to hold a grand reception upon their return. That will certainly help, the family is well-connected, despite ...'

'—being Chinese, you mean?'

'Lucy, there is no need to be flippant. You must appreciate the difficulties involved. Heavens, when we're young we may have friends from all sorts of backgrounds, but marriage! Altogether a different question. Families, inheritances, reputations—so much is at stake.'

'Not happiness?'

'My dear. Happiness may take many forms, one of which is that our families are free to enjoy their rightful place in the social order. A child born of any—irregular—union is unlikely to know that kind of happiness.'

'Perhaps such a child may know other joys.'

Aunt Bertha looks at me with bemused affection. 'You're very young, my dear. However, we must deal with this situation now, and while it's proper for you and your father to attend the reception, sadly, your Uncle Edward and I may not. Elspeth is coming out this year and must naturally be free of any hint of scandal.'

'Naturally.'

'I do appreciate your understanding, Lucy. You may, of course, call upon me for any assistance, I shall be only too happy to help.'

I manage to thank her politely. Later, at dinner Papa says, 'When Edward and Bertha were here I found myself wondering what your Mama, God bless her soul, would have said—and you know, I had to stop myself from laughing out aloud! Our father, Edward's and mine, was a farm labourer. 'Rightful place in the social order' be damned.'

I laugh. 'Aunt Bertha said that to me too.'

He puts down his cutlery and sighs. 'She was not an easy woman, Lucy, your mother. Those avant-garde artists, that extraordinary furniture—hardly a man's idea of comfort. But she sailed with me before you children were born and afterwards too, whenever she could—never complained, no matter what. How she loved the sea. You're like her that way.'

He hasn't spoken so much in three months.

'She'd not have made light of Rosa's situation, but by God you'd have heard no mealy-mouthed platitudes either. Well, we must live up to what she would have wanted of us. We shall stand with Rosa and Sam.'

'They're here, Miss, they're here!' calls Alice.

Papa and I hurry to the front veranda. Sam helps Rosa out of the carriage and they walk together up the front steps. They seem to glow with happiness.

'Well!' says Papa. 'Well! Oh, my girl,' and he hugs Rosa tightly, then pounds Sam on the back. 'By God, Mr Lee, I should clap you in irons for insubordination!'

Inside, Alice squeals at the beauty of Rosa's ring and Mrs O'Brien dabs her eyes. Over tea and cakes in the drawing room Rosa and Sam talk about their honeymoon at Daylesford, taking the waters and strolling in the countryside. When they glance at each other I'm fascinated to notice Rosa's cheeks grow pink and Sam's eyes gleam.

They bring gifts—a blue linen blouse for me for when I'm out of mourning, a fine woollen scarf for Papa (oh, good, I think), lace handkerchiefs for Mrs O'Brien, a leather wallet for Harry and a lilac scarf for Alice, who has never seen anything so beautiful in all her life.

Papa takes Rosa into his study to discuss her settlement and Mama's estate and Sam and I are left in the sudden quiet. He looks at me.

'I'm so sorry, Lucy. Such deceit was unkind, to you most of all. I knew it was impossible when Rosa first turned to me, but she was distraught and helpless and ... you see, I loved her from the moment she walked onto the ship.'

Of course. 'Sam, dear Sam, it doesn't matter. You were my friend and now—my goodness, you've become my brother. In the midst of so much loss it is sweet to have gained something.'

He breaths out with relief. 'Good Lord, do you mean I've gained *another* little sister! But the teasing, the interrogation, the sharp-eyed criticism—how am I to survive it all?' I laugh, and after a moment he says, 'And while we were gone, was it very difficult? Gideon, especially—how did he deal with the news?'

'Very poorly, I fear. I doubt he will ever forgive any of us.'

'Ah. Was there talk of raddled—?'

'Yes.'

'I'm sorry you had to experience that. But perhaps, over time, he'll come around. Despite his temper I believe he has a good heart.'

'I fear we hurt him terribly, Sam, and now he's gone. We heard he shipped out two days ago—third mate on a steamship, Fremantle to Singapore run.'

'Third? He won't like that, but anyone starting in steam would have to do the same. He'll rise quickly enough.' He hesitates. 'Have you seen anything of my family?'

'Yes, I talked to your mother and your uncle too. They gave me tea with flowers in it, which was very nice. And your mother has had an idea.'

'Ah. Has she decided we should go away to—let me see—Broome, perhaps?'

'You guessed!'

'Broome,' he says, his dark eyes happy. 'I shall enjoy that.'

'And she's going to hold a wonderful reception for you both, too.'

'And Rosa will enjoy that.'

'What will Rosa enjoy?' she says, coming into the drawing room with Papa.

'A reception, a wonderful affair says Lucy, to be held by my family to celebrate our union and put paid to any lingering scandal.'

'Yes indeed, Sam, I will enjoy that.' They smile at each other.

7. THE FIDDLE

Rosa looks marvellous. In black of course, but a black silk from Min-lu's warehouse with a shimmer of bronze that lights up her red-gold curls and frames her shoulders like a cameo. (My black dress is plain and cut high at the neck, as deemed suitable for a girl not yet out.)

It appears all of Williamstown has come to the reception and half of Melbourne too. The Mayor and his schooner-launching wife are there, along with the bankers, the lawyers, the businessmen, the ship-builders and the prosperous traders. 'Aunt Bertha will be furious she missed this,' I whisper to Papa, 'I'm sure she never dreamt it would be so glorious.'

On the receiving line, busy with curtsies and handshakes, exquisite Rosa stands with broad-shouldered Sam, beside them Min-lu in emerald silk, Bao-lim in a long robe and Papa, handsome in his formal suit.

I'm pleased to see Mr McPhee and Sig the Bosun arrive, cigars jaunty in their mouths, and Danny too. He's looking splendid in a frock-coat, with his curls cut short and his earring glinting, escorting a woman in pink who seems to giggle rather a lot.

To murmurs of admiration the doors to the great ballroom are opened by pigtailed men in embroidered robes. The orchestra strikes up and women in jewelled satins and chiffons and taffetas begin to swirl around and around with their dark-suited partners in the flickering candle-light. Banks of scented roses fill every corner, and as the heat and chatter increases the long windows are opened to the quiet autumn night.

After a time we pause for refreshments and then the speeches begin. Speeches to laud the power and prosperity of the Lee family, speeches to celebrate Sam's prospects (women whisper, father's a Lord, you know) and speeches to praise Rosa's charms (men murmur, by God, I'd be in a hurry too).

When the dancing starts again Min-lu takes me to see her two little girls, Sam's half-sisters, who've been asking to meet me. On this special night they've been allowed to stay up late in a salon just off the ballroom. Moments after we enter, a servant calls Min-lu away and I'm left with the children.

They're both in frilled white muslin, their dark wavy hair pulled back with ribbons the colours of their sashes, pink for the younger child and blue for the older. She looks at me and says firmly, 'I'm Filipa and that's Izabel. She's seven but I'm nine. I like to be called Fili.'

'Oh. You don't have Chinese names?'

'Silly,' says the younger girl. 'Our daddy was from Macao so we have Portuguese names. He got a fever when I was two and he died.'

'I'm so sorry.'

'I remember him, he gave me a doll. Here, look.'

'You don't remember him,' says Fili scathingly.

'I do, I do!' cries Izabel.

'I can remember things from when I was very little too,' I say.

'*See*, Fili?'

'You're our new sister, Sam told us,' says Fili.

'In a sort of a way. I think I'm your, oh, step-sister-in-law. But we don't have to be friends if you don't want.'

'I don't mind,' says Fili. 'Let's get some cake.'

The salon is next to the dining room, where a magnificent supper is laid out to be served at midnight. Izabel takes my hand and shows me the tables covered in pies and savouries, roasts and buns, cakes and trifles and puddings.

'Well, perhaps we can take a few things from here and there, we don't want to spoil the display,' I say. 'Oh, I see some cordial over there, too.'

We feast side-by-side in the salon and Fili says, 'Our mother told us you like ships very much. I like horses, and Izabel—she's such a baby—she only likes dolls.'

'I like ships a little bit,' says Izabel bravely. 'But I like cats too.'

'I like cats. What about dogs?'

'Oh, yes,' says Fili, 'dogs are nearly as nice as horses.'

We chat in amity by the fireplace, then after a time Izabel, then Fili, yawns and falls asleep on the sofa. I nibble on a meringue and gaze at the flames, thinking how strange and incomplete everything seems without Gideon here too.

I love my old ship-board friends as family, and it's hard to reconcile the good-natured first mate of *Willowmere* with the bitter stranger who was so unkind to me. But grown-up men have many faces: they fight, they rage, they swear. Papa says they carry near-unendurable burdens of worry and responsibility (although Mama would always smile to herself when he said it).

In truth, Gideon's harsh words were no worse than those I used to hear every day on the ship, and of course he had cause for anger —we'd deceived him deliberately, all of us. But now he's gone away, his heart full of bitterness. Will he ever forgive us?

I go to the door of the salon to watch the great ballroom. Crowds of people are twirling and laughing and chatting so loudly they almost drown out the orchestra. Min-lu is waltzing with her lawyer, the handsome silver-haired man, and I can see Danny's friend, the woman in pink, in the arms of an eminent businessman with a walrus moustache.

'She only came with me to make Mr Moustaches jealous,' says Danny, leaning on the wall nearby. He looks past me at the sleeping children. 'I see you survived your first encounter with Sam's sisters.'

I laugh. 'I think we found some common ground in domestic animals.'

Danny smiles, then gazes at the dancing crowd. 'I passed for master and I'm shipping out, girl. First mate on a barque carrying grain to Falmouth.' He pauses. 'I leave tomorrow.'

'First mate?' I say steadily. 'Congratulations.'

'Aye. The previous first jumped overboard, the second's an alcoholic and the third makes the Finn look sane, so I'm the obvious choice.'

He comes into the salon and stands near the fire. 'You'll all be fine now. Sam and Rosa will prosper mightily wherever they are. Your father's coming good—'

'Yes, he is.'

'And Min-lu's no fool, she'll take care of you.' His eyes have never been so green. 'I've left my fiddle with Sam, don't want to take it on a hard-case ship. You can use it if you want.'

'Thank you. We'll miss you, Danny.'

'Write to me now and then and tell me how you're doing.' He puts his hands lightly on my shoulders and kisses me on the cheek. 'There, your first kiss, and from Danny Whalen too. You're a lucky girl.'

I protest, smiling, 'That's not a real kiss.'

'Well, it's all you're getting from me.'

'And it's not even my first kiss. The Swedish boy ...'

'I'll be damned—the young devil. And did you like it?'

'Yes,' I say, laughing.

'All to the better, then.' He takes a breath. 'Goodbye, Lucy.' And he's gone.

I sit down and stare into the fire.

Sam and Rosa are soon embarking on the steamship to Fremantle, in Western Australia, where they'll catch another ship to take them along the wild coast to Broome, a place as far from Melbourne as anywhere in the country. Thomas the Islander and Borue the Koepanger are going as well: they want to work on the luggers.

'But what *is* a lugger?' I ask Sam one evening.

'A kind of boat especially for fishing pearlshell.'

'But what about the pearls then?'

'Good ones are very rare. The business is really in the shell itself and it's remarkably lucrative, £150 per ton last season.' He smiles. 'Once I berthed at Broome and saw the pearling fleet, hundreds of luggers, all sailing out together. It was a marvellous sight, Lucy.'

'I wish I could see them too. Rosa's so lucky to be going to Broome.'

'It won't be easy for her. The heat's extreme, the housing primitive and there are few white women in the town. She'll be lonely and bored, at least until the baby's born.'

'But after that you'll come back?'

'It depends on the business, how Rosa copes with the climate, many things. We shall see.'

'Perhaps Papa and I can come and visit you instead,' I say, suddenly hopeful. 'Then I could sail out on a lugger and find some pearls for myself.'

Sam says gently, 'Lucy, I'm sorry you've had to bear so much over the last few months, and now we're leaving you behind with only your father for company. But you do understand you're able to ask my mother for anything?'

I nod.

'And should I find two little pearls I'll have them set into gold earrings for you, and then you won't have to bother sailing anywhere to search for them.'

I rise and stand at the window for a moment, my eyes stinging.

'But Sam, don't you see that's what I would most like to do?' Then I turn and smile as best I can. 'How foolish of me. What a kind thought.'

The steamer's horn blares. Sam and Rosa wave from the upper deck, as do Borue and Thomas from second class. Men on the wharf release the hawsers and two tugboats nudge and shepherd the ship away into Port Phillip. Min-lu holds Izabel, who's crying. Fili, Bao-lim and the servants from the great house cheer while the ship recedes.

Papa blows his nose and says, 'Well, well.'

The wind off the water is biting; winter is here. We stay until the ship is a distant smudge, then turn and walk silently back to the carriage.

A few weeks later I'm sitting by the fire, a book on my lap, rain flurrying on the windows. Papa is in the city with his brother, visiting their stockbroker. He keeps himself busy every day, reading the newspaper, pointing out stories that interest him, then retiring to his study to work on small business ventures he's embarked upon in partnership with Uncle Edward.

Aunt Bertha was indeed furious she'd excluded herself from what *The Age* described as *the most sumptuous soiree of the season*, and almost wept when she read the list of guests. Every now and then she takes on an air of grievance, as if it were somebody else's fault she wasn't there.

One night she says firmly to Papa I should go back to school now. A young lady of fifteen should not be sitting at home, unoccupied. (Something in her tone implies this is the source of what she calls 'Rosa's *difficulties*.')

'Sixteen, Aunt Bertha,' I say, but she's not to be diverted. Boarding school, perhaps, a fine young ladies' establishment in the country, she even knows the headmistress personally. I'm horrified and say later to Papa, 'I cannot. How could I possibly live with girls who've experienced nothing in their lives after all we've been through? Please don't send me away.'

Papa agrees. He could not have endured me to go at any rate. 'But you must do something suitable for a young lady. Min-lu will know.' (I think Papa is rather taken with Min-lu's brown eyes, although he'd never admit it.)

Before leaving for Broome Sam gave me Danny's fiddle, but since then I've not had the heart to get it out of its case. Today, sitting alone, the ticking of the clock seems to fill the room. I sigh. Perhaps, as Papa suggested, I should go and talk to Min-lu.

I tell Mrs O'Brien where I'm going, put on my waterproof and take an umbrella from the stand. I tramp through the wet streets, leaning into the wind. The man at the great carved doors knows me by now. We smile and bow to each other then he shows me into the drawing room. I warm my toes gratefully by the fire; one of my walking boots has a leak.

Min-lu enters, in cherry-red velvet today, her black hair swept neatly up with her usual gold ornaments. I tuck a loose tortoiseshell comb back into my windblown hair. We sit side by side on the sofa while a servant pours us jasmine tea.

'Lucy, your dress is only cotton, far too thin for weather like this!' says Min-lu. 'Do you not have something warmer?'

'Not really. I suppose, with—everything—I haven't got around to new clothes.'

'I have a lovely worsted in the warehouse, fine but very warm, a charcoal with just a hint of blue. After six months I would imagine you may lighten your mourning a little. We shall go to my dressmaker in the morning.'

'That's so kind of you, Min-lu. Aunt Bertha wanted me to go shopping but I could not bear to go with her. Mama always made certain Rosa and I were fitted with new winter dresses every autumn, but—'

To my surprise I'm sobbing. Min-lu strokes my hair every now and then, but doesn't say anything. At last I take a deep breath and she offers me a handkerchief.

I wipe my face. 'I'm sorry. I didn't know I was so—so—'

'Lucy, you're still grieving. You cannot expect yourself to recover immediately.'

'But just a *year* ago we were at home in Greenwich, packing for the voyage, planning our new life here. I never imagined such losses.'

'Poor child, we've overlooked you in all the fuss.'

'I'm sixteen, Min-lu, not a child. It was my birthday in March, just a few weeks after Mama … well, there was nothing to celebrate. But lately I cannot sleep. I wake up, gasping for breath, but there is no one to tell. I'm so tired.'

Min-lu stares into the fire. 'When Leo died—the girls' father, five years ago—I thought I would die. Like you, I would wake, unable to breathe. It takes years, Lucy, not months, to come back to life again. But this terrible time will pass, I promise you.'

'How did you survive? What did you do?'

'I worked, my dear. I worked so hard I had to sleep. I had to think of so much outside my grief, eventually it eased a little, then a little more. It will never be gone, but now I am alive again.'

'Did you feel like that too when Sam's father went away? Oh, I shouldn't ask. Aunt Bertha says I'm impertinent—'

'Of course you may ask. No, not then, I was young and proud. When Freddy came out to Hong Kong we fell in love, but he went back to England to see his family and did not return. He bowed to his parents' wishes and married the Honourable Edith instead. I discovered I was pregnant but refused to tell him, and he didn't find out about Sam until some years had passed.'

She smiles wryly. 'The Honourable Edith turned out to prefer her women friends to her husband and the marriage was childless. So he has always been very good to Sam.'

I look at Min-lu in amazement, then we both begin to laugh. When Min-lu has recovered she says, 'Well. If the secret is work, Lucy, what shall we find for you to do?'

Min-lu at the office is a very different person from Min-lu in high society. Her concentration is intense and her dress plain (albeit of fabulously expensive fabric). We tell Aunt Bertha I'm seeing a tutor at the Lee company premises and I start spending part of every day there.

Min-lu and Bao-lim have elegant offices at the front of the building. Next is a room with two sensible secretaries and behind that a well-lit space with eight clerks, half of them European, the rest Chinese.

The swift clatter of their abacuses fascinates me and Bao-lim shows me the power and simplicity of the wooden devices. Min-lu teaches me book-keeping, and I help the secretaries, inking the imposing phrases of business correspondence and sealing the letters with red wax.

Sometimes I go with Min-lu to the warehouse. Elderly Chinese women look after the stock and chatter to Min-lu, who translates for me. I gradually begin to understand a few simple phrases and cause great delight when I repeat them. The women tease and scold the two muscular young Chinese warehousemen who linger nearby to try to flirt with me.

Min-lu teaches me about fabrics—shot silk from Siam, satin from China, prints from Japan, wool from Manchester, brocade and chiffon from India. Bao-lim teaches me all about pearlshell, their different types and qualities and regular consignments to the Mother O' Pearl auctions in London.

I love the rhythm of the day. When we stop for lunch, servants bring us steaming containers from the great house with rice and meats and crisp vegetables, more delicious than anything I've ever tasted before.

I learn the names of the dishes and which of the mysterious flavourings from the warehouse have gone into their making. I learn how to use chopsticks.

At three o'clock I put on my coat and walk home again past the ships and the wharves, ignoring the wind, my mind buzzing. I tell Papa an edited version of my day's efforts, then sit contentedly with him after dinner, reading or playing Danny's fiddle. I begin to sleep well once again.

Rosa writes to us in August 1907, after they settle in Broome:

The house is small and appears primitive, with open verandas and wood and iron walls, but we soon realised it is most suitable for this climate. Now it is the end of what they call winter here—and such a winter! Cloudless blue skies, gentle warm winds—I do not envy you bitter Melbourne at all.

Broome is a crude young town, with its foreshore camps for the pearling crews, a few dusty streets and more public houses than provision stores— but its isolation has produced a kind of amiability among the races: and indeed, you could not imagine the mixture of races here!

Min-lu's midwife friend Emilia will assist with my confinement. She is from the Philippines and so good and wise I trust her utterly. Her daughter Cristina, just a little older than you, Lucy, is a ravishing girl, although I fear she has few prospects here.

The voyage treated me kindly. I'm now six months with child and feeling remarkably well. I could go and on and on about this odd place, with its red rocks and turquoise seas, but Sam wishes also to speak, so I will finish now—your loving daughter and sister, Rosa.

Sam's more measured handwriting follows:

Rosa has given you our news but I would also tell you we have purchased four good luggers, and are having several more built. The existing four shall start work soon and 'go outside' for a few months, then at the end of the year be overhauled in the 'lay-up' season—there, Lucy, now you have learnt some of the pearlers' jargon!

Rosa is indeed very well, and has already cut a swathe among the pearlers and their wives at a musical evening and a dinner. We are most content in our plain little house, and regret only that our families are so far away. I trust you are all well, and remain your affectionate son- and brother-in-law, Sam Lee.

'Red rocks and turquoise seas,' I murmur.

'Cloudless skies and warm winds,' sighs Papa.

Rain spatters against the window-pane and we move a little closer to the fire.

The next letter is dated in October. Rosa writes:

> *It's hot now and they tell me it gets hotter, but I love it. I rest in the day and when the little wind comes in off the sea at night I'm reborn. In the early mornings I've taken to settling myself with a paintbox to try to capture something of this glorious scenery. I'm not very good at it yet but I do enjoy it.*
>
> *Sam—or Captain Lee, I should say—is content and well. Every evening he comes to tell me of the progress of our precious luggers. I've not the faintest idea of frames and stringers and hollow heels, nor the respective merits of kauri and cajebut and jarrah, but I nod wisely and he's a happy man.*

Sam breaks in here:

> *Anyone with a lugger in Broome may style themselves a captain—or an admiral! But I am indeed a happy man. Lucy, if you could see the carpenter, a Japanese artisan, you would be amazed at such beautiful work.*
>
> *So far our luggers—two of them skippered by Borue and Thomas—have brought us in a good quantity of shell, but sadly no fine pearls as yet.*

Rosa's writing again:

> *We must finish here—the steamer is leaving soon with the mail. Did we tell you we saw Gideon recently? He's first mate now on one of the Singapore vessels that stop here every few weeks.*
>
> *Alas, he has already forgotten me! He tells us he's engaged to a very well-connected young lady from Perth and seems as merry as ever. All my love, dear Lucy and Papa—your Rosa.*

Sam finishes:

> *Indeed, I was very happy to see Gideon so well, it has weighed on my mind how unkindly I treated his trust. We spent a cheerful evening together and shook hands over our aching heads next day—all was forgiven. I remain, yours affectionately, Sam.*

What marvellous news: Gideon and Sam reconciled and—good heavens!—Gideon engaged, only six months after our bitter parting. I feel relieved. Perhaps we might all be friends again one day.

Rosa sent me one of her watercolours with the letter. She's always had a fine line and a steady hand but this small landscape glows like gemstones.

I prop it on my mantelpiece and gaze at it, and yearn.

Just a few weeks later, in November, the telegram arrives.

ELIZA ANNABEL BORN THIS MORNING SEVEN THIRTY STOP MOTHER AND DAUGHTER VERY WELL STOP WILL WRITE SOON STOP SAM

'Eliza Annabel! I'm an auntie!'

'Good Lord, and me a grandfather. Annabel, eh? That would have pleased your mother. Such good news. By God, such excellent news.'

'But Papa, don't forget Min-lu's plan. We can't tell anyone, we must bite our tongues until the time is right to announce it. Oh, how on earth are we to keep such wonderful tidings to ourselves!'

A few weeks later I realise there is someone I can tell, after all. I finally hear from Danny.

I assume Rosa and Sam have had their child by now—give them my congratulations (if warranted). I expect Broome is still reeling from the experience.

The voyage from Spencer Gulf to Falmouth was hard. The grain shifted in a storm and we nearly broached to. Luckily the weather abated and we were able to restow.

I got to play King Neptune again for a couple of apprentices, but I'm giving up the job—the power's starting to go to my head.

I saw your old shipmate Nilsen—he's third on a Norwegian whaler and sends his regards. You may want to consider a long engagement—whalers smell pretty dreadful. I'm going out soon with a cargo for Bombay. Take care of yourself, girl. Your friend, Danny Whalen.

I reply with all my wonderful news: Eliza Annabel, Rosa's watercolours, Sam's luggers, Gideon's engagement, and a list of my new achievements—accounting with an abacus, using chopsticks, writing business correspondence, and even speaking a little Chinese.

Every day I'm becoming more content, although when the anniversaries of the double loss of Mama and *Willowmere* come and go in February 1908, for a time the house seems large and sad.

In March, when my seventeenth birthday arrives, Min-lu organises a small celebration. Uncle Edward and Aunt Bertha attend, with my new friends from the office—one of the secretaries, a clerk with a broad grin and an old Chinese accountant who can paint flowers with just a few brush strokes.

Min-lu's daughters are there, and Bao-lim, who has cut off his long queue of hair (something to do with Chinese politics) and looks rather dashing.

For my birthday Papa gives me a moonstone necklet, while Min-lu's gift is a dress in silvery silk which drapes in an Empire line, the very latest Poiret style. Aunt Bertha finds it all rather bohemian and hints that her own present, a hairbrush set, is far more suitable.

The days become easier. One pleasure is growing close to Min-lu's pretty daughters: Fili, at ten, is straight-backed and graceful, and little Izabel is plump and tender-hearted, with a mass of dark curls.

I play fiddle with Mr McPhee and Sig the Bosun, but their repertoire is dominated by gloomy Scots ballads and Norse dirges, and I miss the clever, intricate Irish tunes I learnt from Danny.

My seventeenth year passes by in contentment and with summer some thrilling news arrives. Sam and Rosa and one-year-old Eliza are coming home for a holiday.

8. At Last It's Me

'I swear I'm no tiger-lily now,' says Rosa, stretching luxuriously, 'but a mother tiger herself. I would claw the throat out of anyone who threatened my baby. Yet had you told me of this extraordinary state before Eliza was born I would simply have laughed. Oh Lucy, it's so strange, so marvellous and terrible and strange, to become a mother.'

Rosa is softer, her bosom lush, her waist tinier than ever: beside her I feel drab and shapeless. I gaze down at Eliza in my arms and she beams with trust. Her small hand reaches out for a fold of my blouse and she begins to chew upon it thoughtfully. I'm enchanted.

'Here are the pictures taken just after she was born,' says Rosa. 'Mr Nishioka took them. Such a good photographer and one of the powers of the town too. He often assists Sam in business.'

There are portraits of Sam and Rosa, Eliza's little face between them, and others with Thomas and Borue, beaming as proudly as parents, and two women I do not know. Both are dark-haired, with full lips and high cheekbones. The older woman is striking, while the younger is simply beautiful.

'That's Emilia Letolo, my midwife, and her daughter Cristina. They were so good to me. I was terribly rude and angry at one point. I wanted it all to be over, it seemed so difficult and painful, and I was afraid … then Emilia gave me a potion and it all became easier and just a short while later—heavens, there was my tiny Eliza. I owe them so much.'

'What handsome women. What is their background?'

'Emilia is half-Spanish, from the Philippines, while her late husband was partly Aboriginal. I believe Cristina's life has been remarkably constrained by that small fact. Did you know, Lucy, there's actually a government official called the Protector of Aborigines? Anyone with even a trace of native blood may not work or move or even marry without his permission.' Rosa laughs. 'Broome makes Sam's ancestry seem almost pedestrian in comparison.'

We're seated on the veranda of the great house and I suddenly hear raised voices inside. Bao-lim speaks rapidly in Chinese, Min-lu quietly, Bao-lim angrily, Sam firmly. I know enough now to understand a few phrases—*home, money, foreign devils* and *bad business.* This is not the first time I've heard their raised voices, it happened twice last week at the office too.

Min-lu comes out to sit with us. I offer her Eliza and she takes her and rubs her cheek against the baby's soft brown hair. Eliza chews on her jade pendant.

'Ah, sweet child,' Min-lu says, and looks up at my inquiring face. 'Oh, it's Bao-lim, so angry at the foreigners in China and the weak Emperor. He supports the Nationalists and sends them money. It was bad enough he cut off his queue, he made the servants cut theirs too and some of the old men wept for days. It just causes trouble for us and it's not good for business.'

'But that can't affect us,' says Rosa. 'China is one thing, Broome another—and we're doing so well now.'

Min-lu kisses the baby's head. 'Indeed. And it's Christmas-time too, a Christmas to enjoy with our small perfect grand-daughter. My bad-tempered brother can hardly find fault with her!'

We take lavish dinners in the summer heat and even Bao-lim seems to enjoy himself, chuckling as Eliza gently pats his face. The following weeks are a pleasure, with picnics and tennis and walks on the Esplanade beach, Eliza squealing with delight at the lapping waves and Filipa and Izabel solemnly enjoying their new roles as her aunties.

In the long evenings we have drinks on the veranda, the moon above the spires of distant Melbourne outlining the swaying yardarms of ships moored on the pewter of the bay. Sam tells me tales of Broome and luggers and storms and pearls, and I'm amused to hear that the wicked Queen City of the North is not quite as sinful as it likes to believe.

'In many ways it's just a small straitlaced town,' he says, 'although it's a complicated place, and it's hard to follow the precise social niceties among the non-whites. There's Japanese, Chinese, Malays, Indians, Manilamen, Ceylonese, Koepangers, Binghis ...'

'Binghis?'

'Aboriginals. Then there are the half-castes and quarter-castes and Lord-knows-what of all the mixed races. Do you recall, Lucy, when I said on *Willowmere* I hoped Broome might be somewhere my race is of less importance than my skills?'

'Yes, of course.'

He laughs. 'I could not have been more wrong—there is nowhere on earth it's so important. But within that strictness there's a surprising freedom, as long as you don't aspire to the white hierarchy.'

'How is that, Sam?'

'The top level—the magistrate, the Cable Station manager, some of the master pearlers—act as if they're running the Raj, not muddy little Broome. Everyone but themselves is either a servant or invisible. For them and their toadies there's no crossing of the colour bar: even a mere friendship with a non-white would lead to them being ostracised.'

'And a marriage?' I ask gently. 'Is it as you once said?'

Sam sighs. 'Rosa should be free to shine at the highest reaches, but because of me she cannot. But I spoke of a freedom too: there's a certain level of society, sophisticated pearlers and prosperous non-whites, where we seem to fit comfortably. Rosa says she's content.'

In January 1909 I receive a letter from Danny in Shanghai, enclosing a photograph taken with the Swedish boy Mattias Nilsen. They're standing beside another shipmate and a Chinese woman in a long silk gown, and Mattias looks handsome and grown-up in a white uniform. He's now second on a Hong Kong passenger steamer and sends his warmest regards, Danny says.

Danny is now first mate on *Callao Queen*, taking nitrate for fertiliser and explosives from the barren Chilean coast to Europe. Nitrate is the hardest cargo of all, lifted only by vessels desperate for trade. I know he's only twenty-five but Danny looks tired and old in the photo.

He's still without command of a ship and the possibility recedes further every day. He says the captain of *Callao Queen* is a drunkard, the food unspeakable, the men bitter. He does his best but she's an unhappy ship: an unlucky ship. Perhaps not unlucky— many a hellship lives on into gracious old age, while good *Willowmere* ... I sigh.

Sometimes I sit with my family on the veranda into the long evenings and we see vessels make ready to leave port. We hear faint yells, squeaking windlasses, distant chanting as the anchor rises. Tiny silhouettes appear on the yards and a sail blooms and another and another, shaking and filling as the ship moves slowly away.

Even after everyone else has gone inside I watch into the twilight until I can see no more.

'Keep still, Lucy,' says Aunt Bertha. 'Yes, that does look very nice indeed, so *romantic*.'

It's certainly beautiful fabric but no matter how the seamstress re-pins the bodice it still fits me poorly, the puffed sleeves unflattering, the white harsh against my pale skin and brown hair. How I wish Min-lu were here to advise me, but she's in Sydney on business and I'm completely at Aunt Bertha's mercy. She's preparing me for my social coming-out: my presentation to the Governor-General, His

Majesty's representative.

The presentation itself passes in a blur of tulle and gloves and flowers, stern footmen and gleeful mothers. We take afternoon tea while the other girls giggle amongst themselves and I sit silently, wondering what to say. I suspect the recent fall in the price of pearlshell is of not much interest to anyone here.

'And now, my dear, we'll hold a ball for your eighteenth birthday,' says Min-lu, home at last. 'Something exclusive, elegant, with friends and family and the best young men in Melbourne—good heavens, Lucy, what's wrong?'

'I never in my *life* want to be seen in that dress again.'

'Was it truly that bad? We can make you a new dress.'

'But I'm so awkward and gawky and I don't know how to chatter about stupid hats or floral arrangements. I only know about things like import duties on rice wine and dried mushrooms.'

Min-lu slowly smiles. 'Then we shall make you a dress so beautiful you won't have to say a word.'

In the warehouse she unrolls billows of her best fabrics, rejecting a bolt of silvery blue lace (too cold), a beige-pink satin (too washed-out), an emerald green silk (too sharp). Then she reaches to the back of the shelves.

'There it is,' she says. 'Hidden away for a special occasion. What do you think, Lucy?'

It's a silk that rustles like tissue paper, deep pink shot with amber, as rich as the ruffled heart of a peony. I touch it and can only whisper, 'Oh, Min-lu, for me? *Really*?'

'For you. We'll see the dressmaker this afternoon, and I promise, no puffed sleeves.'

On the night of my coming-out ball I stay at Min-lu's house. The hairdresser fusses over me for what seems like hours, then I put on my new silk underwear and stockings. A maid buttons up my dress, and eases my feet into satin slippers with little heels and pointed toes.

Now at last I'm by myself for a few moments. I take a deep breath and stand before the long cheval mirror. My glossy brown hair is entwined with ribbons and my neck rises like a lily out of the amber-pink silk, tailored to flatter my slight bosom and narrow hips.

My eyes are large and dark, my lips and cheeks flushed. Droplets of garnet and seed-pearls, a gift from Rosa and Sam, hang at my ears and throat. I think, Oh, Mama, you wouldn't know me tonight—and it's only silks and jewels, it's not really *me*. But what fun to pretend!

Min-lu brings Filipa and Izabel into the room, who squeal in admiration and kiss me and spin me around, careful not to crush my skirt.

'Min-lu, it's so *beautiful*, I didn't imagine—'

'My dear, you may think it's the dress that's so beautiful, but I promise, it's you too. Come now, we must meet your guests. Fili, Bella, you may watch from the top of the staircase.'

In the receiving line I greet Uncle Edward, who kisses my cheek, and Aunt Bertha, who will never again miss one of Min-lu's events. Her eyebrows lift at the sight of my dress.

'Surely that colour is a little improper, Lucy.'

'But Aunt Bertha, I thought pink was always appropriate for young ladies.'

'Yes, but ... well, you look very nice, my dear, although I feel white suits always you better.'

Papa kisses me. 'Oh, my girl, your Mama would have been so proud.'

'This can't be my little sister, the apprentice upper yardman!' says Sam.

Rosa hugs me. 'Not a wallflower now—I see I'm utterly overshadowed.' I laugh. No one in Melbourne could overshadow Rosa.

'And we have a surprise for you, Lucy,' she says, and it's as if the noise, the people, the lights, simply fade away. I see just the golden head and broad shoulders, the pleading blue eyes.

'Please give me a chance to make amends, Lucy,' Gideon says. 'I've been in torment over my cruelty to one who had treated me only with kindness. May we speak?'

'Oh, Gideon, of course!' I say in delight, 'How well you look.' He moves away, smiling over his shoulder, and I turn to the next guest in the receiving line.

I dance with Sam, who asks, 'Have we done the right thing, Lucy? Sometimes I fear I'm too forgiving, but our small band of friends— of shipmates—would be incomplete without him.'

'I'm so glad you brought him, Sam. He truly is one of us.'

I dance with handsome young men: some I like, some I dislike, and one or two I've dreamt about; then at last Gideon claims me.

'To be part of this fine company again, Lucy! It's a cold world indeed without one's closest friends. And in truth, may Rosa forgive me, my disappointment was fleeting. What seemed misfortune was instead a stroke of good luck which led me to my fiancée, dear Angela.'

'Oh, Gideon, how wonderful!'

'I am eternally sorry for my brutal words. I'd been too long at sea, my temper was frayed, my hopes were dashed. Will you let me apologise with all my heart for my unkindness?'

'Of course I will. We've missed you so.'

Gideon has returned to Melbourne while he awaits a new position, and over the next few weeks he fits as neatly into our circle again as if he had never left. Papa is delighted to see him again and so is Uncle Edward. They talk one evening over brandy and next day take him to meet their broker (an excellent head for business, our Mr Meade, Papa confides to me). They start holding convivial meetings in Papa's study and at Uncle Edward's club in the city.

Sam takes him to the company offices, to be greeted by the ribald squeals of the warehouse women and the demure glances of the secretaries. Although fond of him for Sam's sake, Min-lu is immune to Gideon's charm, but Bao-lim likes him enormously and they often sit together in the evening over wine and cigars. I can see Sam is content at the return of his old shipmate, and Rosa rather enjoys his gallantry towards her as a married woman.

Yet, despite a sense of harmony restored I sometimes feel an anxiety I don't understand, and wonder if it is to do with the time of year—autumn leaves and the scent of woodsmoke and my memories of loss, now two years past.

Or perhaps it's a premonition. One morning, waking from a confused dream, I can hear the telephone ringing and footsteps and worried voices. I put on my dressing-gown and slippers and meet Papa at the foot of the stairs.

'My dear, we have had what may be unhappy news.'

We sit down and he clears his throat. 'The newspaper reports— and the shipping office has confirmed—that Mr Whalen's barque *Callao Queen* has been lost in a Pampero off the Amazon Basin. Dreadful conditions, they say. There are several survivors, but we cannot be confident Mr Whalen is amongst them.'

'Danny? No. Oh, *no*.'

'We must prepare ourselves for the worst, Lucy.'

'I cannot, Papa. I cannot believe it.'

I sit in my room, his fiddle on my lap, my fingers tracing the curve of the scroll. I gaze at the faint letters carved on the neck, *M. Whalen 1883*. Danny's father Michael made the instrument the year Danny was born.

I think of the old joke he once told me: the difference between a violin and a fiddle is that no one cries if you spill beer on a fiddle.

But a spill of sea-water—what has sea-water done to my violin on *Willowmere*? To Mama? And now, perhaps, to my fierce, kind friend?

Sam and Rosa visit every day hoping for news. Sam is deeply distressed and I remember Danny saying, 'I'd die for Sam Lee and probably he for me,' and I think, yes, it's true. Gideon visits too, but often ends up discussing business with Papa. There's not much else to do.

We reassure each other that Danny is a strong swimmer, the waters are warm, the ship was not far from the coast. I try not to think of the swift, dreadful forms I saw, afire with blue-green phosphorescence, that night of the Pampero.

A week of agonising suspense passes, then finally a few misspelt names appear on the fourth page of the paper (the wreck is already forgotten news). It seems five men have been saved from *Callao Queen*, including one Mr Wellin. Is it Danny?

Telegrams fly back and forth and at last, to overwhelming relief, the word arrives that First Mate Daniel Whalen has survived.

As the only officer left alive from the wreck he reports to the British Consul at Rio de Janeiro, then takes passage on a steamship to Fremantle.

I lean against a pile of pillows on a bed at the great house, holding a dozing Eliza while Rosa packs a large trunk. 'Danny stuck on a steamship!' I say. 'He'll be bored.'

'We'll be in Perth in three weeks, so shall meet him then.'

'You never liked him much, did you, Rosa?'

Rosa smiles. 'Not very much. He was too aware of my bond with Sam and could not hide his disapproval. But I like him better now, and Sam—and you—both love him, so what am I to do?'

'He's my friend, Rosa, and when I thought he might have died ...' I gaze at sleeping Eliza. 'Yet I'm not certain that is love. Surely love is something more thrilling?'

Rosa sits down beside me. 'Perhaps it is, but a good friend, well, that is sweet too. But what of Gideon? Is there perhaps something warmer for you in that direction?'

Gideon is certainly a fine-looking man and, two years after the event, one passionate outburst can hardly be held against him. (In retrospect it even seems a little thrilling.)

'Of course not,' I say firmly. 'He's engaged.'

'Wouldn't bother me,' says Rosa with a shrug. 'But yes, the utterly perfect Miss Angela Percival. I wonder if we'll meet her in Perth too?'

Gideon is taking the steamer with Sam and Rosa to Perth to join his command, his first command at last! He's been appointed master of S.S. *Hydra*, a small steamship on the Fremantle to Singapore run, stopping regularly at Broome. He spends his days now dashing between uniform fittings and soirées celebrating his good fortune.

My puzzling sense of anxiety has at last eased. At the crowded pier with Papa, Min-lu, Filipa and Izabel, I embrace Rosa and Sam and little Eliza. Gideon holds my hand and kisses me tenderly on the cheek and I redden a little.

'Dear Lucy, I feel eternally grateful for your forbearance. I promise one day to return the favour.'

'It's been wonderful having you back, Gideon. I wish you the best with your fine S.S. *Hydra*.'

He laughs and slaps the shoulders of friends, and finally mounts the gangway with his familiar warm smile back at me. He stands beside Sam and Rosa and Eliza, and they wave together as the ship draws away.

A few weeks later at the office Min-lu says, her face grim, 'Come for a walk with me, please Lucy—such a fine, bracing day.'

We stride against the wind (somewhat more than bracing) towards the Esplanade. After a few minutes of silence Min-lu says fiercely, 'It's gone, *gone*!'

'What has?'

'Most of our capital, put into terrible investments. I cannot believe my brother would risk the company's money—Sam's money!—on such hopeless prospects. And what hasn't been squandered has been donated to the Chinese Nationalists. They may be working for reform but I hardly wish it to be with my money!'

'Not all is gone, surely?'

'Enough. We could lose the great house and I must close part of the company. There will certainly be no more parties. Oh, Lucy,' her voice shakes, 'Sam's portion, the backing for his venture in Broome, his profits from last year—all gone.'

'But don't forget there's Rosa's money too, her marriage settlement and share of Mama's estate. Not a vast amount, but enough to keep them afloat at least.'

Min-lu thinks for a time. 'Of course, yes, if Sam and Rosa can keep going, perhaps I can bring at least some of the business around. I still have a few resources of my own my foolish brother couldn't get his hands on.'

As I walk home I think with relief, *that's* why I've had such a knot in my stomach. Somehow I must have known things were wrong with the business. But just a day later I enter the sitting room and see Papa's face.

I sit beside him and take his hand. 'Tell me.'

He sighs deeply. 'I've been very careless, my dear. Seemed such certain prospects, everyone else was making money. I had good advice, the very best, but the market ...'

'What have we lost, Papa?'

'I made profits at first—skipper's luck, Gideon called it. Then I started to slide. I kept trying but it was just good money after bad. He and Edward got out, but I kept going—'

'Are we destitute?'

'Certainly not!' He pauses. 'We may have to leave this house and take somewhere smaller.'

'Is that all?'

'No, Lucy, it's not all.'

'Mama's legacy? My marriage settlement?'

Papa closes his eyes. 'I had hoped to increase them for you.'

'And now they're gone.'

He does not reply.

In my room I hug a pillow and look out at the sky. What a cruel coincidence Min-lu and Papa have both been caught up in financial misfortune! I can believe Min-lu will overcome her difficulties, but what will Papa and I do?

I become aware of a curious hubbub from the kitchen. I run downstairs to find Alice helping Mrs O'Brien to a chair, crying out for help. Mrs O'Brien is bleeding from her head and face, holding her ribs, bent over, gasping and sobbing.

Harry rushes in the back door with a look of fury. 'They got away, the bastards, the black-hearted, cowardly bastards! Oh Jesus, Sally, are you all right?'

I didn't know her name was Sally, I think in confusion. 'Harry—Alice—what has happened?'

'She was taking the peelings to the garden, Miss, and I heard her cry out,' says Alice. 'There was two of them, hard-looking fellas, hitting and kicking her. I grabbed the bucket and threw it at one of them—hit him too! And the other yelled something ... oh Miss, I can't repeat it.'

'Say it, Alice.'

'He said, *I was sent to tell this raddled old harlot never to interfere again.*'

Harry gasps. 'Raddled old harlot? The dirty mongrel! Interfere in what? She don't interfere!'

A prickle of shock runs over me. Two years ago I heard those bitter word from Gideon's own mouth when Mrs O'Brien ordered him out of the house. Yes, once she did interfere.

And now I must wonder if I have been utterly deceived.

Could it possibly be true? In those terrible days of losing Mama my shipboard friends were my only solace: of course I trusted Gideon. But then I remember his face, wishing I would suffer as he had.

With increasing horror I think of his evenings with Bao-lim and the loss of the company funds, and Papa's forays into the market—skipper's luck, Gideon said. Was he urging him on?

I try to talk to Min-lu and Papa about it but they don't take me seriously.

'Perhaps he wants to destroy us all because of Rosa and Sam!'

They look puzzled. Min-lu says, 'Even Gideon cannot manipulate the stock market, Lucy.'

'But he can manipulate people to invest poorly. He goaded Papa, he charmed Bao-lim—'

'Good Lord, he's a master mariner, Lucy, I cannot believe it. And why should he wish to hurt Rosa, having his own fiancée in Perth?' says Papa frowning (he does not care for this talk of manipulation).

'And in any case, such an odd way to go about it,' says Min-lu. 'Think, Lucy—to cripple a business, ruin your father, simply because a woman prefers another? That's hardly how a gentleman deals with what is, after all, a common enough disappointment.'

'But it wasn't just Rosa, it was losing *Willowmere*, too.'

'Again, Lucy, he is a sailor!' says Papa. 'He understands what's at stake when a ship goes to sea.'

'It's not possible, my dear,' says Min-lu. 'Please don't fret in this way. These events are merely a series of sad misfortunes.'

Min-lu and I sit together and read Rosa's letter from Fremantle.

We met Danny and the other survivors at the dock. They'd had a truly harrowing time—twenty-five hours in the water before being rescued. Danny himself is much changed and says he will never return to square-riggers. I fear he's drinking rather a lot too.

We have persuaded him to come to Broome with us and he's agreed to take on managing Sam's foreshore camp for a time. We met Gideon's divine Angela at last—she's pretty enough but not quite as I might have expected the daughter of an eminent politician.

Sam says I'm simply jealous, but as a couple they puzzle me, their affection a little cool, perhaps. Still, any woman would have a hard time competing with Gideon's beloved steamship: he departed on the Hydra last week for Singapore.

'You see. He's not in love with this Angela, she's just a cover for his real feelings.'

'Lucy, it doesn't say that at all!' says Min-lu, exasperated.

'No, it doesn't.' I sigh. 'Oh, Min-lu, I'm exhausted, thinking these terrible things about our friend. I fear I've suffered too many shocks and now I'm jumping at shadows.'

She takes my hand for a moment. 'My dear, you know I have little fondness for Gideon, but even I believe that to be so. And in any case you've got more important things to think about. You and your father must soon decide upon a course of action. What will you do?'

'Papa says he wishes to leave Melbourne, to be away from curious eyes. He sits for hours on the veranda watching the bay and it worries me. That's how he was after the shipwreck.'

'But what do you want, Lucy?'

'There's only one thing I want: to go to Broome. It's almost winter there now and Rosa says it's so lovely. We could see little Eliza and Sam's luggers and find out how Danny is. But Papa would never agree—he says it's too wild for a young lady and I'd never get married.'

'Let me speak to him. We could say it's just for six months and you'd be back in time for next year's season.' She hesitates. 'That gives me an idea, too. You know Bao-lim has left for Hong Kong and the great house is to be sold?'

'Yes.'

'How would you feel if the girls and I moved into your father's house while you were away? I'd pay a good rent, which would ease his financial concerns. But I'm a little uncertain ...'

'But that's a marvellous idea!' I gaze at her in consternation. 'Why would you feel uncertain?'

Min-lu smiles at my expression. 'Lucy, we are all constrained by our fears.'

'You, Min-lu? I've never imagined you constrained by anything.'

She hesitates. 'I had an unusual upbringing for a Chinese girl. My father adored young Queen Victoria and wanted me educated as an Englishwoman. My governess was the widow of a minor British noble, impoverished and stranded in Hong Kong, and she taught me everything about speech, manners, dress. But when I was nineteen I met Freddy.'

'Sam's father?'

She nods. 'My governess realised her time of influence was over. She became bitter and stole some of my jewellery—pieces I'd happily have given her! When she was dismissed she said things to me, terrible things, and it was only then I understood. I would be tolerated by Europeans as long as wealth shielded me, but should that shield ever disappear ...'

'Oh, Min-lu, far more than tolerated! You're part of our family now, our kindest, wisest friend. You are welcome to live in our house, and Mama would certainly have approved of it.'

It takes a little longer to convince Papa we should go away to Broome, but in the end Min-lu's arguments (and brown eyes) are too persuasive for him to resist.

As we make our plans he gradually emerges from his despair and teases me, 'There's crocodiles there, you know, missy—*crocodiles*! And wild natives and spiders and snakes as well. You'll be begging me to come home again after a week.'

I simply laugh with delight.

Our staff are happy to stay here, supplemented by Min-lu's cook, butler and nanny. Alice is glad to become part of such a grand household, but says she's nervous about the sharp cleavers the Chinese cook wields so casually. Still, he certainly has a twinkle in those cheeky eyes, she says.

It seems to take forever to organise the packing for Broome, but in August 1909 Papa and I embark. At last! At last it's *me* on the ship, leaving the shore behind.

In my cabin at night I feel the familiar, comforting rolling: my body has not forgotten. Like *Willowmere* but unlike too, because there's no creaking of rigging or calls of men on the yards, just the throb of engines and muffled feet in the carpeted corridor.

We run into a storm and Papa and I stand at the bow, rugged up and reminiscing about the hurricane that hit us in the South Atlantic. He seems better than he has for years, his grey hair ruffling, his eyes on the sea and clouds, as content as if he were back on his own deck.

After Perth, we embark on S.S. *Gorgon* for the voyage along the west coast to Broome. Even after two thousand miles travelled from Melbourne there are another twelve hundred to go. At the tiny pearling port of Onslow I see my first real luggers when two low ketches, *Ibis* and *Redbill,* cruise past the jetty with an air of trim competence. Their Asian crewmen wave and I wave back, fascinated by the silvery shell lying in heaps on the decks.

Further up the coast is Port Hedland, hazy with heat and red dust. At each stop a few passengers come and go, along with bags of mail, piles of timber, horses, cattle, and once even some camels.

Then comes the long beach they called the Ninety-Mile. I can see faint streamers of smoke in the desert beyond, and one of the stewards tells me they are the cooking fires of Aborigines. But how could anyone possibly survive in that wilderness?

In the distance now I can make out a red bluff with patches of green. Gantheaume Point, the steward says, we're almost there. He calls it Gan-thee-um, and I whisper it to myself. On the high tide we steam into Roebuck Bay, its waters of deep turquoise stretching to distant orange hills. When it's low tide, Rosa told me, the bay becomes pale green like Min-lu's jade pendant and ships berthed at the famous long jetty must sit bolt upright on the mud.

As we approach I see a small beach to the left of the jetty, and on the other side a stretch of copper-coloured foreshore that leads through mangroves to the township, a mile or two away. A handful of boats are pulled up on the sand and behind them are sheds of lattice-work and white-painted corrugated iron.

The crew throws hawsers, men on the jetty catch them and tie them to bollards. The grumble of the engines rises suddenly, then stops.

9. THE TURQUOISE BAY

Sam and Rosa are waving to us from a small crowd of people dressed in tropical whites. I run down the gangway, Papa following, and we hug. We push through the hubbub towards a horse-drawn tram running along the jetty, as people call out to Sam and lift their hats to Rosa.

Two tall, fine-looking men come up to us. Sam nods and says, 'Please, let me introduce my father-in-law, Captain Nicholas Fox, and my wife's sister, Miss Lucy Fox, just in from Melbourne. Captain Fox, Lucy—this is the Broome Shipping Master Captain Gregory, and his brother Dick, late of the Indian Army.'

Papa shakes hands and the two men lift their hats to me. Captain Gregory gives me a dazzling grin and says in a deep Welsh lilt, 'Please do call me Greg, everyone else does.' He turns to Sam. 'And may I have a quiet word with you, Captain Lee, about this latest lunatic nonsense from the Fisheries Department?' They move aside.

'Have you been long in Broome, sir?' Papa asks Dick Gregory.

'A recent arrival, Captain Fox.'

'Do you like it?' I ask.

'Had rather a rough welcome,' he says smiling. 'On my first outing we hit a cyclone off the Ninety-Mile. One hundred and twenty men and forty boats were lost, a shocking business.'

'Good Lord,' says Papa, taken aback.

'Then this December past we had another blow. Forty sailors, fifteen luggers and two schooners lost. Nearly did for my brother as well. He had to swim for it when *Kelander Bux* went down.'

I'm astonished. 'You cannot mean—surely not—one hundred and sixty men lost in a single year from a tiny town like this?'

'Mostly indentured workers, Lucy,' says Rosa briskly. 'Not from Broome, of course. They come from all over the East to work here and they understand the risks. Our boats were quite safe, most of our men are locals, they know when to get out of danger.'

I look out at the pretty aqua-blue waters and feel chilled.

A few moments later Sam rejoins us and the Gregory brothers bid farewell.

'Your luggage will be delivered later, so let's take you home now,' says Sam. We board the horse-drawn tram and ride to the shore. In this heat I'm glad not to have to walk down the jetty: Sam says it's almost half a mile long.

We climb into a carriage waiting under a tree. Eliza is there, bouncing on the lap of her Aboriginal nanny Bettie, who smiles shyly when introduced, while Eliza chortles with pleasure when I hug her. Sam takes the reins and we amble along a road, red dust vivid against a grassy verge. We pass the Customs House and Shipping Master's office, no more than large sheds, then two blocks further is the Continental Hotel.

'They hold a Cinematograph with moving pictures on the Conti lawn three times a week,' says Rosa. 'Quite pleasant in the evenings.'

Another block and we start passing handsome bungalows in large green gardens. 'The White Quarter,' says Sam. 'About as far away as it can get from Japtown. We live more-or-less between the two.' He and Rosa exchange wry looks.

I sigh with delight at the warm air, the violet sky, the turquoise water. We reach the house, made of corrugated iron and timber, with pathways of crushed shell beneath palms and pink-flowered bushes. On two sides of the building are wide verandas, shaded by lattice-work and shutters.

In the hot afternoon I doze in my room beneath a cloudy

mosquito net, and in the evening we take dinner on the veranda, candlelight glinting on silver and porcelain, served by Ahmet, an elderly Malay man.

'I cannot believe it, Rosa, such beauty!' I say. 'And I thought you were exaggerating.'

'Nothing in this odd town is exaggerated,' says Sam. 'Part petty-minded village, part wild Asian seaport, it hardly knows what it is at all.'

'And our good Mr Whalen,' says Papa. 'He is recovered from his ordeal?'

'He is well,' says Rosa, 'but the experience seems to have marked him, perhaps not for the better. He is an excellent manager of our boats, it is true, but we don't see much of him otherwise—by his choice, not ours.'

Next day Sam takes Papa and me to the foreshore camp, a few hundred yards away across grass and red dirt. I'm in my lightest dress and under a parasol, but I'm soaked with perspiration by the time we reach the tin building and a cluster of sheds.

Sam calls out and a familiar figure appears, Danny in a grubby shirt and canvas trousers, wiping his hands on a cloth. No—a Danny who seems suddenly unfamiliar.

'You're both looking well,' he says.

'You too, Danny.' It's a lie. His lined green eyes squint against the light, and furrows run down his cheeks through ginger stubble.

'Captain Fox, Missy?' says a quiet voice behind us.

'Borue! How wonderful to see you!' I shake the small man's hand, relieved to be able to take my eyes from Danny. 'And Thomas, is he here too?'

'He outside, Missy—pearlfishing at Lacepedes. He come home in two weeks. My shellopener get sick so we come back this morning.'

'He's in the hospital,' Danny tells Sam. 'Beri-beri and a touch of typhus, but he's going to live. We're doing some work on the lugger now.'

'Ah, do let us see one of these famous ketches! Lead on, Mr Whalen,' says Papa.

We walk around the white building to the shore, lined with green mangroves. Ripples over the pink sand reflect the sky so the water itself seems tinted purple. A large wooden boat sits upright in a trench in the sand, with two deckhouses painted yellow. Below the waterline she's covered in sheets of greenish copper.

On the hull above us is her name, *Honeyeater*, and her licence number B266. Sam has already explained that no boat may engage in pearlshell fishing without such a registration. Just beyond *Honeyeater* sits *Egret*, B270, her deckhouses painted bright blue.

'Goodness, they're much larger than I thought they'd be,' I say.

'Yes, about forty feet long on deck,' replies Sam.

'Well, well,' says Papa. 'Fine-looking vessels. And is that another over there?' He points to a bow visible between the mangroves.

'That's our oldest boat,' says Sam. 'Now we've got the new ones we don't need her, but the fittings will come in handy one day.'

We stroll along the sand past the old lugger. I can see the name *Sparrow* faint on her side.

'My first lugger, Missy,' says Borue. 'Fine sailer but needs too many repairs now.'

'Do you name all your boats after birds, Sam?' I ask.

'Yes, so far we have *Honeyeater, Sparrow, Moorhen, Lyrebird, Mudlark, Egret, Currawong* and *Shearwater*. Working well, so I'm hoping it'll be a good season. What do you think, Danny?'

'Aye, perhaps.'

We turn and saunter back towards the camp. When we're saying our farewells Danny avoids my eye. Then he looks at me and I wish he hadn't.

'What's *wrong* with him, Sam?' We're sitting in the office to one side of the house, piled with accounts and bills and folders.

'The wreck I suppose, but he won't speak of it. The captain was drunk and Danny had to take charge, and he blames himself so many were lost. He doesn't see it's to his credit that anyone survived at all.'

'He always had the makings of a fine master. The men were what mattered to him. He wasn't bothered about the rank or the uniform—'

'Unlike Gideon, who has very different priorities.' Sam smiles. 'Despite my fondness for the man I'm hardly blind to his shortcomings, Lucy.'

Soon after I arrived I told Rosa and Sam my fears concerning Gideon. They reassured me and now, with the clarity of passing time, it's embarrassingly obvious how turmoil and coincidence had led me astray.

'Oh, Sam, I've been feeling such a fool about that. How could I have held such unkind thoughts?' I say, sighing. 'I suppose I fear he will never forgive any of us.'

'Gideon has his own life now, Lucy—a fiancée, a ship to command. Remember, he's a seaman, and of necessity hard and unrelenting.'

'But you're not hard and unrelenting.'

'Perhaps I was never intended for a life of command then,' says Sam, smiling. 'Do you recall, on *Willowmere*, when I told you I did not like being anything but a sailor?'

'Of course.'

'And yet—' he looks around ruefully, 'here I am drowning in bills and stern missives from the Fisheries Department.'

'Perhaps I could help. Your mother taught me all about business, and I rather enjoy the work.'

'But you're here on holiday.'

'I don't like sitting around doing nothing, Sam. Broome's a lovely place but I shall need to find something to occupy my time. And Bao-lim did teach me a great deal about pearlshell.'

'Well, we should ask your father's permission first, but in truth it would be a relief to share my woes with someone other than Rosa. Thank you, little sister.'

Rosa and I take the carriage into Japtown one morning as she wants a new dressing-gown for Sam. We're going to Nishioka's store, the finest in Broome.

'I shall introduce you to Mr Murakami,' she says. 'He's been a great help to us—found Sam his best diver. He took those photographs of Eliza, remember?'

'I thought that was Mr Nishioka.'

'He uses the name Nishioka for the business, after his wife Eki's first husband, but his real name is Yasukichi Murakami. His wife's a photographer too, quite extraordinary for a woman. He's highly influential in Broome.'

The Nishioka store is off a lane in the middle of Japtown, surrounded by flimsy buildings and the boardwalks leading to the foreshore of Dampier Terrace. Heat shimmers off corrugated iron walls and the lane smells of spices and incense and inadequate drainage.

Mr Murakami, in a high-collared suit, is behind the counter. He has a strong chin and thoughtful black eyes, and he greets us with a bow. Rosa introduces me and his formal expression softens.

'The men from the camp have told me about this new young lady, so fond of luggers,' he says. 'Welcome to Broome, Miss Fox.'

His wife Eki, a tiny woman in a kimono, comes over to serve us. She spread dressing-gowns out on the glass counter and as Rosa is deliberating between the blue or the crimson, a tall man enters the shop: the Shipping Master, Captain Gregory, who met us on the jetty a few weeks ago.

'Ah, Mrs Lee, Miss Fox, I do hope you're well this beautiful morning! And has Captain Lee fished you some fine pearls lately to keep you both in the luxury you so rightly deserve?'

Rosa laughs. 'I'm afraid you won't get any clues from me, Greg, you'll have to ask him yourself.'

'But he won't tell me, *cariad*. A hard man, he is.'

He turns to Mr Murakami. 'And good morning to you, Murakami-san. Might I have a word?' He nods to us, and goes into a rear office with Mr Murakami.

Rosa chooses the blue dressing-gown and Eki takes it away to wrap. Gregory comes out of the office, raises his hat to us and leaves.

Rosa whispers, 'He's just bought four luggers with the secret assistance of Mr Murakami.'

'Why is it secret?' I murmur, as Eki returns.

'Oh, thank you, Mrs Nishioka. Good day,' says Rosa.

Outside she continues, 'Aliens—Asiatics—aren't allowed by law to own luggers, but they discreetly lease or part-own half the boats in town. It's called dummying, and it keeps everything afloat when times are hard. Most of the pearlers do it, although they like to pretend they don't.'

'But that's silly. Why can't they legally own pearling luggers?'

'The yapping fools who call me a prostitute for marrying Sam—yes, to my face, Lucy—are terrified of hard-working Asians and wish to deny them advancement in the industry.'

'Then why is Sam allowed to own any luggers at all?' I ask.

'His family took up residence in Australia before Federation, so they're grudgingly permitted to remain and work. But under those laws Sam is allowed to own precisely one lugger, the rest have to be registered in my name. It's absurd, I'm not even interested in the smelly old things!'

Outside the Chinese provision store we meet Danny, carrying canvas bags of groceries, accompanied by two women. Rosa introduces us, and one is Emilia Letolo, who helped deliver baby Eliza, and the other is her daughter Cristina, a beautiful girl with chestnut hair, high cheekbones and full lips.

Emilia is not only the town's chief midwife but she runs a boarding-house too, where Danny lives. After polite chit-chat, Rosa suggests they come to tea the following afternoon—no, not you Danny, she says, you smell too much of tar—and he laughs quietly. He looks in better spirits than last time I saw him and I'm glad.

Rosa's afternoon tea goes well. Emilia is an amusing woman with an endless supply of gossip, while shy Cristina blossoms as we chat. Papa is drawn in by our laughter to take tea with us and he seems to enjoy himself. He always did rather like brown eyes, I think, pleased.

Before the tea-party I was working in Sam's office in a simple cotton gown, so I feel a little dowdy beside Cristina, exquisite in lace, but I enjoy our conversation. Yet as we say farewell she gazes at me from under her lashes with a smile that doesn't quite reach her eyes.

Is that a hint of unfriendliness? Surely not. But then I remember the day before, and how close to Danny she was standing.

Broome's only reason for existence is pearlshell, and slowly I get to know this odd little outpost with its veneer of European respectability overlying a busy Asian seaport. While parliaments thousands of miles away may pompously proclaim laws to regulate the races, here they're simply constraints to be sidestepped.

Those who swagger into town with the arrogance of Empire— the second sons, the restless, the lazy, the dregs—must learn they don't need to like a man's race to work well beside him, or they soon find themselves on the road out of town again.

Broome supports seven hundred Europeans and a few hundred free Asiatics (like Sam's family), plus two thousand indentured Asians, the 'aliens' who actually work the luggers. They are brave divers and fine sailors who, at the end of each season, are marched onto ships and sent home again.

This is not at all as the Melbourne newspapers would have it: according to them Broome is a racially immoral free-for-all. Now I see it is far from that and, apart from the utterly blinkered, most people here know what is at stake: Broome could not survive without the Asian and Aboriginal workers that sustain it.

As I begin to understand the small town I also learn the fine art of lugger management. Some of the larger pearling masters have their own schooners and can re-supply their luggers out at sea, but Sam's boats must return to Broome every few weeks to unload their shell and get everything they need, from curry spices to firewood to dinghies. Slowly I bring some order to the chaos.

In hot November, when everyone is yearning for the wet season to begin, Sam proposes a sail along the coast to Willie Creek for a picnic. We'll go on *Mudlark*, the lugger skippered by Thomas, which has just returned to port because the diver was hit by the bends. 'I like being skipper now, Missy,' Thomas tells me, laughing. 'No more diving. Leave it to Japs, they don't care about danger.'

Just after dawn we walk to the foreshore with cushions and hampers, while nanny Bettie takes charge of little Eliza. At the camp we greet Emilia, alone today because Cristina dislikes boats. Captain Gregory sends his apologies, but his brother Dick is there with a dark-haired young man. He introduces him as Alain Bourdon, an agent for a French pearl-buying syndicate.

The men, barefoot with their trousers rolled to their knees, help us into the dinghy and in several trips row us out to *Mudlark*, bobbing beyond the mangroves. A certain amount of enjoyable fuss gets us all up the rope ladders and onto the deck.

I walk to the bow and look back over the lugger. Two green-painted deck-houses lead to small cabins below, the forward one reserved for the ladies, says Papa. It has a couple of covered buckets 'for necessities' and six small crew bunks.

In the middle of the boat is a hold with the air pump and a fireplace for cooking, and near the stern is the main cabin. I notice Danny is already aboard when we arrive but he stays at the tiller, murmuring occasionally to Thomas and looking out to sea.

I sit on a deck-house as the anchor is raised and *Mudlark* moves away. The men hoist the sails, fresh air fills my throat, turquoise water slaps against the hull and I feel a sense of utter joy. Soon we're heading towards the open sea past beaches covered with gigantic orange boulders.

When we round Gantheaume Point we turn north and the rusty cliffs give way to golden sand. The sky is hazy, the air soft. Comfortable in my white blouse and blue cotton skirt, I sigh with pleasure and lean back against a cushion. Emilia and Rosa pour glasses of cordial and the French pearl agent sits down beside me with two glasses and hands me one. He's slim and tanned, in a white shirt and grey trousers.

'Oh, thank you. And how long have you been in Broome, Mr Bourdon?'

'Please, just Alain. I have been here half a year. It is such a fine life, so different from Europe. And you, Miss Fox?'

'Do call me Lucy. Almost three months. I love it too.'

'I would like to stay but I do not know what my father will say. He is a jeweller in Paris and sent me here to learn more about the trade and to buy stones—I mean pearls—for him.'

I smile. I already know the local slang as well as anyone. 'Your English is very good.'

'My mother is from London, so I have spent time there too.'

'We used to live in Greenwich, but left three years ago to come to Melbourne.'

'I know Greenwich well,' says Alain with pleasure. 'Did you ever go to the Gallery of Naval Art?'

'One of my favourite places!'

He's twenty-two, he tells me. He has dark eyebrows, a narrow face, a quick laugh and expressive hands: his faint accent is charming.

We sail along a wide surf beach with only the occasional fisherman to be seen against its expanse. 'That is Cable Beach,' says Alain. 'The telegraphic line surfaces there after running along the ocean floor all the way from Java.'

'The cable is an astonishing invention, isn't it? Fancy getting the overseas news in just days, not weeks. How fortunate we are.'

'Eventually the council will stop bickering about goats and pot-holes and build us all a good road out to that beach,' he says. 'Then I may have the pleasure of taking you there in my carriage one day to watch the sunset.'

'I hope we stay long enough in Broome to do that. But I fear my father wants us to return to Melbourne soon.'

'Are you quite certain of that?'

I look towards Papa, leaning against a stay in his shirtsleeves, his face brown, his hat tipped back on his head, laughing at something Emilia is saying to him.

I smile. 'Perhaps I may be able to look forward to that sunset after all.'

By midday we're off the crystal waters of Willie Creek. We go ashore in the dinghy and spread blankets in the shade of gum trees for our picnic of cold meats and damper and fruit-cake. Thomas and Danny build a small fire to boil water for tea.

Thomas calls out to someone and I see a small group of Aborigines coming towards us. The men carry spears, but I'm not concerned. In this part of the country relations are peaceful between the natives and the newcomers. The men squat by the fire to put two dead goannas onto the ashes to cook.

The women come over with cries of greeting to Bettie—she's apparently an auntie to several—and gather around Eliza, admiring her curls. A small brown girl strokes my cheek shyly, then bursts into laughter. I'm enchanted by her large eyes and long black lashes, and moved by her twig-thin arms.

The men bring us welcome news of a missing lugger safely ashore about fifty miles north, and Sam, pleased, offers them supplies from our stores. As we're packing up, the laughing women give him a small piece of carved pearlshell—an oval carved with the outline of a lugger, red ochre rubbed into the incisions.

As we're heading home in the sunset, Sam hands me the carved shell as a souvenir.

'I haven't forgotten those pearl earrings I said I'd get for you, Lucy, but I'm afraid so far we've needed every stone we can find to support the business.'

'It doesn't matter, Sam. A day like this is better than any jewellery.'

'I've never heard such rubbish, Lucy,' scolds Rosa lazily. 'You're clearly no sister of mine.'

To the east the full moon lights up the shoreline. We make tea over the lugger's small fireplace and I carry mugs to the stern, where Thomas and Danny are at the tiller. Thomas drinks then says, 'I go check jib, too loose I think.'

Danny and I are left alone. He's been avoiding me all day.

I look behind us at the black-silver sea and, recalling a night on *Willowmere*, say lightly, 'Christ, Whalen, that wake's as crooked as a snake.'

He turns surprised, then laughs quietly. 'Straight as an arrow, girl. Were you ever getting an answer about the silver highways and the roads? Fair worried Brownley for weeks.'

Poor dead Brownley. 'Your fiddle is still with me and safe—' I say.

'Keep it. I've no use for it right now.'

Far on the horizon lightning flickers among clouds.

'Reminds me of the night of the Pampero,' I say, but he's silent.

After a pause I try again.

'Don't you miss it, Danny—deepwater sailing?'

I see his knuckles whiten on the tiller. 'No, I don't miss it.'

'But how can that *be*?'

He takes a breath. 'When we were in the sea after the wreck— mind you, that'd be the wreck off the Amazon, not the wreck off Cape Otway—there was an apprentice, Will, just fourteen I think. The sharks took his legs and he kept crying out for his mother. Then, thank Christ, they finished him off. No, I don't miss it at all.'

I gather the mugs then go to sit on a corner of the forward deckhouse. I watch the coastline pass by, my fingers tracing the lines of the small carved pearlshell Sam gave me. After a time Alain comes near and leans on the shrouds.

'Mr Whalen is a very bitter man, I think,' he says. 'Why is that so?'

I remember Gideon's words: *Danny will never leave sail, he would sooner die.*

'He lost the life he loves and he wishes he were dead.'

The summer lay-up arrives and the luggers sail home to Roebuck Bay, bedraggled and stinking of rotten shellfish. They're hauled out, propped up with sandbags, repaired and stripped of their gear, their seacocks left open to the tide to flush out rats and cockroaches.

Men sort through hillocks of shell in the sheds and layer it into wooden cases. Sam and I tally them, pleased with the haul. One night in the lamplight he takes a matchbox out of the safe and shows me a small silvery handful of pearls. Our insurance, he says.

The indentured men are paid off and under the stern eye of the Sub-Collector of Customs they board ships for Koepang or Singapore and leave. And then the Wet is upon us.

Towering thunderstorms sweep in every day, leaving ponds of red mud and turning the air into a steambath. We take siestas in the afternoon, then sit in the evening with cool drinks and watch sheets of lightning and curtains of rain passing by. We keep the sandflies and mosquitoes at bay—barely—with pungent ointments.

Early in the new year I see an advertisement from Captain Gregory in the *Broome Chronicle*, announcing details of the 1910 Yacht Club Regatta.

'Sam, it says there'll be three lugger races, one for the Heinke Cup, worth—heavens—one hundred and thirty pounds. But why will special consideration be given to ketches?'

'Well, the first luggers were schooners, faster than ketches, but ketches are more common now, better for pearling, and being slower they get an advantage.'

I sigh. 'There's still so much I don't know. I'd love to see a lugger being built, for a start.'

'I won't be doing any this year, I'm afraid. But the Japanese carpenters will be working on other boats and perhaps you could watch them.'

'Perhaps, but I'm not certain when Papa will want us to go back to Melbourne. He says his arthritis is much better here, so he doesn't seem to be in a hurry.'

'Arthritis, eh?' says Sam, and we smile at each other. 'And what about you—don't you long to be the belle of Williamstown once more?'

'I miss your mother and Filipa and Izabel, but I don't think I could bear a real winter again.'

'You know you've been a godsend to us, Lucy, I'll be very sorry when you leave. Lee and Co. would have struggled this year without your help. I wish there were something we could give you in return.'

I gaze at the sunlight on the aqua-green bay, then turn to Sam. 'I've had an idea. If we stay, I want to keep working for you, and there's something else I'd like too—but let me talk to Papa first.'

10. SPARROW

On the day of the Regatta the new steamship *Koombana* is decked out in bunting from stem to stern. '*Koombana* is the finest steamer on the coast, you know,' says an earnest young officer, leaning on the ship's railing. 'Three-hundred and forty feet long, every compartment water-tight—she's unsinkable!'

'Oh,' I say, and turn a dazzling smile upon him. 'But how tragic, her sails appear to have been misplaced. Excuse me, I must speak to ...' and I drift away in a graceful move I learnt from Rosa.

'Remarkably well done,' says Alain Bourdon, smoking a thin cigar, falling in beside me. 'He can hardly argue with that.'

'I'm so tired of people telling me about these wonderful steamships. They're boring.'

We hear the signal for the start of the Heinke Cup, and watch the stately progress of the luggers towards a distant buoy. The course is twelve miles long so there's plenty of time to wander the deck with Alain, sipping a lemonade. When we meet Papa and Emilia, my father and I fall back a little.

'Papa, we must soon decide. What are we to do? Shall we return to Melbourne, with autumn on the way, or shall we stay here longer, where your arthritis is doing so well?'

'You're teasing me, I know full well, missy. My arthritis is not really—' he stops and takes a breath. 'Lucy, how would you feel ... It has been almost three years now since your mother ...'

'Yes, Papa?'

He clears his throat. 'You understand I hold Emilia in the highest regard. It is hard for a man to live alone and I should like, perhaps, to consider re-marriage.'

I'll always miss Mama, but I like Emilia and she makes my father happy when I'd despaired he would ever be so again.

'Papa, I know you've been lonely, so I wish you and Emilia every joy. And it means I can stay here in Broome too.'

'But that's not fair to you, my dear. You must find a husband soon.'

'Papa, look around. There are more men here than I would ever see in a year in Williamstown.'

'Hardly eligible men, Lucy! Scoundrels, some of 'em—drunkards and foreigners the rest.'

'But not all. Someone suitable will come my way. Please, Papa.'

He stops and gazes at me. I think how well he looks now, with his grey hair and strong nose and tanned face. He nods. 'Very well, my girl.'

We hug, then catch up with Alain and Emilia at the bow of the ship. I take Emilia's hands and say, 'I'm overjoyed for you both.' Emilia kisses me then says to Papa, 'Cristina is down on the jetty—let us go and tell her the news.'

She calls out to Cristina, who waves, her other hand tucked into Danny's arm. He looks up but does not wave. I wander off by myself and sit in a quiet corner for a time, thinking. A little later Sam and Rosa saunter past, having also just heard the good news.

'It's settled, Sam—we're staying. And now I'd like to make that request we were speaking of.'

'Anything at all, Lucy, we owe you so much. What is it?'

'That lugger, the one you're not using—*Sparrow*. With your help I'd like to fix her up. I want *Sparrow* to belong to me.'

'Good heavens! I hadn't imagined ... but of course, I'd be happy to help. After all, other women in town have luggers—Mrs Gonzales, Miss Withers—why not Miss Fox? But we must ask Rosa. It's she who officially owns our vessels, after all.'

'Darling, you needn't ask *me*,' says Rosa. 'But wasn't *Sparrow* your first boat, so she's registered to you?'

'My only boat, you mean,' he says ruefully, then thinks for a moment. 'But of course—if we transferred *Sparrow* to Lucy I'd be free to get a bigger one in my own name, perhaps even a schooner for a mother-ship.' He grins at me. 'Little sister, you may actually be doing me a favour.'

A record three hundred and fifty vessels are ready to go out for the 1910 season. On a breezy day in March I stand in the crowd at Lookout Hill, as sails begin to blossom on the bay, one by one. Amid cheering and crying and the angelic singing of mission children, the luggers slowly turn and move like a flock of great seabirds towards the ocean.

Next year, I think, next year my *Sparrow* will go out with them.

As we stroll home Sam says, 'Now we can put your boat under the shelter and start work on it. Mr Egawa will be available from next week.'

'Will he let me watch, or even perhaps help?'

'I doubt it, Lucy, he'd probably be shocked at the idea. How would you clamber in and out of the hull anyway?'

'I can wear a divided skirt like bicyclists. It's quite acceptable nowadays.'

'But have you thought about how it might appear,' says Rosa solemnly. 'Usually only certain sorts of females go down to the foreshore camps you know, Lucy.'

'Oh. I hadn't thought of that.'

'I'm only teasing! But just to annoy the gossips, Eliza and I will keep you company. We'll sit in the shade and read and relax while you jump in and out of your smelly old boat.'

'Oh, Rosa, thank you.'

'I'm just being practical. If our other luggers sink, your *Sparrow* can save the family fortune!'

'What family fortune?' says Sam. 'Min-lu's last letter says the company's still struggling. Still, she seems in good cheer—apparently Alice has stopped putting milk in the jasmine tea, and Mrs O'Brien and the Chinese cook have drawn a truce in the kitchen.'

As Sam predicted, Mr Egawa is horrified at the thought of a woman helping with the boat, but grudgingly agrees I may watch as long as I do not touch. This edict lasts long enough to satisfy honour all round, but is quickly discarded when his assistant Jiro is busy and he needs another pair of hands.

'You hurry, missy, give hammer. No that one, yes,' he says one day, and from then on I'm permitted to pass tools or hold nails. One day Mr Egawa cuts his hand badly with a chisel and stands stoically when I insist on binding the wound with my clean handkerchief. After that he begins to explain to me what he's doing in more detail.

As the days move from autumn to winter the foreshore becomes a delightful place, the mornings fresh and the sky translucent blue. Rosa lies in a deckchair reading or sewing, while Eliza plays nearby on the pink sand. Tiny scarlet crabs shuffle between the roots of mangrove bushes, disappearing suddenly whenever Eliza toddles towards them.

'Oh my,' says Rosa one morning, yawning voluptuously. 'I shall so long for these days when I wallow like a whale again in the summer.'

'Rosa, you could never wallow like a—oh! You mean a baby?'

'In November. Eliza will be just three, so it's a good time. Sam's very pleased.'

'Me too. And that's when *Sparrow* will be finished as well. What fun we shall all have.'

Rosa looks at me with exasperation. '*Fun*! Well, you'll find out for yourself one day. That's if any man is mad enough to marry a woman who has her own lugger.'

July brings the annual Bachelors' Dance, organised by the energetic Captain Gregory. My peony pink dress is too warm even for wintertime Broome, so Rosa has one of her gowns altered to fit, a blue silk with lace panels.

Sam takes us in the carriage to the Literary Institute, where the veranda is hung with lanterns, flags and palm fronds, and sprays of scarlet bougainvillea arch over the stage and tiny orchestra.

I'm pleased to see Alain Bourdon. He's been away in Singapore working for his father's firm so we haven't met since the picnic, but he claims me for three dances.

'I have barely returned to Broome,' he says, 'but already the season has begun and I am swamped with business. Sadly I have no time for more enjoyable pursuits.'

'I thought your work would not begin until after the season was over and the pearling masters sell their precious stones.'

'Ah, I am not dealing in the pearls belonging to the masters, Lucy. Out on the luggers, the shellopener—the white man—watches vigilantly for stones, but the wily crews purloin their share.'

'That seems unfair to the masters.'

'It is not the masters who suffer the heat, the sharks, the cyclones. The crews see it as fair compensation—and they get only the smallest pearls, the shellopeners are not stupid. But I believe you too are very busy? I have heard of your interest in an old lugger, although I find that difficult to reconcile with blue silk.'

His amused eyes glance at my bodice, and I become aware of his strong arm around my waist, his hand enfolding mine. What a wonderful night.

Work progresses on *Sparrow*. We replace some of the ribs, rebuild the two tiny cabins and lay a new deck. Jiro and I nail copper sheets to the hull and squeeze oakum and tar caulking between the planks (my fingers are filthy for weeks). I decide the cabins and trim should be a raspberry colour.

'This paint pink!' Mr Egawa says in horror when I first produce it.

'No, Egawa-san,' I say. 'Pale red, like the sign on the Japanese Club.' That sign has faded from Imperial crimson to something akin to my peony silk dress, but Mr Egawa is mollified.

The great day arrives to raise the masts, and Borue and Thomas the Islander come to help. Sam places a Chinese silver dollar under the foremast step and says, 'I'm told with a coin there you will never want for cash.'

As the foremast is swaying into place, Captain Gregory hails us, striding along the shore from his camp not far away. He greets Rosa, graceful in her deckchair, with a broad grin—Rosa pregnant is still Rosa magnificent—then looks over *Sparrow* with the same professional eye.

In his deep Welsh lilt, he says, 'Morning Captain Lee, Miss Fox. Coming along nicely, a fine-looking vessel. Ah, Egawa-san, would you be free for a repair on *Idalia*, next week perhaps?'

'We doing rigging then, but I fit it in Tuesday, right?'

'Good man.' He turns to me. 'So, Miss Fox, you're our newest one-boat admiral? I hear you plan to seek your fortune now along with the rest of us poor fools.'

I smile. 'I'd simply like to know a little of the pains and pleasures of maritime life, Captain.'

'Ha!' His dark eyes gleam. 'You'll become acquainted with the pains, I warrant, but the pleasures are precious few—what say you, Sam Lee? Remember that hard-case mate on *Andorinha*?'

He turns back to me. 'Your brother-in-law, Miss Fox, was but a snivelling apprentice and I was second mate. Swansea to Cape Town, 1901, and he saved my life, he did—pushed me out of the way of a falling spar. I still owe you for that one, boyo.'

'And I'll collect on it yet, Greg,' says Sam, laughing.

Greg turns to me again. 'Do you plan to work your crew yourself, young lady?'

'*Sparrow* will sail with Sam's men, I shall simply be a silent partner,' I gaze at him, amused. 'After all, I believe it's a common enough arrangement here in Broome.'

His smile broadens. 'So it most certainly is, my dear. And should this scurvy dog fail you by even a coil of rope, do not hesitate, I am at your service. Good day then, Captain Lee, Mesdames.'

When he's gone, Sam says, 'I hardly saved his life either, the spar bounced away on some rigging. But he does enjoy telling the story so. Still, I'm glad he's in better spirits. No doubt you've heard of the loss of the *Kelander Bux*? It hit him very hard, so it's good to see him cheerful once more.'

August brings O-Bon Matsuri, when the whole fleet returns to town for a day to remember the dead at the Japanese cemetery—the horribly well-populated cemetery—with rituals to comfort the souls of the departed and the hearts of those left behind.

Rosa, Sam and I arrive at sunset, when the light is golden on the incised rocky slabs used as gravestones. Broome at night is always glowing with lanterns, but those made for O-Bon Matsuri are especially beautiful, with crystal beads and mirrors and silken tassels. They flicker on the graves beside dishes of food, incense and flowers.

Twanging samisens play as the moon rises, and Japanese women dressed in silk step and dip and flutter their fans in ceremonial dances. In the crowd I meet a dignified Mr Egawa, very different from the sprightly carpenter of the foreshore. We bow and he introduces his wife, a sad-eyed woman in a beautiful kimono.

'Our son Takura was lost in cyclone two years ago,' Mr Egawa says. 'We do not have his body to bury, but tonight we know his soul is content.'

At midnight it's time to take the carriage to the beach near the great jetty. For every person who has died this year there's a carved replica lugger, three or four feet long, laden with food and flowers and little lanterns.

One by one they're launched onto the moonlit water. I stand quietly in the crowd, watching the bobbing golden lights grow fainter and fainter, and finally disappear.

'Now I see how we got it all wrong,' says Danny, coming up beside me. I can smell the drink on his breath. 'We built those bloody great ships to go a-sailing and we forgot the dear little soul boats for when the big ships sink. Damned careless oversight, I'd say.'

'Danny, please don't.'

'Mr Egawa's other son Yoshi works for Sam, too. Will you send him out on your lugger to drown like his brother? Or maybe you're a-building a soul boat for Brownley and Piet and the Yankee?'

I take a few steps away, then stop and turn and gaze at his moon-lit face.

'How dare you Danny! Why try to hurt me? I didn't wreck your ship.'

'No.' He takes a breath that's almost a sob. 'But you're such an innocent, playing at sailor. Like me once, lacking the slightest comprehension—'

'Are you insane? Lack comprehension! Do you not remember what I *lost*?'

Silence. He wipes a hand over his face and turns and walks away.

Mr Egawa is showing me how to thread ropes through blocks for *Sparrow*'s rigging—'It goes this side, not that side'—and I hear an echo of Gideon's kind voice teaching me knots on *Willowmere*.

My fears that he'd engineered our misfortunes have long since passed. I understand now how distressed I was—haunted by *Willowmere* and in shock at the near-loss of Danny—and still redden with embarrassment whenever I think of it.

Although his ship *Hydra* stops at the jetty every two months, Gideon rarely has a moment to spare, and a year passes before we meet again.

One day Sam and Rosa bring him home for afternoon tea, accompanied by Papa and Emilia. On the veranda Gideon takes my hand and kisses me on the cheek. 'Such joy,' he says.

'How did you manage to get time off, Gideon?' I ask, pleased.

'Engine trouble. We must wait for a new bearing to be sent from Port Hedland. But I don't mind, no matter how head office complains—at long last I may see you all again.'

'You have of course heard of my great good fortune,' says Papa, smiling at Emilia.

'Indeed, and I raise my teacup in congratulations to you both. When is the happy event to occur?'

'In four weeks,' says Emilia. 'You would be most welcome to attend.'

'Alas, in four weeks I shall be in Fremantle supervising *Hydra*'s loading once again: she's an unrelenting taskmistress. But tell me, what is this astonishing news I hear? Lucy soon to be a lady pearler? It's the talk of the nor'-west!'

'Hardly a pearler, Gideon,' I say, laughing, 'I'm simply taking an interest in an old lugger.'

I gaze over the rim of my cup at him, touched by the affection in his blue eyes. He was so kind to me on *Willowmere*, so courageous during the wreck, so wounded by his friends' betrayal.

I say, 'And your fiancée, Miss Percival—she is well?'

The happiness leaves Gideon's face. 'Miss Percival preferred not to share my affections with a steamship and we agreed to go our separate ways. Probably for the best.'

There's a murmur of condolence, then Sam slaps his back. 'The truth is she discovered you've got a wife in every port.' Gideon smiles ruefully.

'Would you care to see my old boat before you leave?' I say impulsively. 'In fact, she's rather magnificent at the moment, freshly painted and ready for the new season.'

Gideon looks at me with pleasure. 'I most certainly would. And I suspect no one can stop you from climbing the rigging of your very own vessel—a clever ploy, young miss. Tomorrow morning perhaps? Then you and Sam may introduce me to this glory of maritime architecture.'

Next day, Gideon is surprisingly taken with *Sparrow*. He talks to Mr Egawa for some time about her timbers and lines, and strokes the smooth varnished surfaces as we stand on her deck.

'Of course,' says Sam confidentially, 'the plumage of a real sparrow is rather more drab than Lucy's raspberry pink—'

'Pale *red*, if you please!' I say.

'And I hear there are mutterings in the pubs my entire fleet will soon be a charming shade of lavender if that Miss Lucy is left unchecked—'

We're all laughing when a Malay man hails Sam and he excuses himself.

Gideon turns to me. 'Of course I love my handsome *Hydra* but you'd be surprised at how much I envy you your life of sail here.'

'It's not easy, Gideon, but yes, it is a good life.'

'Lucy,' he says quietly, 'I wish you to know something. I feel the most profound shame over your father's venture into the stockmarket. I cannot forgive myself, but I could not make him see how unwise his position had become.'

'Indeed, he can be very stubborn.'

'And Bao-lim, that devious devil! I suspected he was set upon a dangerous path and tried to warn Sam, but I had no idea he would move so quickly. How is Min-lu doing now?'

'We've just had a letter telling us her company is becoming profitable again.'

'Excellent news.'

I gaze at the aqua bay sparkling in the morning sun and say hesitantly, 'Gideon ... did you happen to hear about our cook, Mrs O'Brien? She was set upon by a pair of bullies and beaten.'

'Good Lord, why? I remember gossip had it she was embroiled in some ancient feud with the publican of the Steampacket, but could never have imagined it come to that. Has she recovered?'

'Yes, she's well now. But her attackers called her a raddled old harlot ...'

He reddens. 'Oh, Lucy, I'm so ashamed I ever used words like that in your presence, or that you should hear them again in such circumstances—' He stops and looks at me in shock. 'You don't conceivably think—you cannot—please Lucy, I would never—'

'No, no, Gideon. Forgive me, for a brief time I wondered ... But I was misled by my own anxieties and now I also feel ashamed.'

'It has been a hard few years for us all,' he says simply. 'You cannot imagine how often I wish we could return to those days of joy we shared upon *Willowmere*.'

In October, Papa and Emilia are married in the small Anglican Church. Emilia wears a dove grey silk gown sent by Min-lu. Cristina, demure, attends her mother, while Sam, his black hair slicked back, is best man to a dignified Papa.

As I watch them at the altar I ponder Broome's absurd racial strictures: Cristina's life is restricted by her touch of Aboriginal blood but, because the Philippines are American, her mother Emilia possesses all the freedoms of a white woman.

After the ceremony I bow to the Murakamis and Egawas, greet Borue and Thomas and shake hands with numerous masters, all curious to know of *Sparrow*'s progress. I chat to kind, sardonic Miss Lizzie Withers, one of the town's few female pearlers, and notice a surprisingly well-dressed Danny in the crowd, but he only nods.

Sam and Rosa, almost eight months pregnant, hold the reception at their bungalow. Seated beside Alain, I drink my first glass of champagne and like it. I like flirting with Alain even more.

After the meal I approach Captain Gregory, who is leaning on the veranda railing, smoking.

'I wonder if I might ask a small favour of you?'

'Of course, Miss Fox. What may I do to help?'

'I have a friend who was in a shipwreck. He has taken it hard but will speak of it to no one, and I fear for him. I believe you too have survived such an experience. Would you talk to him, as if by chance, and perhaps ease his mind a little?'

Gregory is silent, his dark eyebrows drawn, then says, 'Such an event leaves its scars, perhaps forever. Even myself—you may find it difficult to credit—I felt it most painfully.'

'I had no idea,' I say untruthfully.

He draws upon his cigarette. 'Of course, taking it hard, being unable to forget such terrible ... I imagine it might happen to anyone—'

'I believe it must reflect well upon the calibre of a man to be touched so deeply. Only a careless brute could shrug it off in moments.'

'Yes, indeed, indeed.' He clears his throat and says, 'I do believe you speak of Mr Whalen. We met once in Antwerp years ago. I had thought to discuss a rigging problem with him, so perhaps I should take a bottle of beer and stay to talk over old times. What say you to that, Miss Fox?'

'You are extremely kind. And please call me Lucy.'

'Lucy. You're a good girl, *cariad.*'

'What does that mean?'

'*Cariad*? Welsh for darling.' He grins, stubs out his cigarette and flicks it away. 'Now I do believe I see barmaid Nell from the Conti over yonder—and for once there's no one else around. I shall try for a dance. Good day to you, Lucy.'

I dance with Alain then he takes my hand and leads me to a quiet corner. He puts his arms around me and kisses my forehead, my face, my mouth; lightly and then for a long time. It feels unlike any kiss I've ever had, even with the Swedish lad Mattias, and is another thing I like about the day.

The newlyweds embark for two weeks in Perth. Papa will move into Emilia's boarding-house when they return, but Sam and Rosa suggest I stay with them and I'm happy to do so. Heavily pregnant Rosa no longer keeps me company at the foreshore but it's hardly necessary: *Sparrow's* eccentric young mistress has become stale gossip.

I don't see my new step-sister Cristina very often because she's busy with the boarding-house while her mother is away. A few weeks after the wedding Sam mentions that Danny has moved out of Emilia's place and is painting two rooms in the foreshore building for himself. I wonder if his friendship with Cristina has faltered, or if he simply prefers not to live with his ex-captain.

He surprises me one day by bringing over an old boom as a spare for *Sparrow*. Mr Bagge the sailmaker recently cut her a new set of sails, and Danny says she's looking very smart. I'm glad to see he seems more content than before.

We hear that Papa and Emilia will return a few days later than planned because *Hydra* is delayed in Port Hedland with more engine trouble. The heat is fierce and the rains begin pouring down. It's November, earlier than usual for the start of the Wet, but no one is much concerned. The big storms never happen at this time of year.

II. THE CYCLONE

I awake suddenly as something thuds against the side of the house. Rain clatters on the roof and the wind rises every now and then to a shriek. I get up. It's dawn but so gloomy that Sam, in his dressing-gown, is lighting the lamps in the sitting-room.

'This is a pretty bad blow,' he says. 'I'm not worried about the house, but Rosa's in discomfort. Lucy, I think the baby is coming.'

'But it's not due for almost two weeks, and Emilia's still away! There aren't any other midwives—what about the doctor?'

'She can't stand him. He told her white women make too much fuss and should have their babies out in the bush like the natives.'

'I'm surprised she didn't slap him. But isn't there a new Japanese doctor—Suzuki, I think—in Napier Terrace?'

'Of course,' Sam says. 'I'll take the carriage into town and get him, and stop at the camp first to see if Danny can come over till I return.'

I fill a hot water bottle to hold against Rosa's aching back. She dozes a little, then moans as a contraction comes upon her. 'It's not as bad as it sounds,' she says after a moment, 'but it helps to make a bit of noise. Eliza's not awake, is she?'

'No, still asleep.'

We hear the back door shut and Danny appears, shaking water from his curly hair.

'How're you doing, Rosa?' he asks. 'You've picked a grand day for it.'

'That's enough of the blarney, thank you Danny, I'm doing very well. Why don't you make me a cup of tea? Lucy, show him where everything is.'

I re-set the fire in the cooker from last night's embers and put the kettle on the hob.

'The tea's up there,' I say. 'Rosa likes it strong.'

'Now why doesn't that surprise me?'

Something hits the roof with a clatter and rattles down the side of the house, and the howl of the wind reaches a roar. I raise the kitchen blind and to my astonishment the rain is not falling straight down from the sky, it's pouring sideways. Trees are bent to the ground and sprays of bougainvillea whip back and forth against an almost black sky.

Suddenly a sheet of corrugated iron comes grinding and screeching along the street, striking sparks, then it flies upwards, gone. Another follows it among a flurry of palm fronds.

'Danny, the fleet—dear God, there's hundreds of boats out in the middle of this!'

He's pale. 'This is no Pampero, over in minutes. This is a cyclone and it's hardly begun.'

'What about the camp?'

'We've been awake all night securing everything—your *Sparrow* too, don't worry—but the men have left the foreshore. They're sheltering at the Customs House now, too much danger from flooding to stay.'

Danny pours the tea and I take it into Rosa but she's dozing. I come back to the kitchen and sit down at the table.

'I hope your rooms at the camp don't get washed out,' I say.

'Just a cot and a few knick-knacks. I'm sure they'll survive.'

The wind screams and a branch tumbles past the window. Danny raises his head, a familiar glint of gold at his ear. 'Had a visitor a few weeks ago, a friend of yours.'

'Oh?'

'Captain Gregory. Came to tell me shipwrecks aren't so bad after all. I was grateful for the news.'

'Oh.'

'Thinks the world of you, though. *Insightful* he said, more than once. I'm glad to see you're making powerful friends—a Shipping Master's always good to have on your side.'

'I'd hoped if you had someone to talk to, Danny ...'

'Aye. But now I'm getting visions of being talked to by friends of yours for decades to come.'

I can't help smiling. 'I'd have given up eventually.'

'Think I'd have cracked first, girl.' There's weariness in his voice but much of the anger is gone. 'No, not *girl*, now, is it? Probably time to start calling you Miss Lucy—you've certainly become a fine young lady in your silks and laces.'

'But I was up in *Sparrow*'s rigging the other day, so I still like climbing.'

'And no end in sight to the questions and curiosity either, that's for sure. What about Miss Fox, Master Pearler, then?'

'I'd find that most acceptable, thank you.'

Through the clatter of rain on the iron roof I hear a groan from the bedroom and go to Rosa. I help her sip the tea, hold her hand during contractions and bring her the chamber-pot, and all the while the howling of the wind grows louder.

Two hours later Sam returns with a slight figure in oilskins, and they dash, dripping, into the house. Dr Suzuki has a thick moustache and a grave expression, and after introductions and bows he goes into another room and changes into the dry clothes he brought with him.

While he's examining Rosa, Sam also changes his clothes, then sits exhausted by the cooker. 'You could not imagine it. Iron and wood and sand flying through the air, rain like a solid wall. The sheer *noise* of it. I don't know how we got back in one piece.'

Danny pours him a whisky and I go to get Eliza, now awake. I carry the little girl to the kitchen in a blanket and give her to Sam. Dr Suzuki returns and washes his hands in the sink.

'Mrs Lee is well and birth proceeding normally. It will not be long now. Miss Fox, please help by sitting with your sister.'

It may not have seemed long to Dr Suzuki but it's long enough for me, holding my sister's hand, the storm outside a continuous roar. Rosa seems in a haze until the doctor says, 'Now—you must push—*now*, Mrs Lee,' and then she's Rosa of old, wilful and fierce, groaning with effort.

I'm holding my breath, panting with my sister, until suddenly there's a wail and a tiny wet baby in the doctor's hands. He cuts the cord, looks the baby over and wraps it in a sheet.

'Healthy boy, Mrs Lee. My congratulations.'

Rosa sobs a breath, holds out her arms and takes the bundle, laughing with relief. I'm in tears.

Dr Suzuki says, 'Miss Fox, I make Mrs Lee more comfortable now. You kindly give Captain Lee good news and tell him he may see wife and new son shortly.'

While Sam and Eliza are with Rosa I realise the wind's howling is becoming less and the rain is no longer continuous. By late afternoon the cyclone is ebbing, although the streets are full of water and debris. Sam takes Dr Suzuki back to town while Rosa sleeps, the children tucked up with her.

Danny and I sit in the warm kitchen over a final cup of tea. 'I'll be off to see the state of the camp now,' he says. 'Christ, why do I always seem to have these long, difficult days whenever you're around, girl?'

'That's Miss Fox, Master Pearler, to you and I'm sure you bring it upon yourself.'

'This time I'm an innocent bystander—' he stops. 'Ah, maybe not. Something I need to tell you. You'll be hearing the gossip soon enough.' He takes a breath. 'Cristina is with child. My child.'

I cannot speak for a moment, then say coldly, 'Heavens, what a lot of unexpected pregnancies seem to occur amongst my acquaintances.'

I go to the sink and start filling it with clattering cups and dishes.

'I was so low, the wreck and all, I didn't imagine—'

'No.'

'She was gorgeous and headstrong and sorry for me—'

'Yes.'

He sighs. 'Oh Jesus, I just wasn't thinking straight.'

'Probably.'

'But I'm not going to let her down, you know. Your father took a letter to Perth for me, seeking permission to marry from the Protector of Aborigines.'

'But Cristina's not ... surely her *grandmother* hardly counts?'

'Even a great-grandparent gives that cold-hearted bastard control over everything in her life.'

'I'd heard of that but hardly believed it could be true. It's monstrous.'

'At least, married to me, she won't be at his mercy any more. I can protect her name—'

'This is Broome, Danny. I doubt anyone here has much of a name.'

He half-smiles. 'No.'

A few days later at breakfast I read aloud from the paper: '*There was no previous indication that anything resembling a storm was approaching ... about 11 o'clock the more flimsy structures began to give way ...* We seem to have had an easier time of it here.'

'You might have had an easier time,' says Rosa calmly. 'It was a little less easy for some of us.' She moves the baby to her other breast. 'And the town?'

'Rubin's store's blown down, Pearlers' Rest unroofed, Yamasaki's store and Mr Nishioka's, unroofed, Tokumaru's and Jock Sing's too. Oh, the dressmakers' shop, goods damaged. Rosa, your blue lace gown!'

'Bother, I wanted to wear that at the christening.'

'A schooner and three luggers wrecked on Cable Beach, but forty-two vessels safe at Barred Creek. Oh. And another thirty, still nothing known.'

'Ours are all right though, aren't they?'

'We don't know about *Currawong*, but the rest are safe near Port Hedland.'

'Probably just stranded up a creek. Did you know *Hydra* finally arrived last night? Papa and Emilia are coming over this afternoon to see the baby.'

They arrive carrying parcels, followed by Cristina, her pregnancy still a secret, with Gideon bringing up the rear. When everyone is seated Rosa says, 'Here, Gideon, meet Peter Nicholas.'

She hands him the baby which he puts straight into Emilia's waiting hands.

'Fine little chap, well done! A family name, that?'

'Nicholas is for Captain Fox, of course,' says Sam. 'But we simply like Peter in itself.'

'He bears my name? An honour, sir.' Papa's cheeks go pink and I can see how pleased he is.

'Will you stay very long this time, Gideon?' says Sam.

'Several days, we're busy unloading material for repairs. What a horror it must have been! Half the town has simply vanished from the face of the earth.'

'How was it at Port Hedland?' I ask.

'Far less intense,' says Gideon.'And your luggers, Sam, how did they fare?'

'Only one is still missing. Danny is out with the search parties now.'

'Good Lord, you've survived a cyclone and produced a baby at the same time,' says Gideon fondly. 'Extraordinary business.'

I notice Cristina is gazing at him demurely, and remember Danny calling her *gorgeous and headstrong*. She's certainly exquisite, but there's nothing about her to suggest a powerful will. What an odd thing for him to say.

'Now,' says Papa, 'we've brought you all presents from Perth. Rosa, my dear, Emilia thought you might like these.'

Rosa certainly does—they're dainty drop earrings with translucent citrines—while Sam receives a gold watch and Eliza a new doll with a painted porcelain face.

'And it's rather obvious what this might be,' says Papa, handing me a parcel. 'Something in advance for your twentieth birthday.'

I laugh and tear the wrapping paper off a black leather case. Inside is a beautiful new fiddle.

Danny comes home with Sam's other boats, but *Currawong* is lost: only her crushed dinghy is ever found. The final reckoning is twenty vessels sunk and forty-nine sailors dead, all but two of them Asian. Only the two white men are eulogised in the newspaper, while Japtown mourns for the rest. An armada of soul boats will be setting sail this year at O-Bon Matsuri.

Sam and I attend the annual meeting of the Pearlers' Association at the Literary Institute on a stifling hot evening. Among the new members are eleven *one-boat admirals*, among them me. There are several other women pearlers too: Miss Lizzie Withers owns two luggers, and Amy Chapple and Rose Gonzales have three each.

I like Mrs Gonzales. Contrary to expectation, she's a tiny red-haired Irishwoman from Melbourne who bore four children to her late Chinese husband, then re-married a Manilaman. 'They used to say women like me *went to the Chinks*,' she told me once with grim satisfaction, 'but we did so well, by God we had the last laugh.'

The meeting becomes animated upon the subjects of dummying, illicit pearl dealing and inflated shell takes. Dr Paton discusses beri-beri, then a proposal for pressure gauges to stop deaths from air pipe ruptures is handed off to a committee. Special thanks are offered to the master pearlers for salvaging luggers after the cyclone.

Then amid a shuffling of chairs the meeting comes to an end. I look up in surprise. 'But aren't they going to say anything about the men who died just a few weeks ago?' I ask Sam.

'No,' he says shortly. ' You know why.'

'Why?'

'Look around, Lucy. There are more women pearlers here than non-whites. You'd think those whinging about the cost of pressure gauges are the ones out risking their lives on the shellbeds. Dear God, I get so tired of the hypocrisy of this place. The casualties taken for granted here would put any port to shame—but only the people of Japtown seem to care.'

Alain often comes to visit me. He stays for supper and we sit on the veranda, chatting over drinks. Sometimes he kisses me when no one's around, but it's rather annoying how often they are. I like being kissed, I like the scent of him, and especially I like the touch of his long tanned hands.

He visits one night early in the new year of 1911. With Sam we sit in the lamp-light, watching the rain sweep across the garden.

Alain lights a thin cigar. 'I have had a letter from my father. He wants me to go home to Paris for a few months, then return towards the end of the year.' He gazes at me. 'Sadly, tomorrow I must depart on the *Koombana* for Singapore.'

Later, Sam leaves us alone. The rain stops and Alain and I lean on the veranda railing together, watching the distant lightning.

'Perhaps one day I shall take you to Paris,' he says, holding the back of my hand to his lips, nibbling deliciously along my wrist.

'Oh, *yes*. I hear French barques are simply magnificent.'

'No, I mean le Louvre, la Seine—not ... Lucy, you are teasing me again!'

I laugh. 'Of course. Ships are fine enough, but Paris would be very nice indeed.'

I gaze at his dark eyes and trace the line of his cheekbone with my fingers. He draws me close and kisses me, stroking my hips, lighting thrills of pleasure in my belly. Then the clatter of Ahmet moving a tray in the next room makes us jump. I rest my head on Alain's shoulder and sigh.

'Lucy, my father worries that if I stay here too long I will not come home and marry a good Catholic Frenchwoman, and have lots of good Catholic grandchildren for him.'

'But what do you want, Alain?'

'I wish to please my family, but I wish to choose my own wife also.' He lifts my chin and kisses my lips. 'I should leave, I must pack. But *chérie*, I hope you understand that I would rather stay here with you.'

'I understand. Take care, dear Alain. I'll look forward with pleasure to your return.'

But later I wonder—did he truly mean he might want me for a wife? It is certainly thrilling to desire and to know that I'm desired in return. But marriage? The thought feels, just a little, as if something is constricting my breathing.

'Extraordinary!' says Rosa, reading Min-lu's letter and nursing baby Peter at the same time. 'Alice the maid has gone and married the Chinese cook and they're going to open a restaurant in Little Bourke Street. And Filipa and Izabel are glad to be aunties again but can't decide which of them owns Eliza and which Peter. Funny little things.'

'Not so little,' says Sam. 'Izabel's all of eleven now.' He gazes at Rosa. 'How time flies when you have your own babies to raise.' She smiles at him, content.

Outside we hear the crunching of a carriage drawing up. Sam opens the door to a distressed Papa and a red-eyed Emilia, who bursts out, 'The letter came from the Protector of Aborigines. He is no *Protector*, he is a despot!' She begins to cry again.

'He's denied Cristina's application to marry,' says Papa. 'Says she'd be in moral danger if he lets her marry Danny. I've never heard anything like it! When I saw him he implied there'd be no problem at all. It makes no sense. He'd rather she have a bastard child alone than enjoy the protection of a husband!'

Later that day I walk over to the foreshore. Danny is up a ladder painting a boat, and climbs down saying, 'Don't commiserate, for God's sake, that's all I ask.'

'I won't. But why on earth did he change his mind? Papa was quite certain he'd agree.'

'Jesus, I don't know. He's probably just a bloody-minded sod. I'll stick by her, of course, but it won't be easy for her.'

'But most people here can hardly criticise, they have their own colourful pasts. Perhaps in time you'll be allowed to marry.'

'Perhaps. I'm not even certain that's what Cristina wants.'

'How could she not want you for a husband?' I say, astonished. 'Not want her baby's father?'

Danny looks at me for a moment, then smiles wryly. 'Not everyone likes babies and boats as much as you, girl.' He turns and climbs the ladder again.

A few days later *Hydra* comes into port and Gideon visits us for dinner.

'Good God, Cristina pregnant to *Danny*?' he says, lifting a piece of roast beef onto his plate. 'I'd have thought such a handsome girl would have better taste than that.'

'Gideon, that's unworthy of you,' says Rosa. 'You're simply annoyed he got to her first.'

'Well, he was a fine chap once, but he's certainly not the man he was.'

'Danny has suffered a great deal,' I say, 'but he's still the same at heart.'

'Indeed, poor fellow.' Gideon thinks for a moment. 'I am being unfair, I see, but I shall atone. As it happens I have remained on civilised terms with Miss Percival's father, a good friend of the Protector. I shall seek an introduction to that obstructive man and plead on behalf of the lovebirds. Would that make you happy, Lucy?'

'Of course, Gideon. That would be kindness itself.'

'They've lost their minds, man, it's the only explanation!' Captain Gregory bounds up the steps to the veranda where Rosa, Sam and I are sitting over breakfast. He flings a newspaper onto the table, sits down, and pours himself a cup of coffee.

Sam picks up the paper. 'Good God.' He reads aloud, '*No permits for indent Asiatics will be issued unless the diver and his tender are both white men.* In less than two years? Both, seriously?'

'But are there any white divers at all in Broome?' I ask.

'Occasionally some boyo thinks he's good as the Japs, but he soon finds out it's harder than it looks,' says Gregory, frowning. 'No, the only good divers are the Japanese, with a few Manilamen and Malays. And by God, without them we'll have no industry at all.'

'How many luggers are there?'

'Three hundred here,' says Sam. 'Another two hundred or so in Torres Strait and Port Darwin.'

'So we'd need five hundred white divers and five hundred white tenders?' I ask.

'But in the entire world there are perhaps a few *dozen* white divers,' says Gregory. 'Compared to the thousands of Asians we've already got, the best *bloody*—I do apologise, Mrs Lee—'

'Not at all, Greg,' says Rosa, sipping her coffee.

'And they expect those white men to live on the boats, eat what the crews eat, earn what they earn and work from dawn till dark. It's madness!'

'But why on earth is the government doing this?' I ask.

'Oh, Admiral Fox,' says Gregory. 'They're simply jealous because they hear we're *rolling* in pearls and champagne, and they're scared those devilish Asiatics want nothing more than to make caramel-coloured babies—'

'Well, we've been doing our best,' says Sam, 'but Rosa thinks she's had enough for now.'

Rosa laughs. 'True.'

'Seriously, man,' says Greg. 'If we could grow the shells in the bay we'd be fine, just pick them like flowers. Indeed, I hear that Mr Mikimoto is now culturing round pearls in Japan. What say you, young Lucy, why don't we just grow our own?'

'You're a dreamer, Greg,' says Sam. 'The other pearlers would never stand for it. The lazy swine would say you'd got an unfair advantage and drag you down.'

'Oh, such a cynic you are, boyo. Don't you trust to the stout hearts of the men who built the British Empire?'

'As it happens, I don't,' says Sam. 'But what on earth do we do about this ludicrous law?'

The Broome pearling fleet is down by over thirty luggers in 1911: not only those lost in the cyclone, but a dozen more whose one-boat admirals have decided to seek their fortunes in calmer waters.

But not me.

This year, just as I'd hoped, I'm down at the foreshore watching my own lugger going to sea. As the tide comes in *Sparrow*'s hull rocks a little, lifts, and then is afloat. Men push her out between the mangroves, while her sails hoist jerkily and fill with wind.

My lugger glides away, her name and number, B273, proud on her bow. Borue, her skipper, yells commands in a mixture of tongues to the stocky brown men busy at work on her deck, while further out, *Sparrow* joins Sam's boats, gathering one by one.

They turn then in slow, wide curves and move towards the other luggers, now appearing on every side. Soon there are hundreds of creamy sails and dark hulls and splashes of brilliant colour bobbing on the turquoise water.

And then the lovely fleet is drawing away from us and growing dreamlike in the distant haze.

'No need to cry, girl,' says Danny. 'They're just stinking fishing boats.'

'I'm not crying, Danny. The same way you're not.'

12. SOUL BOATS

Shopping in Japtown a few weeks later I meet my step-sister Cristina. She's pink-cheeked and striking in cream muslin, her chestnut curls caught back in a ribbon, her waist trimmed with corsets.

'You're looking extremely well,' I say.

'Oh Lucy, I certainly felt sick a few months ago, but now I feel marvellous.'

We're near the entrance to Roebuck Lane, and I notice three men wandering noisily towards us from the hotel at the other end. One of them, a pimply young shellopener I vaguely know, looks Cristina up and down then spits at her feet.

'Binghi *slut*,' he slurs, then stares at me. '*Chink* lover.' He staggers after his friends.

We stand shocked. I can see tears coming to Cristina's eyes and I take her hand.

'He's a drunken pig, don't pay any attention. Let's go and get an iced squash.'

The Broome Cafe is cool, the lemon drink sweet. My breathing returns to normal and Cristina wipes her eyes.

'That was hardly the first time, Lucy. Some of the men in this town are loathsome, but I will not let them stop me going about. I refuse to hide myself away.'

'When is the baby due, Cristina?'

'In May, in eight weeks time.'

So around last year's O-Bon Matsuri, I think, when we had that terrible argument. Oh, Danny.

Cristina dabs her eyes again. 'I thought we'd be married by now and going to London or Paris. I dreamt I'd wear pretty clothes and travel on a steamship. And *now ...*'

'But perhaps you'll be allowed to marry one day, and then you can be be happy together.'

Cristina looks at me, her eyebrows arched in surprise. 'But *Danny* can't help me now.'

'He's the baby's father, Cristina, of course he can help you. He'll be good to the child.'

'Danny wants to stay here, in this hateful place. But I *must* get away, and if he won't take me I'll just go with somebody else!'

I stare at her in surprise.

She becomes suddenly demure. 'Oh, heavens, what *am* I saying? Those terrible men have upset me so. I'm sure everything will be better once the baby is born. Of course I didn't mean it.'

I do not believe her.

I walk home, my thoughts confused. She really is as headstrong as Danny said, but I've only ever seen the charming exterior. What else have I misunderstood?

King George V and Queen Mary ascend the throne in June 1911, and Broome celebrates along with the rest of the Empire. There's a fancy-dress procession with a noisy band, marching sailors and a truck brightly decorated by the Japanese, while at the Recreation Ground little boys throw crackers at each other around a roaring bonfire.

Later tonight there'll be fireworks, organised by Captain Gregory with his usual nautical efficiency. At the Recreation Ground I meet Sam strolling with Rosa on his arm. He offers his other arm to me, saying, 'Escorting both of you I shall be the most envied man in all of Broome.'

'Speaking of envy,' says Rosa, 'isn't that a rather greenish Gideon over there with *la belle* Cristina and Danny?'

Cristina's baby was born six weeks ago without fuss, and she's back in her pretty dresses again. She couldn't think what to name the child so Danny suggested Liam, and Liam Letolo it is.

All babies are heart-wrenching, I tell myself: Liam's not special. But he is—calm and sweet-natured, with a beautiful smile and wispy red-brown curls.

We join them and Gideon moves to my side. 'As promised, Lucy, recently I was able to prevail upon Angela's father to introduce me to the Protector of Aborigines. I told him I'd known Danny for years—good moral influence on Cristina, should be permitted to marry, all the rest—but he just said flatly he would not alter his decision. I'm extremely sorry.'

'You did your best. Thank you, Gideon.'

Suddenly a swell of drunken singing rises to one side of the crowd, which shifts and swirls around us and I become separated from the others. I wander in the dark until I find myself a quiet spot near the bonfire. Two Japanese people are watching the flames, the woman in European dress. I recognise the photographer Mr Murakami and we bow to each other.

'Miss Fox, let me introduce Miss Murata,' says Mr Murakami.

'How do you do, Miss Murata?'

'Please, call me Theresa,' she says in an Australian accent.

'My goodness, you're local-born! Do call me Lucy.'

Theresa Murata is exquisite and very young. We chat for a time and I'm charmed at her gentle wit and her accent—I haven't met an Australian-born Japanese before. Mr Murakami, who I know has recently celebrated his thirtieth birthday, cannot take his eyes from her.

Danny appears out of the crowd. 'Ah, there you are.'

There are further bows and introductions, then polite farewells as Theresa puts her hand on Mr Murakami's arm and they walk away.

'His wife's not going to be very happy about that,' says Danny.

'I'd heard it was a marriage of convenience.'

'It's been convenient for them both, but I doubt Eki will let it go lightly. Now—Sam and Rosa are over there. Ah. Well, they were over there a minute ago. We'd best stay here and let them find us.'

We stand by the bonfire in silence. I gaze at his face in the flickering light and it's more at peace than I've seen for a long time. He smiles to himself and turns to me.

'Done checking me over for cracks in the hull, girl?'

'Well, you must admit, Danny, last year you'd run into one or two reefs.'

He laughs. 'Indeed I had.'

'But I'm glad you're happier now. Liam is just so—so—'

'That he is. I'm a lucky man.'

'*Here* they are,' says Sam, emerging from the crowd with Rosa.

The fireworks start with a bang, and everyone gasps and cheers. Penny bungers explode in a series of deafening crackles, brilliant catherine-wheels on fenceposts sputter and whirl, and rockets swoop high in the air then fountain down in reds and blues and greens.

People scream with pleasure, even when a large catherine-wheel flies off its nail, flinging fiery sparks through the air. More bangs and more rockets, the last one bursting into a wobbly Union Jack before flickering down into the dark, and everyone claps.

A moment later Gideon and Cristina push their way through a family of laughing Malays towards us. Cristina's white skirt is smeared with soot and she's clinging to Gideon's shoulder, sobbing.

'The sparks fell on her dress but she's not burnt, just shocked,' says Gideon, his arm around her waist. 'There, there, my dear. Here's Danny to look after you.'

Cristina, wiping her eyes, turns her head away from Danny when he speaks to her. She lets me help her through the crowd to find Papa and Emilia, watching the festivities from their carriage. They take her, now silent, into the carriage and leave.

A light breeze wafts sandalwood incense towards me. The samisens finish playing and the dancers, with their high black hair and pretty kimonos, turn and bow behind their fans. They stand still for a moment, then move quietly away.

'Delightful,' says Gideon. 'But I suspect some of them are women of ill repute from Shiba Lane.'

'It's O-Bon Matsuri, Gideon. How can that matter when the souls of the dead may be with us? In any case, I like their dancing and music in the moonlight, it's so mournful and strange.'

He smiles fondly. 'Lucy, is there anything at all you don't like?'

I gaze at Danny, leaning on a fence with Liam asleep on his shoulder. Cristina is nearby, laughing with some friends. 'I don't like how things are for Danny and Cristina. It's not fair.'

'You know, that's exactly what I said last year to the Protector.'

'Last year? But didn't you meet him just recently?'

'No, I'm certain I mentioned it to him in December, not long after the cyclone.'

'But—you didn't find out about Danny and Cristina until a couple of months ago,' I say, puzzled. 'I recall the dinner when you said you'd seek an introduction to the Protector.'

'I was simply being polite, Lucy. It's hardly the done thing to mention such a delicate situation until you're officially informed of it.'

'How did you find out last year, then?'

'Oh, Lord. I'm afraid Emilia and your father were less than discreet when we were stuck in Port Hedland. They were naturally very concerned.'

'Oh well, I suppose the Protector would have made the same decision in any case.'

'Of course, absolutely. He was adamant, perfectly adamant. I did my best for them, Lucy.'

'I understand. You and Danny have been friends for a long time.'

'Well, not precisely *friends*. Don't get me wrong, Danny's a good chap, salt of the earth, finest sort of Paddy as they go. But ...'

'I see. On board ship is one thing, on land another.'

'Exactly!'

Cristina looks over and waves to us with a glorious smile.

'So of course,' says Gideon, 'you can understand my amazement at the thought of that angel with someone like Danny. Even with the Binghi blood you could take her anywhere in the world and still be the envy of all.'

I'm a little shocked at his careless words. After a pause I say, 'And shall you be here at midnight for the sailing of the soul boats?'

'Sadly not. I'll be busy on *Hydra*, we leave port soon afterwards.' He laughs. 'I expect we'll swamp half the little blighters on the way out to sea.'

Cristina strolls towards us but ignores me.

'How very fortunate there are no fireworks tonight, Captain Meade.' She gazes up at him through her eyelashes. 'I shall not need rescuing this time.'

'Fireworks or no, Miss Letolo, I am always at your service.'

For O-Bon Matsuri this year Mr Egawa has carved a soul boat especially for my mother. Rosa and I kneel on the beach and tuck flowers into the hatches, then light the candle inside the lantern. Moonlight wavers on the ripples as the other soul boats are launched to soft cries of farewell and muffled sobs.

We stand and push our little vessel out on the water as far as we can. The candle-flame flickers golden as it draws away and soon it's difficult to tell which is ours.

'Mama would have loved this,' I say. 'She always did like things in the Japonisme style.'

Rosa looks at me in surprise and laughs. 'Of *course*. Oh, fancy that, Lucy! We had to come all the way to Broome to find the perfect way to say goodbye to her.'

There's a moment when our tears of laughter become simply tears, but it passes and we wipe our eyes and hug. 'Come now,' says

Rosa. 'Sam's over there with the carriage.'

'You go ahead, I'll stay a little longer. The Egawas said they'd bring me home.'

I wander along the beach greeting friends here and there till I reach the long jetty. *Hydra* is at the far end, lights blazing, engines rumbling as a crane swings a load of timber into her hold.

Most of the carriages have left now so I'm curious to see one approaching. It stops not far away and Gideon steps down and pays the driver. He lifts out a suitcase, then helps a woman in a dark coat descend. The carriage drives away and Gideon looks up, surprised to see me.

'Ah, Lucy. All the little soul boats go sailing away, did they?'

'Yes, they did. Hello, Cristina. Are you farewelling Gideon?'

'No,' she says calmly. 'I'm going to Perth with him.'

I cannot speak for a moment, then burst out, 'But what about Danny and Liam?'

She shrugs. 'My mother will look after the baby, and Danny's not my husband. *He* wouldn't take me away from this horrible place, but Gideon will.' She gives him an intimate, dazzling smile.

'Gideon! How *could* you?'

'I'm only helping a damsel in distress, Lucy. You know I'm a gentleman. I have to do whatever the lady wants.'

Cristina giggles.

I gaze at Gideon: his beauty, his arrogance. 'You did it, didn't you?' I say flatly. 'In Melbourne. Papa, Bao-lim, Mrs O'Brien.'

Gideon is indignant. 'I said I'm a gentleman, Lucy. I certainly did *not* encourage your father or Bao-lim along their paths of financial ineptitude: they were doing it well enough by themselves.'

'And Mrs O'Brien?'

'Ah, that. Well, I will not be told what to do by any woman on earth—no man would tolerate such impertinence. She deserved it.' His eyes gleam with pleasure. 'But I thought my invention was rather good. A feud with the publican of the Steampacket, wasn't it?'

I stare at him in horror.

'Oh come now, Lucy, that's how the world works. Women have to know their place. Good God, if you'd only get over this unladylike phase in your own life you'd be a charming little thing.'

Cristina's eyebrows arch and he adds, 'Not, of course, that you could compare to the delightful—the exquisite—Miss Letolo.'

He turns to Cristina. 'Shall we go, my dear? Your vessel awaits.'

Cristina gives me a look of triumph and takes Gideon's arm. He picks up her suitcase and they walk towards *Hydra*. I stare after them until they reach the ship and climb the gangway. I see the hawsers being let go, and hear the engines grow louder, and watch *Hydra* move away.

I turn towards Mr and Mrs Egawa, waiting by their carriage.

'Was that not—?' says Mr Egawa politely.

I nod, exhausted.

I don't sleep for hours, then wake next morning to the sound of hasty footsteps on the shell path. I sigh, put on my dressing gown and go out to the veranda.

Papa roars, 'The scoundrel! He's enticed her away!'

'Who, Papa?' says Rosa, looking up from the breakfast table.

'Gideon—he's taken *Cristina*!' says Emilia, sobbing. 'She left us a letter.'

Rosa laughs. 'Don't be silly, they hardly know each other.'

I sit down. 'It's true, I saw them, after the soul boats. They boarded *Hydra* and left.'

'Why didn't you *stop* them!' cries Emilia.

'I tried to but they ignored me. Cristina said doesn't care about the baby or Danny, she just wants to get away. And now I'm quite certain it was Gideon who turned the Protector against her marrying Danny in the first place.'

'He may not have wanted him to have her,' says Sam, 'but I doubt he'll marry her himself.'

'Are you certain, Sam?' says Emilia, wiping her eyes. 'Perhaps ...'

'I'm so sorry, Emilia. I'm afraid I know him too well.'

'Broome is one thing, but Perth entirely another,' says Papa, worried. 'She has no family there, no friends. She'll be known as Gideon's kept woman, utterly compromised.'

'Would it be any use to go after them?' asks Rosa. 'The *Minderoo* will be in port in a week.'

'No,' says Emilia. 'She says she will kill herself if we try to bring her back. No, better we wait. When she finds out what she's gotten into perhaps she will be wiser.'

'Gideon is well-off,' I say. 'That will be some protection at least.'

'Indeed,' says Papa with a sigh. He takes Emilia's hand and says, 'There, there, my dear. We'll weather this storm. And little Liam— he'll be no burden to any of us.' He shakes his head in disbelief. 'I cannot comprehend how anyone could leave such a sweet-natured child.'

Rosa hands around cups of tea. 'Papa, you don't seem to have much luck with your disobedient daughters and step-daughters.'

'You took a year off my life, young lady, and this is probably worth another, too. Lucy, should you ever be planning to elope, please just *go*. Don't leave us any letters.'

I'm tired and restless from the shocks of the night before, so I take Eliza for a walk to the foreshore camp. In the late winter afternoon the sand is deep pink, the water beyond it the palest green-blue.

Eliza is almost four now and I love her sensitive little face and mop of dark curls. Mrs Egawa often babysits her and she's a favourite of Sam's divers too. They believe she brings them good luck, so they always stop by the house before leaving port and pat her gently on the head.

Mr Egawa is in his workshop, making a doll-house for Eliza. We exchange glances and I leave her there with him. I climb the steps to the veranda where Danny is seated at a table, smoking and gazing at the bay.

He pulls out a chair for me and says, 'It's all right. I know.'

I sit down. 'She told me she dreamt of wearing pretty clothes and travelling on a steamship.'

'Probably more the *Mauretania* she had in mind, not Gideon's grubby little coaster.'

'He *lied* to me, Danny. He'd already spoken to the Protector about Cristina long ago, and I'm sure he turned him against you.'

'We worked well enough together, but we were never friends,' says Danny. 'I expect a few centuries of English history keep getting in the way. And he's had bad luck with women—Rosa, Angela—so maybe he thought he'd steal one from someone else for a change.'

'Oh? What happened with Angela? He told us they'd mutually agreed to part.'

'Not quite.' His earring glints. 'She fell for someone I know, an Irishman, too. Gideon was not amused.'

'You're smiling! You don't seem very upset.'

'I always knew she was desperate to get away and it didn't matter who'd take her. It was never going to be me.'

Memory strikes and I say in distress. 'Danny, he *admitted* he'd arranged the attack on Mrs O'Brien—I wasn't wrong about that after all. Dear God! He thought it was *funny*.'

'Lucy, listen now. Gideon is gone. He's out of our lives, he can't hurt any of us. And the baby'll be just fine with your father and Emilia.'

'Not with you?' I say, surprised.

He gazes steadily at me. 'I've no claim to him, girl. We've only her word he's mine.'

'Danny, he's got your smile, your hair. Don't be silly.'

'No denying he'll be a handsome devil once he grows a few teeth. But still, I've no claim. It depends on what his grandparents want for him.'

'So if my step-mother is his grandmother, that means I'm his step-auntie—*is* there such a thing as a step-auntie?'

'I expect not, but I doubt you'll let that stand in your way.'

'You do know,' I say solemnly, 'I'll *always* look after Liam, no matter what.'

'Well, I'd be more certain of that if he were rigged for sail.'

I laugh despite myself.

'Ah, forget Gideon, the man's an utter fool,' says Danny. 'Your young Alain's coming back soon, isn't he?'

'It won't be long,' I say, pleased.

'Well that'll be something to look forward to. Now, is it true what I've been hearing, there's a fine new fiddle come into your possession?'

'Oh, yes! It's not as sweet-sounding as yours of course, but then it's not as old.'

'Nor as scruffy either, I expect.' He gazes at me, one eyebrow raised. 'I'd be curious to hear how it sounds.'

13. KOOMBANA

'Look at my skin, Lucy. It's like leather.'

'Rosa, don't be absurd, it's perfect.'

'If I stay in Broome much longer I'll turn into a crocodile. We've been here for four years and oh, how I'd *love* not to have to worry about snakes or spiders or cyclones—'

'You don't have to make excuses. You need a holiday.'

'But it's too expensive,' says Rosa. 'We can't go away, not when we're just starting to get ahead.'

'We've had a good haul this season, the business can cope.'

Rosa gets up and settles Peter in the cradle, then sits down again beside me on the veranda, gazing at the deep blue October sky, the red-dust road, the emerald trees.

'You know I love it here, Lucy, but I do need to get away, at least for a time. That unspeakable woman, the Councillor's wife, was so rude again—last week she hissed 'slant-eyes' at me. Why does she bother? We all know she's from a dockside pub and she wasn't just serving the beer.'

'That's why she does it, of course,' I say. 'The nasty little strumpet can only try to hurt you through Sam. But you know how well-loved both of you are are by those who really matter in Broome. You can't worry about the fools squawking 'White Australia' like cockatoos on a fence.'

Rosa laughs and I say firmly, 'In any case, your protests are over-ruled. Sam's already made the bookings—a few days in Perth then a steamer to Melbourne. You're going to have a lovely cool Christmas in the south with Min-lu and the girls whether you want to or not.'

'A bloody Royal *Commission*, it is! Well, we can all rest easy now.' Captain Gregory sits down and swings his feet onto the desk.

Sam leans forward. 'But at least a Commission might make it obvious we'd have no business without the Asian men.'

'Did you see in the paper we're being asked to take on some white divers?' I ask. 'Hasn't been much of a rush to sign them up so far.'

'It's gone beyond a joke, young Lucy,' says Gregory. 'Some of the pearlers are using this to settle old scores. Remember Fred Everett? I prosecuted him once for not having lifebuoys on his luggers.' He lights a cigarette. 'Now I hear he's saying I'm in the *pay* of the Japanese!'

'But you've got to stop getting more shell than him, Greg,' Sam shakes his head sorrowfully. 'You just don't seem to know the rules.'

Gregory laughs. 'Rules are there to be broken, boyo. Still, I'm off to Britain for a while, and all this nonsense will be over soon enough. I've left a surprise to amuse you, too. Let my house to a friend. Mr Murakami felt like getting out of Japtown, bit of strife at home I hear, so I thought he might enjoy the White Quarter instead.'

Sam raises his eyebrows. 'That won't go down well with our fine fellow pearlers.'

'All of them freemasons or arrogant swine or both, without the wit to realise that waving a gun at the coloureds won't cut it any more,' says Gregory fiercely. 'You don't let anyone walk over you but, by God, you work with the Japs today or you can forget pearling in Broome.'

'Is Mr Murakami's strife at home in connection with Miss Murata?' I ask.

'Ah, you know about young Theresa, then?'

'I met them some months ago. He seemed very taken with her.'

'He married Eki when she was widowed and they were happy enough then. But she's past having children and he wants a family now. Still, it could take some time to untangle their affairs and Eki's never been a forgiving sort of woman.'

'I feel sorry for her—she's always been good to me.'

'You've a kind heart, Admiral Fox,' says Gregory, ashing his cigarette. 'But now on more interesting topics, how's your catch going for the year?'

'Four and three-quarter tons, and I think we'll easily top five by the lay-up.'

'Well done! I see I'll have to look sharp now to keep ahead of ambitious lady pearlers.'

I laugh. 'I think you're perfectly safe from my single lugger at the moment.'

'Ah, we all started out small, don't you forget.' Gregory stands and shakes Sam's hand. 'I wish you a fine trip to Melbourne, sir, and you a merry Christmas here in Broome, *cariad*.'

After Gregory leaves I open a folder. 'Sam, I've completed the papers for next year's crews and the discharge forms for this year's lot. I just need your signature on these letters now.'

He signs the papers then gazes at me. 'I feel so guilty going off and leaving you, Lucy. There's such a lot of work to be done during the lay-up.'

'Sam, we've already been over this. Danny handles the camp very well and Papa will advise on the business. You'll only be gone for four months, it's hardly forever.'

He smiles. 'I must admit I'm looking forward to it, and Rosa certainly deserves the break.'

'And you do too. Oh, I just remembered—the Sub-Collector of Customs told me he's sent the notice of *Currawong*'s loss to Perth, but he couldn't do *Sparrow*'s transfer to me. She's got to have a new survey first.' I wave a piece of paper at him then clip it into the folder.

'That's a nuisance, I'll be away. Still, Danny's got his ticket, he can do it.'

'Good. Now you've got my gifts for Min-lu and the girls, so just forget about the office and go and help Rosa with the packing. And don't *worry*.'

'You're not even twenty-one yet, little sister, and you run things as strictly as my mother,' he says laughing.

'Well, she did train me, after all.' I stand and put the folder on my desk. 'Now go.'

We hug, and I gaze at him with affection: his straight black hair sun-tipped with auburn, his Chinese mother's tawny skin and kind eyes, his English father's firm jaw and broad shoulders.

'Go, dear Sam. *Go*.'

We sit down to a traditional Christmas dinner followed by an untraditional confection of mango. Papa carves the turkey and Emilia brings out food until we can eat no more. Liam, seven months old, watches placidly with large hazel eyes, then falls suddenly asleep in Danny's arms.

In the evening we sit on the veranda and Emilia reads us Cristina's latest letter. It doesn't mention her son or Danny at all. She's clearly content at being Gideon Meade's kept woman, writing of nothing but parties and dresses and jewellery.

'She could at least visit and see Liam sometimes,' I say.

'Better she doesn't,' says Danny. 'He's happy enough with Emilia and you as joint foster-mothers.'

Emilia tuts indulgently and beams at me. 'And what is the latest news from France, Lucy? I thought your handsome young man would be back here by now.'

I look out at the night sky and sigh. 'I had a letter yesterday. Alain made the mistake of telling his father he cared for me, so his father has sent him off to Amsterdam to study the diamond trade.'

Emilia tuts again, this time in disgust. 'Poor Lucy. Well, he will be one very sorry young man indeed. In Perth you'll have so many suitors you'll forget him in a moment.'

I'm surprised. 'I wasn't planning to go to Perth right now.'

'But you must, Lucy. You will not find a husband here, not one worthy of you.'

'Let's wait till Sam and Rosa are back before you pack me off to the marriage-market,' I say lightly. 'Too much interests me here in Broome—and who'd teach me Irish fiddle in Perth?'

Danny laughs. 'Now there's a reason to be forgoing your entire future.'

'Oh, you know what I mean. And the pearlshell business, and my lugger *Sparrow*?' I'm silent for a moment. 'My life is here, Emilia.'

A few weeks later, in the new year of 1912, a letter arrives from Rosa in Melbourne:

> *We had such a sweet Christmas. Izabel is still the same soft-hearted girl, but Fili's interests have shifted significantly from horses to boys with horses.*
>
> *Eliza loves to visit the wharves with Sam and I fear she has inherited your odd fondness for ships, while baby Peter has started sleeping like an angel—what a Christmas present!*
>
> *Business has picked up and Min-lu is pleased. She's made peace with Bao-lim, although he remains in Hong Kong and thankfully has no further access to the company funds.*
>
> *Well! Another six weeks in this cool paradise and I shall be a new woman entirely. I've taken up my paintbox once more to do a few small views of the sea and sky.*

She sent me one of her watercolours, a silvery view of Melbourne spires across the bay from our old house in Williamstown. It's a pretty scene, but as I look out from the veranda at sprays of pink bougainvillea and swaying green palms, I smile in contentment.

My lugger *Sparrow* needs a marine survey, so Danny spends an afternoon crawling around the bilges, tape measure and notebook in hand. He emerges with a list of *Sparrow*'s measurements and spends the evening at Emilia and Papa's house writing up the survey.

He hands me the form as we sit with drinks on the veranda. 'There, ready for when Sam's back.'

'Thank you so much, Danny. That was above and beyond the call of duty.'

He takes a mouthful of beer. 'Tell the truth, I rather liked it, despite the reek of shellfish. The carpentry's a good job too. When I was a lad I helped a joiner in a small shipyard—it's a fine place to spend your time.'

'Perhaps you'll have a shipyard of your own one day.'

Danny smiles. 'I'm happy where I am, running the foreshore camp.'

'You wouldn't return to the sea then?' I say carefully. I'd asked him the same thing two years ago when he was recovering from a shipwreck and the response had been brutal.

Danny gazes at me. 'You may be on dangerous ground, girl.'

I meet his green eyes. 'I don't want you to lose something you care about, that's all.'

He nods. 'I do think about it, but no, not yet.' After a moment he says, 'In any case you should be worrying about your own future. Alain's a good lad but you'll find someone better in Perth.'

'And you may be on dangerous ground yourself. I do think about it, but no, not yet.' I sigh. 'I've lived through so much, Danny. It would be foolish to pretend to be a sheltered miss, and after Broome I'm certainly not. That won't appeal to young men wanting a wife.'

'Ah, they'll just see those gorgeous grey eyes and won't care if you come with a lugger attached.'

'Gorgeous grey eyes? On *Willowmere* you said I looked like your pet monkey!'

'Well, you did when you were fifteen—an inch of fluffy hair and getting into everything.' He covers his face and groans. 'Jesus, that time up the rigging.'

I laugh with delight at the memory, but my anxiety still niggles. I say hesitantly, 'Danny, I'm worried, truly. I don't want to be sent away.'

'You won't. Sam and Rosa'll be back soon and they'll always look after you.'

A few weeks later Papa, Emilia and I stand in the crowd milling around steamship *Charon*'s gangway. I see Rosa at the top, elegant in a white hat, with four-year-old Eliza by the hand, followed by a steward carrying little Peter.

'There they are! Oh, Rosa, you're looking marvellous.'

'I had such a wonderful time,' says Rosa. 'Emilia, how are you? Papa, would you take Peter?'

Papa looks around, puzzled. 'But where's Sam?'

'Oh, some tedious business delayed him in Perth so he's going to catch the next steamer home.'

At the house Rosa leans back in her chair, sipping a cool drink. 'How's little Liam? And Danny? Did you have any problems with the business?'

'Not at all. Everyone's well, and the men are ready to sail once the weather improves.'

'So what is it that's keeping Sam in Perth, my dear?' asks Papa.

'He had to dash off to see his lawyer about some business, and rang me at the last minute—he couldn't get back to the ship before we sailed. But he said he'd follow us in a couple of days.'

'Did you meet my daughter?' asks Emilia hesitantly.

Rosa sighs. 'Yes, at a restaurant one night. She's enthralled by some new friends who sound like rather a fast crowd—theatre, scandals, drinking—even opium, for heaven's sake. Sam says Gideon is somewhat less enchanted by it all.'

'Do you think she will come home to us?'

'I don't know, Emilia,' says Rosa gently. 'Probably not at the moment. I'm sorry to bring you bad news.'

Emilia wipes her eyes. 'No, no, it is good you met. Cristina will see sense one day. Nothing is to be done and I will not let it worry me. We have much better things to think about!'

'Emilia has organised a magnificent repast to celebrate Lucy's coming-of-age tomorrow,' says Papa. 'Such a pity Sam must miss out on it.'

'He told me to give Lucy our present nonetheless,' says Rosa, handing me a small parcel. 'Happy twenty-first birthday, little sister.'

I unwrap a layer of tissue and inside is a small leather box. I press the catch and there, lying on a cushion of silk, is a pair of rose-gold earrings with drops of creamy pink pearls.

'Thomas on *Mudlark* fished the pearls last year,' says Rosa. 'Min-lu designed the earrings and Sam had them made up for you in Melbourne. He said to tell you it might have taken rather a long time, but here they are at last!'

I put them on with shaking hands. 'Oh Rosa, I never expected anything like this!'

'Such fine pearls,' says Emilia. 'All of Broome will talk about them.'

'They talk about everything else, so why not?' says Rosa, laughing.

Later that night I come awake as a rumble of thunder echoes and fades away. Rain splashes on the iron roof and in the distance lightning flickers. Another storm is passing by.

I glance at the bedside table. Yes, there are my earrings, the most beautiful jewels I've ever seen. I turn, pull the sheet up over my shoulder and fall asleep again.

My twenty-first birthday is an evening of good-natured gossip, laughter, food and wine. I wear Min-lu's gift from Melbourne, a sapphire silk dress that turns my grey eyes to blue, while my new pearl earrings glow against my shiny brown hair.

Emilia and Papa's present is a dainty watch and Danny's a leather-bound book—the *Coastal Pilot*, a guide to the ports around the world I can only dream of visiting. Mr Murakami and lovely Theresa Murata bring me a pair of translucent vases, and *Sparrow's* carpenter Mr Egawa and his wife give me a set of fine carving tools.

By the end of the evening I've enjoyed three whole glasses of champagne, and as everyone says their goodbyes I hug them solemnly.

Danny is the last to go and as he puts on his coat he says, laughing, 'You're absolutely sozzled, girl. Too many tots of rum, if you ask me.'

'Nonsense,' I say with dignity. 'I'm just appallingly happy that's all.'

'Well, congratulations on reaching twenty-one, at any rate. I had my doubts you'd ever make it.'

'You helped me get here, Danny,' I say solemnly. 'Willowmere—teaching me fiddle—everything. You've been such a good friend.'

He gazes at me for a moment, his face still. 'It's you've been the good friend to me, you know. More than you'd realise.'

I step forward and hug him. He feels warm and rangy and so welcoming I sigh and rest my head on his shoulder. Dear Danny. After a moment he pushes me gently away and bends and pecks me lightly on the cheek.

'That's not a real kiss,' I say, mock-indignant.

He grins. 'Well, it's all you're getting from me.'

'You said that at Sam and Rosa's magnificent ball, too,' I laugh and shake my head reproachfully. 'Oh, Danny, you don't remember.'

'Indeed I do,' he says. 'You'd be surprised at what I remember.'

He looks out at the night, where the rain has stopped but thunder is still grumbling in the distance. 'I'd best be off now, and you should go and get some sleep too. Sam will be back tomorrow.'

'Good night, Danny.'

I sit down on a chair with a sigh. This wonderful evening would have been even better had Sam been here too.

His absence makes me feel something that reminds me oddly of the time I had scarlet fever. It went from almost nothing at first, just an ache when I swallowed, then bloomed into days of anxiety, delirium, pain.

I sit up, surprised. Good heavens, why on earth did I think of that? I stand and carry some plates out to Emilia and Rosa in the kitchen.

So this is what they mean by a hangover, I think when I wake up dry-mouthed next morning. It's not very nice. By the evening the headache has worn off and as I'm finishing some letters in the office, I hear the carriage crunching on the gravel. At last! Rosa's back from the jetty with Sam.

I walk out to the veranda but see she is alone.

'What a *bother*,' she says. 'The ship's been delayed. There was a cyclone and they went out to sea to avoid it. The telegraph is down now so we don't even know when they'll land.'

Next morning I take Eliza for a walk to Lookout Hill, where other people are waiting and watching the bay. The turquoise waters sparkle, dainty puffballs of cloud dot the violet sky, the copper soil is outlined with swathes of emerald. But all we can see is the horizon, empty of the smoke-smudge that would let us relax and turn away and smile at our fears.

'Why is Daddy not here yet?' asks Eliza, as we walk home.

'Oh, his ship's running late, that's all.'

Papa and Emilia come to dinner. Rosa refuses to be concerned and Papa is equally assured.

'*Koombana*'s the finest steamship on the coast,' he says. 'Watertight doors, excellent engines, stable, strong. I'm certain she's at sea somewhere, probably dealing with repairs. They say her workshops would put a land-based factory to shame.'

Next morning the weekly *Broome Chronicle* appears. A small

paragraph is headed KOOMBANA CONSIDERABLY OVERDUE, but the losses and strandings of luggers in the storm receive much more attention.

The telegraph line to the south works briefly, then goes down again. All we can find out is that *Koombana* was last seen leaving Port Hedland three days ago, heading out of harbour to avoid the cyclone. Still, news of her arrival further north, at Derby or Wyndham, is expected any day.

Emilia hears someone say the ship has arrived safely at Derby, but then nobody knows for sure because the lines are now down in every direction. A few days later the telegraph to Port Hedland is restored. It brings reports of two ships wrecked, a lugger lost, two lighters swamped and at least forty people dead. No word of *Koombana*.

On Thursday the line going north is reconnected and a message finally comes through. The postmaster types out a notice and displays it on the board: *Koombana is not at Derby*.

'She's drifting out at sea,' says Rosa, her chin firm. 'That is all. They'll find her any day now.'

Search parties walk the coast, luggers set out for Pattersons Shoals, and ships steam to the Monte Bellos and the Rowley Shoals and along the Ninety-Mile Beach.

The following Saturday the *Chronicle's* headline is A TRYING TIME FOR SHIPPING. Engineers who know the *Koombana* are interviewed. Masters of vessels that survived the cyclone are interviewed. The paper maintains, *It is held in well-informed circles that she is still afloat, disabled*. In the list of passengers I read 'Capt. Lee' and my throat tightens.

Danny comes over to the house to play fiddle music with me as usual. The intricate reels and jigs and hornpipes keep my mind busy, but when we play a sad, sweet air I have to stop because my eyes keep filling with tears. Danny makes tea for us in the kitchen while I find a handkerchief.

'I've heard *Koombana's* propeller was out of the water when she

forded the bar at Hedland,' Danny says, rubbing his chin with a
callused hand. 'So she wasn't in ballast at that stage—wouldn't
have got over the bar otherwise.'

'They probably planned to fill the tanks out at sea.' I sip the
comforting tea.

'And perhaps the storm hit before she was loaded, or the pumps
failed.'

'But, Danny, the engineers say she's very stable.'

He shakes his head. 'She's a top-heavy bitch, never been as stable
as they like to say. But Christ, there's a hundred and forty people on
board. She's drifting somewhere, *got* to be.' He looks as if he hasn't
been sleeping either.

Two weeks after *Koombana* forded the bar at Port Hedland,
fragments of her wreckage are found seventy miles out to sea.

ALL HOPE ABANDONED says the *Chronicle*.

The search is called off.

We attend services at the Anglican church, the Catholic chapel, the
small iron mosque and the Japanese cemetery. At the Anglican
church I see Gideon Meade, master of *Hydra*, seducer of Cristina,
and Sam's oldest friend. Afterwards he stands uncertainly before
me, his hat in his hand. All the beauty is gone from his face.

I gasp and hug him. 'Oh, *Gideon*.'

He clings to me then stands back, his hand to his eyes. I lead him
to a quiet spot beneath a tree. He wipes his face with a
handkerchief and whispers, 'Dear God. Dear *God*. This is beyond
all—Rosa? How is she? I saw her at a distance but simply could not
...'

'Bearing up for the sake of the children,' I say, but it's not true.

'Lucy, there is something I must tell you. The last thing Sam did
—' Gideon takes a shuddering breath. 'The last act of that
extraordinary man ... was to save my worthless life.'

'Your *life*?'

'It was the day Rosa sailed home to Broome. Cristina announced to all and sundry she was going to Britain with a theatre director who would make her famous.'

'Oh, Gideon, I'm sorry.'

'No. No kindness. I deserve every measure of grief!' He wipes his face. 'I—swallowed laudanum. When I realised how stupid I'd been I rang Sam and he took me to hospital. They pumped out my stomach—dreadful, disgusting beyond endurance. Then he stayed with me until he had to depart on that fateful ship.'

'But why on earth did you ...?'

His face crumples, his jaw clenches. 'Cristina had an opium habit, Lucy. And after she packed and left me, I simply could not bear to go on.'

I sigh. 'So *typical* of Sam, such goodness. Gideon, please come and tell Rosa.'

He shakes his head. 'I've stayed too long and *Hydra* must sail. But I had to tell you, you've always been good to me, Lucy, and I've treated you shabbily. Never again, I swear. I'll protect your family just as Sam would have wished.' He half-sobs. 'Forgive me, I *must* go.'

He hurries to a waiting carriage. I gaze after him, tears of horror and pity in my eyes.

'The strangest thing is, I feel nothing for those poor souls on the *Titanic*,' Rosa whispers. 'So soon after *Koombana*, and ten times as many people, but I don't care. I'm so cold.'

Despite the heat she wraps herself in her shawl and sits for hours on the veranda. When the children come near she strokes their hair, then hands them back to Bettie. She weeps until her face is a swollen mask.

I weep too, and rage against the lawyer who'd so fatefully delayed Sam from sailing with Rosa, but Danny just says sadly, 'It's no one's fault, girl, it was just bad luck and the sea.'

I don't see him cry, but his eyes are as bruised as mine, so I know he does.

'But what shall we do?' I run my fingers through my hair in despair, wrenching out a comb. 'I wake up in the early hours and I don't know what to *do*.'

'We'll do what Min-lu told you years ago. We'll work,' says Danny. 'The luggers must still find pearlshell to support Rosa and the babies. We've got to do it for Sam.'

'Min-lu! Dear *God*, what she must be feeling.'

One day Emilia brings baby Liam over to the house for a few hours. I give him to Rosa to hold and he smiles at her with his slow sweet smile and strokes her cheek, as compassionate as a Buddha in a Japtown shrine. She buries her face against his red-brown curls for a long time, and murmurs later, 'Peter was born in a cyclone and makes me remember too much. Liam helps me forget.'

Gideon visits, and Rosa hear his sad story and hugs him. He keeps his oath to protect Sam's family: when *Hydra*'s schedule allows, he helps Rosa with legal matters and amuses the children so she might rest. After a time she begins to deal with the household again, her cheekbones sharp, her eyes shadowed.

Sam's estate is complicated, but is slowly untangled by Papa and a lawyer Min-lu sends to Broome, Harold Browne, a friendly middle-aged man. Min-lu herself writes restrained, comforting letters to me: I hope my own in return offer her a little of the same ease.

I receive heartfelt commiserations from Alain too. He wants to return to Broome—to me—within a year, once he's financially free of his father.

I remember his warm lips, as I often do before falling asleep, and think oh, how I'd welcome the comfort of his arms. But the only diversion I have in the world is my work, and I sigh and put Alain's letter in my bottom drawer.

14. MOONRISE

Six long, slow months after Sam is lost, a letter arrives from Min-lu telling us she's leaving Melbourne and moving to Perth with her daughters, to the suburb of Victoria Park. We all need a change, she says.

At breakfast on the veranda one morning soon afterwards, Rosa puts down her spoon and says, 'I've decided I need a change too. I'm taking the children to Perth, to stay with Min-lu and her girls for the summer. We'll go to concerts and exhibitions and walks by the river.'

'Oh. But what shall I do?' I ask.

'What do you want to do, Lucy? I'd love you to come, but I know you enjoy being here.'

'True, and there's so much to be done over the lay-up. But Rosa, would you trust me to keep the business going? Of course Danny and Papa can help—'

'Yes, of course I trust you. I'm only worried you might be lonely by yourself.'

'Emilia wants to give up her boarding-house, so it might suit her and Papa to move in here,' I say.

'Good. Their presence will keep you safe from the gossips, and Bettie can help with Liam.'

'Aren't you … afraid now of going on the steamer to Perth?'

'No. I'm not afraid of anything any more,' says Rosa. 'Apart from the children there's nothing could hurt me now. I don't expect this to make anything better, but at least it will be something different.'

In November I wave goodbye to Rosa and the children as they depart on *Hydra*. It's painful to see them go—Peter in his tiny sailor suit and Eliza's solemn little face under her brown curls.

Then I spend the next few days helping Emilia and Papa move into Rosa's house. We hold a small dinner to celebrate and invite the lawyer who's working on Sam's estate, Harold Browne. He comes from the port of Newcastle, New South Wales, where his father owns three barques that carry coal to Chile, nitrates to San Francisco and timber back to Newcastle.

Over dessert Harold Browne says, 'Mr Whalen, perhaps when you have grown tired of these toy luggers you may wish to return to true sailing vessels. My father is always on the lookout for reliable masters.'

'Shame, Mr Browne,' I say. 'Luggers are far from toys and you know it.'

'Forgive me Miss Fox, I most certainly do! I've had to wade through a mountain of documents from the Registrar, the Minister, the Departmental Secretary, the Harbourmaster and the Sub-Collector of Customs, and I find to my horror I'm expected to take them very seriously indeed.'

'Like every sailor afloat I've been to Newcastle, but I've no desire to return to deepwater sail,' says Danny. 'Luggers'll do me fine for now, thank you, Mr Browne.'

'Keep it in mind at any rate, sir. As more and more officers move into steam there are fewer good men for the sailing ships, yet they still carry the lion's share of cargo.'

Later, when the lawyer has gone and Papa and Emilia are in the kitchen, I say, 'Well, at least you didn't bite his head off for suggesting it, Danny. That's promising.'

He laughs. 'Be fair, I can at least consider the prospect now. And sometimes ... ah, old dreams.' He shakes his head.

We begin to clear the table. 'I saw Captain Gregory when I was shopping today,' I say. 'He's back from Britain, ready to take on the town. He was horrified to hear about Sam—he went so pale I thought he'd faint. He knew of *Koombana* of course, but hadn't realised ...'

I sit down and put my hands over my face. 'The night of my birthday party I had such a painful foreboding and now it never leaves me. Oh Danny, when will it stop *hurting* so much?'

He touches my head for a moment. 'I don't know, Lucy. I just don't know.'

I become very thin and my monthly courses cease. I go to see Suzuki-san, the doctor who delivered Rosa's baby, who prescribes an iron tonic and reassures me that all will soon be well with my body. He can do nothing for my heart.

In early 1913, sitting on the veranda watching a summer rainburst, I read a letter from Rosa:

> *Christmas passed quietly, although we made an effort for the children. I mostly walk a lot and sign papers the lawyers send me. They say the estate is almost—oh dear, I don't remember the words—but I shall be quite comfortably off, which is a relief.*
>
> *Gideon remains our Rock of Gibraltar. Min-lu finds comfort in his schoolday tales of Sam, and he's kindness itself with the children. His incautious adventure with Cristina and the laudanum appears to have taught him a lesson. How often I think of my dearest Sam beside him, helping him, before embarking on that final voyage.*

Gideon is trying to prove he's a changed man I suppose, and why not? He must have learnt from his sad experience. But how odd for someone so confident to collapse into despair and take an overdose of opium! Thank God he was able to ring Sam in time to help him.

The sweet-scented rain patters onto a red-mud puddle in the garden, pink bougainvillea swaying beyond it. The ripples expand and criss-cross and spread out and as I watch them I grow very still.

Why?

Why did Gideon think Sam was still in Perth to ring in the first place, when as far as anyone knew he'd already left for Broome with Rosa? Unless, unless ...

My heart thuds. Of *course*.

The hair on my scalp tightens and I can barely move for grief and rage. Some time later Danny arrives and I stand painfully and take him into the office.

My voice shakes. 'I've just realised something dreadful.'

'Jesus, what?'

'Gideon told me he'd taken opium and rung Sam after Rosa sailed. But how did he even know Sam was still in Perth? No one knew! I think Gideon was that supposed lawyer who called Sam away. *He* was the reason Sam died in the cyclone!'

Danny stares, horrified.

'I felt sorry for him, you know,' I say. 'But he was lying—lying again. He just can't help himself. Dear God, we must tell Rosa. He killed Sam and he's worming his way into her life, the children's lives, he's deceiving us all!'

'But she's just getting back on her feet. Another shock? It'd be too cruel. And you can't be sure—'

'Why does no one ever *believe* me!' I cry.

'I do. I do believe you. Christ, I'd believe anything at all of that man.' Danny rubs his forehead distractedly. 'But think, think! What would Sam want us do? He loved Gideon, he'd have stayed behind to help him, no matter what. It was the cyclone really killed him.'

'No, no! It was Gideon. I'll never forgive him, never.'

Danny grips my hands. 'But you must, you'll choke on your own bitterness if you don't.'

'Well, you'd certainly know *that* well enough, Danny.'

'Damned right I do. I learned it and the hard way too. Let it *go*, girl!'

He drops my hands and slams the door and I put my head down and sob.

I should just stop. Go to Perth, become a well-groomed young lady, marry, have babies, forget. Forget, not just Sam and Gideon and Danny, but this strange life too. Even in easy-going Broome I know I'm an oddity.

I sit, my head in my hands, then wipe my eyes. I cannot think for this stifling heat, the air itself seems a solid thing. There's nothing I can do. *Nothing.* Just keep going, keep working.

I loosen the collar of my blouse, dip my pen in the inkwell and start writing a letter.

The following day Harold Browne comes to the office to continue working on Sam's estate.

'Lucy, how are you today? With your permission I'd like to finish off a few notes.'

'You're welcome, Harold,' I politely lie.

Half an hour later he closes a folder and says, 'How odd. Your lugger *Sparrow*—I cannot locate her latest certificate of registration. Yet she's a merchant vessel, registered at Fremantle, is she not?'

'Yes, of course, but I thought the certificate was in that file you've been looking at.'

'No, there's only an old one, the ownership as Lee and Co.'

'Oh, I know what's happened,' I say, feeling tired. 'Is there a survey form pinned to it?'

'From early last year.'

'We had to complete a new survey before she could be transferred. Danny did it while Sam was away in Melbourne, but when he—did not return—I forgot about it. But it's not a problem, is it? We can just submit it now.'

'Not quite that simple. The boat is still part of Sam's estate, you see, so you will need the signature of the inheritor, that is, your sister, for the transfer to take place. And until probate is declared, that cannot occur.' Harold taps the papers neatly into place and smiles at me. 'Still, I expect all will soon be in order, then at last I shall be free of these troublesome little ships.'

After he leaves I sit, surprised at my rush of feeling. I walk to the window. Far away, heat shimmers above the camp's tin roofs and streams of jade water meander through the red mud.

I think about our endless cycle of labour, season after season, caring for the men, rebuilding the boats, bringing to light the silvery shell and luminous pearls of the deep blue sea.

Later I walk over to the foreshore camp and knock at Danny's office door. He's at the desk ticking items off a list when I enter and I sit down in the chair opposite.

'I'm sorry, Danny. What I said to you was unforgivable.'

He grins. 'I suspect, in the reckoning of unforgivable words, girl, you're still a long way ahead of me. But why the sudden mildness?'

'Harold Browne found out today I'm not *Sparrow*'s legal owner yet—there's some silly formality with the estate. But when he told me I was astonished at how much owning her meant to me! And I suddenly realised I don't want to give up and go away—'

'You wouldn't be doing that?' says Danny, startled.

'Well, for a time there I was wondering what on earth I was doing in Broome.'

'There's quite a few of the other pearlers wonder that too, but they're not as good at their job as you.'

'I know everyone thinks I like luggers the same way spinsters like kittens, but it's not so. Don't laugh, Danny, but it suddenly seemed to me as if our caring for the men and the boats and the camp all together creates some sort of curious device for discovering pearlshell—I said don't *laugh*!'

'That wouldn't go down too well at the Conti,' he says grinning. 'Most of our noble pearlers would rather choke on their beer than care for their men.'

'But you've seen yourself how the take goes up when the luggers are sound, the men eat well, the right crews are brought together.'

'The pearlers'd claim we were just lucky.'

'You know it's not luck! Every pound we've spent on the men we've got back fivefold in shell.'

He nods. 'But that's a truth this town despises. They already whisper we've gone native if we use a few words of Malay, and they'll whisper far worse if they hear you say that.'

'I don't care. I've decided I won't let *anything* stop me now, Danny. Not cyclones nor cruel gossip nor a need for respectability.' I take a deep breath. 'And I won't let bitterness about the past stop me, either. Not even bitterness about Gideon.'

Despite my brave words I need all my resolution some weeks later when I hear Gideon's deep voice speaking to Ahmet on the veranda. I rise and go out. He's regained his good looks, I notice, as he shakes my hand. We chat politely while Ahmet brings afternoon tea.

'Papa and Emilia are shopping. They'll be sorry to have missed you.'

There's a silence. Gideon clears his throat. 'Lucy, there is something I wish to explain.'

'Oh?'

Gideon's peaked cap is small in his enormous hands, his thumb restlessly stroking the gold embroidery of the band.

'At the time of the shock of Sam's loss and Cristina's betrayal and my—hospitalisation—I became confused as to the unfolding of events and I fear I may have misled you. It seems I rang Sam before Rosa departed on the *Charon*, not after.'

'Yes.' I'm trying to breathe evenly.

'In his discretion, good Sam Lee told an untruth. It was no lawyer he hurried off to visit, of course, it was me. When he stayed behind to save my life it led in turn to the loss of his own on *Koombana*.'

'Ah.'

Gideon gazes at me. 'I see you understand.'

There are new lines around his blue eyes but they only enhance his beauty.

'I realised what must have happened a while ago,' I say.

'You certainly are a clever young lady, Lucy. And how do you judge me? Do you find any forgiveness in your heart at all?'

'It's not for me to forgive.' My pulse is pounding. 'That's up to Rosa.'

'Rosa knows.

I stare at him.

'I told her. Rosa knows and forgives me. She wishes to forget the past. She understands, in the end, it was a cruel act of nature that took Sam from us.'

'I see.'

'Lucy, I said once I had learnt from my mistakes. What I did not realise then was how many more mistakes it is possible for a man to make.' He takes a breath. 'I need your understanding too.'

He sits very still, his head bowed.

Dear God, what would *Sam* want of me? Gentle Sam, who never held a grudge in his life? Half-Chinese Sam, protected by this man when they were only boys together dreaming of the sea?

I sigh, and after a time say hesitantly, We are all so interwoven since *Willowmere*. Like a crew, like a family. Perhaps, whatever happens, even a disaster like this ... Sam would want us to carry on, to pull together. To forgive each other.'

Gideon breathes out softly. 'Thank you. Thank you indeed, Lucy.'

He stands, tall and golden, and places his cap upon his head. 'And now I have a message from Rosa too. She says she wishes you would come to Perth to discover a new life, just as she has.'

I nod, rise and offer my hand in farewell.

Gideon takes it and says earnestly, 'I must agree with her, Lucy. You should be making a good marriage, not chasing pearlshell in this grubby little town.'

I shake my head. 'This is where I prefer to be.'

He pats my hand, smiling. 'Time will tell.'

We are busy at the foreshore making Sam's luggers ready: it is March, the start of the 1913 season, the first he is no longer here to witness. Papa, once master of a deepwater barque, is content now to organise the loading of mere boats, Danny is settling an argument between two divers and I'm helping Borue stow supplies in a dinghy, my shoes spattered with red mud.

A group of people stroll along the road nearby, one the Councillor's wife who so dislikes Rosa. Her husband hails Papa and they exchange polite greetings. I hear the woman snickering and look up to see her whispering to a young man and gazing pointedly at my feet.

'Tell her it's the latest fashion,' says Danny in passing.

'She's such a fool she'd believe it too.'

There's a murmur around us and I realise the luggers are starting to lift on the tide. One by one their sails are hoisted and we watch as they move gracefully out through the mangroves and away.

Papa says, 'What a sight to see them afloat, my dear.'

'And what a miracle we got them afloat at all,' says Danny, shaking his hand. 'In no small part due to your assistance, Captain Fox.'

Papa beams. 'A pleasure, sir, a pleasure.'

As the lovely flock moves towards the open sea, the weight on my heart lifts for the first time in a year. 'Goodness, we did it. Sam would have been happy.'

'Indeed he would,' says Papa. 'Now, I do believe Emilia has prepared something special for tonight to celebrate the sailing of the fleet and you're invited, Mr Whalen, of course. Your lad is chattering a treat lately, such a bright little fellow.'

Danny smiles but I notice, not for the first time, something like pain in his eyes at the mention of his son.

That evening Emilia brings Liam to see us before dinner, freshly washed and ready for bed. The child, almost two, says solemnly, 'Night-night, Aunt Lucy.'

I bend down and breathe the scent of his hair as he kisses me. He turns to Danny, who lifts him onto his lap. 'Did you make the boats go sailing out today, Papa?'

'Ah, we all did that together, little man. Perhaps you can come and help us next year.'

Liam grins, his eyes so much like Danny's I almost laugh.

'Oh, *yes*. Night-night, Papa,' he says and kisses him.

'Off you go now. Grandma and Grandpa will tuck you in.'

We sit in silence, then I ask, 'Is something wrong, Danny? Are you worried about Liam?'

He raises his head and says hesitantly, 'You remember I told you I've no right to him, not being married to Cristina? Well, it goes deeper than that. You see, I'm not even sure if I'm really his father, and the uncertainty is eating away at me.'

'But I was just thinking how very alike you are!'

'Something I never told you. Cristina left the father's name blank on the registration and when we were arguing one day she said it was because it wasn't me.'

'She was lying of course, trying to hurt you. Danny, it's not true —he's *so* like you.'

'Sometimes I think, yes, there's a look of my own father. Other times?' He shrugs. 'She was a wilful woman, Cristina, and she'd have done anything, used anyone, to get away from here. When I didn't fit the bill she found Gideon.'

'Her being wilful doesn't mean you're not Liam's father.'

'But I wasn't the first man in her life and, she said afterwards, not the only one either.'

'Oh.'

'When she had Liam I really hoped we'd stay together. He's a darling boy and I'd do anything for him.' The light leaves Danny's eyes. 'But legally I'm not his father. And I worry what will happen if Cristina wants him back.'

Rosa writes to me:

Gideon told me you said Sam would want us to forgive each other, to pull together as on Willowmere—so typical of you!—but true.

Please come to Perth, Lucy, you must start thinking of your future. Gideon said you were wasted on a provincial town and I think he has a point.

And a rather exciting thing has happened. Min-lu and I decided to stop renting this house and have bought it together instead!

There's plenty of room for you, and as an added incentive, Min-lu has opened a small business in pearlshell export and says she'd love to have the advice of a "real pearler."

So do come, we all miss you. Love, Rosa.

'Sounds like an excellent plan to me,' says Papa, as he cuts the top off his boiled egg. 'Indeed, just the other week Emilia and I were discussing something similar. My dear, you're almost twenty-two and time is running out to find a husband.'

'But I don't want to go away, I want to keep working here.'

'Lucy,' says Emilia earnestly, 'that was suitable while your sister could chaperone you, but now, well—I'm sorry to say, I am hearing rumours.'

I put down my cup. 'If it's that awful Councillor's wife—oh, Emilia, you know that's just Broome, people here live for gossip.'

'Lucy, I have seen too many good girls compromised in this town and I could not bear it if you suffered Cristina's fate. You must go away, you *must* marry.'

'And you could always come back with your husband,' says Papa. 'But now your character is under attack, day after day.'

'The other pearlers are simply jealous of our success!'

'I would not disagree in the slightest, my dear, but the outcome is deeply damaging to you.'

'Go and see how you like it, Lucy, then come back,' says Emilia. 'You know everything will be all right here without you for a few months, and you might enjoy Perth society more than you think. You're so pretty, after all.'

That night I sit at my mirror. Am I pretty? My wavy brown hair is glossy in the candlelight and in a cooler climate my tanned skin will become desirably fair. But I'm not fashionably buxom and my dark eyes are direct and curious, not shyly downcast as is proper in a young lady.

It has been two years since Alain went away, two years since a man kissed me and sparked ripples of delight through my body. Of course someone else may want me, but would he also want me to leave behind this life I love?

One evening a week later I take the accounts down to the foreshore office for Danny, and find him sitting on the veranda sharing a bottle of beer with Captain Gregory.

'I hear you're leaving us, Admiral Fox, swanning off to the wicked south!' says Gregory. 'Take a seat and let's pour a glass for you in celebration.'

'Yes, please. And I've been informed it's me that's wicked, too wicked for Broome at any rate.'

'*Cariad*, I hit a man the other night who dared—' He clears his throat. 'Well, they're all just hypocrites, liars and gossips, don't you take the slightest notice of them.'

On the dusty blue horizon a translucent moon is brightening, while golden clouds cast the last of the daylight onto the ripples shimmering between the shadowy mangroves.

'Ah, and what will you do in Perth without that great silvery moon to admire?' Gregory says, leaning back, contented. 'Nothing like it anywhere else but Broome.'

I nod, gazing at the lovely sight, and sigh.

Danny says, 'I was just congratulating the Skipper here on his new appointment.'

'Oh yes—new Superintendent of the Pearling Act. Well done, Greg! Will it be an onerous job, do you think?'

'Well, I've ordered a crate-load of carbon paper,' says Gregory gloomily. 'Lists of vessels to be sent to Fremantle every three months, in triplicate, and pecked out on a typewriter, dear Lord!'

He looks ruefully at his large hands. 'And all the luggers must have licence numbers on their bows exactly twelve inches high. Do I have to swim out to them with a measuring stick?'

Danny laughs. 'If it makes the politicians happy.'

'Well then, I'd better do some work to keep them off our backs.' Gregory drains his glass and stands. 'To your safe journey, my dear. I'll make certain my boats leave just enough pearlshell for Mr Whalen here to keep him busy while you're away. Do come back to us soon.'

After he leaves I say, 'I cannot *believe* that tomorrow I'll be heading south to the cool autumn.'

'Ah, well,' says Danny, 'we'll just keep slaving away here in the tropics, while you play the Great White Pearler to the horde of suitors they've got lined up for you. Mind you impress them with tales of the giant Broome octopuses now.'

'Of course, once I've told them all about the man-eating clams.'

Danny stretches and yawns. 'Did you hear *Sparrow* came in this afternoon with a leak? We fixed it once she was ashore, but part of the caulking had gone.'

'The caulking? Not the section I did, I hope! Let me see.'

In the dusk we walk across the sand to the lugger's stern.

'There,' says Danny, pointing.

'Oh, Jiro did that section, not me,' I say. 'Thank heavens, I'd hate to let the dear thing down.'

'I thought she was a curious device for discovering pearlshell, not a kitten.'

'You know I'm not sentimental about the luggers, Danny. But this one's special. She's *mine*, Sam gave her to me and I couldn't bear it—I *can't* bear it—' I stop, my throat aching.

'She'll be fine, don't worry.'

'But I don't *want* to go away! They're all so certain I should marry, but what if it's someone who won't understand me? Remember when you said Sam and Rosa would look after me?

Now there's no one left in the world who cares what *I* want! Danny, I'm so *afraid*—'

My words catch on a sob.

He says, 'Ah, there, now,' and puts his arm lightly around my shoulders.

I lean my head against the comfort of his chest and weep with relief for a few moments.

'Come on, girl, it won't be very long. We'll all be here, your *Sparrow* too, when you come back.' He kisses the top of my head.

I rub my eyes and murmur against his shoulder, 'That wasn't a real kiss.'

He laughs softly. 'Well, it's all you're getting from me.'

I look up at him, curious, alert, alive. 'Is it?'

I lift my hand and stroke the line of his smiling cheek. I lean into him, nuzzling his face, my fingers cupping his curly head, his earring smooth against my palm. He closes his eyes for a moment, then opens them, no longer smiling.

His arms tighten and I can feel the muscles quivering. I brush my mouth across his face, along his lips, tasting the salt of him. I move closer, my arms, my breasts, my hips yearning for contact, and he pulls me against the long sinewy warmth of his body and kisses me over and over.

I can smell him and feel him, and the world is still, and perfect, and utterly focused. I hear the lapping of ripples on the sand and the call of a night bird. We stand quietly, our mouths touching, breathing together for a long time.

Then the peace is shattered: voices from the crew quarters arguing over cards. Danny lifts his head, dazed, and groans.

'No, sweet, we must not, I've already caused enough damage. No, no.'

He puts his hands on my shoulders and pushes me gently away from his warmth. I stare at him in disbelief. I'm trembling, furious, *bereft*.

I say coldly, 'But shouldn't you help me practice for the horde of suitors they've got lined up for me in Perth?'

'No. Yes. *No*! You'd be better off with any one of them, I've nothing to offer you. Oh Christ, I'm sorry, Lucy, I'm so sorry.'

15. THE PEARLSHELL PENDANT

The foreshore grows smaller across our foamy wake: Emilia and Papa and Liam are now just dots on the jetty. Danny did not come to say goodbye.

I'm travelling south on S.S. *Hydra*. The days pass easily, with landings at dusty jetties, occasional luggers in the distance, more scrubby trees and less solid heat, the reverse of my voyage from Fremantle nearly four years ago.

So much has happened since then. Picnics, launchings, regattas. Festivals for the dead.

I'm haunted by memories: Mama laughing on *Willowmere*, Rosa bearing Peter in a cyclone, Liam left behind by his mother, Sam calling me 'little sister.' And Danny, always Danny.

Sometimes, grateful for my cabin to myself, I weep into my pillow, then lie quietly for hours.

When I meet Gideon he jokes about my lack of love for anything without sails, but I grow fond of *Hydra*'s quiet, efficient routine and it pleases him when I tell him so. One evening after dinner, promenading on the passenger deck, we stop to look out at the ship's silver wake.

Gideon lights a cigarette, his hand cupping the flame against the breeze. He draws hard upon it, his golden brow outlined, his eyes in shadow.

After a pause he says, 'Lucy. There's something I'd like to ask you, regarding Rosa. I'm wondering how you might feel if, after a suitable time, I courted her.'

'Marriage?'

'It's never been a secret how I feel. My God, it's been seven years since we first met. I'm a fool I know, but no one can say I forget easily.'

Has he changed? He's selfish and he lies, but in that is he very different from many other men? He's also been surprisingly good to Rosa and the children, and I suppose in the end it must be her choice.

I say, 'It has not been very long, of course, since ... but really, it's for to her to decide. On my part I believe you'd do your best to make her happy.'

'With all my heart.'

'Then I wish you well, Gideon. I wish you both well.'

I gaze at our wake and am struck by memory. 'Do you remember on *Willowmere*, when I wondered if Rosa were fond enough of the sea to be a captain's wife? Such a long time ago now.'

'Indeed.' He flicks his cigarette into the sea. 'Thank you.'

The house in Perth has carved fretwork on the veranda and coloured glass around the door. The hall smells of beeswax and orange oil, and bowls of roses sit on the sideboard.

'All rather easy on the eye,' says Rosa. 'Now, I'll just get the tea. Oh, they're back—'

'Aunt Lucy!' calls Eliza, running in and climbing onto my lap. 'I saw such a pretty barquentine!'

Her face has filled out, her eyes are bright, her brown curls caught back in a ribbon. Peter toddles in the door led by Izabel and Fili, Min-lu's pretty half-Portuguese daughters.

'My darlings, how good to see you! Fili, you're so tall, and Izabel, what wonderful curls. Oh, little Peter, don't you remember me?' He looks at me solemnly and shakes his head.

Another figure is at the door: petite, elegant Min-lu, grey streaks now in her black hair and fine lines in the golden skin around her eyes. We hug for a long time.

Autumn in Perth brings us bright days and cool nights. We go to the theatre, to concerts and regattas, and it's a relief to simply shop for clothes, chat over afternoon tea, play with the children.

Sometimes I walk in the park with Min-lu. Admiring eyes glance at me, the smart young lady, then disapprovingly at the Chinese woman—in their park! Then they see Min-lu's fashionable outfits and expensive jewellery, and nod knowingly. A princess, a rich oriental potentate: that's all right then. Wealth trumps race.

Haltingly I tell her what happened with Danny in Broome. She last saw us together six years ago in Melbourne, Danny a twenty-four-year-old ship's officer and me a bereaved girl of sixteen, but she doesn't seem surprised.

'You were so fond of them all—Sam, Gideon, Danny,' says Min-lu, as we sit on a bench in the shade of a tree. 'And they of you, such a charming, curious child. I always wondered about Danny—so self-effacing and cynical, yet strong beneath. Sam thought the world of him.'

'But Danny used to be with Cristina, glorious, desirable Cristina. He wouldn't want me.'

Min-lu laughs. 'Oh, Lucy! Of course he wants you. You're lovely, and better than that, you're kind. He has always cared for you, but he seems to believe he is not worthy. Give him time.'

She shrugs. 'On the other hand, perhaps Danny is not the man for you. He is not well-off. He is not ambitious. He clearly does not appreciate your affection for him.'

I look at her in surprise.

'You owe it to yourself to enjoy your time here, to meet young men and find out how you really feel. You've been away from society for too long and perhaps a different kind of man will catch your attention, someone who may have more to offer you.'

'I did rather enjoy spending time with Alain,' I say shyly.

'A pearl-buyer! Shall we never get you away from Broome?'

I laugh. 'It doesn't help that you're dealing in pearlshell now,

Min-lu!'

But I do try. Sometimes eligible young men come along on our outings, all of whom I like perfectly well, none of whom interest me in the slightest. Edward—or is it Thomas?—kisses me one quiet evening.

He's pleasant enough, but the world does not become still, or perfect, or focused in any way.

Gideon is growing more pompous, heavier at the jaw but still handsome in his uniform and he's undeniably kind to the children. Eliza, puzzlingly, holds back a little but Peter adores him.

Rosa, thank God, has put on some weight and the stark misery of her eyes has eased. Gideon's presence clearly gives her great comfort. He takes her to meetings with the lawyers and afterwards gently explains what they mean.

Sometimes he murmurs in her ear and she smiles.

It will soon be a year and a half since Sam's death, and Rosa starts to give up her mourning clothes. She orders new gowns in the jewel-rich colours that suit her, and with her red-gold hair lavishly dressed and her eyes shining she dines with Gideon in fashionable restaurants.

Min-lu is a serene presence, as always. She enjoys Gideon's good humour but sometimes I notice her watching him with a thoughtful air. Entirely natural I suppose. She must compare him to Sam and anyone on earth would suffer in such a comparison.

Her new business, Pearlshell Ltd, sells shell directly to local jewellers without the overhead of it travelling to Britain for the auctions then back to Australia again.

One night at dinner she says, 'If only the pearlers here would co-operate with each other, stop undercutting, do more for themselves. There's not a single pearlshell button factory in the country yet that's where the big profits are. So short-sighted.'

I laugh. 'Yes, pig-headed, arrogant, short-sighted! That's Broome.

You'd think it has centuries of tradition behind it instead of a few brief decades in the north-west. I don't understand it either.'

'But surely it's the difference between being an adventurer and working in commerce?' says Gideon, carving the roast. 'Pearlers can be gentlemen, lords of their tiny fleets—but a factory, well that's quite another matter! Clerks, invoices, machines, warehouses. Appalling. Of course they'd rather relax and leave the Japs do all the hard work.'

Min-lu blinks and looks away. 'Then they're fools.'

Autumn turns to winter. After a brisk walk one evening with Peter and Eliza, I come into the sitting room and rush to the fireside.

'I'm frozen—such a wind out there tonight. Good heavens, champagne!'

'We've been waiting for you, Lucy. We have some wonderful news,' says Gideon.

'Three lots of wonderful news really,' says Rosa.

Min-lu stands and shakes coal onto the fire, jabbing it with the poker.

Gideon pours the champagne and hands it around. 'Our first lot of news is that probate on the estate was settled last week. The second is that I've been offered a promotion.' He smiles at Rosa. 'That led me to aspire to the third—to risk all! I have asked Rosa to be my wife and she, brave woman, has agreed to it. A toast to her fortitude.'

'A toast to you both. Lovely news.'

I can see Min-lu, straight-backed, unsmiling, from the corner of my eye.

'And your promotion, Gideon?'

He straightens his shoulders. 'The Fremantle to London run, the flagship vessel on the prime schedule. No more cattle and lumber, first class luxury instead.'

'Congratulations!'

'But you haven't given Lucy all the news yet, Gideon,' says Min-lu. 'Tell her what you told me earlier.' Her hands are clasped in her lap, her face controlled.

'Indeed. Regarding the estate,' says Gideon. 'Naturally, Rosa must rationalise her assets now, liquidate some investments, capitalise on others. Her new life will have different priorities—she'll be absent from this country for long periods.'

'Yes ...'

'Well. This means we've decided the shell-fishing business is no longer a suitable investment. Lee and Co. is being terminated and the assets sold. We'll get an excellent return.'

'Terminated? Assets?'

Rosa says, 'The boats, Lucy. I'm sorry but I can't run a business from a steamer on the England run. There are better investments available.'

'The boats? What about my *Sparrow*? You were to sign the transfer once probate was settled—you've done that of course, Rosa, you've done that—'

I stare from Rosa to Gideon, my scalp prickling.

'Lucy,' says Gideon. 'Rosa and I have discussed this and what I'm about to say is purely for your own good. You must give up this nonsense. You need to settle down, have a family. We cannot let you throw your life away so casually—'

'Sam gave me that lugger. It's *mine*.' My heart is pounding.

'Lucy, he was simply humouring you,' says Rosa.

'That's not true!'

'The point is, you do not own it legally,' says Gideon, glancing at Rosa. 'However, we did appreciate you might find this painful and decided, in the light of your informal agreement with Sam, that the sum the boat fetched should go into your own bank account for you to spend on whatever you desire.'

'I desire to have my *lugger*!'

'Not possible, I'm afraid. The company's been closed, the boats put on the market. Most have been snapped up already.'

'*Sparrow*?' I whisper.

'Eight hundred pounds, Lucy,' says Rosa. 'An excellent price. I'm sorry, I know this is painful but I'd never have agreed if I didn't think it was truly the best for you.'

'Rosa, how *dare* you—' I stop. I take a breath and say, 'What about Papa? He was so enjoying ... and Danny, what will happen to Danny?'

Gideon sips his champagne. 'We've had an exchange of telegrams. He understands the situation and he'll have no difficulty finding another job. I shall naturally give him a good reference.'

'But he was happy doing *this* job—' my voice shakes.

I stand and leave the room before I weep in front of that despicable man.

I rise late the following day, my eyes swollen, my head aching. I find Min-lu in the morning room.

'Min-lu, what should I do? I cannot think.'

'I'm so sorry, my dear. I had no idea he'd stoop to this. I knew he wanted Rosa but now he wants her assets too. Assets built up by my poor Sam.'

'You know, I've misread him so often. When he was careless, as with Papa and Bao-lim, I thought him wicked. But when he's been truly cruel—hurting Mrs O'Brien, seducing Cristina and now *this* —I thought him merely pompous. I've been so blind.'

'You mention Cristina. I've heard it was he who encouraged her drug-taking, not her theatrical friends,' says Min-lu. 'She was completely addicted when she left him.'

I look up. 'Poor Cristina. His favourite curse on a woman was to wish her opium-raddled and a harlot, yet she was neither until Gideon met her.'

'And now this dreadful man is to marry your sister and be father to my grandchildren.'

'Perhaps Papa ...?' I say.

'Gideon spoke to him in Broome and he has already agreed. It was Gideon's idea in the first place to separate you from your lugger, to protect you, he says. Emilia loathes him, as you may well imagine, but he persuaded even her.'

I'm silent. Then I ask, 'And did ... did Danny know too?'

'No. He'd never have gone along with it. Oh my dear—'

I wipe my eyes and say, 'Perhaps if we explain things to Rosa?'

'She'd think us merely bitter. No. She has made her choice looking to her future, and her wilful heart and passionate nature have already compromised her. Everyone in Perth knows what's between them—he made certain with great subtlety that they did.'

Min-lu's eyes are bright. 'But here is something Gideon does not know. Sam's estate is more complex than his lawyers assume.' She smiles. 'I made absolutely certain of that. He may find the spoils not quite as accessible as he'd hoped.'

She sits and takes my hand. 'This is what we shall do, Lucy. We shall bide our time and smile as falsely as Gideon. Since we cannot prevent it we shall bless their wedding and they will sail away for six months.'

'And then?'

'We will make certain we escape from his grasp, so he can never hurt you again like this.'

My smile fades. 'But while he has Rosa and the children we shall never escape his grasp.'

Emilia sends me a photograph of Liam, round-cheeked and laughing, but I hear nothing at all from Danny. Papa writes, saying he agreed with Gideon it might be better for me to be separated from my lugger (oh, Papa, how could you?) and was exceedingly happy my sister would find marital joy once again: but he'd never imagined for a moment the whole company might be sold. He was so very, very sorry.

I try but I cannot hide my bitterness. Then one day, as I'm feeling for a stray earring in my jewellery box, my fingers touch the small oval pearlshell incised with the lines of a lugger that Sam gave me long ago, and an idea comes to me.

I withdraw five pounds from my bank account (thank you *Sparrow*) and go to see a jeweller. He fashions the pearlshell into an iridescent pendant, lined on the rim and in the grooves with rose gold.

I wear it to dinner and Gideon says, 'Good Lord, one of those Binghi shells. Doesn't look like a real boat though, just the idea of one!'

'I think that's why I like it.'

'It's exquisite, Lucy,' says Min-lu. 'Wherever did you get it?'

'From Sam, soon after I first went to Broome. Remember, Rosa, when we went out on *Mudlark* for a picnic at Willie Creek?'

Rosa pauses then says, 'I remember. Wasn't that the time Danny bit your head off for not being able to mind your own business?'

She folds her napkin, stands and leaves the room. I glance at Min-lu then follow, catching up with her at the end of the hall.

'I'm sorry Rosa, I didn't mean to upset you.'

'It's not me you're upsetting. How do you think Gideon feels? You never stop reminding us of Sam! I'm trying to make a new life, Lucy, for the sake of the children. Dear God, I loved Sam completely, but Gideon's a fine man and he's been loyal to me for years. I'm trying to do what's best for us all.'

'But what Gideon got you to do wasn't best for all of us! You let him hurt Papa, Min-lu, me! And you call him *fine*? Have you forgotten poor Cristina so quickly?'

'Cristina got herself into trouble long before Gideon! And how can I make my way in the world without a man by my side? You're a cold, hard girl, Lucy.'

'I'm not cold, I just don't fall into bed with every—'

Rosa flinches, her hand over her mouth. I throw my arms around her and say, 'I'm so sorry.'

'I'm sorry too,' she says, tears in her eyes. 'I'm sorry about your boat, but I've got to think of the future now.'

'I want you to be happy, Rosa, and yes, Gideon can be a fine man —but sometimes he's not, and I'm afraid he'll hurt you.'

She draws back and looks at me. 'I understand him, Lucy. The children need a father and I believe we can be content.' She takes a deep breath. 'Come now, let's go back to dinner.'

She pauses and touches my pearlshell pendant. 'It shocked me to see it again, but it truly is beautiful. I'm glad you have it.'

One night, aroused by quiet footsteps and murmurs in the hall, I turn over in bed and think bitterly, why does everyone else in the world except me seem to enjoy sweet romances?

But I know the answer: I yearn for a life no sane woman would ever contemplate, and I'm not feminine or dainty or desirable. Why should any man want me? Even Danny, my dearest Danny, does not.

Then at last a letter arrives from him, and it offers the first comfort I've known for many months.

Don't take it too hard, girl, I knew the business was on borrowed time. I don't need to tell you to be careful and watch out for Gideon—he's slyer than even I'd given him credit for.

He'll probably treat Rosa well enough, but he's got little regard for anyone else. However he justifies it, there's not many in Broome think much of what he did with Sparrow.

You'll rest easier I hope knowing it was Captain Gregory who bought her. He's a good man with luggers, although I think the colour of the trim's got him worried.

Well, the news is I'm leaving Broome next week. Harold Browne got me a job in Newcastle, NSW, as owner's agent for several companies. Liam will stay with Emilia and your father.

I don't know what to write about the last time we met. I've felt every kind of fool since then, and wish I could go back and fix things up. Look after yourself, Lucy. Your friend, Danny Whalen.

That night I lie awake wondering what it was he wants to fix. Then I realise that soon we'll be thousands of miles apart and I'll never know.

16. RETURN TO BROOME

On Gideon and Rosa's wedding day, Min-lu and I smile as falsely as we'd planned. Filipa and Izabel and little Peter enjoy themselves but Eliza is quiet, and Rosa says she's gone to bed with a stomach-ache.

The reception is held in the saloon of Gideon's new command, due to leave for London that evening. The best man makes jokes which seem to please everyone, about battleships and the noble Empire and the foolish Kaiser.

The papers have been full of news lately about wars in places with odd names like Servia and Montenegro and Roumania, and over the wedding breakfast I ask the best man his opinion of the Balkans.

Before he can say anything Gideon interrupts, laughing. 'Those squabbles are nothing, but war between the great powers may yet arrive and by God, *let* it. The British Empire will not tolerate a rival for mastery of the high seas. Still, there's no need to concern yourself, Lucy, our ships are perfectly safe. Civilian vessels will never be a target.'

Finally I stand with Min-lu and her daughters on the wharf and wave to Rosa and Peter on the first-class deck. Eliza is in her cabin, although I slip away for a few minutes to kiss her goodbye, and Gideon is in all his glory on the bridge.

In the carriage on the way home Min-lu says slowly, 'Barely twenty months since *Koombana*. Rosa is—fortunate—to be able to put it behind her so quickly. You know, last year I thought I could not bear to visit Broome, where Sam was so happy. But now? Now

I believe it's where I would most like to be.'

'What about the girls?'

'Filipa will soon start boarding school here, but I think Izabel would enjoy the experience. Don't you wish to return too?'

'Of course! But I'll be lost. No Rosa, no children, no work, no luggers.'

'Not necessarily. I've decided Pearlshell Ltd should open a branch in Broome.' Min-lu's eyes sparkle. 'I imagine it will need a manager —someone who really knows the trade.'

We're almost there. The green and red shoreline is dotted with small white buildings, the air is soft and hazy, the turquoise sea vivid, astonishing, familiar. It's the end of the year so most of the luggers will soon come home for the lay-up.

Just a few are drawn up on the sand: is one of them *Sparrow*? Or is she floating at the Lacepedes or somewhere off the Ninety-Mile?

'That's the town and Dampier Creek along to the right—see all the mangroves?' I tell Min-lu, 'and there, the foreshore near that red bluff halfway to the town, that's where Sam's camp is ... was. I don't know who has the lease now.'

Papa and Emilia meet us on the jetty. Papa carries Liam on his shoulders and Izabel says, 'Oh, the pretty child! Is that Liam?'

'Yes, that's our darling.' I reach for the little boy and cuddle him, then put him down to let Izabel take his hand. 'He's grown so much, Emilia,' I say. 'And you both look well.'

A deep voice calls my name and I turn.

'Oh, *Alain*!' He takes my hand and kisses it.

Emilia says teasingly, 'Ah, we knew Monsieur Bourdon would return to Broome eventually. Who could stay away from such attractions?'

Papa shakes Min-lu's hand affectionately—they've known each other since Melbourne days—and Emilia, an old friend, hugs her. As Alain is introduced to Min-lu I think, heavens, he's twenty-six now, still slim and quickly-spoken, his dark eyes creasing in laughter, his lithe brown hands just as I remember. My face goes warm.

Alain helps Papa load our luggage onto the steam-tram and promises to visit when we're settled in. The whistle sounds and the tram trundles along the jetty, then turns at the shore and rattles slowly along the tracks.

It stops part-way into town so we can disembark near Sam and Rosa's old house, although now it's where Papa and Emilia and Liam live. I recall Sam telling me Broome's White Quarter was as far away as it could get from Japtown. 'We live more-or-less between the two,' he'd said, sharing a wry smile with Rosa.

And it's true. Ever since half-Chinese Sam entered our lives and Rosa flung all wisdom and propriety to the winds and eloped with him, our whole family has been living more-or-less between two worlds. But I wouldn't have changed it for *anything*.

To have known Sam himself, to have found Min-lu after losing Mama, to have learnt and felt and enjoyed so much: it's all been worth it.

Home again. I lean on the veranda railing and look at the evening sky and smile. And how good to see Alain again too.

Min-lu rents a small office on Dampier Terrace and lets it be known that Pearlshell Ltd is in the market for select parcels of jewellery-grade pearlshell.

In the first few weeks we receive a steady stream of callers curious to meet Sam's mother, happy to welcome me back and eager to offer their opinion on Gideon's deviousness.

One day Thomas the Islander comes to visit, looming at the door of the office, hat in his hands.

'Thomas, how wonderful to see you!'

'Welcome back, Miss Lucy,' he says shyly. 'Sorry to hear Captain Lee's business closed down.'

'Do you have another job now?'

'I got work with Streeters. But their boats not as good as Captain

Lee's.'

'And Borue?'

'He still with *Sparrow*, working for Gregory now. We glad you back, Missy.'

'Oh, Thomas. I can't tell you how happy I am to be back.'

Captain Gregory drops in one day, tanned and handsome. He expresses his condolences on Sam's loss with a kindness that so touches Min-lu she goes to recover in the little kitchen at the rear of the office.

'And my *Sparrow*? You're treating her well?' I ask.

'Without question, *cariad*! And what a fine vessel she is. Though the trim needed a touch-up, of course.'

'What colour?'

'A dark red—Egawa-san was very pleased.'

'I'm glad somebody was.'

'Now then. It's better she comes to me than to someone who doesn't look after their luggers.'

'I agree, but I'm warning you Greg, one day I want her back.'

'You'll have first refusal, I promise.' His dark eyes are alight with mischief. 'So did you hear about the ruffled feathers on the council, then?'

'Arguing about who's on and off the electoral roll?'

'Oh, even better than that. Last night the ratepayers voted to dismiss the whole sorry lot of them!'

'My goodness. What will happen?'

'Sly prevarication until the elections I suspect—the council's not so easily outmanoeuvred. But I'm thinking myself of sticking them a bit of ginger.'

'Oh, Greg. You're going to stand for election? They won't know what's hit them.'

'I do like a challenge, Admiral Fox. Time for a change. Wouldn't that make a good headline?'

Min-lu rents a house near ours and Izabel starts making friends at the small convent school. Min-lu and Emilia and Papa enjoy each other's company, and Min-lu grows fond of gentle Liam, now almost two and a half years old.

Alain becomes a regular visitor to our house. When he first takes my hand and draws me close, the familiar pleasure begins, but then I'm surprised at how shy I suddenly feel.

'So much has happened, Alain. I need time to get to know you again.'

He kisses the top of my head. 'I understand, *chérie*. Now I am back I shall court you properly.'

A few days later I'm at Min-lu's house, helping her try a new hairstyle from a Paris journal. Sunlight streams over the lace of her bedspread as I weave gold combs into her glossy hair.

'There,' I say. 'Oh, that does suit you.'

Min-lu looks critically left and right in the mirror and smiles. 'That's very nice, Lucy, thank you.'

'I love your combs. You've worn them as long as I've known you.'

'Leo Peres gave me those. A set when each of the girls was born.'

'You must miss him, and miss being married too.' I sit down on the bed.

'I've had other men friends over the years, Lucy. Don't you remember that handsome silver-haired man in Melbourne?'

'I thought he was your lawyer!'

'Well he was at first.'

I laugh then say, 'But if you loved each other, why—?'

'He was already married to a wealthy invalid. He'd never leave her and I'm not certain, after the first few dizzy months, whether I'd have wanted him to anyway.'

'Oh.'

'Society can be so unkind to young women.' Min-lu says thoughtfully. 'Yet it's the mature women, widows like myself, who threaten propriety more than foolish young girls. We know what love is, we wish to be close to a man and we know how to prevent babies.'

'You know how to *prevent* babies?'

'After I had Sam I learnt from the old ladies in Hong Kong, and then told Rosa the herbs and practices to use too. Such methods are not infallible of course, but at least no modern woman needs have a baby every year unless she so wishes.'

'It would be terrible to be unmarried and in child. Perhaps that's why I feel restrained with Alain.'

'You're very wise to be restrained. That is not a situation I would wish upon any woman.' Min-lu gazes at me. 'But perhaps fear of the consequences is not the reason. It occurs to me—how do you feel about being here, now, without Danny?'

After a pause I say, 'I don't know. Even if he were here, I fear he wouldn't want me.'

'It takes courage to risk yourself in love, Lucy, and you may pay dearly for it, but you must not be afraid. Life is too short.'

I often wake before sunrise and go into town before the heat grows intense. One morning while it's barely light I round the corner and almost trip over two people sitting on the bench outside the office.

'Murakami-san! Theresa?'

Theresa, clearly pregnant, is crying and Mr Murakami's arm is around her shoulders.

'Please, let me get you some tea.'

When I return with tea and cups on a tray Theresa has wiped her eyes. I pour the tea and we sip in silence as the sky grows pink over the bay before us.

Theresa takes a deep breath. 'I'm sailing to Japan this evening. I've never been there before and I'm a little afraid. I'm going to live with Yasukichi's family for a time.'

'They will take care of Theresa and one day we will marry,' Murakami says.

'Are you travelling alone?' I say.

'A friend of my mother's is coming with me. I must leave Broome. My parents—and Mrs Nishioka—are furious.'

'Theresa, if there's anything I can do to help—'

'Thank you.' She hands me the cup and says, 'You're not shocked, Lucy?'

'No, I think you're very brave, much braver than me.'

The new year of 1914 begins and as usual the rains pours down. I watch this year's departure of the fleet from the veranda in front of the office. I see Sparrow in the distance with Gregory's boats and for a moment my eyes sting.

Alain and I spend time together—carriage rides to Cable Beach, the Roebuck Stadium Pictures—and I enjoy his kisses but still keep my distance. I can tell he's disappointed but I feel confused and do not know what to say. I try not to think about Danny.

Captain Gregory is elected to the council and noisy arguments become the staple topic of the local paper; probably because there's not much else happening except the usual incomprehensible to and fro in the Balkans.

It is Emilia who first realises something is wrong with Liam. He's hot and very quiet, and soon a grey patch forms on the side of his throat, the mark of the *strangling angel*—diphtheria.

After three days he's limp and pale, and I can see how swollen his neck is. The doctor simply shrugs. Children either recover or they don't.

I feel frantic with anxiety, then suddenly think of clever Dr Suzuki. I drive the carriage into town and find him at his rooms.

'I have samples of new antitoxin from Japanese laboratory,' he says. 'Not approved by Health Department but I believe effective. Risky, of course.'

'I'd prefer risk to no hope at all. Please help us!'

He packs his medical bag and we quickly drive back.

'Oh thank God, thank God!' sobs Emilia as we enter. 'He's blue, he can't breathe!'

Dr Suzuki examines him. 'Must perform tracheotomy, now.

Please bring boiled water.'

He wipes Liam's throat with cotton wool dampened with disinfectant from a bottle in his bag.

'Hold his arms please, Miss Fox, he may move.'

I stand on the other side of the bed and hold the limp body. The doctor picks up a scalpel, wipes it with the moist cotton wool and cuts into Liam's swollen neck. He inserts a rubber tube and the boy's chest lifts convulsively as air gurgles into his lungs. His cheeks flush with pink.

'Hold him still, Miss Fox, while I prepare antitoxin.'

He injects the fluid deep into the child's thigh, then returns to work on his throat. I help him fix the tube into place with a bandage and wipe the blood away.

'Still very ill, you understand,' says Dr Suzuki. 'Antitoxin works quickly and some danger will pass, but perhaps more to come. Once throat opens up I will remove tube and he may have fluids. Please nurse him carefully. Miss Fox, you are contagious now, so you must stay at home.'

'Papa will drive you back into town, Dr Suzuki. Thank you, I cannot tell you—'

He gazes at me with his steady brown eyes. 'You are good nurse, Miss Fox. I remember with your sister's baby, no fuss, very careful. Thank you too.'

I spend nights awake by Liam's bed. I watch his small face against the pillow, his red-brown curls and strong brows, his long-lashed eyelids flickering as he dreams.

I can see the traces of his mother's ancestry and sometimes feel a pang of fear for him. Will that remote ogre the Protector have any claim on him, the great-grandson of an Aboriginal woman?

Gradually the crisis passes. One evening I'm sitting beside Liam's bed sewing a small shirt for him, when I hear footsteps on the shell grit path outside, coming up onto the veranda.

Liam whispers, 'Papa.'

'Papa's in the kitchen, I think.'

'*My* Papa.'

I look up and Danny is standing in the doorway. He says slowly, 'You always did say you'd look after him, rigged for sail or not.'

When I can speak I say, 'How did you know to come?'

'Your father sent a telegram. He said my place is here with the boy, although we both know how fast—' He pauses. 'Caught the first steamer back. It's been a long couple of weeks.'

He's exhausted. I say, 'Sit with Liam while I get you some food.'

As I pass him he touches my shoulder and I stop, gazing down. All I want to do is breathe the scent of his skin.

He says quietly, 'I won't be going away again.'

At breakfast a few weeks later Min-lu asks, 'When does Danny take command of *Gemstone*?'

'Tomorrow. I'm so glad he's back where he needs to be.'

'Master of a ship or in Broome?'

I smile. 'Both.'

'And have you had a good talk yet?'

My smile fades. 'No, and I wonder if we ever will. We never seem to know what to say, we're suddenly so wary. I don't understand it.'

'You've both suffered a great deal—wariness is not surprising. Have courage, my dear.'

Liam recovers. Danny comes to see him at bedtime and usually stays with us for dinner. Papa calls him Captain Whalen and we talk about his new job as master of *Gemstone*, an eighty-ton supply schooner. Thomas the Islander is sailing as the mate and Danny is so quietly pleased about it my heart ache with joy for him.

One night Papa and Emilia say they're tired and withdraw earlier than usual. Min-lu remains sitting with us on the veranda for a few minutes, then unexpectedly says good-night and leaves too. I look after her in surprise.

After a silence, Danny turns to me, light glinting from his earring. 'I hear Gideon and Rosa'll be back in Perth soon.'

'Oh. Yes. Heavens, it's been seven months since Min-lu and I returned to Broome, so I expect it's time they ...'

Oh, what a blithering fool I am. Have courage, say it.

'Danny, when you wrote, you said you wished you could go back and fix things up. What did you mean? What would you fix?'

He stands and walks to the railing. After a time he takes a deep breath and turns to me.

'You know I've got nothing to offer you, girl. You should marry a rich lad like Alain, I'm just a sailor, and not for you. I can't change that, but I just couldn't bear you thinking I didn't want you then, in every way possible—' He rubs his forehead. 'Jesus. Talking out of turn again.'

'I'm a woman of twenty-three now, hardly that naive child you once knew.'

He smiles. 'I remember, up the foremast. Christ, I was terrified. And the accident, your hair all cut off—'

'Like your monkey—'

'The monkey would've had the good sense to stay out of a hurricane.'

'I just wanted to *see*!'

'So you did.' He sighs. 'Ah, Lucy, so you always did.'

I stand and walk to him. 'But my hair has grown now. Look.'

One by one I remove the pins that restrain my waves, and let them drop to the floorboards. I run my fingers through the coil to loosen it as we gaze at each other. I put my hands on his chest and his heart is pounding.

'You see, Danny, you can't just decide all by yourself you're not for me. It's too late for that.'

He shakes his head. 'Sweet, you don't know what you're—'

I touch his lips. 'Shh. I want to be brave now.'

He kisses my fingers and sighs, then wraps his arms around me and buries his face in my hair. I laugh with joy.

As if on a perfectly respectable stroll in the mild autumn evening, we walk to his lodgings, two quiet rooms just a block away. In the candlelight I tremble as he unbuttons my dress, and then I become bold and help him take off his shirt.

Now I can smell him and feel him, and whatever else we are wearing becomes simply an obstacle to be discarded to allow touch and texture and pressure and pleasure. Such pleasure.

And then, at last, the world once more becomes still and perfect and utterly focused.

Nestled in the crook of his arm I murmur against his shoulder, 'I never imagined it could be like this. Now I understand why people take such risks.'

'Well, it's not always quite this amazing, sweetheart,' says Danny, his eyes glimmering with happiness. He kisses my neck and I run my fingers—my newly-educated fingers—slowly down the length of his spine.

He gasps, and laughs quietly. 'And whether I'm for you or not, I'm far beyond caring. Nothing now could keep me from the skipper's daughter.'

I smile and murmur and caress his hair, his face, his shoulders. His lips find the curve of my breast and his hand eases between my thighs, gently, rhythmically, insistently. I sigh and shift and move my hips to meet his.

He lifts his head and whispers my name and brings his mouth down to mine. Again.

Danny is away on *Gemstone* for a week at a time, but when he's back I go to him at his lodgings, slipping out at midnight and returning just before dawn. I am noticed of course, but this is Broome and anyone else awake then has secrets of their own to keep.

We return to the easy give-and-take of playing music together. We plan to marry at the end of the year and he gives me an engagement ring set with a sea-green emerald. I cannot stop myself admiring it.

The local paper reports coyly, *Our young Lady Pearler has finally found her Master.*

Apart from us, the most newsworthy items lately have been rumours of rivals for the position of Mayor (including Captain Gregory) the loss of two unnamed Asians in a storm off the Ninety-Mile, and the finding of 'several nice stones' by a local lady pearler. (I notice Miss Withers looking rather pleased with herself at the bank.)

The diving-suit maker Heinke donates a decompression chamber to the hospital. The council announces another inquiry into the ramshackle jetty and calls for tenders to repair the roads. The deadline for replacing Asian divers with whites is pushed back to 1918: a most sensible decision, everyone agrees.

The only crisis worthy of mention is that of Home Rule for Ireland: the King urges compromise and a spirit of generosity. Danny almost falls off his chair laughing.

Gemstone supplies fresh water and stores to the luggers working hundreds of miles out of Broome, and on one trip Danny takes Liam with him.

The boy comes home chattering of shells and diving suits, then spends hours drawing lopsided ships in wave-torn seas, with spiky Danny-figures at their helms.

We talk about setting up a boatyard after we're married. With some assistance from Min-lu we'd have enough capital, but there's no need to hurry. In the scented nights we hold each other, caressing, murmuring, drunk with pleasure, content beyond understanding.

How could we have imagined how brief this moment would be?

17. CULARDOCH

I see a small article, *Heir to Austria-Hungary Throne Shot,* and think, why do things like that always seem to happen in places with silly names like Servia? I don't pay much attention to the weeks of dull pronouncements that follow, but suddenly great Austria has invaded little Servia, massive Russia has mobilised, war-mad Germany has also mobilised, and the headlines are looming black with ultimatums.

'*If Austria goes beyond a certain point Russia must invade Galicia,*' I read aloud at the breakfast table. 'Where's Galicia? Why must Russia invade it?'

'Christ knows,' says Danny.

'*With Roumania attacking Austria next door*—what's Roumania got to do with it?—*then Germany would violently attack France in the hope of profiting by Russia's slow mobilisation; finally the British fleet might make a swift dash to annihilate the German fleet.*'

I put down the paper, shaking my head. 'What on earth are they talking about, Danny?'

'The war they've been itching to have for years, sweetheart, and it looks as if they've got what they wanted at last.' His face is grim.

Within a week in August 1914—a single week!—Europe has collapsed into war. The local newspaper roars, *Let encouragement to the weak and defiance to the tyrants be emblazoned upon your brow!* The Broome lads rush away to Perth to enlist, convinced if they don't get a hurry-on it'll all be over before they get there.

Towns whose names no one can pronounce become famous as

battlefronts. Skirmishes take place between tens of soldiers, then hundreds, then thousands. One day a cable from Alsace reports thirty thousand casualties. I'm convinced it must be a misprint but no correction follows.

'*The necessary retirement was executed with precision and was a complete success.* What's a necessary retirement?' I peer at the print in the lamplight.

'A retreat,' says Danny. 'A nice successful one.'

'But they mean the Allies, not the Germans, and the French have moved their government to Bordeaux. How can it possibly all be over by Christmas?'

'It can't,' he says quietly.

People gather outside the post office and in the pubs and cafes, talking and waving their hands. Papa sticks a map on the wall and uses coloured pins to mark the lumbering choreography of armies.

Obscure placenames become synonyms for disaster, and the name *Ypres* appears for the first time in the newspaper. 'Wipers?' says Papa and Alain gently corrects him.

'My cousin was killed last month at Amiens,' Alain tells me. 'I tried to enlist once but I was rejected as I have a small deformity of the foot. My father insists I should stay here to keep the business going, and I do not know what to do.'

'They're taking only the fittest, Alain,' I say, 'so you'd still be rejected if you went home. But if it all goes on for, God forbid, another year, then perhaps you can think again.'

'Another year? Surely not. They say the breakthrough will happen any day now.' He sighs. 'You understand, Lucy, when you and Danny ... It pained me greatly, but please know I will always be your friend and protect you honourably when he goes away—'

'He's not going away!' My throat is tight. 'Danny's a Master in Sail, he knows nothing of battleships. And he's too old now to return to the foc's'le deck. He's not going away.'

'I'm only thirty-two, girl,' says Danny, stroking my mouth with his thumb. 'Prime of my life. And a war's not all dreadnoughts and destroyers, you know. Coal and grain's got to be carried too, and that's just the job for square-riggers.'

He's silent for a moment. 'It might be my last chance ever to command a deepwater ship.'

I sit up and stare at him in horror. 'You've been thinking about this.'

'Of course I have. And I've already had a couple of letters from shipping firms, they're desperate for experienced men.'

The sheet slips down to my waist. Danny smiles and draws me closer. I pull away, then move back to fit myself against him. 'You said you wouldn't go away again, you *promised* me. We've had so little time, Danny. What would I do if ...' I'm silent then, but my tears trickle onto his shoulder.

'Lucy, it won't be this year or even next year it will end,' he says gently. 'Both sides are too well matched and there'll be none of those breakthroughs the papers keep talking about. The only thing will end it is if all of us do what we can.'

'Not you, my love. Not *you*.'

'If the sharks off the Amazon wouldn't eat me, sweet, I'd have to be pretty indestructible. Come here now.'

The offer of a command arrives suddenly and now there's no chance for us to marry. I take the steamer to Fremantle with Danny and on the jetty before we leave, unusually, small Liam cries. Danny holds him for a long time.

Thomas the Islander comes with us, saying he's not going to let Captain Danny go away to a new ship without him. In Perth we stay at the little house near the park with Rosa and Gideon.

Danny is fitted for his merchant captain's uniform and it suits him as if he's worn it all his life. The headlines are more terrible every day, and the only comfort is Danny's happiness, his great glowing happiness, in his ship.

She's called *Culardoch*, a steel four-masted barque launched a decade ago from the Glasgow slips and named for a Scottish mountain. She's twice the length and five times the capacity of *Willowmere*.

We have dinner at a fine restaurant one evening. Rosa looks marvellous in a satin gown and a diamond necklace Gideon bought her in London. I wear my peony-rose silk dress, with the pearlshell pendant and my emerald ring.

I'm introduced to Mr Pat Doyle at the dinner. He's to be first mate on *Culardoch* and is an old friend of Danny's—they apprenticed together out of Dublin as lads.

Pat Doyle is as stocky and dark as Danny is rangy and russet, and I watch them together, charmed by their banter and soft accents. With a small sense of relief I decide Mr Doyle will be someone Danny can rely upon.

Rosa is unusually quiet during the evening but Gideon fairly glitters with braid and good humour. As soon as war broke out out he joined the Royal Navy and now enjoys some sort of liaison job (hush-hush, he winks) with the Australian government.

He's devastated not to be at sea he says, but will rest easy knowing that men like Danny and Pat will be out there doing such a sterling job. I flinch, Pat's eyebrows rise, but Danny just looks at Gideon, shakes his head laughing and raises his glass.

'The best of luck to you too, shipmate,' he says dryly.

The days disappear as if in a nightmare. I buy Danny's kit and pack it while he goes to briefings. He supervises the preparation of the ship and gets to know his crew: it's another comfort to know Thomas the Islander has been appointed second mate.

Culardoch will load coal in Newcastle, New South Wales, sail to the Americas, then proceed around the Horn to Britain. No one is to know exactly where they're going and even Danny won't find out until they embark.

Today Danny is away at another briefing and, dry-mouthed in the heat, I stand at the dock watching as boxes of supplies are hoisted from railway trucks to men on the ship, then quickly stowed below.

In shirtsleeves and carrying a clipboard, stocky Pat Doyle greets me. 'Miss Fox, please come and have a cool drink below. If you're knocked over by a truck the skipper'll never forgive me.'

'I just want to see what's happening, I don't want to get in the way.'

'You'd never be in the way, I promise. Come now, you should be more comfortable.' He leads me up the gangplank and along the deck to the saloon at the stern of the ship, where he asks someone to bring us cordial.

The saloon is much larger than *Willowmere*'s old-fashioned quarters and we're silent for a moment as I gaze around us.

'You mustn't concern yourself, Miss Fox, we're a merchant ship, a square-rigger. This war isn't about vessels like *Culardoch*.'

'Oh, the Germans are aware of that?' I say tartly.

Mr Doyle smiles. 'I think so. Both sides want the glory of sinking battleships—what honour could there be in a barque with half the speed and none of the armaments?'

I sigh and sit down. A man brings us a tray with glasses and a carafe of lemonade.

Doyle offers me a drink. 'The word is that a few of the square-riggers have been stopped by the Germans but they always let them go on their way.' He pauses. 'Well, there was the one they blew up with time-bombs, but they got the crew off first.'

'That's supposed to reassure me?'

'Ah, you know what I mean,' he says with a grin. 'But I'll tell you now, I'll do whatever I can to look after Danny Whalen. I'm proud to be sailing with him.'

I look into his kind eyes and can see that he means it. I nod. 'Thank you, Mr Doyle.'

Danny returns a few minutes later. 'Good, you're both here,' he says, hanging his uniform coat on the back of a chair. He sits down and takes a long drink of lemonade.

'Skipper, I've just been begging Miss Fox here to throw you over and marry me,' says Mr Doyle, 'but she's quite the stubborn one.'

Danny smiles a little as he gazes at me. 'Oh Pat, that she is.'

'What's the news, Danny?' My throat is tight with fear.

His green eyes are gentle. 'Tomorrow, sweetheart.'

He looks up. 'Mr Doyle, tell the men. Loading to be complete and everyone aboard by 2200. We sail at dawn.'

The last night is upon us. We dine alone, not eating much, then go to bed. I can feel the tension in Danny's back, but he makes love to me as if we have all the time in the world. As my pleasure ebbs I find tears filling my eyes and hide my face against his shoulder.

He nuzzles the top of my head. 'If anything happens—you know —I want you to promise me you'll go on. Marry some other lucky bastard and have all those babies you want. Lucy? Promise me.'

I cannot speak.

'Lucy. Please.'

I take a ragged breath. 'I can't—'

'Promise me.'

'Very well, I'll go on. But, oh Danny, come *back*—'

'God willing, I shall.' He sits up and takes out his gold earring, puts it into my palm and closes my fingers over it. He says quietly, 'Mind this for me until then.'

He gets out of bed and begins to dress.

'I have to go now, sweetheart.' He tries to smile. 'If I stay the night I doubt I could ever leave and I'd be done for desertion before I've even sailed.'

I try to smile too. I watch him gather his last few belongings, check his pockets and go through a mental list with a far-away look.

Then he sits beside me on the bed and kisses me, and goes.

Early in the new year of 1915 I receive my first letter from Danny, posted from New South Wales.

> *Apart from a few rough moments in the Bight the trip to Newcastle went very well. Now we've loaded up the coal I've just got time for a few lines before we leave. We've seen good sailing so far.*
>
> *Culardoch handles like a dream and the crew are not a bad lot. To be master of such a vessel is hard work, but she's well-found and so lovely in sail I feel myself a lucky man. Still, I must be getting old—thoughts of what I've left behind haunt me too, sweetheart, day and night.*
>
> *Indeed, at Newcastle I met an old shipmate of ours, also now captain of a four-master—Mattias Nilsen, the Swedish lad. Pistols at dawn were on the cards at the news of our engagement, but still he wishes you joy (obviously puzzled at how that's possible with me).*

Dear Mattias, I think, remembering the boy from *Willowmere*. I smile at Danny's words, relieved to hear he's safe.

A diversion from my anxiety is the arrival in Perth of Alain Bourdon and Captain Gregory for a few days. Alain is here on business and Greg is on the way to Melbourne to visit the family of his new fiancée, Miss Villiers.

'I'm getting on now—thirty-six soon, can you believe it! Time to settle down. My mother's not well and my brother has rejoined his regiment. I must do my bit for the family, you know.' He shows me a photograph of a good-looking woman. 'I believe she's strong-willed enough to keep me on the straight and narrow,' he says almost shyly.

'Then I wish you both the greatest happiness,' I say, pleased for him.

We're at a restaurant with Alain and Rosa and Gideon, and Alain quietly tells me he's now become reconciled to staying in Broome, then a photographer comes to the table to take our group portrait to commemorate the evening. In wartime everyone wanted photographs taken, just in case.

When we receive the pictures a week later there's Alain and Greg, both dark and fine-looking, myself bright-eyed between them,

Gideon laughing heartily and Rosa, quiet beside him. I sigh. If only Danny could have been there with us too.

In a few months Gideon is leaving to work in Britain, but Rosa plans to stay here. I try to be cheerful for the childrens' sake and Peter is content enough, but I'm surprised at how subdued Eliza often seems. I ask Rosa if Eliza is unhappy because Gideon is going away.

I'm startled by her laugh. 'I doubt it.'

I begin to notice the strain between Rosa and Gideon. That night at the restaurant her wrist was bruised beneath the evening bracelet she wore, although I'd thought little of it then. Now I notice another blue mark on my sister's jaw, half-covered by her hair.

I ask her to walk with me in the park and we sit on a bench beneath the trees at the river's edge.

Rosa says, 'You're examining me again, Lucy.'

'Last time you said that you were pregnant.'

'Well, I'm certainly not pregnant now and unlikely to ever be.' Rosa laughs bleakly. 'I've made my bed as they say, but at least I'll bear no children in it.'

'Things are—difficult—with Gideon?'

She pauses for a few moments then sighs. 'It started in London after the wedding. One night at Covent Garden we met Cristina with her latest Count or Duke or God knows what.'

'Heavens. Wasn't that embarrassing?'

'Only to me. Gideon and Cristina seemed to much enjoy the encounter—and others, I've every reason to believe took place later. But Gideon does not feel I have any right to dislike the situation. So.'

'But Rosa, you have *bruises*.'

'It's better it's me he punishes.'

'*Eliza*?' But she's just a child!'

Her mouth is bitter. 'He punishes any female he believes slights him.'

'You're as transparent as a window, Lucy,' Gideon says. He leans on the mantelpiece, looking at me in irritation. 'I suppose Rosa's been complaining. I'm not that bad, you know.'

'Sometimes a person may be evil without thinking they are.'

'Well of course.' He looks puzzled, then bursts into laughter. 'Oh come now, you don't mean you think I'm evil? A raised hand is hardly *murder*. Most men would behave exactly as I do.'

He is sadly correct.

He continues, 'I have occasionally slapped Rosa in sheer exasperation. And of course I chastise the children when they're naughty, as is my duty.'

'Why do you chastise only Eliza?'

His eyebrows rise in astonishment. 'Because she's the only one who requires it, you foolish girl. Lucy, you seem to be under the impression you have some right to stand in judgement upon me.'

'Can I not make my own—'

'You seem to believe it was you who forgave me, you who returned me to the fold. Have you ever considered that I gave my good name to your sister despite your shameless public eccentricities?'

I stare at him, astonished.

'I've proffered the hand of friendship, Lucy, over and over. I've accepted much from you I'd accept from no one else. In your own way you've been very dear to me.'

He walks to a picture on the wall and adjusts it, then turns to me.

'I told you once I do not forget easily but I suspect you did not quite take my meaning. I also forgive with great difficulty.'

There is a long silence.

'I did not intend to hurt you,' I say carefully.

Another long silence, then Gideon sits down and sighs. 'Oh Lord, I don't know, Lucy, I have such a temper. You've only heard Rosa's side of the story of course, and judged me accordingly. Would you not also hear mine?'

'Very well.'

He rubs his lip. 'I thought to ask Cristina to write me a letter, a letter stating Liam was truly Danny's. I know how much that odd child means to you all, and I've heard the Protector is considering a new restriction—without written proof of parentage any part-Aboriginal would be deemed full-blooded.'

'That's ridiculous. I don't believe you.'

'Lucy!'

'Oh, Lord. I find it difficult to believe—is that better?'

'Yes, much.'

'But is it true?'

'Well, in one move the Protector would give himself enormous powers over the North-West, so why not? He's an ambitious man. But you understand, of course, Liam could be taken and sent to a mission orphanage. God knows, his mother is never returning to him.'

'And did she give you the letter?'

A small smile comes to Gideon's lips. 'After some persuasion, yes she did. Whatever happens, Liam is safe.'

'I suppose that puts things in rather a different light.'

'Rosa simply does not believe me although I've tried—well, perhaps some day. But ...'

'Gideon?'

'I am truly sorry, Lucy,' he says sincerely. 'All I've done was with your best interests at heart. You've been a good friend and I find your eccentricity almost—endearing. And I do respect your ambition, no matter how unladylike it may be.'

It's been a pleasant evening, easing the small dread that's always with me now. We dine at a good restaurant and laugh at a comic operetta. Rosa seems happier and Gideon has some surprisingly thoughtful words on the progress of the war.

So it's all the more shocking find the house in a shambles on our return: a downstairs window forced open, curtains billowing in the breeze. I dash upstairs to my room, then sit heavily on the bed. It's too much, too *much*.

My jewellery box lies smashed and scattered at my feet. Thank God my pearl earrings are safe in the bank vault, but all my other precious things are gone: the garnet and seedpearl set, my moonstone necklet, Danny's gold earring, my pearlshell pendant from Sam. All gone.

Then I grow cold with horror. Lately I've become thin and my emerald engagement ring loose, so this evening I'd left it at home. I fall on my knees and scrabble in the pieces of the box. No, no, not *that*!

I sit back against the side of the bed and cover my face and weep.

After a time I hear Gideon's raised voice. I wipe my eyes and go downstairs. 'My port,' he says, rubbing his face in disbelief. 'My thirty-year old port from the Admiral—gone. My gold cigarette case, my ruby tiepin. Gone. The *scoundrels*—'

Rosa sits stunned, her empty jewellery box open on her lap. Her diamond necklace and a string of pearls Sam gave her have been stolen too. She'd taken them out of the vault for occasions in honour of Gideon's imminent departure for Britain.

I know how much Sam's pearls mean to her and there are tears on her cheeks. Eliza and Peter and their nanny have awoken in the hubbub and the children are clinging wide-eyed to Rosa.

Two policemen arrive but they offer little hope. They stand outside the open window and shine a torch on a tangle of footprints in the muddy earth.

'Can't you take an impression and match it to the shoes of the suspects?' I ask desperately.

One policeman says, 'You've been reading those Sherlock Holmes books, miss. Doesn't happen in real life. And we don't have any suspects, apart from every petty thief in every pub in Perth—'

The other policemen harumphs and the first one goes quiet and shines his torch around busily. He bends and triumphantly lifts up something clotted with mud, dangling from a chain. I gasp: it's my pearlshell pendant, filthy but intact.

'That's nothing,' says Gideon. 'Pity it's not the diamonds. Oh God, sorry, Lucy.' He rattles the window and says, 'I just don't understand it. This window has two good locks, it simply cannot have been forced.'

'Looks like they were left open,' says the talkative policeman.

'That's not possible,' says Gideon, 'unless someone in the house —' he stops and looks around, frowning. 'I shall speak to the servants. Thank you for attending, constables.'

It becomes obvious it was the nanny who left the window unlocked. She protests her innocence, but we all know how she likes to lean out to flirt with the groom. She is dismissed and the insurance company is generous, but that does not bring back our precious things.

I clean my pendant and put it away. My left hand aches at the absence of Danny's ring.

Gideon is changed after the robbery. He seems almost vulnerable and drinks more than usual. He's soon to leave on a steamship for London but cannot stop reading the newspaper listings of battles and casualties and sinkings. Especially sinkings.

One night we're sitting in the drawing room and he puts down the paper, shaking his head.

'Drowning, Lucy. So many years a sailor yet all I can think about is drowning. It's my greatest fear. I have no idea how Danny survived that wreck and even went back to sea.'

'It took him some time to come to terms with,' I say cautiously. I'm still unused to a Gideon who admits to the slightest chink in his armour.

'He must have great courage. I do regret how much I've misjudged him.' Gideon looks at me solemnly. 'When I get to London—if I get to London—I'll have more than a drink with

Danny. By God, I'll buy him the best dinner he's ever had and toast his good health.'

'Of course you'll get to London,' I say with more firmness than I feel. 'You'll even be there before him. He'll still be battling the Horn while you're slipping quietly through the Suez.'

Neither of us mentions the U-boats, now preying like sharks upon the allied navies. The great comfort, repeated often, is that they treat merchant ships in a more civilised manner. Or so far they have.

'Now don't worry, I'll give Danny your letter, guard it with my life, and I'll tell him all about the robbery,' says Gideon. 'And here's a thought. Has he a photograph of you? I can give him a print of that one from the restaurant—you looked very becoming that night.'

'What a kind idea. Yes, I'd like him to have that.'

'And Lucy,' he pauses and takes an envelope from his inside pocket. 'I will entrust you with this. You're the best person to have it in any case.'

I open the envelope and read the page inside. I'm familiar with Cristina's impatient, misspelled hand from her letters to Emilia, and now here is her statement, dated and witnessed, swearing that Liam Letolo is the natural son of Daniel Whalen.

'You see? I was telling the truth, you know.'

'Oh Gideon, *thank* you. There's nothing in the world means more to me.'

Gideon leaves at the beginning of March 1915, expecting to arrive in London in six weeks, and we wave him off at the wharf. Peter and I sniffle a little but Rosa and Eliza are quite dry-eyed.

Later Rosa says, 'Are you quite certain you haven't been taken in by him again? You were suspiciously touched at his departure.'

'Not this time. But I was thinking of Cristina's letter. It will mean everything to Danny.'

'Well, I'll always have my doubts about anything Gideon says regarding Cristina. But how on earth could Danny not believe he's Liam's father? The resemblance is striking.'

'But there's no legal proof and Cristina's reputation leaves her with little credibility,' I say. 'At least this statement will protect Liam and give Danny great comfort.'

'Speaking of comfort, how very sweet it is to be by myself again,' says Rosa. 'Time to paint and walk and think without the endless pressure of having to listen to Gideon and admire Gideon and obey Gideon. Oh, Lucy, what a fool I was to marry that man.'

'But he's so plausible, who could blame you! He believes every word he says and I find myself wanting to believe him too.'

'Don't be misled,' says Rosa, frowning. 'He lies to himself and he lies to others. He's no buffoon. He has a very dark side.'

'I understand that, Rosa—whatever Gideon wants Gideon must have. But he's a link for me to the past, you see, to Mama and Sam and *Willowmere*. Sometimes I find I still have a fondness for him no matter how badly he's behaved.'

'And that he certainly has,' says Rosa. 'Dear God, I'm grateful to Min-lu's lawyers. If they hadn't safeguarded my estate he'd have bankrupted me by now.'

'Speaking of Min-lu—'

'Of course. You'll be going home to Broome soon?'

'I miss it terribly. It's where I want to be when Danny returns.'

Before I leave, a letter postmarked San Francisco arrives from Danny, dated five weeks before.

Well, sweetheart, now you may know where we've been. From Newcastle we took coal to Valparaiso. There we loaded nitrate for San Francisco, where I'm writing this as we stow a cargo of timber.

I cannot tell you of course where we sail next, but I plan to enjoy a drink with a pompous shipmate from Willowmere at the end of it.

We've taken on a cat here, or perhaps she took us on—the rats have been dreadful. A little grey thing, sits on my feet when I write at the desk. She's curious and keeps me warm and climbs the rigging. Rather like

you in many ways.
Now others may see this so I cannot write my thoughts in full. But
perhaps you will understand when I remind you of my small house in
Broome and the rain on the roof and the scent of the night air.

I smile at the memories. Darling man. If he sailed soon after writing this, with good winds he'll be close to the Horn by now. Then another two months to Britain, arriving in late May perhaps.

Gideon will give him my letter in London and then he'll be able to write to me again. Oh, but it takes so long and he's so far away!

A few days later I board the steamer to Broome. Once there I begin working again with Min-lu, desperate for time to pass more quickly. After some weeks Rosa writes to say Gideon has arrived safely in Britain. That's good to hear, but I know Danny and *Culardoch* must still be somewhere at sea.

Early May brings us some appalling news: a giant passenger liner has been sunk off Ireland. The *Lusitania* was torpedoed by a submarine without any warning at all and twelve hundred people died.

Everyone around me seems to be chattering that this means that a barbaric new era of warfare at sea has begun, until I want to scream at complete strangers to shut their damned mouths.

Then, in the last week of May, Gideon—God bless him—sends me a telegram from London: DANNY HERE SAFELY STOP LETTER SOON STOP GIDEON.

I feel weak with relief.

18. FASTNET ROCK

Six weeks later I receive the longed-for letter from Danny in London. I read it quickly then curl up on a couch and read it again.

The voyage around the Horn was so cold the cat spent most of the time in my bunk—she was welcome but I'd have preferred you. When we reached the Bay of Biscay everything happened at once—a hurricane, leaks in the hull, a lost topmast.

Still, we limped home, very glad indeed to see the Thames. We'll be here for a month as Culardoch must go into dry dock for repairs. There was some unhappy news when I picked up my mail.

One of my sisters wrote to say my mother has died. It happened two months ago so there's nothing to be done. She was ill for a long time and it seems to have been a mercy. Now I've no family at all in Ireland—my brother is in America and my sisters are married and moved away to Liverpool—so perhaps I shall have to make my home in a little pearling town instead.

I'm sure it will be a fine living as long as I have a curious young lady with long brown hair to share it with. Or even one with short hair who looks like a monkey—I'm not particular.

I must finish now, I'm off to have dinner at a posh restaurant courtesy of Gideon. I'll try not to embarrass him too much. Sweetheart, I'll write again soon.

I sigh with pleasure. If they have to stay a month in London surely he'll have time to write me lots of letters. I open a second envelope, this one from Rosa.

I've just heard from Gideon. He says he had a fine dinner with Danny, who apparently wanted only to hear of you, rather than Gideon's hard work at the Department (I think he spends most of his time at country houses, hunting, fishing and shooting).

But here's the most extraordinary news! Last week I happened to look in a jeweller's window and saw your garnet and seedpearl earrings, the ones I'd had made for your coming out. So on a hunch I went in and asked if they had any pearl necklaces. And out of the safe they produced MINE! (Sam had our initials engraved inside the clasp.)

I remained terribly calm—you'd have been proud of me—and went straight to the police. Well! The jeweller has been charged with receiving and we shall soon have some of our gems back. Your moonstone necklet was there too but, I'm sorry to say, no sign of your engagement ring. Still, I am just so content to have Sam's beautiful pearls back again.

'So Danny's probably sailed already,' I say to Min-lu. 'I wonder when another letter will arrive.'

'Lucy,' says Min-lu, 'when I was a girl the mail took a good four months to get across the world—if it got there at all—so six weeks from Europe to Australia seems a miracle to me.'

'I know I shouldn't be so impatient.' I roll a piece of paper into the typewriter. 'But oh, I wish I knew where he was. I wish I could *see* him.'

Min-lu shakes her head in mock despair.

'Yes, I know.' I smile. 'The only solution is work.'

An hour later the bell above the door tinkles. I lifted my head smiling then my face seems to freeze. The telegram boy asks, 'Miss Lucy Fox?' and hands me an envelope, and leaves.

I stare at Min-lu in sudden terror. She comes to my desk and says, 'Courage, Lucy,' although I see her hands are suddenly trembling. I open the telegram and we stare at it.

REGRET TO INFORM YOU CAPTAIN DANIEL WHALEN DECEASED STOP SHIP CULARDOCH TORPEDOED JULY SIXTH SUNK OFF FASTNET ROCK STOP

'Where is Fastnet Rock? What does it mean?'

Min-lu's voice is shaking. 'Danny has been lost at sea, Lucy. His ship was torpedoed.'

'But he was just having dinner with Gideon, he was in London.'

'No darling, remember you were telling me his ship had already sailed.'

'Yes. Yes, so it had. Min-lu, what must I do?'

'We shall close the office and go home now.'

I rise obediently and go with her. I do not cry as Rosa did, extravagant in her loss. I simply feel puzzled. I've always wanted to understand and now something has happened that's beyond all understanding.

People come and go, notices appear in the paper. I had not realised how well-loved Danny was: such astonishing kindness. Yet I barely weep.

'I can't seem to believe it,' I say to Min-lu. 'They haven't found his body, after all. Perhaps he was washed ashore, his memory gone. Perhaps he's wandering in the wilds ...'

'Darling, Ireland is not deepest Africa,' she says gently. 'There are villages all along the coast. It would be impossible for someone to be washed up, alive or dead, without it being reported to the Admiralty.'

I yearn to receive Danny's letters from when he was still in London, before *Culardoch* sailed down the Thames and across to Ireland to be lost off a rock called Fastnet: I know very well now where Fastnet lies. Yet, terribly, no more of his letters arrive and it's another puzzle, another incomprehensible grief.

Others write. Rosa, Captain Gregory, the Pearlers' Association, Lizzie Withers, Mr Murakami, the Egawas, Mr Bagge the sailmaker, Mrs Gonzales, Aunt Bertha and Uncle Edward all sent their kindest thoughts. And a missive arrives from Gideon.

My dear Lucy, I cannot express my sorrow at your tragic loss. When I

last saw Danny, over our excellent repast at The Cavalier, he was a
happy man. The voyage had gone well and he had every prospect of
future joy with you.
Sadly it was not to be. (Confidentially, he has been commended and
may yet receive a posthumous award.) Naturally I gave him your letter
and photograph that night and we passed a cheery time reminiscing.
Although we did not meet up again I will always remember the evening.
You must surely be proud he died in the service of his country.

I could not care less that he died in the service of his country, I
think bitterly. His country didn't need him nearly as much as I did.
Stupid Gideon. And if they'd had such a good time at dinner, why
didn't they meet up again? Danny was there for a month after all.
Gideon was probably too busy hunting and fishing and shooting at
country estates to bother.

And a letter arrives from Thomas the Islander, who mercifully
survived the sinking.

Dear Miss Lucy, I cry every day thinking about Captain Danny, so
brave. He stays behind to get rid of code books and goes down with ship.
Germans from submarine laugh at us in lifeboats and we row for a day,
no food or water, until navy ship finds us. I am so sorry Captain Danny
is sad, I try to help but he does not want to talk to me.

What on earth could he mean? It rings true, more so than Gideon's
unctuous commiserations, but in the end what does it matter? All
that matters is that no more letters will come from Danny and that
somehow, beyond belief, there is no more Danny in this world to
write them.

Min-lu packs his belongings into an antique camphorwood chest.
On top she places the lovely old fiddle Danny's father made for him
and I set mine beside it. I cannot imagine a time when I would play
music again. She locks the chest and gives me the key, and I hold it
in the warmth of my hands for a long time.

Finally His Majesty's Admiralty writes to me to explain what the
telegram could not, and to end even the slightest possibility of

hope.

> *We write to inform you further regarding the loss of your fiancé Captain Daniel Whalen. The Culardoch was torpedoed at approximately 1800 on 6th July 1915. On the following day the lifeboats were found by a naval cruiser and the crewmen taken to Queenstown.*
>
> *First Officer Patrick Doyle floated ashore alive at Barley Cove, where three bodies also washed up. Mr Doyle formally identified them to the local authorities.*
>
> *One of the deceased was Captain Whalen, who performed his duties with honour and was the last to leave his ship. He was buried in the churchyard near Barley Cove. The Admiralty expresses its deepest regrets for your loss.*

That evening, catching sight of Danny's schooner *Gemstone* on the bay, my breath catches on a sob. Next morning I surface with a dizzying rush from the depths of sleep to meet a wave of grief that seems to have been suspended above me forever.

The wave breaks.

Pearling struggles to survive: there is little demand for beauty now in the abattoirs of Europe. The paper prints letters from the soldiers, many once shellopeners, identified by their masters. Connor (out for Blackman) loses his right hand at Gallipoli.

Hornsby (out for White) is badly wounded. Lenton (out for Russell) writes lovingly of an ancient pearl necklace he saw in an Egyptian museum, but soon his letters speak only of shrapnel and bayonets and dysentery.

Dobson's cheery note to his mother—*I am writing this in a hole about 5ft in the ground*—appears in the same edition as the report of his death.

Within the span of a few months, Telford is killed in action, along with Monger, Chandler, Ulrich, McRae, Timms, Aarons, Fraser, Horsfall, MacDonald, Barnsley and Caporn. King stops two bullets; Haldane, Townsend, Rodgers, Vowles, Castles, Moffin and Howe are wounded. Hill is missing.

Lenton writes from hospital, *The things we did in Gallipoli during the first few weeks fairly make me shiver when I think of them in calm moments here.*

Charlie Blackman says, *It was heartbreaking to see your pals shot down, some with their heads blown off or cut off.*

Vic Kepert writes, *It is quite true about men being 5 or 6 deep, you had to walk over them in some places. Some are still lying unburied. The flies are an awful nuisance here.*

The soldiers' letters sit beside advertisements for Asahi Beer and Charlie Chaplin films, and become more and more grotesque as they try to convey the incommunicable. After a time the paper prints only the blandest of them.

Still, there is no relief from the horrors. Because so little happen in Broome itself, the paper's pages are always filled with grim cables. After Gallipoli, the Broome lads are sent to the Middle East and the Western Front.

Then the telegrams begin again: five local boys die on a single day at the Somme.

In this war Japan is a stout ally of the British Empire. When the new Emperor is crowned in late 1915 there are lanterns, processions and a model warship which fires flags by day and sparkling fireworks at night. I meet Mr Murakami near the Japanese Club and ask after Theresa Murata.

'Because of the war I cannot go to Japan, she cannot come here,' Murakami says, his face sombre. 'All the traders have trouble now and I must close the Nishioka shop after so many years.'

'What will you do, Murakami-san?'

'Captain Gregory has bought the Dampier Hotel so I work there. I bring in the Japanese and get a share of profits. It goes well, Miss Fox, but I wish I still had my own business.'

I nod. Prices for pearlshell have plummeted and our company's trade is very slow. Not that it matters to me. Nothing interests me. Every movement is an effort, every day shadowed in gloom. I feel as if I've been initiated into a great mystery and can now recognise all the other initiates—those like me who've come to know complete loss.

That Christmas of 1915 is unspeakably sad. A year ago Danny was alive, sailing his beloved *Culardoch* towards London.

Sometimes I lie on my bed in the afternoon with small Liam beside me looking at picture books and chattering about ships and puppies. I hug him and smell his soft hair as he drifts away into sleep and wonder what will happen to him. And to me.

Early in the new year a vicious little cock-eye storm hits Broome at night. I take the tram to the Customs House and walk to the foreshore. I meet Captain Gregory, his face dark with worry.

'A thousand pounds,' he says. 'That's just the damage, mind. Three boats loaded with stores too, all ruined. A bad business.'

He sees where I'm staring. 'I'm sorry, *cariad*, she got the worst of it. Just about beyond repair now.'

'I don't care. I'll give you fifty pounds for her. You can have the rigging, it'll rot otherwise.'

'Ah, she's not worth fifty pounds. Look, I'll see what I can do, maybe she can be patched up. She's done me proud you know, fished me three fine stones.'

I walk to the tramline and wait in the shade of the Customs House. From there I can still see *Sparrow* on her side, her bow smashed in, a tangle of ropes and splintered wood on her deck.

At times I believe I'm beyond feeling anything ever again, but every now and then I find I'm mistaken.

The bleak months drift slowly by. Every night I go to bed desperate for oblivion and every day I wake to despair. I know Min-lu aches for me like a mother but there's nothing she can do to help.

Alain is kind and supportive and amazed by the depth of my sorrow. I'm utterly numb but I let him kiss me occasionally. It seems odd, neither sweet nor unpleasant. Perhaps I'm dead too.

Time passes disregarded. In mid-1916, a year after losing Danny, I open a letter from Rosa. She says she's coming to visit Broome with nine-year-old Eliza and five-year-old Peter, and bringing two good friends from Perth.

Visitors? Despite my bleakness I feel a spark of interest, and when I see my sister and little Eliza and Peter waving to me from the ship I feel almost glad.

Rosa's friends are Mr Anton McKee, who teaches her painting, and his sister, Miss Ellen McKee. Anton is a bearded, pleasant-faced man with glasses, while Ellen is fair, with deepset blue eyes and a quick smile: it's easy to like them both.

They stay with Emilia, Papa, Liam and me, while Rosa and her children go to Min-lu's house. Min-lu's pretty daughter Izabel has just turned fifteen and thinks she's far too grown-up to play with Eliza and Peter, but quickly changes her mind.

When we walk around the town, Anton stops every few minutes to sketch something or discuss some effect of light and colour with Rosa. I realise he's very fond of her. It's not the facile worship she usually evokes, but a respectful warmth that makes me like him even more.

His sister Ellen charms me too. One day Anton jokes about 'when Ellen flees the nest' and she glances up smiling.

'I want to be a nurse,' she says. 'My parents have always been opposed, but soon I come into a legacy so I shall quietly outmanoeuvre them. My mother says my head was turned as a child by the story of Florence Nightingale, but nursing is something I simply must do.'

'I've felt that compulsion too,' I say. 'Needing to work, to be involved in the world, despite the efforts of those who assume they know what's best for me.'

Rosa reaches out and touches my hand for a moment. 'I fear I'm one of those who tried to divert her from her calling. Never again, little sister, I promise.'

'I'm not quite sure what my calling is any more,' I say lightly. 'Pearlshell and luggers have had their day and Danny ...' I stop.

'I'm deeply sorry for your loss,' Anton says gently. 'A cousin of ours, too— '

'Yes, so terribly many.' I change the topic. 'I hear you're planning an exhibition of students' work that may even include a small piece of Rosa's?'

'A small piece!' He laughs. 'A number of her canvases will be shown. Her work has a depth and maturity most of my students will never discover.'

'Rosa, will you become one of those avant-garde Cubists like Monsieur Picasso?' Ellen says.

'I doubt it,' says Rosa with a sigh. 'I suspect I'll only ever be Mrs Gideon Meade and she's not likely to be permitted to be a Cubist. Should I *want* to be a Cubist, Anton?'

'Not such a terrible fate. But their style is not yours, Rosa, you have your own integrity.'

Rosa glances at him then busies herself with the teapot. The three small children bustle into the room, and Eliza says to Rosa, 'Look, Mummy, Liam did a painting.'

Rosa smiles and shows it to Anton. He gazes at it then smiles and says, 'A good joke, Eliza! Now who really did this?'

'Liam,' she says, and 'Liam,' echoes Peter.

'But he's only five,' says Anton, puzzled.

'He did it, Mr McKee, truly,' says Eliza.

Liam watches with large eyes as Anton passes the paper to Ellen and me. It shows a lugger at sea with small brown men helping a diver on the deck. The curves of the sails, alive with movement, echo the lines of the waves.

'Yes, that's his.' I hand it back to Anton. 'He's rather good at painting.' Liam beams at me.

'But it's quite extraordinary. Would you mind if I gave him a few lessons while we're visiting?'

'I'd like that. It's been almost two years now since he last saw Danny. It would be good ...'

'I understand. So young man, I shall see you tomorrow at eleven. Will that be suitable, Lucy?'

I nod and Liam whispers, 'Thank you, Mr McKee.'

He turns and runs out the door, Eliza and Peter following, chattering.

'Liam, Rosa—is *everyone* in your family an artist, Lucy?' says Ellen laughing, then stops and goes red. 'Oh, I do apologise. I was thinking for a moment Liam was your son. Oh dear.'

'It doesn't matter, Ellen. His mother Cristina is my step-sister, and Danny fathered him long before we became engaged. It's complicated, rather typical of Broome.'

'So despite the complications, Lucy, are you an artist too?' says Anton.

'No. I used to play music. Not any more.'

It becomes a springtime of simple pleasures, childrens' games, reading aloud, singing around the piano. We have picnics on luggers and take the carriage to Cable Beach, and talk endlessly of art and politics and war. Emilia and Min-lu hold dinner parties: Emilia's table rich with spicy dishes, Min-lu's with savoury delicacies.

Alain is away working in Singapore during this time but I don't miss him. I'm content with this engaging new company. I've had few friends my own age before, and none like Ellen, a woman as determined as myself. An easy comradeship grows between us.

Liam flourishes with Anton's tutoring too. The reserve he's shown since the loss of Danny seems to lift. Anton thinks his painting, 'Gemstone in the Wind', is almost good enough to be hung in a student exhibition.

And far from being unable to help me, I discover it was Min-lu herself who arranged for Rosa and her friends to visit Broome and ease my despair. Sometimes I wonder if I'll ever be able to repay the kindness that small, wise woman has shown me since the day we met.

One day Rosa mentions something about Min-lu's older daughter Fili, who's just finished boarding school in Perth. Filipa has grown from an imperious child to a fashionable eighteen-year-old, with her mother's creamy-gold skin and her Portuguese father's dark curls.

'Heavens, Fili's *eighteen*? It seems only moments ago she and Izabel were little girls at Min-lu's wonderful ball—remember, when you and Sam were just married?'

Rosa smiled. 'That was a lovely night, wasn't it? Sam looked so handsome.'

'And your dress was glorious too. I had to wear that horrible black sack because I wasn't yet out.'

'I doubt Danny cared.'

'Danny never noticed me then,' I say, surprised.

'Oh Lucy, Danny always loved you. *Always*. I knew that even when he barely knew it himself.'

I sit down and begin weeping with deep, wrenching sobs. Rosa sits beside me and puts her arm around me. After a time I take a shuddering breath and wipe my face.

'Rosa. Does it get any better? After Sam ... when you married Gideon, did that help?'

'Sam was my passion, my dearest love. Gideon? A nightmare I've stumbled into. I wish—' Rosa stops and sighs. 'I still miss Sam but every year the pain is a little easier. The children help, and now I have my painting too. I forget everything when I'm doing that.'

'And Anton?'

Rosa laughs ruefully. 'Remember when you accused me of falling into bed rather too easily? Not this time, little sister. Anton?' She shrugs. 'He's a good man, too important to me to take chances. Gideon will be home sooner or later. I don't know what I'll do then.'

After a moment I say, 'Danny made me promise to go on if anything happened to him, to find someone else. But I don't see how I can.'

'Of course you can, you *must*. You're too warm-hearted to be alone, Lucy. What about Alain? He's always cared for you.'

'And I for him.' I shake my head. 'But I just don't know.'

19. A FAR GREATER DARKNESS

Towards Christmas Ellen returns to Perth to begin her nursing training, but Rosa and Anton decide to stay longer. I'm sorry to see Ellen go, but by then I've grown clear-eyed and calm. I walk again in the early morning and gaze with pleasure at the luggers on the foreshore. To my surprise Captain Gregory has even managed to patch up dear *Sparrow* and she's working again.

At the start of 1917 the reports from the trenches are not as dreadful as usual. But the war grinds on, a shadow over everyday life. Most of the the young men have enlisted and one third of the luggers are laid up.

Alain comes back from Singapore and we meet at a dinner soon afterwards. He gazes at me over the candles as we talk, his narrow brown face as handsome as ever, his eyes full of good humour. Later, behind the lattice, he holds me and kisses me and my body curls against him like a cat.

The moment returns to me over and over. A week later I'm alone at the office because Min-lu has left for a concert at Izabel's school, and I stretch and prepare to go. As I lock the office door I breathe the warm night air, scented with frangipani, and sit down in the dark on the bench facing Roebuck Bay.

I close my eyes and recall the warmth of Alain's mouth, the pleasure of his touch. Far away I can hear a distant swell of cheers in the pub, the chatter of voices in rooms nearby, the crunch of carriage wheels rolling along the street.

It's more than two years now since I last saw Danny; eighteen months since the Admiralty's telegram gouged the chasm of Before and After in my life. He's dead, I tell myself, and all those boys at the front are dying, but I'm alive and I promised him I'd go on.

Oh Danny my darling. My poor lost darling.

I sit for a long time then stand and walk through a nearby laneway to a staircase. It leads to Alain's comfortable rooms, where I've taken tea before but have never visited at night. I breathe deeply, walk up the stairs and knock. Alain answers, his dark eyes pleased.

'Lucy, how marvellous! Come in, please.'

I'm grateful he makes no comment on my late-night visit but pours me a glass of wine and sits beside me on the balcony, chatting of everyday things. We gaze at the faint lights of boats on the bay and after a time silence falls between us.

'Lucy, perhaps I should escort you home now?'

'I think I'd like to stay here, Alain. I'm tired of feeling nothing. I'd like you to hold me, if you wish that too—'

He stands and takes my hands and draws me towards him and gazes at me, stroking my hair back from my face. He kisses me and murmurs, 'Please Lucy, I wish that very much.'

Next morning, through the glass doors onto the balcony, I can see the pink dawn over Roebuck Bay. Alain sighs and turns in his sleep. His shoulder is outlined against the light, not as broad as a sailor's shoulder but still strong and pleasing to touch.

My thighs and arms ache a little from the unfamiliar activity. I stretch slowly then fit myself closer to Alain's back. His hair does not coil into russet curls and his ear wears no golden ring, but as I drift again into sleep I feel a peace I'd almost forgotten could exist.

Alain makes me coffee in the morning, and we've been friends for long enough there's no more than a moment of shyness between us. As I'm driving home in the carriage I'm entranced by the colours and movement and scents of the day.

The pain in my heart is still there of course, but the world is alive again.

While walking one evening I meet Captain Gregory standing uncharacteristically still and gazing at the bay. His ongoing feud with the editor of the local paper has hit a new low.

'You've seen what he's writing about me?' he says glumly. 'Lacking *patriotism*? Why do I get all the stick for keeping the business running while my brother's at the front? Somebody has to do it.'

'I don't understand it, Greg. Plenty of men younger than you are still here.' I glance sideways. 'Wouldn't have anything to do with flirting with Mrs Editor would it?'

Gregory can't hide a small grin. 'I'm a happily married man I'll have you know, young Lucy.'

'Of course. Have you heard from Dick recently?'

'Still with the Camel Corps in Palestine. It's been quiet for them lately.'

'Good, they probably need the rest. By the way, I notice your loudest critics are your business rivals—complete coincidence, I reckon.'

He laughs. 'You always cheer me up, you do, Admiral Fox.'

'I'm not an Admiral any more,' I say dryly. 'You've still got my lugger.'

'Ah, I'll give it back one day. But listen now, I've had an idea. See all those little boats rotting away? We need bigger luggers, ones that can carry engines.'

'But we don't have the carpenters—white ones that is, and the Japanese carpenters aren't allowed to build boats any more, only to do repairs on them.'

'So very true,' he says, lighting a cigarette. 'But what if a Jap repaired one of those old things to be, say, longer by twenty feet?'

'Surely that'd be a complete rebuild.'

'What if you tell the Department it's just a repair? And don't tell the Registrar the new size either. Will they run up to Broome with a tape measure to check it?'

'If you used timber from the old lugger,' I say slowly, 'I suppose it's a *sort* of repair. It could keep the same name and crew permits —'

'But the Japanese would build it in half the time at half the cost.'

'What a wonderful idea!' I stop. 'You'd never get away with it.'

'Not right now, but after the war perhaps, when those yapping fools won't be able to touch me.'

'After the war ...' I sigh. 'Do you think Broome will ever be the same?'

Gregory shakes his head. 'The lads coming home will be very different. But pearling will go on, people always want beautiful things.' He grins. 'And come the grand rebuilding of the luggers, *Sparrow* too, of course, we'll be ready to take on the world.'

'A new *Sparrow*! Might she have a clipper bow, like a square-rigger?'

'Now there's an idea. What a fine-looking vessel that would make. So we'll do it, Admiral Fox?'

'We'll have to see. Do I get my lugger back?'

My love affair with Alain prospers and everyone says how well I look. After a few months he lightly mentions marriage. I'm taken by surprise and just as lightly evade the topic. I don't know why—I understand marriage and children are important to his family. Perhaps I'm just not sure what they mean to me.

I always use Min-lu's Chinese potions to prevent pregnancy but perhaps they're not as reliable as I'd hoped. One day I feel a pain in my belly which becomes worse and worse.

My monthly courses have always been irregular but this is different, and after a time I wonder if I have an inflamed appendix. Then I begin to bleed heavily.

Min-lu finds me white-faced and doubled over, and quickly calls the doctor. It's not our old friend Suzuki-san, but a new Japanese doctor whose spotless surgery and quiet efficiency have made him just as popular. He examines me carefully then gives me an injection of morphine.

When I return to consciousness I'm in my bed beneath a clean sheet, weak and in pain. The doctor is sitting in a chair nearby, writing notes.

'What's happened?'

'Miss Fox, you have miscarriage, very serious one. You lose baby. You very lucky young woman, if you not so healthy you might die.'

'And will I—in the future—'

'There is damage, much damage. I do not think you will have baby again. I am very sorry.'

I look at him in bewilderment then lie back and curl up on my side. I tell Alain when he comes to see me with a bunch of flowers. He's silent for a few moments then says, 'Perhaps it is better not to bring new life into this terrible world.'

He does not mention marriage again and now I know he never will. I'm oddly relieved.

It takes me many weeks to recover. I lie in bed looking at the passing clouds through the window and think, Mama, how strange: I will never have babies like you or Rosa. But at heart I don't care. I only ever wanted Danny's child.

My own loss is simply an overture to a myriad of new losses, now dragging us all into a far greater darkness. Ypres begins to dominate the news for the third time in as many years, and the death notices are no longer large and black-bordered but simply a few terse lines.

I meet Lizzie Withers outside Tokomaru's store one day and express my condolences—her younger brother Ernest died a few weeks ago—and I'm haunted for days by the grief on her broad, kind face.

Alain becomes very quiet and I realise our time of warmth and consolation is drawing to a close. One evening he looks restlessly for one of his thin cigars and goes out to the balcony to light it. I follow him and put my arms around him, my head against his back.

'You want to go, don't you?'

'Yes. I am so sorry, Lucy. The French army would take me now without hesitation.'

'Then you must go.'

'I do not want to leave you—'

'We'll meet again, darling. In Paris, after the war, perhaps. And then you may show me l'Opera and le Louvre and la Seine.'

'And of course we will go to the docks to see the square-riggers too,' he says. 'Ah, *chérie*, I have been so happy with you.'

It hurts when Alain goes, but not as it did with Danny. Perhaps I'm getting hard I think. But no, I'm not hard, I'm just tired. Please Lord, let him be safe.

In late 1917 Rosa and Anton decide reluctantly it's time to return to Perth. Seven-year-old Peter doesn't object, but Eliza, just turned ten, sobs bitterly as they sail. She's heartbroken to leave her best friend, one of Mr Egawa's grand-daughters, with whom she chatters quietly in Japanese.

Business is the worst it's ever been but I try to keep going. Just as I'm closing the office one evening I notice a large figure sitting hunched on the bench outside the office, his trembling hand holding a flimsy paper.

'Captain Gregory?'

He looks up and I stop, shocked at his face.

'I was walking but did not know where to go. I sat down here for a moment and now I cannot, I cannot ...'

'No, no. Not *Dick*.'

'In Palestine, of wounds, they say. Oh, my poor little brother ... my poor mother. He was always her favourite, you see, the fine cavalry officer—no wicked sailor he.'

'I'm so sorry, he was a dear man. Oh, Greg.'

He puts his large hands over his face and his broad shoulders shake. I return to the office and call Mr Murakami, and sit with

Greg on the bench until the car stops in front of us. Mr Murakami helps him stand and settles him in the front seat.

'Thank you,' he says. 'You know that my own brother died too, a few months ago? Greg was very good to me then. I will take him home to his wife now. Good night, Miss Fox.'

I can see the lines of sorrow on his face and think, dear God, we all look like that now.

After *Culardoch* took Danny to his death I came to loathe the great sailing ships. Now even the luggers on the foreshore leave me unmoved. They're falling into disrepair, some as broken as the bodies of the soldiers who once worked them.

Alain is gone and business is pointless. The news is ugly, the summer hard, the rains sparse, the sun unrelenting.

One stifling afternoon Min-lu says, 'I've just had a letter from Filipa. She wants to get married.'

'But she's only nineteen.'

'Indeed. I'd like to meet this Captain Barratt before giving my permission. Filipa tells me he was at Gallipoli and had his foot amputated, and now he breeds horses. He's apparently well-off, but I wonder if she's mature enough to take on a man so damaged.'

I gaze at Min-lu: the streaks of grey in her glossy black hair, the beautiful bones of her face, the lines around her brown eyes.

'The *Minderoo* is due in this week,' I say. 'Why don't we go to Perth to see Filipa and her Captain? I'd really like to get away, I've nothing worthwhile to do here, Min-lu. The losses never seem to end and they all remind me ...'

Min-lu nods. 'I want to be somewhere else too.'

Gregory drops by before we leave. He clears his throat and says, 'Thank you for calling Murakami-san when—the other week. Particularly helpful of you.'

'Greg, it was nothing, he's the helpful one.'

'It's a very odd thing you know, but sometimes I suspect, in this entire town, the only fellow I can truly count on is that Jap.'

'It's not odd at all, Mr Murakami is a fine man,' I say. 'And he's probably the only one in town who matches you for cunning too.'

Gregory smiles. 'You may be correct. But he's far more trusting than me, mind. Have you heard about Eki's revenge for Theresa's baby? She secretly collected all the money owed to the business and now she's run away to Japan with the lot. He's probably bankrupt.'

'Poor Mr Murakami.'

'I'll do what I can to help, of course—I've put off a few creditors already. But he has a hard row to hoe.'

'It's been hard for too many of us lately. That's why I want to go away.'

'Well, don't you forget my scheme to rebuild the luggers now, Admiral Fox. You will come back, won't you?'

'I'm not so sure, Greg. Luggers don't seem very important any more. Nothing does.'

At the start of the new year of 1918, Min-lu, Izabel and I sail for Fremantle docks. It's been three years since I was last in Perth and it seems a darker place. As we drive into town I'm shocked to see so many maimed ex-soldiers begging on street corners.

That afternoon we meet Filipa's young man Eric Barratt over tea at Rosa and Min-lu's house. He limps a little but he's fair and strong-faced.

'When we drove through Perth, Captain Barratt,' I say, 'we saw returned soldiers begging on the streets. Surely there are facilities to assist them?'

'Only charities, Miss Fox, and they are overwhelmed. You understand I'm extremely fortunate. I was discharged early in the war and I work with horses, so my injury is not a disadvantage. But there are few as lucky as me.'

'How can you call yourself lucky, Captain Barratt?' asks Min-lu, surprised.

'Those less injured than me had to return to the Front, where they usually died. The few who survived are broken men, some of them once the bravest I ever met. You cannot imagine how fortunate I feel, especially since meeting your daughter.'

'You do not foresee disadvantage in becoming tied to an Asian family?' asks Min-lu coolly.

'Good Lord, no! Everything has changed now. Men of all races have fought their hearts out for the Allies and that will surely be appreciated after the war. We must never again return to the corrupt old world that dragged us into such a disaster.'

'You are more confident than I, Captain Barratt,' says Min-lu, 'but I hope you are correct.'

Later Min-lu speaks privately to Filipa and next day gives her permission for an engagement. The ceremony will take place later in the year, at a church near Eric's farm. Filipa has been passionate about horses all her life and I'm glad to see she's discovered a like-minded soul.

Min-lu holds a small party for family and friends. Some of Eric's old comrades are there, one in a wheelchair, an angry-looking man whose legs end at mid-thigh.

Another seems fit until I realise his hands never cease trembling, while the right sleeve of the best man's suit hangs empty. In the happiness of the evening that doesn't seem to matter, at least not until I see him gazing in despair at people dancing in each other's arms.

Over dinner one evening Anton McKee tells us about an exhibition of Rosa's paintings he recently organised. Two-thirds of the canvases sold and a reviewer called Rosa an extraordinary new talent.

I can see the affection runs deep between him and my sister, but even now it seems platonic. Rosa says, looking at a candle through her glass of red wine, 'Gideon plans to soon grace us with his presence. They seem to have run out of things to hunt and fish at the great estates of Britain.'

'He may find life much changed on your part,' says Ellen.

Rosa shrugs. 'He'll have to make do.'

Ellen grins. No-nonsense and practical, she has finished her first year of training and is now nursing in a ward for injured servicemen.

'Ellen, I saw so many crippled men in the streets,' I say. 'Don't you find nursing makes you sad?'

'Lord, no. If nothing else it makes you grateful to be in one piece yourself. What's sad is to see so many wounded, yet too few nurses to help them.'

Min-lu says thoughtfully, 'Dr Suzuki said you'd make a good nurse—remember, Lucy? When Liam had whooping cough.'

Rosa says, 'Heavens, yes—and when I was having Peter you were absurdly calm too.'

'Anyone would have seemed calm compared to the cyclone,' I say, laughing.

'No, you've always been like that, Lucy, forever bandaging cuts and broken arms down at the foreshore,' says Rosa. 'It never seemed to bother you.'

I say nothing for a moment, overwhelmed by the memory of Liam's small face flushing back into life when the doctor cut open his airway.

As the conversation moves on I think, surely nurses must be strong, careful, wise—and I'm none of those, I'm unhappy and directionless. Could someone as lost as me possibly help those poor wounded men?

I look up and realise both Ellen and Min-lu are watching me, smiling a little.

'Do you truly think I'm capable of being a nurse?' I ask Min-lu next day. 'Such responsibility.'

'Yes,' she says firmly. 'You need something new in your life Lucy, something worthwhile, and I believe you should try.'

20. WOODMAN POINT

Matron Chisholm seems unusually young but her manner is brisk as she appraises me.

'Obviously we have applications from girls who think it's all terribly romantic then faint at their first amputation and simply waste our time. I need nurses who don't have illusions, nurses who can work like oxen. Do you think you'd manage?'

'I can work hard and I've experienced quite a lot.'

'Yes. Nurse McKee told me you'd had an unsheltered life. That's certainly useful.' After a pause Matron says, 'You'd have to live in the Nurses' Home of course. Shifts are twelve hours, starting at six in the morning, and you're woken at five. Naturally you don't take public holidays.'

'Naturally.'

'Very well. I'll send a note to Housekeeping. Your room will be ready on Sunday, so be here at three in the afternoon to collect your uniforms.'

'Yes, Matron.'

Anton and Rosa drive me to the hospital on Sunday then farewell me. The room the housekeeper takes me to is small. A narrow bed and tiny desk and cupboard are the only furnishings.

I find my way to the hospital laundry, with its massive chimney and blasts of hot steam, where I collect a stack of uniforms starched stiff as cardboard. The cuffs, collars and belts are separate so they can be boiled and passed through giant ironing presses. The cap is flat and somehow has to be moulded into a curved shape.

I sit down on the bed and think, oh God, what have I done?

Ellen taps on my door before I fall into complete despair and shows me the trick of shaping the cap. Then we go to the dining room and have roast lamb, string beans and potato, followed by pudding with custard which, if nothing else, is substantial.

Next morning it's still dark when I wake from a deep sleep to loud knocking on the door and someone calling briskly for Nurse Fox. In a daze I realise that's me.

I struggle into the ankle-length blue dress with its stiff white collar and cuffs, the full apron, the wide belt, the cap, the sensible shoes. Min-lu has given me a silver nurse's watch and I pin it to my apron bodice. I stare in the mirror for a moment, then rush away to my new duties.

At the end of that extraordinary day I collapse onto my chair. I've hardly eaten and my stomach is a knot of exhaustion. The edge of my collar has chafed blisters into my neck and my feet hurt in ways I never imagined possible. If I close my eyes for a moment, sights and sounds and smells seem to echo: blood, pus, excrement, cries of pain.

How can I possibly do this? I get up groggily and go to wash, then fall into a dreamless sleep.

It seems just moments before the knocking begins again on my door and I want to weep. Another appalling day arrives, then another. Waking at dawn and working till I drop seems to be all I know. Later I don't remember much about this time, just impressions: the red of a blood-soaked sheet, the clang of bedpans in the sterilising room, the sweet smell of gangrene, a boy's face as he dies.

Suddenly it's my day off but I'm so tired I can't get out of bed for breakfast. At lunch Ellen says, 'The first week's the hardest. It's easier when you know where everything is.' I wince at the memory of one Sister's contempt at my incompetence and go back to bed.

On my next day off I manage to get myself to Rosa's house for afternoon tea, but find I cannot say anything much about the job—

it seems indescribable.

They're surprised when I return to the Nurses' Home before supper, but I feel oddly relieved to go back to my little room, prepare my uniform and fall asleep by nine o'clock.

Weeks pass in a blur, then it's time to go to training school. We're given lectures by wild-haired doctors and dignified senior nurses, we take notes on diseases and practise giving injections, we measure drugs and set limbs. So much that had puzzled me on the ward suddenly makes sense and now I can hardly wait to go back with my new understanding.

'Don't get too carried away,' says Ellen. 'No matter how much you know they still die when you least expect it and survive when you think it impossible.' And that's true too.

Now, after my shift, I have enough strength to take tea with other nurses in our rooms, or go out to a cafe, or sit and gossip. There's a simplicity to it all, from the intensity of the day to the sweet peace of evening.

Then I go on to the night shift and that's different again. In the early hours, when everyone on the ward is asleep or unconscious or lost in their thoughts, I sit by the green-shaded light and write notes or read textbooks.

Then I walk soft-footed along the rows of beds, taking pulses and temperatures, listening and watching over my charges.

I begin to feel a strange contentment at my lot.

In mid-1918, revolutionary Russia makes peace with Germany, freeing hundreds of thousands of German soldiers to fight on the Western Front. The numbers of our patients rise dramatically, as day after day men are unloaded from ships at the docks.

They bring unhealed amputations, lungs melted by mustard gas, buried shards of metal, red-raw burns, and the bizarre malady they call shellshock.

They also bring home a wave of influenza, and along with some of the other nurses, Ellen and I are struck down. I burn up with fever, my head and bones aching, and for days afterwards I feel weak.

But by August I'm back on the ward, happy I'm well again in time for Fili's wedding. I unstitch the seams of my peony-pink silk gown, now long out of date, and make a stylish new dress from the fabric.

It has a wide neckline, long sleeves, a slim waist and a draped skirt which falls to just past mid-calf. Swirling in front of the mirror, I feel prettier than I have in a long time.

The wedding is a small affair but Filipa looks beautiful in layers of lace. There are not many young men at the reception but I dance with Eric Barratt's friends—Dave, the one-armed best man, and Bill, the soldier with shellshock.

They're both much improved and I'm pleased to notice Ellen and Bill seem to be growing fond of each other.

One surprise is Filipa's younger sister Izabel, just turned eighteen. She was always a pretty, plump child but now she's grown elegant and startlingly attractive. We sit together at the wedding breakfast and she tells me she wants to be an actress like vampish Theda Bara.

With her sooty eyes and lush mouth and high cheekbones she'd certainly suit such roles, but she's always had a tender heart and I wonder how she'd cope with such a life.

'You'd have to go away to London or Hollywood, Izabel, and be separated from your family. Could you bear that?'

'Yes. I *really* want to do this, Lucy. I've been working on my dancing and singing more than anyone knows, and I've been studying all the female roles from the classics, too.'

I've known her since she was a vulnerable small child, dominated by bossy Filipa, and I can see how passionate she is. I take her hand and say, 'Darling Izabel, I hope you succeed in achieving whatever you want in life.'

She beams and she's breathtakingly lovely.

I feel a twinge of—what—fear? Yes, fear for such a beautiful girl in a world that might exploit her, perhaps even misuse her. Then I'm amused at my forebodings and tell myself she'll probably marry some nice lad and settle down, and in the end forget all her dreams.

But then, I didn't forget my dreams. At least not until I lost Danny.

In the world at last there's good news—the Americans have joined the fight. They march tall, clean and confident to the Front, only to fall back again as exhausted as the red-eyed Allies hunched in their trenches. But there are so many of them, well-fed and well-armed, and the Allies take heart.

In September 1918 the long dreamt-of breakthrough begins.

A few weeks later Matron Chisholm calls us together for a meeting as each shift comes off duty. We assemble in the cold hospital hall murmuring, our chairs scraping on the floor. On the stage beside Matron is a man with a distracted air, Professor Brenton, Head of Infectious Diseases.

Ellen and I glance at each other, puzzled.

'Quiet please, nurses,' says Matron. 'We've brought you here to inform you we've just been contacted urgently by colleagues from overseas. They tell us that the influenza epidemic from earlier this year has broken out again in many locations worldwide. Unfortunately it's now far more serious, as it's accompanied by a severe and often fatal pneumonia. Professor Brenton will describe it to you. Professor?'

Brenton clears his throat and says, 'Nurses, we appear to be facing a previously unknown infection which produces inflammatory, suffocating, haemorrhagic oedema of the lungs. It's extremely contagious and death may occur within days, even hours, of the initial symptoms.'

The hall is silent.

'As you all know, the war may end at any time,' says Matron. 'Vast numbers of servicemen will be coming home and some will almost certainly be infected. Starting from next Sunday all shipping into Fremantle will be quarantined for a week.' She looks at Professor Brenton.

He nods and says, 'Because of the war, the countries involved have suppressed their mortality figures. However, you need to know that in the past months perhaps two hundred thousand people have died in Great Britain alone from this pneumonic form of influenza.'

There are gasps all around the hall.

'I fear that is the least of it,' he says sombrely. 'Already there have been more than five hundred thousand deaths in the United States, and I am told by reliable sources that millions of people in the East have already succumbed.'

Nurses murmur. Matron Chisholm coughs and silence returns as she says, 'One small mercy is that those who suffered influenza earlier in the year appear to be immune to this outbreak, which includes a number of you, I know. I shall be seeking volunteers to work at the Woodman Point quarantine station if and when the need arises. Are there any questions?'

A nurse puts up her hand. 'Where is Woodman Point, Matron?'

'Several miles south of Perth, on the coast.'

'And if you didn't get influenza before what will happen?' says another nurse timidly.

'We shall take all precautions to protect you and the people of this state by making certain the disease is contained by quarantine.' Matron pauses. 'There is nothing else we can do.'

'A nurse! Oh *God*, Lucy. Other women roll bandages and hold fund-raising teas but you've got to get right in amongst the bedpans. Really!'

'And welcome home to you too, Gideon. I trust your voyage was pleasant?'

'Crowded, but luckily we just managed to avoid quarantine. That would have been a bore.'

'Didn't you hear about the pneumonic influenza epidemic in England?'

Gideon sits down on the sofa, glass of whisky in his hand. I see his beauty has coarsened over the years he's been away.

'I believe it got quite sticky in the slums—logical I suppose after four years of privation. The order at the Department was to downplay it, not give heart to the enemy, that sort of thing. But you can't seriously imagine it could happen here?'

'Yes of course. That's why quarantine's been imposed.'

'Oh, Lucy! Always galloping off on your white charger to save the world—I'd almost forgotten your funny little ways. Yet nursing must suit you, you have something of a glow. Aha! A handsome young doctor on the scene, perhaps?'

'No, not at all. After Danny died I—walked out—for a time with Alain Bourdon, but he went to France a year ago to fight. We write but I don't expect him to return.'

'Ah well,' says Gideon. 'Every family needs its spinster aunt and I'm sure you'll find fulfilment in Rosa's children. They clearly adore you.'

'And I them,' I manage to say.

'To be frank, I doubt you'd have found happiness with Danny, in any case. He was so uncouth.'

His face is petulant and I look away to hide my dislike. I take a breath. 'Do tell me, Gideon—I've heard that Danny was unhappy about something in London. Was that your impression the evening you had dinner together?'

'Oh, good Lord, no, we enjoyed a magnificent repast. Afterwards he said, Gideon old man, that was the best meal of my life. No, it was very jolly, very jolly indeed.'

You're lying, I think, you can't even stop yourself. Why *bother*? I feel overcome with a terrible sadness. To change the subject I ask about his job prospects.

'Just between the two of us, I'm being considered for a vacancy at a rather exalted level of my old shipping line, if you take my meaning.' He winks.

'You're lucky to have work, Gideon. I doubt most of the returning soldiers will have such opportunities.'

'Lucy, you little Bolshevik! I never expected to hear such sentiments in my own house.' He guffaws at his own wit.

'It's Min-lu and Rosa's house.' He isn't listening. 'Gideon, so much has *changed* while you've been away. New ways of—'

'Good thing I'm here to put everything back on track then.'

Rosa appears at the door taking a scarf off her hair.

'Darling, how was your walk? Now Lucy, doesn't my dear wife look marvellous? It so warms my heart to be with my family again at last.'

He leaps up and hugs Rosa vigorously. She gives me a look of despair over his shoulder.

Men are still being sent to Europe even as the Armistice terms are being argued. At the end of October two troopships sail: *Boonah* for South Africa and *Medic* for New Zealand. Shortly after they reach port they're signalled to return home.

It's the 11th of November 1918, and the war to end all wars is finally over.

We hold a picnic in the park with the children to celebrate. Filipa and Eric come along too, no longer newlyweds but still immersed in each other. As Eric whispers in Fili's ear I feel a familiar pain.

The war is over at a cost beyond reckoning, and part of the cost was one man, the centre of my own small world. I get up and walk restlessly towards the water.

Rosa and Gideon are a short distance away, arguing. 'You will, you *bitch*!' he hisses, then turns his back and strides back to the picnic. He refills his glass and sits down, chatting charmingly to Izabel, Filipa and Eric, the essence of urbanity once again.

I stand beside my sister, who's staring out at the river.

'He wants me to stop painting,' she says.

'To stop seeing Anton too, I suppose?'

Rosa laughs. 'Yes. To stop seeing a man who respects me and has an open mind. A man, dear Lord, who encourages me to work.'

'When he's settled down again things might improve,' I say doubtfully.

'Unlikely, Lucy. He's been with other women while he was away and now he expects me to be just as compliant—and I will not.'

There's a fierce note in Rosa's voice, familiar from childhood. I touch her shoulder and say, 'I'll help you however I can.'

When we return in the evening I'm tired and the children are grizzling. Min-lu is thoughtful, Gideon silent, Rosa distant, and Izabel lost in a dream. Filipa and Eric, wisely, left earlier.

A sad letter from Papa awaits us: Emilia has just been informed that her daughter Cristina recently died in London of pneumonic influenza.

Gideon goes pale, grabs the letter and reads it for himself.

Rosa says coolly, 'Counting the weeks since you saw her last? Don't worry, you'd have got it by now.'

Medic returns to Sydney with over three hundred soldiers already ill with influenza, while *Boonah* arrives at Woodman Point in early December and three hundred and fifty men are rushed into quarantine.

I'm sent to nurse there at Woodman Point and it will haunt my dream forever.

When new arrivals are ferried ashore we give them disinfectant showers and fumigated clothes. Those who are still healthy wait out their time at the barracks. The others are taken to the observation block or the isolation hospital, behind a high stone wall.

One of my patients is Private Jimmy Betts, and I will never forget his plain, good-natured face. Jimmy is playing cards in the observation block when we first meet, and the men around him are smoking, reading, talking, waiting restlessly for this final service obligation to be over.

One by one I record everyone's temperatures. Jimmy winks at me and says, 'Come on Sister, we're all right, open the gates and let us go. There's a pretty young thing waiting for me—looks a bit like you, I reckon.'

'I'm a Nurse not a Sister, as you well know Private, and you'll have to wait like everyone else.' I look at my notes. 'In fact, you ... and Barnes ... and Warren—come to the clinic, please.'

The others call out ribald jokes as they get up to follow me. I take their temperatures and pulses again, and listen to their hearts while they cough on cue into their handkerchiefs.

'All right, Barnes, you can go back. Betts, Warren, come with me please.'

'Not the plague block, Nurse,' says Warren nervously.

'It's an isolation hospital, Private, just a precaution. I'd like to keep an eye on you.'

'Sounds good,' says Jimmy Betts. 'You can keep an eye on me any time, Nurse.'

He's laughing, then he looks down at his handkerchief. There are tiny red flecks on it.

By the time I walk them both over to Isolation, only fifty feet away, Jimmy is holding his belly, his teeth clenched. By the time he's in bed his face is scarlet and he's pouring with sweat.

After I return from dinner I check on him. He's hacking bloody foam into a pan and I set up a bowl of steaming water and zinc sulphate to ease his throat. It helps for a time.

He says hoarsely, 'You know, you'd like my girl Annie. She's kind and careful like you.'

The doctor arrives and gives him a strychnine injection and prescribes calcium lactate every four hours. Later I put a hot-water bottle under Jimmy's feet and gloves on his hands—they've started turning blue as his lungs fill with fluid. There's nothing I can do about the tips of his ears.

When I come back on duty next morning he's still coughing, almost without break, spitting blood and mucus into a bowl. The tips of his ears have turned black.

His eyes are glazed, and as he tries to focus on me, he says, 'Annie, love, I never told you—'

I try to make him comfortable, then turn to go.

'*Annie!*' he sobs.

I attend to him between my other duties, steaming his throat again, cleaning him as his bowels and lungs void black tissue. His coughing gradually slows along with his agonised gasping. His face is blue, his lips are black.

He says nothing more, but as I feel for his pulse he opens his sunken eyes and gazes at me, then closes them again. I sit down and hold his hand and a little later his chest stops moving.

I stop the openings of Jimmy Betts' body with folded gauze and dress him in a clean gown. The orderlies wheel him to the morgue while I wash my hands over and over again.

Jimmy Betts is only the first. Day after day, patients collapse with raging temperatures and within hours they're coughing up blood. Their ears, fingers and feet are cold and blue, dying from lack of oxygen as they drown in the fluid engorging their lungs.

The doctors try all sorts of treatments but the only thing that seems to help is nursing care, and often that's not enough.

We work desperately but some of us have no immunity, and as the patients drop, nurses and doctors drop with them: four of my friends do not recover. Ellen and I attend their burials with military honours in a little cemetery beneath dark trees.

As more patients arrive the pressure intensifies, and the joy of Armistice is a distant, forgotten dream.

But slowly, slowly, the numbers of new cases become fewer, and in late January 1919 government officials confidently declare the epidemic is contained.

They are sadly premature. Almost immediately the disease escapes quarantine and takes hold everywhere. In the great cities of Sydney and Melbourne the papers report ten, twenty, fifty people dying every day.

Yet here in Perth, astonishingly, the flood of new cases at Woodman Point slows and stops. One glorious day only convalescents remain in our care.

After three months of labour, lockdown is lifted and we are allowed to take leave.

21. THE TIPS OF HIS EARS

When I arrive at Rosa's house only Gideon is there, red-faced and drunk. He leads me into the sitting room and picks up a glass beside a half-empty bottle of whisky.

'She's throwing me out, the bitch,' he says bitterly. 'I'm supposed to pack and leave today.'

'I've been rather—busy—at the quarantine station. I didn't realise it had come to this.'

'She looks so sweet, your sister, but she's a harridan. I'm better off out of here anyway.'

'Where are you going?'

'The Grand Hotel. I rather fancy the suite.' He sighs. 'You're the only one left, Lucy, they've all abandoned me,' he says with alcoholic melancholy. 'So many years. I gave everything, now she won't even let me touch her. You're the only one who still cares. You do care, don't you?'

'Of course I want you to be happy Gideon, but you need to be happy with someone other than Rosa.'

He sways. 'That's just what I was thinking. You're a jolly little thing, you know. Perhaps you'd like to visit me at the Grand—a champagne dinner, what do you say?'

I laugh weakly. 'I'm too worn out to do anything, let alone have an assignation. Come on, I'll help you pack and then you should be off. You must do as Rosa asks.'

He draws himself up and pushes a lock of hair back from his sweaty forehead. 'The offer still stands, Lucy. You've always been dear to me. Perhaps after so long it's meant for us to be together.'

I gaze at him, exasperated. 'I don't think so, Gideon.'

He grows very still. He lifts his head and his eyes are dark with rage. 'That's right. You'd rather screw a Paddy bog-trotter than an honest Englishman. How's Danny's little half-caste now, by the way? Are you still worrying the Protector is coming to take him away?'

'He's well. Gideon—'

'I've got another piece of paper, you know.' He smiles horribly. 'That bitch mother of his would sign anything if you got her addled enough. It says the boy's real father is Big Alfred. Remember him? The Binghi gardener always in the lockup for drinking? Yes, I see you do.'

'Who'd believe that?'

He shrugs theatrically. 'Cristina's dead, Danny's dead. Who's to deny it?'

'Emilia, Papa, me!'

'Against a witnessed document signed by the late lamented mother? I doubt it. You have your own reason to lie, after all—you want the boy for yourselves.'

I stare at him, my heart pounding. Surely he can't be serious.

With exaggerated care he takes his wallet out, removes a piece of paper and unfolds it.

'There—see? Her words, her signature. Oh dear, you've gone terribly pale. No, no!' He whips the paper away from me as I try to grab it. 'You won't get it that easily.'

'Gideon *don't*—'

'That's it, oh yes, I do like a few tears. Well, if you really want this paper, Lucy, you'll find me at the Grand Hotel. Give me plenty of warning so I can chill the champagne.'

I return to Woodman Point, my thoughts in turmoil. Is he serious? Surely no one would believe that ridiculous story. No, I tell myself, even Gideon isn't cruel enough to hurt gentle little Liam. I will *not* let his threats upset me. He's just a fool, a petulant fool.

I force myself to concentrate on the job, and back on the ward I hear several new patients have been admitted. When I make my rounds I'm both horrified and delighted to see Thomas the Islander resting in an Observation bed.

'Thomas! Heavens, what are you doing here? Are you all right?'

'Miss Lucy! You a *nurse* now? Goodness me.' His strong face glows with pleasure.

'Oh, *Thomas*—it's wonderful to see you again. How are you feeling?'

'I be good, Missy, got pearldiver's lungs after all.'

I laugh. 'Let me look at your chart.' I'm relieved to see his symptoms are mild.

'Would you like to go down to the beach in a wheelchair? Some of the other patients are there at this time of day, and we can have a nice chat.'

Thomas is shy about me seeing him in his pyjamas but I get him a robe and reassure him. Soon I'm pushing his wheelchair down the path to the beach. We find a shady spot with a boulder for me to sit on, and we gaze over the water to Garden Island.

'I come in last night from London on a transport,' Thomas says. 'A few of us are sick, not too bad, just ordinary flu I think. But they say we must stay here and wait.'

'Well, that's probably a good thing and at least it means we've met up again. But what have you been doing these last few years, Thomas?'

'I been on coastal freighters most of the war, Missy. Got promoted to first mate. Had a few close calls but nothing like *Culardoch*.'

In silence we watch the sparkling water, while seagulls cry and wheel around us, then land and sidle away squabbling.

I take a breath. 'Thomas, tell me about it. I've wondered for so long. Please.'

He looks at me. 'Are you sure you want to hear it, Missy?'

'All, Thomas. Tell me all.'

'Well,' he says slowly, 'We stay in London one month loading scrap metal for New York. Then we sail to Ireland, to Queenstown to take on provisions, then we go. After one day we are near Fastnet Rock. You know where that is?'

'Yes. Yes, I know where that is.' My throat is tight.

'It is evening, warm, fields behind us. I smell hay on the wind.' He sighs. 'I am checking lifejackets in deck locker and I see Captain Danny looking sad. I try to cheer him up. I say, glad we're out of port now, Skipper. He says to me in gruff voice, Thomas, in London you help me very much. I'm so surprised. I say, of course I help you, I help you *always*. That makes him smile and he says, thank you Thomas.'

He wipes his forehead and takes a deep breath. 'Captain Danny goes to helm, talking to mate, Mr Doyle. Suddenly there is noise, hull clanging like bell, terrible sounds from rigging, everything shaking. Captain Danny calls out *Hard a'starboard, all hands on deck*! Men come from below, we wait, all quiet, looking at each other.' Thomas shakes his head slowly in distress. 'Oh, Missy, it was such a beautiful evening.'

He's sweating freely now. I dare not move.

'Captain Danny sends men to check holds, then Mr Doyle calls out, *There, sir*! We see bubbles to starboard. I pray to God, and that torpedo misses us. We know U-boat corrects for next one, so Captain yells *Hard a'port*! I think, if they miss us one more time they forget about us, we not worth the ammunition. Oh, I remember it all. So real even now.'

'Don't stop, Thomas. Please.'

He takes a deep breath. 'Suddenly there is big explosion at stern. Backstays snap, mainmast falls, broken cables whip through air. They ... cut. Shipmates are screaming.'

There are tears on his cheeks but I wait, implacable.

After a few moments he swallows and continues. 'Helmsman is

dead. Wheel is spinning, rudder is lost ... our wake behind is long, long curve. We start to settle by stern. Ship is slower now, sinking deeper and deeper. Captain Danny yells out *Abandon ship*! *Abandon ship, you lubbers*!

'Men run for lifeboats. I see Captain Danny heading below, I call out to him. He says he must get code books, we must abandon ship. Me and Mr Doyle help men into lifeboats, then we are so happy to see Captain Danny coming back. He throws the code books far away into the sea.'

Thomas looks up. 'He was always very careful like that, Missy.'

'Yes, Thomas.' I wipe my eyes. 'Even if the ship was sinking he knew that was his duty.'

'Two lifeboats get away, and beyond them I can see that black submarine that attacked us, evil as sin. Water is coming over stern now. Me and Mr Doyle and deck boys try to launch another lifeboat, but Captain Danny yells, *Go, go now,* and throws lifejackets at us. We pull them on, I see him looking for another one. I yell out, Skipper, starboard locker, *starboard locker*! I think he hears me—but he roars, *Jump, Thomas.*'

Tears are rolling down his face. 'I want to stay, but he is my captain. I *must* obey him, Missy.'

'Of course you had to go, Thomas, he didn't need you to stay.' My jaw is rigid with anguish. 'What happened then?'

'Me and deck boys and Mr Doyle jump into sea. I swim and get to lifeboat, but the others are not such good swimmers, they are still in water. Almost dark by now, but I think I see Captain Danny jump. I call out for him, again and again, *Captain Danny.*'

He puts his hands to his head. 'The sails are like ghosts, they are all white and shivering. Ship is sinking and air bubbles are exploding from holds. Then one great wave comes up, and rolls over everything, and afterwards ... afterwards, there is only wreckage. *Culardoch* is gone.'

He wipes his face.

'We yell for Captain Danny, for Mr Doyle, for the deck boys, but nobody answers. Germans from that black submarine laugh at us for crying for our ship. They steal our rations and go away. We row for very long time, until the Navy finds us. Ashore, later, we hear good news that Mr Doyle is safe.' He sighs. 'But not such good news for anyone else. That is all. Thank you, Missy.'

'What for?'

'I never tell anyone before. It feel a bit better now, you know?'

I stare at the sparkling water in front of us, the water that had closed over the head of my beloved. Seagulls cry and the wind rustles through the scrub, and a final question remains.

'Thomas, remember the letter you sent me after Danny died?'

'Of course.'

'You said Danny was unhappy in London, and now you say he was sad on the ship. But I don't understand. Gideon told me he was happy when he saw him.'

'Mr Gideon not telling the truth, perhaps,' he says quietly.

'No doubt of that. But I don't understand why he'd lie, or why Danny was so unhappy.' I rub my eyes. 'Please, Thomas ...'

He looks at me curiously. 'Because of you, Missy.'

I gasp. 'Me?'

'Captain Danny comes back from dinner with Mr Gideon very sad, very drunk. I help him to cabin. He asks me do I think Miss Lucy will be happy with that Frenchie, Mr Alain.'

'What?'

'Mr Gideon shows him photo of you with Mr Alain. He says you don't write him letter, but you send back engagement ring and Captain Danny's earring because you don't want them any more. You finish with Captain Danny, you marry Mr Alain.'

I stare at him in horror. 'But I *sent* Danny a letter! And his earring and my beautiful ring—they were *stolen* from me—how on earth did Gideon have them?'

Realisation hits and I fold in anguish.

'My God, my God.'

How I had misunderstood. Gideon, in London, entrusted with

my letter. Gideon, blaming the nanny when the jewellery was stolen. Gideon, threatening gentle Liam. Spiteful, *relentless* Gideon, who would never, ever, forgive.

And Danny had died believing me untrue.

A ship comes in that evening from Singapore with seven cases of raging influenza. Most of the patients are ship's crew, but one is an elegantly-dressed passenger. I help them into the ward, take their temperatures, wrap their clothes in paper parcels and write up notes on their conditions.

All the while my mind is in a crystalline state in which everything is sharp, remote and vividly real. I estimate the elegant man is perhaps half an hour from death, but with good nursing and much luck the rest, hacking and gasping for breath, may survive.

The elegant man dies twenty-five minutes later. I collect his parcel of infected clothes and take it by torchlight to the incinerator shed.

Then I have a sudden thought and stop and open the parcel. It holds a handmade shirt, tailored trousers, shoes, socks, underwear —and a handsome silk scarf.

I fold the scarf into one of my uniform pockets, rewrap the parcel, leave it for burning and return in the dark to the ward.

'Well, well, well—you've changed your mind,' says Gideon, leaning against the doorframe, his blue eyes looking me over. 'Do come in. Sorry, haven't had time to chill the champagne yet.'

I arrange myself gracefully in a velvet armchair opposite him, my handbag with its silken, infected gift beside me.

'I've thought about what you said, Gideon. I must admit, once I got over the initial shock—well, it's no secret we've always been fond of each other, and I suppose if we both get what we want—'

'Absolutely correct, old girl. Why don't you come over here to the sofa?'

'We can only speak tonight,' I say demurely. 'It's not quite the right time for me, you understand.'

'Damn. When, then?'

'I'll come back in two days, Gideon. There are just a few little things I need to clear up.'

He's wearing the ruby tiepin he claimed was stolen in the burglary. I point to it and laugh. 'Oh Gideon, you naughty boy. There wasn't *really* a robbery, was there?'

He looks charmingly abashed. 'Lord, Lucy, your sister was keeping me on a very tight rein at the time and the pawnbrokers saved my neck. I'm sorry you lost a few little things, but you did get the insurance money for them yourself. I'd never have tried to take that, of course.'

I gaze at him from under my eyelashes. 'Of course not. But a little bird tells me Danny got his earring back, Gideon. How could that be?'

'It was just a *joke*, Lucy.' He clears his throat and coughs. 'Honestly, I've no idea why he took it so badly. I was going to explain, but he left in such a fury and wouldn't return my calls.'

'And my letter, Gideon?'

'Didn't get a chance to give it to him. I planned to, after we'd had a good laugh about it all.' He loosens his tie and wipes his forehead. 'Still, I'd hoped it might make him think twice about you.'

'Oh?'

'Well if you'd married him, God forbid, he'd have been my brother-in-law! Would have appalled my parents, we deserved better.' He rubs his eyes and sighs. 'It's been a burden you understand, a terrible burden I've had to carry all these years. Nobody knows how painful it's been for me.'

'I can hardly imagine it.' My pulse is like a drumbeat in my throat.

He walks restlessly to the half-open window and pushes the brocade curtain to one side. He takes several deep breaths then sits down heavily on the sofa.

'Truth is I'm not feeling very well right now,' he says in a puzzled voice. 'Probably a good idea to put our celebration off for a couple of nights anyway.' He grimaces. 'I saw the quack today and he reassured me but, Lord, I feel awful.'

'In what way, Gideon?'

'Oh, aching everywhere, bad throat, hot one minute, chills the next. I'm sure it's nothing.' He coughs, takes out a handkerchief and coughs again and again in a spasm that lasts for a long time. Then he draws in a choking breath.

'Show me your handkerchief,' I say.

His face and eyes are red and sweat beads his forehead. He holds out the handkerchief in a shaking hand: it's covered in flecks of blood.

My training takes over, my silken revenge forgotten. 'Gideon, you must go to hospital *immediately.*'

He stares at me in horror. 'Not the hospital. I can't bear those places, you know I can't. When they pumped my stomach—dear God! Sickness is so *vile.* There's nothing wrong with me, really. I'll rest, get into bed, that's all I need—'

He begins coughing again.

'Gideon you *must* go, you must!'

'No, I can't, I won't. I'll stay here. You're a nurse, you'll look after me won't you, Lucy? For the sake of our old friendship?'

'You could ask that of me, after—?' I stop, outraged. After Sam and Rosa and Liam and *Danny?*

He's bent double, making a dreadful noise that goes on and on, and I gaze at him as if from a great distance.

'Well. Is that what you truly want, Gideon, to stay here? Are you quite, *quite* certain?'

He takes a long shuddering breath and groans. 'God, yes, no one must see me like this. You're the only one I can trust, Lucy.'

The tips of his ears are turning blue.

At the funeral Rosa looks fetching in a black silk hat and one of the new, shorter skirts. Her children and Ellen and Anton stand with her. Min-lu is as reserved as ever but her bearing holds a fierce satisfaction.

Soft-hearted Izabel sobs. Poor child, she's known her brother's friend, beautiful Gideon, all her life. She cries, 'Oh, *why* didn't you make him go to the hospital, Lucy?'

'He simply wouldn't go, darling. There, there. Life can be so cruel sometimes.'

Min-lu comes over to me and squeezes my hand.

'He drowned from the fluid in his lungs, you know,' I say. 'Drowning was his greatest fear.'

22. INVERLEY

Thomas the Islander is wrong about his good health. He collapses, his massive shoulders clenched in spasms of coughing, his lips spotted with blood. Desperately ill, he's moved into Isolation.

Even when my shift is over I stay with him, assuming bleakly he'll be dead by morning. Once, when I'm sponging him down, his large eyes open and he whispers, 'Missy,' with an air of wonder. I doze in a chair beside his bed, dreaming of the night I spent beside Mama so long ago.

To my surprise he's still alive when I wake up. There are no other acute patients on the ward, so I'm able to spend much of the day nursing him and he holds on. By next day he's coughing less, and a day later he can speak hoarsely and eat a little.

And miraculously, a fortnight later Thomas is well enough to be discharged. I go with him to wait for the truck that takes people to the jetty, where he'll catch a ferry to Fremantle and the steamer home to Broome.

As we stand in the shade of a tree Thomas says, 'You saved me, Missy.'

'I think it was more likely your pearldiver's lungs saved you, Thomas.'

After a moment says, 'No, you are wrong. I would truly die if you are not there, and all those other sick boys too. We would all die without you.'

I say bleakly, 'People die whether I'm there or not.'

He shakes his head and smiles. The truck comes down the road trailing a cloud of dust. Thomas throws his bag into the back and climbs in, breathing heavily.

'Don't forget, give my love to Liam,' I tell him. 'And say hello to Borue and Captain Gregory and Mr Murakami—'

'I will.' As the truck starts up again he calls, 'Bless you, Missy!'

I wave and watch the truck bumping away down the road.

'Bless you, dear Thomas,' I whisper.

Influenza flares up again, then fades away as immunity spreads. They say twelve thousand people died in the pandemic, but since they don't count Aborigines or foreigners it was probably many more.

Papa writes to tell me Thomas arrived home safely and is starting a ship-chandling business with Borue the Koepanger. Captain Gregory has just been elected the new Mayor of Broome, and Theresa and Mr Murakami are soon to be married.

I put down the letter, smiling. My friends are carrying on with their quiet lives and Liam is safe now forever from Gideon's venom.

One day I overhear a Sister saying, 'I really must speak to Nurse Fox, especially after that episode with the enormous—what, *Polynesian*? How on earth can one of my nurses be familiar with such a person?'

How very fortunate I am to be familiar with such a person, I think, and a few days later I resign. The hospital doesn't need so many nurses now the pandemic is over and I'm tired. But I don't know when—or even if—I'll ever go home to Broome.

In any case Min-lu is suddenly too busy to think about business, as Izabel falls suddenly ill. Fortunately it's simply appendicitis, not influenza, and she enjoys her bossy convalescence.

Min-lu says grimly she wouldn't mind a rest in a nursing home herself, because Izabel is still fiercely determined to be an actress despite her mother's carefully-marshalled arguments.

I receive a letter from Alain, who survived the war with a minor wound and some ugly memories. He says he will never forget me, but for the sake of his family he is marrying a distant cousin. He sends me a brooch with an exquisite sapphire, which rather pleases me.

Not long after Gideon's death Rosa holds a new exhibition that the critics call daring and perceptive. After a time she begins to be seen in society with Anton McKee.

People are kind. Gideon was not much loved.

One day in mid-1919 I come in from a wintry walk in the park to find Min-lu sitting on the sofa beside the fire staring at nothing, with a letter in her hand.

She says in wonder, 'I've heard from Freddy, Sam's father, do you remember? Left me pregnant in Hong Kong and went home and married the Honourable Edith. We've written to each other occasionally through the years of course, but *this*! My goodness.'

'What is it?' I sit down, laughing at her expression.

'Edith has died and Freddy wants me to visit England with Sam's children. He's desperate to see them.' She smiles to herself. 'And to see me.'

'Oh, that's wonderful!'

'Yes, isn't it? He's sending me tickets, with one for a companion. Will you come too?'

'But what about Rosa?' I say.

'I think she's too preoccupied with Anton and painting. We'll ask, but if she doesn't want to go and doesn't object to the children going without her—'

'Of course I'll come.'

It's decided that Izabel will stay behind with Fili and Eric at their farm. She's joined an amateur dramatics group in a nearby town and say she couldn't bear to leave now. (Min-lu says her headstrong daughter will soon find out for herself that acting is simply unglamorous hard work.)

After a few weeks of packing and farewells we board a steamship. When we pull away from the dock Peter feels unwell so Min-lu takes him below. I lean against the railing with Eliza, both of us pleased to see the lights of the shore disappearing in the dusk.

'Aunt Lucy,' Eliza says, 'will you be happy to see your old house in Greenwich again?'

'We're just going to drive past. It's been, oh, thirteen years since we left. My life is in Australia now, but I'd like to see—' I hear an echo of Danny's voice. *You always wanted to see.*

'That was in the olden days, wasn't it? When you used to wear corsets and long skirts.'

I laugh. 'Eliza, it wasn't the olden days! Well, perhaps it was, the war changed everything. If nothing else I'm glad we don't wear those awful corsets any more.'

'I like your new haircut too,' she says. 'It's very modern.'

I ruffle her dark brown curls. 'Oh darling, when you're all grown up you can have yours bobbed too if you want.'

We're silent for a time, watching the waves.

'Aunt Lucy, do you still miss Captain Whalen?'

I look at her, surprised. 'I didn't know you even remembered him.'

'I was nearly eight, and he was always so nice to me. He'd call me Lizzie Lee and give me toffees and swing me through the air.'

'That's right, so he would. Ah well. Yes, I still miss him.'

'It never seems to me that he's really gone. Not like Daddy and the *Koombana*.'

'Darling, you were closer to your Daddy so you'd feel the loss more.' I think, oh child, if only you knew how much I've hoped he wasn't really gone either.

We reach London in early October. As we steam along the Thames in the grey dawn I gaze at the drab warehouses and damaged wharves and wonder if Danny saw them too, when he sailed down the river and away to the waters of Fastnet Rock.

As we dock, Min-lu clings to my hand. 'It's been such a long time. What if Freddy doesn't—'

'Min-lu, you're as beautiful as you ever were.'

'Oh dear God, there he is.'

I see a broad-shouldered man with white hair and a wide moustache, waiting on the dock. He catches sight of us and begins to wave, a huge smile on his face.

'I think he recognises you, Min-lu, and he looks rather pleased at what he sees.'

The Honourable Freddy is more than pleased. He clears his throat and hugs Min-lu with what looks remarkably like a blush on his weatherbeaten cheeks. In minutes we're sweeping through customs, our baggage loaded into a large car by a chauffeur.

'And these are Sam's children,' Freddy says in wonder. 'Good Lord, our own *grandchildren*.'

'I've brought photographs too,' says Min-lu softly. 'Pictures of Sam and Rosa in Broome.'

'Thank you, my dear, I'd love to see them.'

They're both so shy they can hardly look at each other, but Freddy's hand slowly reaches out and takes Min-lu's. We drive along twisting streets and over a bridge to the south of the river, to Greenwich where my family lived before we set sail on *Willowmere*.

'It's all very grey, Nanna,' says Peter uncertainly. He and Eliza are perched on the folding bench facing the rear seat, where I sit beside their grandmother, who's unaccountably holding hands with a white-haired giant.

'We're almost—just down this street,' I call to the chauffeur. 'And to the right, yes, along here for a bit. There! On the left, number 32.'

We stop. I gaze at my old home, a semi-detached with a path leading to the front steps. Mama's beloved apple trees used to grow on either side of the garden but someone has cut them down and planted ugly bushes instead. The door is no longer blue but brown, and a pile of boxes sit untidily where Mama once had neat pots of lavender.

'Is that really where you grew up, Aunt Lucy?' asks Eliza.

'Yes. I can't believe how it's shrunk, and it's so untidy too.' I smile ruefully. 'Well, let's go now. We've got a long drive ahead.'

I silently watch the grimy streets of London pass by. Fields start to appear and we stop by a stream to eat the lunch Freddy has brought along. We drive on through the autumn afternoon, and the sun has set by the time we reach his farm near the South Downs in Hampshire.

'Just a little place really,' he says. 'Sheep, a few cereal crops, some fishing, that sort of thing.'

The old stone house is large and comfortable, with warm fires and fresh linens in the bedrooms. We eat a light supper the cook has left out, then the children go to bed. Soon afterwards I say I'm tired and follow them.

Min-lu and Freddy sit beside the fire and talk late into the night of the lives they've led apart for so many years. Then they climb the stairs together to Freddy's room.

We spend two weeks at the farm and the children love the dogs and horses and sheep. The days are brisk, sunny then cloudy then sunny again, the trees turning orange and gold.

It seems Freddy went to school with one of the Air Commodores of the new Royal Air Force, so we visit an airfield and Peter can't stop talking about Sopwith Camels for weeks.

Another of Freddy's school friends just happens to be a Lord of the Admiralty, so to Eliza's particular joy we spend a day at Portsmouth Naval Base.

I feel only an obligatory sense of awe at the vessels of the Royal Navy, so I sit on a bollard watching the water while a young commander discusses battleships with Eliza, Peter and Freddy, all equally enthralled.

Min-lu asks, 'You don't care for this kind of ship?'

'Not much.'

'You don't care for anything much,' she says gently.

'I feel so lost, Min-lu. My past no longer exists and I can't imagine any sort of future.'

She gazes at me. 'Freddy has suggested something. He'd like us to visit his estate in Ireland. He says it's peaceful and beautiful there.'

'Ireland? I can't go to *Ireland*—'

'It's nowhere near the place *Culardoch* was lost, Lucy, it's on the east coast. But I think you should go for another reason.'

I stand and walk to the edge of the jetty, hugging my arms for comfort.

Behind me Min-lu says, 'Did you know Danny's first mate Pat Doyle now works for Freddy?'

'Pat Doyle?' I recall the kind face of the man I met in that hectic time before Danny left. The man who survived when Danny didn't.

'He also sailed with Sam in the old days and Freddy was delighted to give him a job. Now Doyle is his estate manager, and I think you need to talk to him,' says Min-lu firmly.

'Need! Why?'

'To end, finally, with Danny. To speak to someone who actually saw his body buried. I'm sorry to be so brutal, Lucy, but you have no future while you cannot let him rest in peace.'

I say nothing for a long time then turn to Min-lu in despair.

'You're probably right but I can't do it. I can't.'

We return to London to stay at Freddy's house in Kensington. He takes us on outings to museums and galleries and West End shows. We watch the Changing of the Guard and visit the Tower of London and go to the docks to see the steamers, and I politely trail along. Then one day we see a great four-masted barque being towed up the Thames. Her name is *Inverley* and I cannot stop staring.

Freddy notices and next evening asks, 'How'd you like to visit that four-master we saw, Lucy?'

'*Inverley*? Yes, I'd like to.'

'Oh, please, me too!' says Eliza.

'Had a chat with a man I know at Clarksons today—they're the shipbrokers for those square-riggers. Not many left nowadays and they're being run out of Finland, of all places. He's written me an introduction to the master, Captain Nilsen, and he'll show us over the ship.'

'Nilsen?' I say. 'There was a boy on *Willowmere* of that name. I wonder if it's him. Probably not.'

Next day Eliza, Freddy and I walk along the dock to looming *Inverley*. Like *Culardoch*, she's a Scottish-built steel giant, and her carved painted figurehead is a lady with a sheaf of lilies.

As I'm walking up the gangway I see Mattias Nilsen. He's as fair as I remember—more muscular, more mature, but still the Swedish lad. He stares at me, delighted.

'My God, *Lucy*!' he says. '*Hej*, we meet again. I remember you often these many years.'

'*Hej*, Mattias.' He takes my hand to help me step off the gangway and holds it for a moment, smiling broadly as I introduce Freddy and Eliza.

'Why is this a Finnish ship now, Mattias?' I ask, as we take tea in the comfortable saloon.

'No one wants barques today, Lucy, so they are very cheap. The Finns of Åland buy them and work them with small crews, bringing grain from Australia.' He laughs. 'Pays well for the shipowners, not so much for the masters.'

'And when do you sail, Captain Nilsen?' asks Freddy.

'Not until late next week, sir. There is a problem getting a piece for the donkey-engine.'

I notice a portrait of a pretty blonde woman and a small girl on the wall. Eliza points and says, 'Is that your family?'

'That is my sister Annika and her daughter,' says Mattias. 'She is a widow, so we share a farm near Stockholm. But you are more grown-up than my niece, I think.'

Eliza beams. 'I'll be twelve in a month.'

'So young lady, you are the daughter of Sam and Rosa. Lucy, have you and Danny children too?'

Freddy says quickly, 'I'm afraid Captain Whalen was lost in the war.'

Mattias is horrified. 'I had no idea. I am very sorry. He was a good man.'

'Thank you Mattias,' I say steadily.

Mattias shakes his head and sighs. 'Too many good men gone.' He's quiet for a moment then says, 'I will show you my ship now.'

'I'd love that.'

The few times I visited *Culardoch* so long ago I'd been consumed with anxiety for Danny, so had barely noticed the vessel herself. But now, upon meeting *Culardoch*'s steel sister, I can recognise *Inverley* for the extraordinary creation she is.

We stroll along her vast curved deck, peering into the enormous cargo holds. We gaze at the giant double wheel of the helm and the roomy deckhouses, their roofs linked by catwalks, and we see the wide space under the poop deck that hold a myriad of sails and miles of rope.

We stare skywards in awe at the masts soaring hundreds of feet, their yards a forest of steel trunks, their stays as thick as my wrist, holding the structure in exquisite balance. We admire the crane and the donkey-engine.

Freddy says the massive winches are most impressive. Eliza declares the anchors are just like baby elephants. I say nothing, but gaze around me in passionate concentration.

'How many years more do you think she'll see, Captain Nilsen?' asks Freddy.

'Ten, perhaps twenty, sir.'

'She's just *wonderful*,' says Eliza. 'You're a very lucky captain.'

'Too much hard work I think, young lady! But yes, she is a fine ship. Perhaps when she is gone I retire, get a nice wife to live with me then.' He smiles at me.

I come back to the conversation. 'Oh yes, I hope so, Mattias.'

'You should come with us, Lucy, travel back to Australia on *Inverley*.'

I laugh. 'I'd love to. But surely you don't take passengers?'

'We take whatever we're told to take. People think, oh so romantic, and our owners think, oh so lucrative. Yes, we sometimes take passengers.'

'It would be wonderful, but we're staying in London for a time yet. Still, I'm so happy to have seen your beautiful *Inverley*. She makes me understand something I never understood before.'

I lean forward, gazing at the fire. 'Min-lu, I loathed *Culardoch* for taking Danny away, I loathed all the square-riggers. But after seeing *Inverley* I understand for the first time what his ship meant to him, why he had to go. *Inverley* is so beautiful—oh, she's more than beautiful, she's a work of art and intelligence, and I can't hate her. And now I can't hate *Culardoch* any more either.'

'Does this change of heart mean you feel able to come to Ireland with us?' says Min-lu, looking up from a sash she's sewing for Eliza.

'I think so,' I say in wonder. 'It's as if I can forgive Danny now for leaving me. Isn't that odd?'

Min-lu smiles. 'Not for you.'

We drive to Holyhead over a relaxing two days, then catch the ferry to Dublin. On the ferry, despite my best efforts, I feel shaken listening to the soft Irish accents around me, and find it hard not to stare at the men with russet curls: the men who seem always to be walking away from me.

In Dublin the following evening, Freddy takes me to a public house near our hotel.

'Min-lu told me you used to love the fiddle. Well, you'll hear some of the best in the country in this pub,' he says, opening the door. 'They take turns playing or they all pop up and play together. Lord knows how they keep track.'

There's a rush of tobacco-scented air as we enter the pub, lit up with coloured-glass shades over gaslights. The chatter doesn't change when we enter: I'm not a novelty, other women are sitting there too. From the back of the room comes the lilt of a tune I know, and my heart leaps.

Freddy pushes through the crowd and finds us a place to sit. Over to one side is a long table covered with ashtrays and glasses of beer. An old man is playing the accordion, his foot tapping, his head to one side. A fiddler joins in and then another, a young woman seated near me.

When the tune ends the young woman wipes her brow and turns to me smiling. 'Jesus, never thought I'd keep up with Billy on that one. And I've busted a string!' She finds a new one in her fiddle case and busily fits it.

'That's a lovely instrument,' I say.

'It's my da's best one, it's very old.' The woman looks up. 'Do you play?'

'I used to, a long time ago.'

Another tune begins. 'Oh, *Harvest Home*!' I say.

The young woman hands me the fiddle. 'Here, go on, I'm off to get a drink. You can do it, just keep up with the others, no one'll mind.'

I tentatively finger the notes as the music rises. Almost everyone is playing now and I softly join in. I lose myself in the rhythm, my hands seeming to remember what to do by themselves.

When the tune finishes everyone laughs and turns to each other and makes jokes about their own small mistakes, and I find myself beaming too.

'There, wasn't too bad, was it?' asks my new friend, returning with a glass of beer so dark it's almost black.

'It was wonderful, thank you so much.'

A man starts a slow, mournful tune on the uileann pipes and a whistle-player joins him. I think, I love this. It's nothing to do with Danny, at least not any more. I love this music for myself.

In the morning a hired taxi takes us fifty miles south of Dublin.

'My family has held this estate for two hundred years,' says Freddy. 'They were the sort of Englishmen who become more Irish than the Irish. Raised a few eyebrows back in London, I can tell you, especially when they kept their tenants on in the famine.'

'What about the fighting at the moment, Freddy?' says Min-lu. 'There's so much in the papers about Unionists and Republicans shooting each other, yet the people seem so friendly.'

'The worst of it's happening over in the west, my dear. Some of the British supporters have behaved reprehensibly so it's hard to blame the independence lot for retaliation,' says Freddy. 'Fortunately this region is quiet. Let's hope it all ends very quickly.'

We drive along a winding road into a valley at the foot of the Wicklow Uplands. On one side is a stream which widens into a small lake, and beside it is Freddy's house, large and shabby, set among trees and meadow grass, its facade of golden stone reflecting the afternoon sun.

When we get out the only sounds are bird calls and the rustle of leaves in the breeze. The front door opens and the butler greets us, followed by the housekeeper and two curtseying maids.

'This is Stafford,' Freddy says, 'and Mrs Walsh, and Bessie and Brigid. Or maybe it's Brigid and Bessie.' The maids giggle. 'I'm certain they'll make you very comfortable. And where's my right-hand man, Mr Doyle?'

'At the horse-fair in Newbridge, but he should be back this evening, sir,' says Stafford. 'We didn't expect you till next week.'

'Had a change of plans—a change of heart you could say,' says Freddy, smiling at me. 'Decided to strike while the iron was hot.'

We sit in the drawing room with its long windows looking out over the lake, and Mrs Walsh serves tea and sandwiches and cakes.

'I do hope I've managed to bake enough for you all, sir,' she says, thinking, he's brought some odd people home at times, but an oriental lady? Ah well, must be a princess or something—will you look at the size of that ruby!

I take a nap in the afternoon and when I come down another lavish meal is served. Then the children are tired and one of the maids takes them upstairs for baths and bed.

'Lucy, we have something to tell you,' says Min-lu. 'Freddy has decided to come back to Australia with us when we leave. He'll stay there for half a year, then I'll come back here for half a year.'

'How lovely! I'll miss you when you're away of course, but six months won't be too long.'

'You don't mind me running off with your Min-lu like this?' asks Freddy.

'You make her happy, Freddy. I'm glad for you both.' I stretch and find myself yawning. 'Heavens, the air here's so fresh it's like a drug. I think I'd better take a stroll down to the lake before it gets too dark.'

Min-lu says, 'We'll be off to bed in a while too, I think—we're not as young as we'd like to believe.' Freddy smiles until she blushes and says, 'Stop that, Freddy.'

He chuckles and says, 'Lucy, there's a path over to the side that loops back through the meadow. No chance of losing your way.'

The sun has almost set but I know the twilight will last. I can smell cut hay and horses and woodsmoke, and from a small rise I see the lake and a cottage beside it with a wisp rising from the chimney.

The path is easy walking at first but becomes narrower, with long grass and bushes, and I have to push through the undergrowth.

Breathing heavily, I start to think perhaps I've lost my way after all, then I see the lake glimmering between the leaves. Almost there. I emerge through the trees near the cottage and find myself on a swathe of soft turf.

My breathing slows. I sit down and wrap my arms around my knees. A few tumbled clouds far away are catching the last rays of the sun, the sky is fading to red-gold and a breeze ruffles the reeds in the lake. It's lovely here, and quite different from anything I've ever seen before.

I gaze at the faint moon lying above the hills and the shimmer of light on the moving water's edge. That's strange. The landscape here is completely foreign, but still it reminds me of something. What is it?

Then I gasp at the shock of recall. Of course: that evening in Broome, golden ripples on the bay and Captain Gregory's silver moon in the dusty blue sky.

The last time I ever touched *Sparrow*. The first time I ever touched Danny.

After so long, the almost-forgotten colours and smells and sensations of Broome flood over me. The violet sky, the turquoise sea, the hot orange rocks, the rustle of palm trees, the tropical flowers, the sweet night fragrances.

Home, I think with joy. That's what I yearn for! Not emerald Irish fields or grey English skies: I want to go home to Broome—to Liam and luggers and pink sand and shimmering pearlshell.

I close my eyes and fall into my memories.

A long time later I seem to hear a soft noise and lift my head and sigh, coming out of my reverie. The sky is darkening, the horizon barely outlined by twilight. Then someone speaks behind me and my heart thuds.

'Don't you move, lad, I've a shotgun aimed at your back.'

'All right,' I whisper.

A *gun*? Has the violence started here as well?

'I'll have no poaching on these lands. Get up.'

I smile with relief. It must be the estate manager returned from the horse fair.

'I'm not a poacher, I'm a friend of Freddy's. Is that you, Mr Doyle?'

'Indeed it is. Let's see you now.'

I stand and turn. I look along a gunbarrel gripped in large hands to a pale shirt, a glint of earring, a face more familiar than my own.

'*Lucy?*'

23. PAT DOYLE

I cannot move my lips to speak and silence roars in my ears. I try to breathe but it's as if I've been kicked in the stomach. Distantly I see the man put the gun carefully on the ground.

'You?' I finally whisper. '*You're* Pat Doyle?'

'I thought you were coming next week,' he says coldly. 'I wasn't going to be here.'

'You're *alive*?' My voice is shaking. 'All these years you've been here and you didn't tell us?' My voice cracks. 'How *could* you?'

'What bloody business was it of yours? I'd washed my hands of the lot of you. You dumped me flat for another man.'

'I didn't, I didn't!' I'm beside myself with rage. 'Gideon lied about it all, I never planned to marry anyone else. He lied and he lied and he *lied!*'

Danny stares at me. 'He lied?'

He sits down heavily on a stump. 'Oh, Jesus, what a fool I am. Of course he lied, he always did, and I *believed* him?' He stands up. 'I'll kill the bastard.'

'You don't have to. I already did.'

'You *killed* Gideon?'

'Yes.' I can feel the blood pounding in my ears. 'But how are you *alive*? Dear God, we got the telegram, the official letter!'

He shakes his head. 'I barely know myself. I was in the water, the little cat was mewling nearby, and I was ready—past ready—to go with the cat and *Culardoch*.' He laughs bleakly. 'I remember thinking, oh Lucy, your silver highways have done for me now.'

'But that was clearly not the case,' I say flatly.

'The holds blew as the ship sank and a wave pulled me under and I blacked out. When I came to it was dark, the lifeboats were gone and I was lying across a plank. I was pissed off—didn't fancy facing down the sharks again. I wanted to let go.'

'Why didn't you then?'

'That bloody cat was beside me on the plank, shivering against my neck, so I couldn't.' He sighs. 'We drifted all night then washed up on a beach at dawn, quiet as a feather. I just lay on the sand for hours looking at the sky.'

'And the cat?' I say coldly.

'Walked off with her tail in the air. Next time I saw her she'd moved in with the local priest.'

I stare at him. 'I'm freezing, I'm going to fall over.'

'Shock. Come along, I've a fire in the cottage.'

He shows me to an armchair and builds the fire up to a blaze. He gets us two glasses of whisky and sits down in the other chair.

'At least you knew I was still alive!' I say bitterly. 'How could you let me believe, go *on* believing, damn you, damn you—'

After a few moments he says in a low voice, 'But I didn't matter to you any more. My mother had died, *Culardoch* was gone. You—Liam—everything—was lost. I lay on the sand and wanted to forget Danny Whalen ever existed.'

'You did a damned fine job of that. But why on earth do people think you're Pat Doyle?'

He shrugs. 'I told them so.'

I stare at him, appalled.

'The farmers came down to help and I didn't want to be *me*. Pat was the last man I'd seen on the ship, the first name I thought of.' He hesitates. 'I think I went mad for a time. Another shipwreck seemed more than I could bear.'

He leans forward and stokes the fire. 'Further along the beach they found the bodies and by God, I didn't expect to see poor Pat lying there. But I knew he had no family, no one'd care if I kept his

name. So I said he was Danny Whalen, and that's how they buried
him.'

I rub my face and take a breath. 'And how did you end up here
with Freddy?'

He runs his fingers though his curls, a gesture so achingly familiar
I have to look away.

'I saw myself buried near Barley Cove. Interesting, that.' He
laughs shortly. 'Then I walked away from the sea, took odd jobs,
kept on the move. One night I ran across a carriage with its wheel
off and an old man by himself. It was no part of the country for an
Englishman, so I helped him.'

'Did you know he was Sam's father?'

'Not at first, though he seemed familiar. Then when I told him
my name was Doyle, he spoke of Sam because he'd once been
shipmates with Doyle—and he offered me a job.'

I sit in silence and sip my drink.

'And you?' he asks. 'After you thought I was gone?'

I gaze at him. 'I mourned like a demented fool. Then I took Alain
Bourdon as a lover.'

Danny gulps a large mouthful of whisky and stares into the fire.

'Alain went away to fight and I became a nurse. Gideon came
home and I found out about the lies he'd told you. So when he
became ill I let him die.'

'Christ.'

'Wait a minute, I nearly forgot about the miscarriage—to Alain—
and now I'm barren.'

'Oh, *sweetheart ...*'

'It's certainly been an interesting few years. Thank you, Danny.'

I put down the glass and walk out.

It's dark by the time I get back. No chance of losing my way,
Freddy? I've lost it completely.

Min-lu and Freddy are about to put out the sitting room lights when I arrive. I stare at Min-lu stony-faced. 'How could you *do* this? Not even give me a warning!'

'What?'

'No wonder you were so damned keen to get me here!'

'Lucy, what are you talking about?'

'You know perfectly well. Danny, here—*alive*. Freddy's helpful right-hand man, Pat Doyle!'

'Freddy?' says Min-lu, turning to him.

'Danny?' says Freddy. 'My Doyle is your lost Captain Whalen?'

I look from one to the other. 'Oh God, you didn't know.' I sit down suddenly on the sofa.

'Of course not. But I always wondered,' says Freddy. 'Many a man wants to put something behind him so I didn't pry. Said he'd shipped with Sam. Good enough for me.'

'How can this possibly be, Lucy?' says Min-lu in wonder, sitting beside me. 'Danny's dead.'

'No. No, he's not. He survived the wreck ... but he wanted to forget us.'

'Forget! Forget *you*?'

'Gideon told Danny I'd broken our engagement ...' I begin to sob.

'Oh, of course,' says Min-lu. '*Gideon*.'

'Gideon?' says Freddy, quite lost.

Min-lu sighs. 'I'll explain later.'

'Scoundrel by the sounds of it. I'll horse-whip him for you, Lucy.'

'No, it's fine,' says Min-lu. 'She killed him already.'

'Good girl,' says Freddy. 'So, d'you want me to promote Doyle or dismiss him?'

I laugh through my tears. 'I haven't the faintest idea.'

At dawn I get up and sit on the window seat for a time, then dress and walk down through the meadow, the path spangled with spiderwebs of dew. When I reach the lake Danny is there, seated on a bench, watching the pink clouds to the east.

I sit in silence beside him. After a time he sighs deeply. 'I'm sorry, Lucy. So utterly, *terribly* sorry. It's not enough, I know.'

'I don't understand, that's all,' I say. 'I don't understand how you could have believed Gideon's lies, how you could think I'd shrug you off as easily as that.'

He looks at me in surprise. 'I thought it was obvious. I always knew I wasn't for you, not really. You were the skipper's beautiful daughter and I was Paddy scum from the foc's'le deck. Why wouldn't you leave me one day?'

'But you were my dearest friend.'

He rubs his forehead. 'And you the best I ever had. But I never quite trusted my luck, and Gideon knew it.'

A flock of ducks land in the reeds. I go to the water to watch them, then say, 'Let's walk along here.' A gravel path leads past the reeds, and our footsteps crunch softly in the quiet morning.

After a pause I say, 'Your fiddle is safe. Min-lu locked it away with mine in an antique chest in Broome.'

'Glad it survived, never had another like it. Are you still playing?'

'Not for a long time but I might start again. I heard some good tunes when we were in Dublin.'

'And Liam ...' says Danny hesitantly. 'Is he doing well? A schoolboy now, I expect.'

'He's healthy and happy. We write and he draws me pictures of luggers and asks when I'm coming home.' Home, I think, my heart aching. No matter what, I can go home.

'Does he live with his mother now?'

I sigh. 'Danny. There's so much you don't know yet.' I take a breath. 'Cristina died almost a year ago. Liam's living with Emilia and Papa.'

'That'd be best for him then, with both parents gone.'

I halt. 'What do you mean *both*? And yesterday, why did you say you'd lost him?'

'He's not my son, just as I'd feared. Gideon showed me—'

'Oh Lord, let me guess. A sworn statement from Cristina?'

'How do you know that?'

'I've seen a few of those. Who was the father this time?'

'Him—Gideon. Said they'd been lovers while she was with me. Lucy, what's so damned funny?'

'I went through Gideon's things when he was dead and burned several papers. One claiming he personally was Liam's father, another gave Papa the credit, and a third had Big Alfred—yes, Big Alfred—doing the honours. The only paper existing now is the one that names you.'

'But after that, how could it be worth anything at all?'

I sit down on a bench and gaze at him, biting my lip thoughtfully. 'Tell me, Danny. Have you ever seen your back in a cheval mirror?'

His eyebrows rise. 'Square-riggers are usually lacking such refinements. I'd have to say no.'

'Then you're not aware you have a brown mark in the small of your back, the shape of a flying jib in, oh, a twenty-knot wind?'

'Not ten knots?'

'No. Definitely twenty.'

He gazes at me. 'Do I really?'

'Yes.'

'Something like that little birthmark on Liam?'

'Identical.'

'Ah.' He breathes out and his eyes slowly crinkle. 'Twenty knots, you say?'

'Perhaps twenty-five. I'd have to check.'

He sits down beside me and takes my hand and kisses it.

'It's the sort of thing we'd need to be certain about,' he says. 'I'd be grateful if you would.'

Danny leans on one elbow looking down at me, his green eyes gentle. He strokes a lock of hair back from my forehead. 'I like your hair cut short. Less monkey, more Highland terrier.'

'You won't get around me with flattery,' I say, caressing his back.

'I seem to have got around you somehow or other.'

'Well, I had to be certain. Definitely Beaufort Scale six. Anyway, I just wanted to see.'

He laughs and we kiss again. A long time later, he carries cups of tea to the bedside table, naked, unselfconscious. I smile at the sight of his strong shoulders and slim hips and long bony legs.

'So what did Gideon die of?' he asks, setting down the cups, climbing into bed and wrapping his arms around me.

'Influenza. I was planning to infect him with a scarf, but he'd already caught it—'

'Then you didn't really kill him.'

'Oh, but I did. Once he was unconscious I could have called the ambulance, but I just sat with him until the end. You see, whatever Gideon wanted Gideon got—and he wanted me to keep him out of hospital.'

'You're terrifying. I always knew you were the woman for me.'

Dust motes spiral through the slanting light as we lie together, late in the day.

'I'm doing well here,' Danny says, nuzzling the back of my neck. 'Freddy's a good boss. I've made some money selling bloodstock too, more prosperous than I've ever been. Could strike out on my own but haven't so far, I like Freddy too much.'

He stops nuzzling for a moment and laughs ruefully. 'I kept your emerald ring, you know—wanted to throw it into the sea but couldn't do it. Stay here with me, sweetheart, and we can get married after all. What do you think?'

'But love, I must go home to Broome,' I say, confused. 'Liam's there and that's where you should be too. Papa's getting old and Liam needs you.'

After a pause he says, 'How can I possibly go back when everyone thinks I'm dead?'

'We can say you had amnesia, shellshock, didn't know who you were. It's common enough.'

He's silent.

'Danny, it's my *home*. It used to be yours too.'

'I've made a new life here,' he says slowly. 'How could I face Broome? I've let everyone down, I've hurt you and Liam beyond all forgiving. I've stolen the name of a good man who didn't deserve it. I've been a gullible fool and a liar too, no better than Gideon.'

He sits up. I roll over and gaze at him as he takes a cigarette and lights it, his hand trembling.

'Truth is, I'm in shock seeing you again.' He rubs his face. 'I'm ashamed, God knows, and I'm afraid too, afraid of going back to sea on a ship. I don't know if I can. I'm sorry, Lucy, I'm not the man I used to be.'

He won't look at me.

I sit up, anguished. 'You don't think this is a shock to me too? At least *you* knew I was still alive! All you had to mourn for was the *supposed* loss of my love, Danny, but I've had to mourn for more than you could ever comprehend.'

'I know that, sweetheart.'

'I don't think you do. In fact I don't see how you possibly can.' It feels as if my throat will explode. 'But back in Broome you could still do something for *Liam!*'

'I'd be ashamed to go near the boy. What sort of a father could I be after what I've done?'

I say coldly, 'And how, precisely, do you plan to improve that situation, Danny? By running away *again?*'

The silence lengthens until the truth is inescapable.

I can't think for pain. I push back the bed-covers, stand, gather my scattered clothes and carefully put them on.

At the door I turn and gaze at him, puzzled. 'No, you're not the man you used to be. Goodbye, Pat Doyle.'

I tell Min-lu and Freddy I'm leaving for London alone. They protest but I'm adamant, and pack quickly.

Freddy orders the local taxi to take me to Dublin and explains how to book for the ferry to Holyhead and the train to London.

'Lucy, are you quite certain?' says Min-lu, as the taxi comes along the driveway.

'Yes. I know what I want to do and now I'm going to do it. Your plan worked, Min-lu. I met Pat Doyle and now I'm absolutely certain Danny is dead.'

Min-lu gasps. 'Lucy, no!'

I hug her. 'I must go.'

'Anything you need, just call us,' says Freddy. 'My lawyer's put a deposit in your bank account to cover all expenses. Now, Lucy, you be careful. A young woman travelling alone ...'

'Freddy, thank you. But I've been shipwrecked, I've been a pearler, I've been a nurse. I even have my own money. I can look after myself.'

'Well, goodness me, yes. I suppose you can.' He brightens. 'But once we're with you in London, you'll be all right.'

I laugh in exasperation and kiss them both, then get into the taxi.

Four days later I embark on *Inverley*.

24. THE SHIMMERING MORNING

I leave after just one day in London, hurriedly organising my passage with Clarksons and just as hurriedly packing. On the mantelpiece I prop a letter for Min-lu and Freddy, saying I'll land in three or four months at Port Victoria, South Australia.

I remember Papa joking, *Lucy, should you ever be planning to elope, please just go quietly. Don't leave us any letters.* Oh well, Papa, going to sea is hardly an elopement.

Inverley is sailing the same route as *Willowmere* thirteen years ago. The winds are constant, the sailing fine, carrying us smoothly past the Bay of Biscay and the coast of Portugal.

It isn't until we near the Canaries that bad weather hits us, causing a corkscrew rolling that makes everyone sick, even me. I come on deck for a short time when the winds calm down.

Mattias says, 'You get your sea-legs soon, Lucy.'

'But I've never *been* seasick before,' I say crossly.

'Even when I am ashore for just six months I get sick the first time back. You will be better soon.'

Inverley begins rolling again and I totter below to my berth.

I'm not the only passenger on board. There are two friendly older women, Teddy and Frankie, who share the cabin next to me, and down the corridor is a young gentleman, George, being sent out to the colonies to make something of himself.

Often there are echoes of the voyage on *Willowmere*. One day we're wallowing through the hot, blue-sky doldrums, when the smell of pitch takes me back to Gideon teaching me to tie sailor's knots, and Danny teasing me about climbing the rigging. So long ago.

I haven't completely recovered from my sea-sickness, and suspicion has fallen on something we've eaten, as Teddy is also still unwell. I've lost quite a lot of weight but since I'm starting to feel better every day I know I'll soon put it back on.

The crew of the four-master is made up of young Scandinavians: it's not as diverse as on *Willowmere*. Some of the lads are friendly towards me, some suspicious, but all are slyly curious about my relationship with the captain. Occasionally Mattias and I are able to talk together in the saloon or charthouse, but there's little privacy on a ship.

Daily life on a giant four-master is not very different to life on little *Willowmere*, although time has brought changes. As on *Willowmere* there are only twenty or so crew, but now brace-winches and an engine help *Inverley*'s men with the massive yards. There are other changes too—the galley may be larger here but the food is meaner and, I suspect from my illness, rather less fresh.

One day Mattias and I are chatting about *Willowmere* and he shows me the old scar on his head, now just a silvery line. But we cannot even find my own scar—Mattias gently parts my hair here and there but the sailmaker's stitching was so perfect it has quite disappeared. (The third mate gazes open-mouthed in amazement and nudges the man at the helm in the ribs.)

The boys hold a Neptune ceremony at the Equator, not as elaborate as *Willowmere*'s but just as unpleasant for the apprentices. It's the first crossing of the Line for the other passengers—young George bravely accepts a drubbing, though the older women are treated more gently.

Teddy, less rotund now since her sea-sickness, gruffly accepts a parchment of welcome and shakes Neptune's hand, while Frankie does some clever drawings of the ceremony.

I remind Mattias about his long-ago role as shy Amphitrite in rope ringlets, consort to Danny's King Neptune and attended by the ramshackle court. (The second mate raises his eyebrows and gives the bosun a significant nod at the sound of our laughter.)

The wind carries us towards South America. When we're off the humid Amazon the weather is calm and no Pampero strikes. This is a disappointment to George and Teddy, who'd hoped for a bit of drama, but a great relief to me and Mattias.

As we cross into the South Atlantic the storms arrive. Yet tempests that might have overwhelmed little *Willowmere* hardly ruffle four-masted *Inverley*, with her ranks of great rounded sails driving her along. The grey days have their own charm, while dark evenings pass peacefully with reading and conversation in the warmth of the saloon.

As the weeks go by I realise Mattias is growing to care for me, yet I know a relationship between us would be impossible. When I talk about my life in Broome he's shocked (Frankie says she'd love to be a pearling master), and he disapproves of my nursing work, deeming it unsuitable for a woman even in wartime (Teddy says, 'Dashed good show').

Mattias is a kind man but naïve, and for all his years on ships it seems he knows little about the world. I'm fond of him, but I've experienced too much to find comfort with someone so untouched.

Or perhaps with anyone at all.

We pass into the Indian Ocean and the days grow warmer. I feel wonderful now because I've put my lost weight back on and even a little more. For the first time in my life I feel womanly—almost as buxom as Rosa, I think with delight.

When we're approaching Western Australia we see a passenger ship far away. Both vessels change course to meet, and people stare and wave at us, the now-rare sight of a square-rigger. *Inverley*'s mate signals the steamer so they can pass on the news of our position.

Two weeks later I see blue-brown slivers on the horizon and the

Eyre Peninsular begins to emerge from the haze. After a day of sailing we turn into Spencer Gulf, heading towards the eastern shore and little Port Victoria.

Inverley must first go to the ballast grounds to unload the rocks and sand that have stabilised her for the outward voyage. The donkey-engine hauls out the slimy ballast and drops it splashing into the sea.

That takes two days, *Inverley* riding higher and higher in the water as she's unloaded. Then we sail to Port Victoria and let go the massive anchors half a mile off the long jetty.

Ninety-six days, we say to each other in delight. A fine passage!

Two boys row Mattias ashore in the afternoon to exchange papers with the Harbour Master, send cables to London and Finland, and arrange onward travel for the passengers. He returns with fresh food and beer for a small party to celebrate our arrival.

I'm sorry to be leaving *Inverley* but eager for tomorrow to come. I still have a long trip ahead. A hired car will take me one hundred and twenty miles to Port Adelaide, then I'll catch a steamer to Fremantle and another to Broome.

We've arrived in late February, midsummer in the Spencer Gulf. For the party I wear my favourite dress but it's a little tight in the heat (perhaps buxomness has its drawbacks, I think, gazing in the mirror).

But I know I look pretty, so I'm surprised to realise Mattias is almost cool towards me during the evening. I wonder if it's because we'll soon be parting.

Later, when everyone has wandered tipsily to their cabins, I ask, 'Mattias, is anything wrong?'

He gazes at me sternly. 'Perhaps that is something you must tell me, Lucy.'

'What do you mean?'

'It is obvious now. You make me believe you are alone, you lose

Danny, you have no man. Yet I think you lie. It must be that you leave a boyfriend behind in London.'

'Mattias, that's not so.'

'Ah, still you pretend. You cannot pretend for much longer, soon everyone will know.'

'Know?'

'Oh, Lucy, come on.' He waves at my waist. 'You are going to have baby. I see how it was for my sister. Sick, then fat in bosom, face all soft. Like you.'

I stare at him, then carefully sit down. I gaze at a half-empty glass, a plate scattered with crumbs, a paper streamer lying across the table. Could it be? Certainly, my courses had ceased early in the voyage, but I'd assumed it was from my weight loss, as in the past, not because—

'But I'm *barren*,' I say, astonished. 'The doctor said I cannot have children.'

'Well that is one not very good doctor, I think! So you do not deny? You have boyfriend?'

'Mattias, when I went to Ireland I ... found Danny Whalen there. He isn't dead, after all. He'd—he'd lost his mind for a time from the shipwreck. He told people he was someone else.'

Mattias nods sagely. 'Ah yes, that happens a lot in the war. So now I understand, you meet Danny, you are together again. But why did you not tell me, Lucy? I start to think you and me ...' He sits down heavily.

'I'm so sorry, Mattias. You're a fine man and I like you very much. But I was trying to forget Danny and simply couldn't talk about it.'

'Forget, why? He is alive!'

'Yes, he's alive. But you see, he doesn't want to live with me.'

'Ah, I understand. So now you have baby and no Danny.'

I smile, tears spilling from my eyes. 'Yes. I have baby and no Danny.'

'Lucy, what will you do?'

I wipe my face, laughing weakly. 'Oh my goodness. A baby? I'll go home, Mattias. I'll go home to Broome and have my baby.'

Young George has decided he likes being at sea, so he signs on for the return passage to England, while Teddy and Frankie are booked for a touring holiday. I get up early to farewell them, then later that morning it's time for me to leave too.

Before I go ashore Mattias takes me aside. 'You will write to me, Lucy? Your family will look after you I think, but I help if I can. Still, perhaps you cannot come to my farm, my sister would never approve.'

'But I wouldn't have suited your farm anyway, Mattias. You see, I don't like the cold.'

'Ah, of course. But Lucy, we are still friends?'

'Always.' I kiss him on the cheek. 'This has been a wonderful time, Mattias—and I hope *Inverley* sails for many years yet. And I hope you find a wife for your farm, too.'

He grins. 'I try to make it so! *Hej då*, Lucy.'

He helps me over the side and I climb down the ladder hanging over *Inverley*'s steel hull to the boat below, where one of the boys helps me to a seat near the bow.

I call out my farewells and we pull away from the ship. The day is warm, the air shimmering, the water calm and very blue. The lapping of oars is the only sound in the dreamlike morning.

After a long row we tie up at a small landing off the jetty. The boys help me out, and carry my bags up the stairs and along to a small shed on the foreshore. I shake their hands, then they climb back in the boat and row away.

I gaze beyond them at the four-master riding high in the water, ready to be loaded once more with grain to feed Europe. Magnificent *Inverley*, I think, thank you for this wonderful time.

And now? I feel an ache of fear and wonder. A baby? I can scarcely believe it yet I know Mattias is right. I was simply denying the obvious.

And yes, I'll go home, although I know even in relaxed Broome there are those who'll treat me with contempt. My family may try to protect me, but it won't be easy.

I sigh and turn to climb the stairs from the landing to the jetty. From there I can see the one or two dusty roads of Port Victoria and a hotel across the way.

Mattias arranged yesterday for a car to come from the hotel with a driver to take me to Port Adelaide. I walk towards the little shed, the sun dazzling my eyes.

As I draw closer I can see the car, and my bags beside it, and a man waiting for me.

Light glints from his earring.

'You took your time,' he says.

'Just when are you going to stop popping up in my life like a smug Cheshire Cat?' My heart is thumping. 'And how did you get here?'

'Steamer. Wanted to get home before you,' says Danny.

'Home? I thought Ireland was home.'

'Not once you'd gone away.'

'Did it take you long to realise that?'

'Until all of next morning. And Eliza—young Lizzie Lee—came and had a sharp word with me. You always did have friends who thought I needed a word or two. She suggested I admit I've been a spineless, ludicrous fool and beg humbly for your forgiveness. May I do that?'

'I suppose you may.'

My knees seem to be trembling. I sit down on a bench outside the shed and gaze at *Inverley*, serenely afloat on the mirror-blue water.

'Trouble was, I couldn't catch up with you to do any begging, you'd taken the only taxi in the village. By the time I got to Dublin you were gone, and by Holyhead you had a day's lead. In London I went to the docks as soon as I read your letter but you'd sailed four hours before.'

'I don't like to hang around,' I say coolly.

'That's for sure. So there was nothing to do but follow you back to Australia. Been here two months already.'

My face is calm. 'Have you visited Broome?'

'I have.' He shakes his head in bemusement. 'No one cared a jot where I've been or even why. They just welcomed me back.'

'And Liam?' There seems to be a bubble of joy in my chest.

'Wants to know when you'll be home, the darling boy. He did you a painting of *Sparrow* with her new clipper bow, courtesy of Captain Gregory.'

'He always said he'd rebuild her one day.' My beautiful *Sparrow*.

'Mr Egawa's done a good job. You'll be impressed.'

'Perhaps.' I glance at him. 'Min-lu and Freddy are well?'

'Flourishing, but now it turns out young Izabel's run off to England to become an actress. Since Min-lu'll be over there much of the time now herself, she's not too fussed.'

I nod. 'I'm glad Izabel's doing what she wants. Did Freddy and Min-lu visit Broome with you?'

'Indeed they did. Freddy's seen an opportunity already and says I've a job going there if I want.'

'But surely you wouldn't return to a *port*?' I say. 'I hear there's a terrible lot of sharks in Broome.'

'Aye, so many you can hardly get a boat in the water.'

'And what about those giant octopuses then?'

'Busy sorting the shell in the packing sheds.'

'And the man-eating clams?'

'Still running the Pearlers' Association.'

I can't help but smile.

Danny sits down beside me. 'You'd a pleasant passage with Captain Nilsen, then?'

'Extremely pleasant, thank you. I was even pressed to visit the farm near Stockholm. Sadly, the invitation had to be withdrawn when he realised I was a fallen woman.'

Danny laughs. 'A *what*?'

'You heard me.'

He takes my hand. 'You're looking remarkably lush and pleased with yourself. I thought fallen women were thin and haunted.'

'Not this one,' I say. 'But I think you'd better marry me before my reputation goes entirely adrift.'

'Well, I just happen to have a fine engagement ring with a sea-green emerald that might be to your liking.'

'Hope it still fits when I'm a lot lusher than this.'

He gazes at me in wonder. 'Not barren after all? I've heard the Irish air is a great curative.'

'I think, myself, it may have been the Irish amnesiac.'

He laughs and draws me close and kisses me.

Some time later he lifts his head and says, 'There's only one problem, sweetheart.'

'Right now, Danny,' I murmur against his shoulder, 'I'd really, *really* prefer no problems at all.'

'Our fiddles are still locked away in Min-lu's antique chest. She won't let me break it open and nobody knows where the key is.'

I gaze at him, content. 'But I have the key, my love. It's always been with me. Always.'

THANK YOU, READERS

Thank you for reading *Silver Highways*. I started it in 2004 and the underlying research began with *Redbill*, four years before that. If you've enjoyed it, please recommend it to your friends and give it a review or rating on your favourite book site.

Silver Highways is the foundation of my other novels. Lucy, who relates this story, is the mother of Mike, the protagonist of *The Turning Tide*, while Rosa's children, Eliza and Peter, relate *Testing the Limits*, set in the 1930s. If you'd like to know more about pearling luggers and Broome history, try award-winning *Redbill: from Pearls to Peace*.

<u>seabooks.net</u> provides links to the books, reviews, extracts, images and background information.

ABOUT THE AUTHOR

 I grew up near Lake Macquarie, NSW. My background is in science and technology, but in 2000 I ran across the story of the charmed life of an old Broome pearling lugger, and discovered the joys of historical research and writing. My first book, *Redbill*, won the Western Australian Premier's Book Award for Non-Fiction in 2004. My second book, *Alan Villiers*, won the Mountbatten Maritime Award in 2009, and my novels include *The Turning Tide*, *Atomic Sea* and *Testing the Limits*. I live with two whippets in green South Gippsland.

ACKNOWLEDGEMENTS

I began *Silver Highways* after *Redbill* was published, but a few complicated years and the writing of *Alan Villiers* intervened before I could take it up again. I'd like to thank my WOFL friends, Gillian Clarke, Alison Shields, Ruth Carson and Lynn Atkinson, and my mother Margaret Lance, who kindly edited drafts.

I'd also like to thank my Irish musician friends for their wonderful sessions in Melbourne pubs so long ago, especially Greg O'Leary, Helen Cahun, Peter Rayner and Morag Logan.

I've drawn on many memoirs of life at sea for this novel. In particular Rex Clement's *A Gypsy of the Horn* for Danny Whalen's ghostly sea story, and *By the Wind* by Captain J. Murray Lindsay for the torpedoing of a four-masted sailing ship during WWI.

One image on the cover is derived from a Wikipedia public domain image by user Daderot, of the painting *Sally* by Joseph de Camp, c. 1907, from the Worcester Art Museum, USA.

FICTION BY KATE LANCE

TESTING THE LIMITS — Kate Lance, Seabooks Press, 2020

The love of the old. The thrill of the new. The turbulence to come.

1930s England: will the sunny days of ships, flying and love ever end? Eliza McKee sails away to a new life in London, where her glamorous aunt Izabel is a star with a secret to hide. Her brother Pete yearns to fly, but he has no idea how much he needs to learn from fierce pilot Billie Quinn. Eliza's friend Harry loves golden Charlotte, but Charlotte just loves gambling with flyboy Pete's heart. And when a great white barque encounters the coast one foggy night, more than an era of sail finds itself tested to the limits.

THE TURNING TIDE — CM Lance, Allen & Unwin, 2014

"It took me about two pages to fall in love with this beautiful Australian book."

Commando Mike Whalen trained in 1942 at rugged Wilsons Prom, and fought in East Timor. Now a widowed academic, and more damaged than he realises, he meets Lena, the granddaughter of his glamorous old friends Helen and Johnny. When Johnny died in the war he left Mike with a burden of secrets, and as Lena draws him back into her family he discovers more secrets existed than he ever imagined. From the Prom to devastated Hiroshima, this is a saga of adventure and passion.

ATOMIC SEA — CM Lance, Seabooks Press, 2016

"Brilliant! Every chapter holds a twist you can't see coming. Fast moving and worth the reading ride."

Chernobyl. Fukushima ... *Broome*? Everyone loves Broome's new nuclear-waste plant—a certain Great Power will even take full responsibility for any problems. Sadly it's lying. When life onshore becomes surprisingly threatening, scientist Lena's only refuge is skipper Simon's old boat: sadly he's lying too. Just offshore is a blue vessel with two corpses and a lethal cargo. The plant is about to open and a cyclone called Cyril is about to hit. And Lena discovers being stuck on a committee isn't her worst nightmare after all.

NON-FICTION BY KATE LANCE

ALAN VILLIERS: VOYAGER OF THE WINDS

2nd Edition, Seabooks Press, 2020. Fully revised and with over 100 photos. **Mountbatten Maritime Award 2009**

> *"A delightful warts-and-all biography of one of the world's most notable chroniclers of seafaring life."*

When Australian journalist Alan Villiers sailed on the last of the giant merchant windjammers in the 1920s and '30s, his writings and photographs made him famous. Villiers crewed on beautiful *Herzogin Cecilie* and tragic *Grace Harwar*, took tiny *Joseph Conrad* around the globe, sailed on Arabian dhows, led wartime landing craft, captained *Mayflower* II across the Atlantic, and inspired sail training and ship restoration projects.

Drawn from his personal diaries, this award-winning biography of the author-adventurer reveals both his mythmaking and his achievements. It is a tribute to the greatest sailing ships ever launched—and to the extraordinary man who loved them.

REDBILL: FROM PEARLS TO PEACE

Fremantle Press, 2004.
Western Australian Premier's Award 2004 for Non-Fiction

> *"Lance has presented the biography of Redbill with quiet passion and exquisite detail."*

Redbill is the true story of a sailing boat's voyage through a century of history. She began life as a Broome pearlshell lugger owned by the buccaneering Captain Gregory, then became naval vessel HMAS *Redbill*, bombed in Darwin during WW2. After the war *Redbill* went pearling in Papua, then worked for Greenpeace in Tahiti, and raised funds for refugees.

Redbill also filmed a Bass Strait voyage, *If It Doesn't Kill You* and reunited a young Aboriginal man with his long-lost family. Finally she took on an epic voyage around the coast of Australia, to return to the North-West to face her greatest challenge yet: Rosita, the most powerful tropical cyclone to strike Broome in ninety years.

www.ingramcontent.com/pod-product-compliance
Lightning Source LLC
Chambersburg PA
CBHW070652180626
46817CB00006B/2338